COMPETITION

COMPETITION

A NOVEL BY

. . . .

J Edward Duncan

Little Bug Publishers
Portland

This book began in conception after the author received his degree in architecture, and was completed when the student loans were finally paid off.

For my Sweetie,
this book could not have
been written without you

With thanks to:

Kathleen Duncan
Marguerite Duncan
Stephanie Martin
Carol Pedersen
Karen Drake
James Gantz

Contents

COMPETITION

Chapter I

Deconstructing an Architect
[Summer 2001]

1

O urs is a generation of addicts; we celebrate our recoveries as if they were rites of passage. But the first step toward recovery is to acquire the addiction. Mine was architecture, a disease of wanting to design too much. By addiction, I really mean a pattern of behavior, a cycle of making the same mistakes over and over. In architecture and in life, my habits grew from choices. And my habits made life unmanageable.

As I tell you this, I'm drawing the hip of a young woman. Although nude, her pose is not seductive. A very shy and delicate woman, I think, although I'm looking at her from behind. The tricky part is capturing the light reflecting from her skin. If I was a more accomplished artist, I could manage it, but the softness of her skin is beyond me.

The hip belongs to a woman who belongs to a painting that belongs to the Philadelphia Museum of Art. It's a traveling show, so in a week the painting will be packed up, shipped to a different city, and hung on a different wall. So sad to have to say goodbye to such an extraordinary work, but I'll have a sketch as a memory. This voyeuristic painting depicts a young woman posing for a sculptor. It's difficult not to feel a little guilty or uninvited when looking at this work, as though the subject of the portrait is unaware that she is being studied.

Drawing, in a sense, has become my patch for architecture. It's a way for me to remain creative without stumbling back to my pattern of compulsive designing. I've gotten in the habit of spending my lunch hour in the art museum, not just to look but to draw. It's an excellent way to study the works of accomplished artists, and it's good therapy. Today, I capture the sensual curves of a hundred-year-old canvas. Yesterday, I finished a rendering of an abstract collage by a local artist. I've discovered that abstract works often don't translate to pencil. Take away the color and the life of the painting goes with it.

I won't pretend to be an artist, but I'll tell you why I like to sketch. I've always admired people who can put pen to paper and render what they see. To me, that is an astonishing ability. No doubt we all see life a bit differently, so anyone who can record and preserve their point of view with an image is a rare communicator, an historian of the commonplace. They remind us not of the important events that shape a nation or an era, but of the simple and the familiar things that often are the most significant.

Perhaps you've always loved Impressionist works showing fuzzy images of busy town squares, stuffed with people, or you've seen paintings of abandoned farmhouses, with desperate nails clinging to splitting boards? To me, each of these images tells a story. I see the old farmhouse, and wonder what it once held. Born from promise and purpose, an endeavor of many, it is a simple reflection of the people who built it. Withstanding winter after winter, the structure now stands as testament only to its own obsolescence. But this one image of a farmhouse creates a metaphor for our own lives and it also serves as a rugged but beautiful monument, inviting the eye to linger.

So, this is why I sketch. I want to be able to tell people what I've seen and felt. Words can't always do this. Words *tell*, images *show*.

To this an entire generation can bear witness. Pictures, colors, patterns, faces. Our televisions and magazines are filled with them; everyone can relate to images. Words are fine but sometimes cumbersome and incomplete. Granted, an image is not always focused, but it feels more personal. Who can stare at the cover of a fashion magazine without believing, honestly believing, that the model is looking back at them – not the camera? Who can follow a television series without finding that they have somehow connected with the stars and starlets who recite the dialogue?

I talk to many who decry the relentlessness of image. "With so many images," they argue, "no one image can be important. It all becomes noise."

Fine.

There doesn't have to be a grand significance to the images we see. This is what I'm talking about - *the commonplace.* It's a lucky person who can find beauty in the commonplace. The old farmhouse is beautiful, but this beauty is often ignored because it lacks grandeur.

Earlier I made reference to an addiction. In fairness, I should point out that I had enablers. In school I was encouraged to study design and to practice drawing and rendering. At each level of my education I investigated color, pattern, shape, and form; at first because I was encouraged and eventually because I grew curious.

Initially, painting intrigued me. For whatever reason, that was the most accessible medium. Inheriting tubes of oil paints and assorted brushes from my mother, I soon found it easy to spend hours mixing colors and preparing a canvas. As much effort and interest was invested in developing colors and consistencies of pigment as there was in applying them to a canvas.

In school I spent hours studying the history of painting and examining photos depicting the works of masters and their compositions, hoping to understand their eye and follow their hand. So much emotion can be conveyed with a stroke of ultramarine or a dab of sienna – it was this fascination with the minutia of composition that led me to the field of architecture.

In this sense, painting was the gateway drug and my professors were all dealers. Being fed images of Renaissance painters and abstract sculptures, I soon developed an appetite for other types of design. My curiosity for images, then forms and spaces, became a fascination for buildings and architecture. I wanted to know how they were built, who built them, and how the design had been conceived.

I confess, I'm inclined toward melodrama, but studying architecture demanded intensity. I was happy to spend long hours working in studio, scribbling over tracing paper, convinced that someday I would see my designs come to life. If substances can create addictions, why not experiences? In this sense, I was a junkie, a design-junkie. I became desperate, disillusioned, and dispirited. In other words, I became an architect.

There is a romantic idea of what an architect is supposed to be. The learned designer, self-assured and self-made – this, I'm told, is an architect. Having spent time in the field, I learned otherwise. Don't misunderstand, I still enjoy design, I still am fascinated with buildings. I will always be intrigued with images and the language of our visual world. I've simply found sobriety through moderation.

2

A museum is an oasis, a place to escape. Once inside, each of us becomes an eye, our only charge is to appreciate. There is little required of an observer, so I've found good therapy in canvases, sculpture, and history. Spending the lunch hour in a gallery became my habit upon completing my degree and returning to Portland. It was here, in this museum, that I took the first modest step toward recovery. I can't recall, now, what I was trying to draw, but it was among the first of my museum sketches.

Competition

I had been in the museum for forty minutes. In ten minutes I needed to finish the sketch and find my way back to the office. Not enough time, so I put down my pencil. Seeing my supine pencil as a signal, a museum docent came toward me.

"Heads down, pencils up. You've got to discipline yourself to draw faster."

"Please offer advice only when asked."

The docent was a young art student, Andrew Klein. If it weren't for work-study, this would be a *starving* young art student, but a small stipend came his way for each month he helped at the art museum. I had known Andrew for some time, both of us frequenting art shows. Time and again, we found each other at the same events, and struck up a friendship. Aloof and self-assured, Andrew was on the cusp of becoming a name in the local art scene.

"If you can find the time, we're opening a new show at the Angry Pear. Not that you architects understand self-expression, but it should be a good one. Lots of paintings, mostly oils. Stop by."

"What's special about this one, any of your work being shown?"

"Nope, I need to get cookin' on some new work. I've been spending too much time cultivating inspiration."

This month, Andrew's inspiration was a somewhat attractive art student. I say somewhat attractive because I always had the impression that someday she would put on weight. Perhaps I expose my own shallow nature, but at least give me credit for being perceptive.

"Andrew, your last show was good, you need to continue developing your paintings. I'm not interested in going if there's none of your work."

"Nick, you need to come. Besides I only get to see you when you come here to do your drawings. Lets talk after hours for once. You'll be there?"

"Details - "

"Good man." Andrew reached into his shirt pocket and pulled out a small card.

J Edward Duncan

*The Angry Pear invites you to a free
presentation of oil paints and photographs . . .
7:30 – 12:00 @ 1310 NW Marshall
Opening – First Thursday*

The first Thursday of each month was the traditional evening for gallery openings. I took the card in my right hand and grabbed my wallet with my left. Smiling at Andrew I inserted the card between a couple of ones and placed it back into my pocket.

"Honestly, you ought to finish a series of oils. You're not yet burdened with a full time job, you won't always have the time to paint."

"You're right, but that doesn't mean I'm interested in hearing it. Any more advice, or may I be excused?" Andrew held his head down in mock shame.

"Look, I'm just saying – spend more time studying your canvases and less time studying your models."

"Nick, what is art without the pursuit of beauties?"

"You waste so much time in pursuit, have you ever stayed with the same girl for longer than a painting?"

He paused, rummaging through the archives of his mind.

"Your problem," he began, "is that you haven't yet been in enough relationships to take even one of them for granted. The pursuit is never a waste of time; sometimes it's the whole point." He paused, waiting for my rebuttal; when I offered none he continued, "Let's finish this at the Pear."

"Alright, I've gotta' get back to work, see you there. I won't show up at 7:30, though. Look for me around nine."

"I'll be looking." He turned around and slowly waved his hand.

I hustled out of the museum and *jog-walked* outside through several intersections under an overcast sky. I was caught unprepared, as the morning had been sunny – the summer showers in Portland often passed quickly but came

8

without warning. I wanted to get back to the office before I had been gone a full hour; not as though anyone would notice. Typically, everyone was so focused on their own deadlines that an empty cubicle didn't even raise an eyebrow. For nearly four years I had been working at Integrated Designs, and had discovered that architects tended not to look far past their own desks.

As I approached the office, the sky released a warning volley of raindrops. I had a little under a minute to make it to safety before the real rain would begin. Clutching the sketchbook to my chest, I quickened my pace. I wanted to avoid letting my drawings get wet, but I also had an aversion to running while downtown. When in the city, I adopt my professional demeanor, which means that I walk at a steady pace and rarely look anyone in the eye. Even to catch a bus or streetcar, I can manage only a quick saunter. If I'm late and a bus pulls away, I refuse to run or shout; another will eventually pull up.

Through the front door, into the elevator, and up to the fifth floor. As I popped out of the elevator I gave a knowing nod to the receptionist and continued toward my desk. Upon arriving, I saw a yellow sticky note clinging to my computer screen.

Any plans this eve???

Written in *distinctless* staccato print, a style cultivated by architects and engineers, I knew that it was from Ron. Not that Ron himself was without distinction, but he was one of the few architects in the office who had ever invested any time learning how to properly letter by hand. I, on the other hand, spent little time on my lettering. Ever since the advent of the dot-matrix printer, I had made it my personal goal to develop the handwriting of a surgeon.

I looked toward the other side of the aisle and saw Ron methodically tapping his mouse. Never has a more jagged mind lurked beneath so mild a face. Ron was a good man to know, but a better man not to be. By this, I mean that he possessed a caustic wit that could only be the result of years and years of bitterness - always amusing, but amusing in a tragic sense. It was as though the burden of his world was so mighty that he only had enough strength left to laugh at his situation. I suppose all people experience brief periods like this, but it was Ron's life.

Slouched in his chair, Ron squinted with intensity at his monitor. His form fitting black pullover revealed a slim but untoned body; and he seemed to adopt a perpetually aloof posture when seated. When standing, it was easier to understand the intensity of which he was capable. When speaking, he stood just a hair too close, his eye contact lingered just a bit too long, and his gestures became just slightly too exaggerated.

When we had first met as students at the University of Oregon, he had been seated, wearing a simple black T-shirt with a pair of khaki pants and sandals. After our first conversation, I had been left with the impression that he was a good bit taller than he was. His black hair, standing up in short unkempt spikes, added maybe half an inch, and could account for the illusion. Now, in the office, his hair lay limp on his head, but he still maintained the same *Banana Republic Black* that matched his pullover and shoes.

Recently, I had engaged in fewer conversations with Ron. Although we sat in close proximity, it seemed that my deadlines had been coming more frequently and with greater urgency. I think we actually spent more time in discussion when our desks were on different floors entirely. I think also, I grew frustrated from the way the conversations were directed. We had common ground when discussing pop-culture, design, or work. I balked, however, when Ron stood up on his social-soap box. It wasn't that he was wrong, rather that he exposed his own jaded nature. For this reason, I considered the note on my monitor, and wondered if I should include Ron in my evening plans.

"The note on my monitor – you?" I asked.

"Me - what are you up to?

"I'm debating," I crossed my arms while attempting a decision. "I'm catching a show at the Angry Pear. Meet you?"

"The Pear. I haven't been in quite a while."

Now it was Ron's turn to debate. Purposely, he all but ignored my question, bobbing his head ambiguously, and maneuvered the conversation toward non sequitur.

"Nick, I've finally figured it out."

"Yes, Ron." I waited; clearly he was savoring the moment. "You going to fill me in on what you figured?"

"I can tell you're eager for my answer, so let me explain. You remember last evening, we were walking to grab cigars and pizza? We walked by Jo-Bar, a trendy-enough spot, good reputation, hip décor - and *nobody* there was under forty. Only Baby Boomers."

"This upsets you?" I asked.

"Northwest Portland is supposed to be a youthful, energetic area, but the Boomers swoop in with their cash and drive out young hipsters like you and me. It was young people like us that first moved into the neighborhood and infused it with energy; then as soon as it became hip, the young were driven out by the Boomers with their cash."

"Ron, I can't agree with you."

"Are you saying I'm speaking half-truths?"

"Well, no. I'm not convinced that even half of what you say is true."

"Come on, Nick – the old are sucking the blood from the young. The aging hipster is little more than a vampire."

I was eager to end the debate, and the quickest way to do that was to agree. "Now that I think about it, you're right. You've figured it out."

"I figured it out," Ron continued, "Precisely. What I've figured out is an opportunity. In a short number of years, the Boomers will retire. After years of toil, they finally will reap their golden harvest and turn toil into grain. Now, as we both know, after the fields have been plucked, gleaners such as you and I will find little leftover but chaff. So, I began to think. After a Boomer has retired, what will they do with their abundance? How will they spend their fat jellyrolls?

Will they build houses? Travel overseas? Engage in a debauchery too ribald to imagine?"

"Ron, have we had this conversation before?"

"No, but we've had conversations like this one. This particular conversation will focus on the direction of money. Tell me what is most prized by the elderly. For what would they sacrifice all else?"

"I suppose everyone is different, people don't all value the same things."

"While you are usually astute, my friend, this time you have stumbled. Every generation, when approaching its twilight, has sought a common prize." At this, Ron tightened his lips and squinted. "I'll first tell you what that prize is *not*. While a young man has ambition, and craves power, the old man has no use for it; truly, it's a burden."

"Ron, to which client do you bill your melodrama? Anyone else in the world could have given me a brief answer, but you give me a soliloquy. The Boomers have more money and power than they need. They've forgotten about sex, so I can't tell you what they want."

"And that is why I am here, to guide you."

"Can you show me a slightly more direct path toward enlightenment?"

"Think of Ponce de León. Think of the Pharaohs of Egypt. Think of Elizabeth Taylor. What do they all share?"

"I think I've solved your riddle. You're talking about the fountain of youth, Boomers want to be young again."

"You, my friend, have achieved enlightenment. Exactly, they want to turn back the clock; they want to prolong life. And why not? Hell, I'm 29, and I already wish I was 24. What we need to do is to get in on the market that sells people lost youth or promises more years. This architecture business, it's for the birds. The future isn't in flashing details, and it's not about addenda or supplements to construction documents. How much longer are we going to wait to pay our dues as architectural lackeys?"

"Ron, the problem is that you could never give up design. Whatever your career, you'll always need to be expressive. Whatever you do, you'll try to turn it into art. That will be your downfall, you're not a businessman. You're an artist."

"An artist who has two sheets of flashing details to complete before 5:30." Ron said this with newly found sobriety.

"Therefore, I'll let you get back to work. Let's not end our conversation, though. Tonight at 9:00, the Angry Pear?"

With a subtle nod, I had my answer. In rare instances, he was a man of few words.

Mid-afternoon minutes crept along. The office had become quiet, as most had slunk off to late lunch or meetings. The space offered few distractions; the hallways were empty. Mounted in these hallways were the accolades the office had accrued over time. Awards were lined up in neat rows; framed, aligned, and suspended from proud nails. Every plaque quietly proclaimed an attention to design and creative problem solving, every plaque represented a happy client, and every plaque was dusted once a week on Fridays – but no plaque was younger than twelve years.

The office had long enjoyed a good reputation, but that reputation was nearly spent.

3

There was an unspoken rule that Thursday evening was the unofficial beginning of the weekend. Granted the work week still held one more day to endure, so Thursday evening became a sort of teaser. The tradition held that some local watering hole would provide the table for our *Feast of Weekend's Eve*. The tradition had a simple brilliance that had to be applauded. Somehow, it trivialized that last day of work, thereby making it more tolerable. It was as though the weekend reached back and grabbed an extra day, in order to better balance the unkind ratio of 2 to 5.

Earlier in the day, a host of other young architects and myself had received an email message providing information about the 'where' and 'when' for our gathering. The message had read:

> *What has your liver done for you lately?*
> *If you wish to put it to use, bring it to*
> *the 21ˢᵗ Avenue Grill (TBFKASM). We'll meet at 5:45*
> *in the outdoor patio. If needed, undamaged*
> *livers will be provided for those interested in*
> *drinking to excess.*

Ron's name was on the address list, but I suspected that he would be absent.

Originally named *Seafood Mama's*, the *21ˢᵗ Avenue Grill* was in the process of an identity change. Not appealing to the hipper-than-thou crowd that lived in The Pearl District, management wisely initiated the face-lift. However, there had been a certain kitsch appeal to *Seafood Mama's*, so those in the know referred to it as TBFKASM, or "The Bar Formerly Known as Seafood Mama's". For whatever reason, that title seemed a hundred times more appropriate, and therefore stuck.

The face-lift could better be described as a makeover – because it was only cosmetic. The menu stayed the same, the drinks were unchanged, and the atmosphere was not appreciably different. However, the clientele grew, and so the Pub enjoyed a reincarnation of sorts. The bar had also featured live jazz in the evenings, the line up remaining identical to what it had been pre-makeover.

The outdoor patio was hidden from the street and contained a modest forest of trees. When the weather was warm and clear, it was difficult to find a better location for deep conversation and potent drinks.

14

After work, I made my way to the bar. Through the main dining area, I found the entrance to the courtyard. I stepped out of the shade and saw Pierce, another architect that Ron and I knew from Rome. Typically he dressed casually, not having to bother with office attire – a short sleeved button down shirt and black jeans. Upon first meeting Pierce, his features struck me as being unusually harsh. His pronounced cheekbones and thin lips granted a severity to his expression that was rarely intended. He was, in fact, a warm person although quite shy. His demeanor masked an intensity that he applied to all of his endeavors. I recall a conversation when he confessed to having tested himself as a boxer, before entertaining ideas of studying architecture. I made no secret of my surprise, considering his slender proportions and quiet nature. Yet his arms were more powerful than they appeared, and his hands quicker than I imagined.

While unexpected, his affinity for boxing fit with his need to continually test and push himself. Upon completing his first degree, he left his home to travel through Scandinavia, spending time in Norway and then renting a small flat in Denmark. Thriving on uncertainty, he decided to live in there before having even landed a job. Within weeks, he found work as a graphic designer. His place of work was situated near an amateur boxing gym, and the promise of a new curiosity to observe brought him in as a spectator. As his fascination grew, so too did his desire to tie on a pair of gloves. His interest propelled him into the ring, where his quick hand speed gave him false confidence. Promptly, he was given a broken nose and hand, thus making quick work of his curiosity, and propelling his interests into more cerebral vocations.

Sitting in the patio outside the bar, ashtray littered with butts, Pierce seemed to have replaced boxing with activities that employed slower methods of weakening his body. Pulling a cigarette from his lips he screwed it into the ashtray and motioned for me to join.

"Nicholas - We've already ordered for you, sit down and relax."

He had claimed a small shaded table. I was glad to see he had chosen to show up. Too often absent, he frequently eschewed groups any larger than four. Several people had arrived, but were distributed among a few tables. There was only one other at the table Pierce had chosen.

"Pierce, this is rare. I see you too seldom," I said.

"I already told the waitress to bring you a Manhattan, you're taken care of."

"Good man."

"I also mentioned to Janet that you and I had studied together in Rome."

I smiled and found a seat under the canopy of a tree. I had not yet met the girl sitting next to Pierce.

"I'm Janet Elliot, good to meet you. I used to work with Pierce."

Janet was an Egyptian statue wearing sunglasses. I could not help but be reminded of Queen Nefertiti, a delicate faced queen immortalized by a stylized sculpture found in every history book that discusses Western Art. She possessed the same elongated neck, and the same fragile cheekbones. Each time she sipped from her straw, her face stretched forward, emphasizing her long slender neck. Her black sunglasses, a pair of dark ovals, complimented her dark hair and brown skin.

"Janet, it's my pleasure. What are you drinking?" I asked.

"It's a lemon-drop. I can only drink alcohol when it's sweet. If it doesn't taste like candy, I'll pass."

"That's no way to drink," I said. "There's perfectly good alcohol mixed in somewhere with that sugar."

"You're missing the point. It's a *Trojan drink*," Janet retorted.

I raised an eyebrow.

Pierce interjected, "She means like a Trojan Horse. You disguise the alcohol in order to get it into your system." He laughed. "A good analogy, no? Make the alcohol sweet and you hardly even know you're drinking it."

"I notice that you're drinking scotch, neat." I pointed at his drink.

"True. I no longer need the Trojan Drink. The enemy has already entered the gate and overrun the city. The battle is over, so there is no more need for disguises." Again, Pierce laughed and took a sip for affect.

"Pierce, I don't believe that your liver has been sacked yet, but don't resort to the sugar drinks. It is better to know thy enemy – far better to let alcohol take its toll up-front. That way, you never have to offer your body an explanation, it was a willing accomplice."

Janet was no longer paying attention.

"Janet, mind if I try some of your lemon drop?" I asked.

"Oh, God - order your own." She licked sugar from the rim of her glass and propped up her chin with a disinterested hand.

Pierce grabbed a piece of calamari and tossed it toward Janet, where it bounced from the table down to the ground.

"Thanks for the calamari, Pierce, that's so thoughtful." Janet offered a syrupy smile while continuing to prop her chin.

"Janet must have lost her appetite, she usually loves calamari," Pierce offered.

"Guys, while I often admire droll wit, you're really not hitting it right now."

The waitress strolled up to the table with her tray and dropped off a glass of bourbon.

"Would you like another Lemon Drop?" She eyed Janet.

"We'd all like a Lemon Drop. Lemon Drops for the table." Pierce waved his finger in a circle.

The waitress scratched a quick note on her pad and departed.

"Janet, why don't you present your dilemma to Nicholas?"

"Oh, this sounds good, I love a dilemma," I said.

Janet lowered her sunglasses and stared at me in mock disapproval.

"Nicholas, you have to promise to be serious and not poke fun – otherwise I tell you nothing."

"I really do poke too much fun, don't I?" I said.

"How about if I just present my quandary?" Janet began. "I've been working in Portland for about three years now and the job has been okay. Not great, but okay." She paused to take another sip of her lemon drop. She turned her head, and lifted a thin arm in awkward fashion while holding her glass.

"Janet enjoys interior design, but she's not been thrilled with the projects that she works on," Pierce added.

"Well, the projects themselves have been fine, but not my role on those projects."

"Janet, you're describing all of us right now. Nobody's satisfied with what they're doing. Some professions are unkind to the young."

"But I know that I can do better. I'm debating whether the time is right for me to work for myself. I've been able to do a little moonlighting on small retail and commercial projects; with a little extra effort, I think I could do that full time."

"Do you have the clientele?" I asked.

She put her drink down, as though to signal that the conversation was now serious.

"A hard question to answer; that's part of my dilemma, I've a *maybe* client. There's potential, but until I know for sure, I can't take the risk and work for myself. I've got my certification and can cover some start up costs, but I can't be guaranteed sustained work."

"How many of these smaller projects can you get? Do you think they could ever lead to something more?" I asked trying to hide my envy.

"Something, yes." Pausing, she turned. "Pierce, you're not out of cigarettes are you?"

He looked at me for approval and then pulled out a cigarette and lighter.

"Pierce, what advice have you offered?" I asked

"My advice was that she order a lemon drop."

"That may be the best advice I've had all day," Janet muttered.

When Pierce and I had been students in Rome, discussions like these happened on a daily basis. The topics changed, but the format was always the same. In the morning, we would gather for coffee and pose our version of one of life's great questions. Then in the evening, we would gather for drinks and offer whatever answer each of us had come up with. The conversations had rarely been conclusive, and always ended with insobriety.

Including myself there were four regulars who would sit up late, talking and drinking wine from tumblers. Sometimes the debates were animated, other times subdued, but they always seemed more sensible at night than they did the morning after. Looking at Pierce now, I realized that the four of us had never all gathered together since our time in Rome. Ron was one of the four, and the other was Angeline, a girl whom I had not seen since our studies abroad.

This question that Janet posed, though, had been sprung on me suddenly. It seemed nearly unfair; I had no time to prepare my answer.

"Look, both you guys know the score," Janet said between puffs, "you can work in an office your whole life and enjoy security, but never be involved in any fulfilling or rewarding work. That, or you can try to get out on your own and see what happens. I want to make a go of it. I just don't think it'll get easier if I wait; I'll only become complacent."

"Janet," I began, "first of all, finish your lemon drop. Then talk to me about how you're going to go about making a go of it."

"Well, the toughest part will be gathering enough capital and enough clients to get me through the first few months."

Pierce began to quiz her, "Nicholas asked about repeat business from your moonlighting. Tell him what you told me."

"Yes, in fact that's what got me started thinking that I could do it. As I've said, I've done some smaller projects on my own. One of those clients approached me to work on a design. He's implied that he has other projects that he would like me to work on."

"Good start," I said. "Where do you go from there?"

She reached for her lemon drop and swirled it around before licking more sugar off the rim and taking a sip.

"I've got a plan. I've been in touch with a design school in town and they need some instructors for some of their interiors classes. If I could do that part time, I could begin my own projects. Then as my projects become more frequent, I do that full time."

"Teaching could help, but how do you know you'd be offered classes every term?" Pierce asked.

"I'm not certain. What's more, it wouldn't happen right away, so I've got to be patient. And if I've got to be patient, you two have to keep quiet. I don't want this getting back to my office, understand?"

"Janet, you can rest assured that Nicholas and my silence can certainly be purchased."

"Yes, I think that another plate of calamari would be a good start. Now, Pierce, you mentioned that Janet had a dilemma. What she described is not exactly a dilemma. It sounds more like an opportunity."

"An opportunity, yes - but I don't know where it could lead. My current job is secure and the paychecks don't bounce; I just feel so nervous about giving that up." She stubbed out her cigarette and then pointed at both of us. "Oh, and listen, I need to have designers that I can work with. Some of these jobs are sort of dreck, but they have a fast turn around time, and I don't want to have to search around for an architect."

"Architectural mercenaries?" I asked.

"Count on it, just give the dreck to Nicholas," Pierce said.

"I'll share the good stuff, if it comes in," she smiled. "Honestly, the client I mentioned could be a good one to work with. I only spoke with him briefly, but he's not afraid to spend a little for design. His name is Jack Harlan, have you heard of him? He's done a few projects in the Pearl district. I've worked with him through my office a number of times."

"Good to work with?"

"Good enough. Things have gone well enough that he's had me do some projects on the side. They aren't all glamorous, but we've developed a business relationship of sorts."

"What sort?"

"Encouraging."

"Meaning?"

"Meaning there's reason for each of us to hope a project comes through."

As Janet spoke, I watched her quick but fluid movements. There was an awkwardness to the way she gestured that betrayed a shy nature. Still wearing sunglasses, even under the shade, she hid her eyes and avoided prolonged glances. However, when discussing her intent, her tone was matter of fact, never seeking approval. That I was taken into confidence at all was testament to Pierce's recommendation, as I was certain she had asked him if I was trustworthy. Just the same, her comments had been directed first toward Pierce, and then to me only out of politeness.

However, I couldn't help but be intrigued by the idea of involvement in the projects she described. I hesitated slightly, having just met her, not knowing if her opportunities were real or imagined. But if Pierce had confidence in her, I concluded her abilities likely matched her ambitions.

Our waitress hurried by, transferred three glasses from her tray to our table, and then proceeded on without comment. The three of us continued talking only for the duration of the last round of drinks, and then Janet stood up.

"Gentlemen, it's been grand. Here's a twenty for my drinks."

"Janet, before you go – Will you be joining us at the Angry Pear later this evening?" I asked.

She smiled. "You'll find out when you get there. See you both later."

Janet waved goodbye and left the courtyard.

4

"Joining 'us' at the Angry Pear? Are you presuming that you'll see me there as well?"

"Come on, what else will you be doing with your time? Show up."

"Past my bedtime."

"Bedtime? When was the last time you were asleep before midnight?"

"Alright, it's not the hour, it's the crowd."

"You and groups; would you have met me here if you suspected more than three would be sitting together?"

"Find out - next week invite four people."

Pierce brought out another cigarette and raised his eyebrows to solicit an endorsement.

"Yeah, go ahead. So will you at least offer a *maybe* to meeting at the Pear?"

Pierce took a drag, turned his head away from me and released a puff of smoke.

"Ask me again before we leave." Quickly, Pierce jumped to another subject, "My friend, it's been too long since we met for drinks." Bringing the cigarette to his mouth, he hesitated and then asked, "How's Ron?"

"The same, but worse. He's not happy."

"No, I don't remember him ever being happy. Do you talk to him much?"

"Quite a bit, our desks are close together. Actually, he does most of the talking, and I'm the ear."

"An ear? As a designer you should always aspire to be an eye." He pointed to his glasses.

I smiled at his reference, recalling a conversation now years old. According to Pierce, the eye was the most important tool that any designer possessed. He had explained his reasoning to Ron and me while the three of us sat on the steps of an unused Roman church.

We each had a different role in a philosophical discussion, which we described as a *phililoquy*. Pierce was often inclined to go for lengths of time without contributing to the conversation. When he did offer his point of view, he did so with energy and skill. Using words with economy, he increased their value, and his cadence lent significance even to his pause.

Ron was better skilled at sustaining conversation, always able to offer one more twist that had yet to be considered. It was often he who goaded us into participating in the verbal jousts.

The three of us were lounging in the shadow of San Girolamo della Carità, a church just a stone's throw from the palazzo that provided our student housing. Holding large bottles of watery Italian beer, we took advantage of the quiet and shade provided by the church.

"Bottle opener, please." I said.

"Siesta, please – find your own opener," Ron responded.

"Inside the bag," Pierce said.

I grabbed at a brown paper bag sitting on the steps and reached inside. Pulling out the bottle opener I wrenched the cap off a dirt-smeared bottle of Italian pilsner. Pierce rubbed his forehead with his bottle, but it offered little cooling.

"Suppose they ever drive cars down this street?" I asked. The alley must have been just a little more than fifteen feet wide from building to building, and only a tiny streak of sunlight was allowed to fall across the rough stone cobbles.

"Not often. Mopeds, though, all the time." Ron responded with authority, though each of us had spent only a week in the city.

"Can you imagine riding one of those mopeds in the states? On a tiny cycle – zip, zip, zoom with a pretty Italian lady holding on tight." Pierce said.

"Holding on tight to you or her cell phone?" Ron mused. "Every pretty lady I see has a phone to her ear while her boyfriend smokes his cigarette – both trying to look indifferent."

"Indifferent, but beautiful," I added. "Tan skin, dark eyes, long legs."

"Yes, but only when they're young. Something happens to them after thirty or so." Pierce said this with a smile before tilting back his bottle. "In order to be happy, you have to find beauty in the ordinary."

"How about an ordinary set of steps? How about an ordinary bottle of pilsner and an ordinary Italian afternoon?" I asked.

"All right, I'll make my point. Do you find this alley to be beautiful?" Pierce asked, eager to begin a debate.

"This alley," I spoke after setting down my bottle, "is not beautiful. It's comfortable, but not beautiful. If for no other reason, take a look at these old stucco buildings that form the perimeter."

"Nicholas," Pierce said, "I'm not asking about the individual buildings, I'm asking about the alley itself."

I took another look around.

"But these buildings create the alley, and there isn't one of them that is endearing. I love old Roman buildings, but not these. They're vanilla buildings, impossible to tell one from the other."

Pierce interjected, "True, I agree with you on that point, each building on its own is unremarkable. But the alley is not one of these buildings, it is all of them together."

"Nick, here, drink some more beer and you'll understand what he's talking about." Ron grabbed my bottle and lifted, trying to pass it to me. I pretended not to notice his offer.

"So Pierce," I retorted, "You don't like any of these buildings, but you're trying to argue that this alley is beautiful?"

"Yes, that was my point. I'm trying to convince both of you that collectively, these ordinary buildings create something beautiful. But, unlike an attractive woman, age adds more beauty."

"Pierce, I'll grant you that I'm content in this alley," Ron began, "but we need a working definition of beauty. We can't each have our own secret list of qualities."

"Agreed," Pierce said.

We sat deliberating within our heads what qualities made a place beautiful. Coming up with an artistic proof is difficult and, I now think, pointless, but there's value in a polemic. Ron sat swirling his bottle while staring at a streak of sunlight. Absentmindedly, his feet shifted position rhythmically. Pierce, looked down at the cobblestones and scribbled in the sand with his finger. I couldn't tell if he was writing or simply occupying his hand while his brain buzzed.

It was Ron who finally spoke. "Beauty is absolutely *not* in the eye of the beholder. I think beauty must be something that anyone could see. Otherwise there's no point in debating, if each person's opinion carries equal weight."

"Of course each opinion has equal weight," I said.

"No." Ron shook his head.

"Don't be dense, your head's all wrong." I said.

"No. I'm saying that there are things that aren't subjective. I think that there are qualities of beauty that we'd agree upon. Therefore, it isn't simply opinions being weighed against opinions."

"Can you name those qualities? The ones that we'd agree upon?"

"Pattern," Pierce interrupted. "We all perceive and appreciate patterns. We see them in nature and in the built environment."

"What about a girl? Don't we each have our opinions about what makes a girl beautiful?" I countered.

"Nick, we're talking about finding beauty in the ordinary – there's nothing ordinary about a beautiful girl," Ron said.

"All right, pattern, we all appreciate pattern," I said.

"Yes, when you look at the façade of a building, you want the windows to make sense; you want to find a pattern. When you listen to music, you want the notes to have an organization; you want to find a pattern."

"Patterns," Ron mused.

"That's one. Another quality of beauty is proportion. Do you enjoy squat proportions or elongated?" Pierce questioned.

"That's loaded," I said. "I think the word 'squat' carries too much baggage. However, I see your point. There are proportions that are beautiful."

"Okay, I've got one," Ron said. "Scale - Size as it relates to context."

"Expand on that," I said.

"Look at the doorways for your vanilla buildings, Nick. The doors themselves are pretty tiny, which might look awkward with these three and four story buildings. But the entrance surrounding the doorway is much larger, which is more appropriate for the scale of the buildings."

"And more appropriate for the scale of the alley," Pierce said, pointing at the air for emphasis.

"Look," Ron continued, "let's revisit our beautiful girl. If you asked for her measurements, she'd give you all of them. Why? Because they only make sense in relation to each other. You appreciate one measurement because of the proportion and scale of another."

"Once again, I think we're getting away from our original question about the alley," I added.

"This still pertains to my question about the alley. These ordinary buildings work because of their context. The alley that they create does have the qualities of beauty we discussed, even though the buildings may not."

"Proportion?" Ron asked.

"Sure," I conceded. "The size of the alley is perfect for a conversation of three. In seriousness, the proportion of the street is appropriate for the height of the buildings. So, Pierce, I'm willing to concede that much."

"I'm drinking to that," he said. Pierce picked up his bottle and filled his mouth with beer then swallowed. "So, do you think the alley is beautiful?"

I took a more considered look around the alley. The buildings were faced with cementitious stucco that was peeling in patches, revealing pinkish brick underneath. Thin fragments of stucco lay fallen in chalky piles at the base of several buildings. Many exterior walls had been stained in a warm hue that had long ago faded. The colors, though, were not flat. As a backdrop, the walls allowed window baskets filled with flowers to draw the eye. Bright reds and yellows spilled down from perches among the baskets. Two buildings, at the top level, stretched a thin rope from window to window, allowing stiff clothing to swing in the breeze. The buildings themselves were very ordinary, but I acknowledged that the alley they created was something more.

Every element of the alley seemed to connect to the next, without any stone or brick seeming random or haphazard. Tightly spaced cobbles allowed the street to flow from doorstep to doorstep without ever acting as a barrier. The materials that composed each building seemed to share a similar ancestry; the brick, the stones, and the stuccoed plaster all were pulled from the earth and then formed by human hands.

As Ron and I sat considering, Pierce asked, "When you look at this alley, what do you see? I see it is beautiful. Not because of our arguments, but I am told it is beautiful by my eye."

"Now you're talking about judgement, your opinion," Ron said.

"I'm not so certain. We can still argue about truth and beauty, but acknowledge the importance of seeing. I think we need to trust intuition."

"Our eyes can be fooled - trompe l'oiel," I chided.

"But, as a designer, what is more important than your eye? What tool can you use to overrule a genuine reaction? If an architect cannot *see* beauty, how can he *create* it?" Pierce asked.

I looked again at the doorways that opened to the street. Each housed a small door, except for the church entrance where we sat. Two large wooden doors met under an arch. The arch itself was contained within another ornamented arch that was twice as large as the first. The doors themselves were restricted to the scale of a young college student, but the arches above expanded to reflect the scale of something much larger.

"Be an eye. As designers we need to be eyes," Pierce said. "To me, this is a beautiful alley. I'm amazed that such a place can be created by such homely buildings."

As we sat on the shaded steps, an older woman opened her door across the street. She seemed unaware of our presence, or at least unconcerned. With slow, deliberate movements, she stepped out of the doorway holding a broom. With an uneven walk she shuffled backward while swishing the broom back and forth. After the stones in front of her door were swept, she grabbed a bucket and emptied it on the street. Then she turned toward a group of large clay pots that contained a modest garden, and began picking at leaves.

Her skin was dark and creased, and she hid her hair in a patterned shawl. I wanted to speak to her, but my Italian was no good. As she continued to pluck from her garden, I wondered if she lived alone. Or, perhaps she had been cleaning the steps because she expected her husband to soon return home.

"Do you suppose she has lived here all her life?" I asked.

"On this street or in this city?" Ron asked.

"Either, I don't know," I said.

The woman placed the leaves in a ceramic bowl and set the bowl on the windowsill. I suspected that she was quite old, but her face was in shadow and her hair covered. Her clothing was faded, but richly textured and layered. I wanted to believe that she had made her dress.

"What do you suppose she thinks about the mopeds that drive by on this street?" I asked.

"They're probably just part of the background, part of the buzz of the city," Ron said.

Pierce simply sat and watched her. He seemed content, and leaned back against the step, ignoring my question.

I had recalled that conversation on previous occasions, but had forgotten how quiet Pierce had become after the woman had stepped outside. As we sat facing each other, I pushed an empty martini glass forward. Dissolved streaks of sugar smeared the rim, and a small splash of Lemon Drop lingered in the bottom of the glass.

"Done drinking? More?" I asked.

"Done."

"An eye. Aspire to be an eye, wide open."

"Certainly, you agree?"

"Yes, I do."

"Fine. But I'd like to add a caveat."

"As expected."

"One should aspire to be an eye, but not just an eye. Shouldn't we also strive to be a hand?" Adjusting his glasses he smiled, then continued, "Because an eye can observe, but not act. It is only the hand that can influence."

"Then let me influence," I said grabbing Pierce's hand. "Join me at the Angry Pear tonight. I only like to go when there are people I know. Call Janet, have her come along. You say yes?"

I laughed and let go of his hand. My laugh tends to sound more like series of short sighs, so I smiled wide to seem whimsical.

"Nicholas, you'll be there this evening?"

"Yes, I've now made enough promises to that effect that I'm obligated. Look, I know you won't say 'yes', but at least say 'maybe'."

"I'll say this much, if I can't make it I'll at least call."

"You've got my cell?"

"I haven't got it memorized, but I've got it."

"Pierce, I think I've got you pinned down for a *maybe*."

The waitress brought by our check and we both did architect math to determine how much each of us owed. In the end, we both left the same amount and agreed that good and bad karma would work itself out in the end.

5

By my watch, it was seven o'clock - Not yet late enough to make an appearance at the Angry Pear. I began to walk from TBFKASM to my apartment located in a part of Portland traditionally inhabited by young architects, Nob Hill, also known as Northwest Portland. The area blends hip paupers with aging trend seekers, desperately clinging to youth. This was the neighborhood that fueled Ron's rant about the Boomers. I suppose it's no coincidence that the two worlds would converge; each group hungrily sucking the blood from the other. The whole situation smacked of an incestuous blood transfusion, yet there was something about it that worked.

The young hipsters had a commodity in abundance to which no adult could aspire. It wasn't just their youth, but their attitude - the melodramatic invincibility that can only by found in those who have never really been tested. And this perceived invincibility fostered an *inspired audaciousness*. Example: I can go into a coffee shop and be served by a snarling twenty year old who believes that he is too good to be behind the counter. This same twenty-year old, nose, nipples, and eyebrow pierced, gives me a look that says, "*How can you even stand yourself? How could you even get out of bed knowing that you are who you are?*" So much *attitude*, in spite of the fact that this youngster is forced to sling coffee from a lack of either ambition or marketable skills.

Pierce has always disagreed with me on this. He said that he'd worked in the food industry for three years before becoming a graphic designer, and this before becoming an architect. He claimed that the most interesting and intelligent people he'd worked with were those in restaurants. I've always believed Pierce too charitable.

"People are more genuine and candid before they decide what it is they want to be," Pierce had said in between sips of cappuccino. "Many that I encountered had ambitions beyond their work, or enjoyed the freedom of their vocation. When a person decides who it is they want to be, they too often lose themselves. It's as though one identifies the person they are to become, and then manufacture that personality. Why not simply be, and discover over time who you will become?"

"Pierce, having ambition doesn't mean losing sight of who you are," I countered. "I believe that ambition pushes us toward discovering what it is that we can accomplish. Doesn't that make one more interesting and more genuine?"

"Have ambition, but not to become someone. Have ambition to learn something."

He had said this just before biting into a scone. With a mouthful of scone, he became silent. No agreement had been reached, but the debate was over.

Ambition is a product of youth, and I suppose one has to be ambitious to pierce three different parts of the anatomy. That's what I mean by *inspired audaciousness*. The barista's contempt, heaped upon me, brought out an instinct that wanted to please. After being served coffee with a snarl, I almost felt like apologizing for not being edgy enough, not being hip enough to order coffee. A neighborhood for the ego, yet I never regretted living in Nob Hill.

I had moved to the neighborhood upon arriving in Portland, and found a modest studio that I could barely afford. My experience was different from that of most young residents. The typical formula worked like this: an aspiring novelist joins forces with a cocky web-designer and a barista with a degree in psychology. Between the three of them, they scrape together enough money for a trendy apartment in an old but once fantastic building. They spend a weekend moving boxes of CDs and unmatching dinner ware, then spend the next weekend combing garage sales for bar stools, a coffee table, and a stain-free sofa. The sofa must be draped in a sheet.

Obviously, the web-designer has a computer, most likely a Mac, while the novelist has a laptop that was current technology when he was still deciding on a college major. And the Barista? He most likely has both nipples pierced.

Once settled in their hipster's nest, the three of them hit the town for some nightlife. The chichi restaurants being too spendy, the trio frequent pubs and cocktail lounges.

The restaurants are the domain of the aging trend seekers, and therein lies the rub. The young hipsters resent the money and position that they can witness but not possess. The oldsters resent the youth that they are pretty sure they once had, but has long since passed them by. In spite of the minor tension, the two groups co-mingle surprisingly well. The copacetic relationship proving that cash is fair trade for energy and optimism.

Next, the young hipsters quickly cultivate a life of earnest clubbing. The truly amazing part is the genuine sentiment of urgency that pervades the lounging done by the nouveau-middle-class. Perhaps the co-mingling of generations emphasizes the limited amount of youth that can be crammed into one body. Early in life, there is so much youth stuffed into one's skin, there's simply no room for creases. Then as the youth is spent, or allowed to leak out, the body begins to sag and wrinkle. With so much aging flesh on the perimeter of a nightclub, it's no wonder the clubbers refuse to rest. Use it or lose it – how long until one gets pushed to the outside and is forced to peer through thick spectacles just to catch a glimpse of a disco ball?

I continued walking past two sushi restaurants, a bookstore, a salon, and a semi-adult card shop. These were the stars in the constellation of my neighborhood, all shining with equal intensity, although the card shop shined with orange neon. It was precisely these peculiar juxtapositions that confounded and delighted. Good thing that I was able to get my sushi, hair-care products, and soft-core porn greeting cards all in the same block – one hates to have to search all over town for the essentials.

Yet in spite of the wonderful oddities and novelties of the area, there was also a sad superficiality that couldn't be ignored. With so much visual noise, it was a struggle to find an identity for the area. And with so much emphasis on being *Hip*, being *Now*, being *Noticed*, it was difficult to relax. In some ways, the energy and motion that gave life to the street also made it a lonely place. Lonely because it was so easy to see all the things going on that one wasn't a part of.

I continued to walk; past another salon, a clothing store, a convenience store, and a bakery that always closed by three in the afternoon. Despite my rants and criticisms, it was an easy neighborhood to love. I realize that in a later station in life, I'd look back on my time living on that street and miss it. But at the time, I just needed to get home.

My apartment was in an old but once fantastic building. The façade was composed of real, *honest-to-god brick*, laid by a mason. What this means is that the brickwork wasn't merely veneer that only resembled brick. These faux brick veneers can be less than an inch thick, and ought to be called *Brik* or *Bricklike-Panel*. In some way, if only in the spelling, there should be acknowledgement that the panel systems are only a shadow of the real blocks of masonry. My building, though, had been assembled block by block, by a mason, who had spent years to develop his craft.

The entrance was a small courtyard, which lead to a vestibule, which preceded a foyer, which met stairs that climbed to my room on the third floor. Inside this small, but charming apartment was a claw foot tub. The tub, which tended to leak, provided an apt metaphor for the building; it was once a beautiful and useful object that had aged and retained only its charm.

The ceilings were quite tall and the floors hardwood. This meant that the ceilings conveyed spaciousness while the floor collected dust.

Because of the character and in spite of the flaws, I had renewed my lease twice. If for no other reason, the apartment included a balcony, accessible by two French Doors, adjacent to the main room. The only reason that I could afford such opulence was that the building hadn't really been maintained in years. The brick exterior, while crafted and elegant, also was clothed with salt deposits and other forms of water damage. A once proud cornice at the building's crown was now chipped and provided a home for all forms of moss and birds. Don't misunderstand, the building wasn't about to fall down, but the rent and the level of maintenance went hand-in-hand. However, that's what's so great about old buildings with character – they suffer if maintained too much.

J Edward Duncan

I walked into the main living area of my apartment and dropped my satchel in front of the closet door. The apartment allowed enough light that there was no need to flip on a bulb. My home enjoyed a spartan decorating style that avoided clutter in all rooms except the bedroom and bathroom. A few pieces of humble furniture sat expectantly, as I breezed past them toward the balcony.

Upon opening the doors leading to the small balcony, the murmur of the street below filled my living room. 21st Avenue was not terribly busy with autos, but did get a good deal of foot traffic, making it ideal for people watching. Below, a woman walked her dog. Clad in her speed walker's sweats, she was moving with purpose and clearly was on a schedule. Behind her, three girls strolled, giggling, peering into shop windows. Not one could be older than fourteen, but each had acquired a lifetime of knowledge about makeup and accessorizing.

Across the street, sitting outside a coffee shop, sat a street-life regular, *the genteel vagabond.* A swollen, pockmarked face poked through unkempt tufts of hair. Fat fingers drummed on the side of a coffee cup as his head bobbed to inaudible music. This sobriquet was self-bestowed, as he was a man who carried himself with a sense of style and confidence typically not associated with those in dire need of a shower. I'd seen him around quite a bit, although we never conversed. From what I understood, he was part street performer, part con man; unfortunately, neither incarnation was ever sober.

Next to him sat an older serious looking sort, with a guitar case. On top of his head he wore a white cowboy hat that was splitting apart in the back. The two traded periodic snips of conversation, although from my balcony I could only imagine the exchange.

Both men belonged to the Nob-Hill area; neither was a *tourist.* The neighborhood, because of its scene, attracted countless such tourists. During the summer, the streets were lousy with them. Anyone who came to the neighborhood strictly for the scene or to shop was a tourist. The guitar player was

34

seasonal, usually appearing when the rain let up. The coffee shop was only one of several locations he used as a forum for his music. On occasion, a woman might accompany him with a tambourine. What amazed me about his music was that every song was composed of only one chord. Not only that, but that same chord would be played in 1 : 1 time while he barked out lyrics. I can't say that the music was good, but there was something endearing in the site of the old fellow standing on the corner delivering the most genuine noise his old lungs would allow.

In the Nob Hill district of Portland, my street was one of two major thoroughfares for foot traffic. The other, 23rd Avenue, was the more upscale of the two streets, housing most of the boutiques, clothing stores, and bistros. My street was tailored for a younger, and less wealthy set. Sure, there were still expensive restaurants and antique shops. The difference was the peppering of lowbrow bars, restaurants, and movie houses along the street. This was where one truly saw a mixed salad society – a cappuccino sipping biker on one street corner, a yuppie sporting dreadlocks on the other.

From my balcony, I was able to feed my inner voyeur with the hum of 21st Avenue. Just as important, however, was the view that continued over the rooftops of nearby houses. My sight hopped from chimney to chimney, making its way toward downtown Portland. I could see the office towers poking up above the city fabric, settling on the edge of the Willamette River. On a clear day, the hazy mountaintops of the Cascades were visible in the distance. While walking along the street to my apartment, I had been aware of nothing more than the street activity in my immediate surroundings. However, only three levels above the ground, I could be part of a world that extended past the city limits, through farmlands, and onto the top of a snowcap.

To my left, on the adjacent balcony, the doors rattled and then slowly swung open. A young woman stepped out with a watering can and moved from planter box to planter box. Her first name was Carmen, but she insisted on being called

Carly; I had to agree that it suited her better. Perhaps four years younger than me, she had recently moved to Portland and into her apartment. She had at one time told me where she was from, but I couldn't recall. I always assumed that it was somewhere in the Midwest, perhaps because she frequently commented on how, "Portland was *such* a big city," in spite of Portland being really somewhat provincial.

"Nick, enjoying the sunshine?"

"Very pleasant today. If it's like this tomorrow we're going to get spoiled."

"When are we going to go for drinks? We keep talking about margaritas."

She was right. I was trying, without success to recall a conversation that hadn't ended in a promise to spend an evening boozing with tequila. I had never really given it much thought. The promise for drinks had always been for some perpetually distant date just a few days into a fictitious future. However, for the first time I found myself intrigued with the offer. The summer just beginning, I hadn't previously enjoyed the sight of Carly in a spaghetti-strap tank top. Now, as she stood in minimal summer apparel with one hand resting on a rounded hip, I found renewed interest in her proposition.

"I've got margarita mix but no tequila. Too bad, with a full bottle we could make our own," I said.

Tilting her watering kettle, she leaned over a leafy plant while nodding. Her thin top clung to the curves of her torso as she tended to her plant. I turned away, feeling guilty for staring, but still filing the image into memory for later. She was too young, too 'girlie'. Then again, that isn't the right word. What I really mean is naïve, not young.

"What are you up to tonight?" I asked.

"Tonight's bad, but the weekend works. Are we making a margarita date?"

"Weekend works for me. What do you have going this evening?"

"Oh, I already have plans – gonna go out," she said, looking away from me and down toward her plant. I allowed her the evasive reply. I stood briefly silent, watching her mind the garden. The only other time I had really been guilty of gawking at Carly, she had been out reading on her balcony. At the time, being new neighbors, we exchanged only smiles, no words. She continued reading, while I sat on my own balcony pretending to read.

Presently, I regarded her plants, green and perky. My own were no more than corpses.

"Carly, I've got to ask you – how the hell do you keep all your plants alive? I've got two house plants and one's almost dead, the other is missing."

"It doesn't take that much time to care for them," Carly sighed. "Let's go to the Farmer's Market this weekend and pick out some plants for you."

Carly's balcony was filled with color & fragrance. Tiny clay pots were clustered on top of a small disco table. Fat, healthy leaves crawled down the side of the pots and overwhelmed the tiny tabletop. She was not so much a plant person as a comfort person. Carly loved to lounge on her balcony and soak up sun, while her little community photosynthesized. I hadn't spent time with her outside of our apartment building, yet I felt that I knew her well by virtue of her garden.

My plants always died because I was selfish and inattentive. My deductive reasoning skills told me that she must be the opposite.

"Okay, the Farmer's Market," I said. "The problem is, I can buy plants, but I can't keep 'em alive. Honestly, I'm the Dr. Kevorkian for vegetables." This got the reaction I hoped for, she laughed and shook her head.

"But it's so easy," she said. "Water is free . . . give it to your plants, don't be stingy."

This time I laughed. Sarcasm was a side of her that her garden did not express.

"Why so critical?" I inquired.

"Oh, Gawd, Nick. Critical? You're too much. Look, you're a designer. Aren't you supposed to be creative and nurturing?"

"I am," I blurted with too much emphasis.

"I'm looking at your balcony and I see one chair, a barbecue and a radio. What evidence is there of a nurturer?"

"I have your beautiful garden to admire, so why do I need to create my own?"

"That," she said with a sly smile, "is what I'm saying. I do all the work and you get to enjoy it. I want to see you put one plant on your side."

"I already agreed – We're going to the Farmer's Market first thing Sunday morning."

"Okay, but I don't want to see a scrawny little fern. Show the creativity. I want to see evidence of some imagination and emotion."

6

Showing disdain for my corded phone, I grabbed my cell and called Ron. One ring, two rings, three rings – finally an answer.

"I'm Ron, who's this?"

"Ron, Nick, it's twenty-five after eight, come on over to my place, we're going to The Pear."

"The Pear, did I ever agree that I was going?"

"Yes, Ron. At work, you gave me a nod. No time to waste, hurry over," I commanded.

I could imagine him sitting in his leather chair, gazing across his room. No doubt, he was considering my offer with a grave expression. Ron took nothing lightly, and he took nothing seriously. I rarely entered into conversations with him casually; it was a venture that demanded preparation. There were two reasons for this: The first, he was intelligent and expected everyone else to be the same. If I were unable to hold up my end of the conversation with adequate wit and acumen, it would not be tolerated; he would find someone with more pith to converse with. The other reason was that Ron was an emotional black hole. He was always entertaining and incisive, but also had a heavy quality that frequently left me drained. This time, though, he would be no match for my persuasiveness.

"Ron, get out of your chair, grab your coat, and come over."

"I'm not sitting in my chair."

"Then you're well on your way, no excuses."

"I won't patronize you with excuses, I'll simply make a decision and commit to it." He paused. "Give me a moment to think about this. I'm imagining myself at the Angry Pear. In my mind's eye, I'm at the bar buying a drink for an attractive brunette. She's wearing tastefully tight denim jeans with a cropped shirt. We're discussing the show, and she reacts with excitement and genuine curiosity to everything that I have to say."

"You see, it'll be fantastic."

"But you're just saying that, you don't really buy into my vision." Now he was playing the devil's advocate, I had to think fast.

"I have confidence that if you don't go to The Pear, the scenario you've envisioned will have a zero percent chance of happening. So are you in?"

After a pause he said, "Yes, I'll be over in ten minutes."

As I waited for Ron to arrive, I stood in front of my closet. Just any shirt and pants wouldn't do for a *First Thursday* gallery opening at the Angry Pear. There was an unofficial uniform required. Anyone who was in the know had an assortment of all-black outfits from which to choose. Personally, I didn't mind color, but tonight I didn't feel like rocking the boat. Actually, bold statements of color were perfectly acceptable, but only certain personalities could really carry this off. Yes, I'd make quite a statement arriving in a bright solid orange shirt with a tangerine vest. The shirt would need to be sufficiently retro, yet not in a patronizing way. The pants would probably have to be a warm color as well, perhaps red? Needless to say, this wasn't me. I've seen people carry it off, but you have to be female, gay, or a fantastic dancer, and I was none of the three. I selected a safe black pullover to accent my black pants and shoes.

My uniform on, I walked in front of my mirror and began a familiar routine. The hair needed just a little gel in front to make it stand up. Add some cologne and I was ready – I could now go appreciate some art.

Ron arrived shortly afterward.

"The sun's finally starting to go down, we can hit the streets," Ron said with uncommon enthusiasm.

"You wanna' drive or walk?" The Pear was only about eight blocks toward the river. It required we walk underneath the overpass, but the distance was easy.

"Might as well walk, that way we can't get drunk and lose the car."

"You're on top of it."

Ron walked out into the hall while I hunted down my keys. As I was locking my door, Carly exited her apartment at the same time.

"Hey, Carly, you're sure you don't want to join us?" I asked.

"Sorry, already have plans, but give me a heads-up for next time. You always tell me about these things half hour before they happen, you've got to get on the ball."

Ron regarded Carly and then looked in my direction expectantly. Being somewhat dense, I was momentarily puzzled by his expression.

"Nick, are you going to introduce me to your friend?"

"Oh, I'm sorry." I shrugged my shoulders apologetically and smiled at Carly.

"Carly, this is a friend of mine from work. Ron, my neighbor Carly."

"Are you heading out to meet someone?" Ron questioned.

"Yes, and I'm way too late. Promise that you'll both invite me next time. I've never been to the Angry Pear."

"Just a word to the wise, those on the inside just call it *The Pear*," I confided.

"Nick's not on the inside, don't be fooled." Ron added. "However, you should stop by 'The Pear' later tonight if you're feeling restless. We'll still be there."

Carly began walking down the hall, waving at us.

"I'll see how I feel later this evening. You both have fun."

As she turned the corner, Ron again regarded me with a quizzical look. Not knowing exactly what he was getting at, I offered back an equally ambiguous look of my own.

"We're going to be late and miss out – let's go," I said.

"You weren't going to introduce me were you?"

"What? Oh, that. I'm sorry, slipped my mind."

"No, I mean, you really should practice your social skills. First, you don't invite your neighbor to the Art Walk until you're nearly out the door. Then you completely neglect an introduction. You're pretty self absorbed, but I don't hold it against you."

As per usual, Ron's words were spoken in a dry unaffected manner that made it next to impossible to know if he was serious or joking. As a matter of policy, I usually assumed that he was not serious; he rarely was. However, I had come to realize that his humor was generally rooted in some truth that he was subtly articulating. It was as though simply stating an opinion was too banal for him, he needed to turn it into a game. So, yes he was usually joking, but there was always a message that he expected one to understand.

"I'll practice my social skills later," I said. Ron maintained his poker face.

We made our way through the hall, down the stairs, and out onto the street. The cowboy hat wearing guitarist was now standing on the corner belting out another of his songs in search of a melody.

"Crazy old guy," Ron began. "If he ever stops playing his guitar, I will truly be sad. No joke. I mean, he can't sing, but it's great to see that guy giving every song equal enthusiasm. This is what he lives for, he does this nearly every night."

"He's a fixture. You ever give him a donation when you walk by?"

"A couple times. He seems to do all right, people love a character."

"True. I don't know that I've ever tossed any money his way. I hope that's not bad for karma."

"No, there's no karma-penalty for not giving him money."

"No?"

"Well, you just won't get any karma-bonus."

"I used to try to store up karma."

"Why'd you stop?"

"I kept using my bonus on worthless stuff. You know, I'd do a good deed for some old lady, and then later that day I'd find a good parking spot."

"What's wrong with that?"

"Nothing, just a low rate of return."

"Shrewd, very shrewd," Ron commented. "Well, you certainly got no bonus for hooking me up with your neighbor."

"Ron, I don't really know her that well."

"Still, a little effort is all I'm asking."

"Fine, I'll remember for next time."

"Fine."

"I'm not even sure that she's suited for you." I regretted my words the moment they left my mouth. Ron stopped walking and simply stared at me.

"What? I'm serious, I don't think you two would make a match."

"I thought you didn't know her well."

"I don't, I'm just saying that she seems pretty high energy."

"That's the conflict? High energy?"

"Well, you're sort of a contemplative person. You prefer to discuss and debate, I don't think she's that way."

"Nick, if you don't want to introduce me to her, fine. It's not a big deal. Especially if you don't see her that much."

"I don't. It was a rarity that I even spoke to her today. Usually, only when we're both out on our balconies."

Ron nodded, but had no comment. We continued walking east toward the Pearl District. Once past 21st, the street was no longer filled with people and no longer was lined with restaurants. Two and three story bungalows now stood in rows along the thin street. As we moved closer to the overpass, the houses would give way to warehouses and parking lots.

Consistently, I walked more quickly than Ron. His steady gait was unaffected by my subtle urging. Typically, at street corners, he would wait until all cars had passed, so he could stroll across the street without having to hurry. Had I been walking alone, I would have been inclined to scurry across the moment a break formed in traffic.

Finally, I resigned myself to walk at his pace, hoping to re-engage him in conversation.

"You've been out on my balcony, no?" I began.

"It's a fine balcony."

"Sure, but it is a little plain, right?"

"Plain?"

"I mean, I never bothered to put plants out there. I've never really spruced it up."

"What are you going to put out there?"

"Haven't decided. But that's not why I'm asking.

"You should put something out there. The balcony could use a little punch."

"That's actually what I'm getting at."

"Plus, it would give you an excuse to spend more time out there. More opportunity to get to know your neighbor. What was her name again?"

"Carly. Actually, she was saying that I ought to put a little more effort into the balcony."

"Smart girl."

"Sure, It's just that I realize how long I've left that balcony plain. I've been a designer for years now, but I never bother to be creative with my own home. Isn't that a little weird?"

"A little weird, but not epic weird."

"Carly, was giving me a hard time about it. Have you gone to much effort to design your place?"

"Of course, you've been to my place. I put time into painting the walls and installed a few light fixtures. Those fixtures, by the way, are coming with me. No way I'm leaving them in the apartment."

"I don't think I've ever done anything to my place. No paint, no plants, no artwork."

"Why not?"

"I suppose I always thought I'd wait until I owned my home. Your lighting is nice, but like you said, you don't want to leave it for someone else. I suppose, it just seemed more sensible to wait."

"So, you've waited. That's why your balcony is plain, you're still waiting."

"I enjoy being creative, but Carly was suggesting there's no evidence of any passion for design in my balcony."

"Well, there isn't, though, is there?"

"I think I'm seeking a way to be creative, but in a practical way."

"You're seeking a more sensible passion, not one that's so frivolous?"

"I think I'm just seeking plants that don't need to be watered so often."

"Same thing," said Ron.

We walked underneath the overpass, past an abandoned shopping cart and a parked car that was missing the driver's side window. Both of us quickened our pace as the fumes from the cars above thickened and became visible puffs of black smoke. Once beyond the overpass, most of the buildings either were warehouses, or had been converted from warehouses to suit some other purpose. Some of the old industrial buildings had been converted into lofts, others now provided studio space for artists. Two buildings originally used to store trucks had been converted into a fine art school, with a new mezzanine being added to serve as classrooms.

The industrial area was undergoing a renaissance as the old brick and heavy timber buildings were re-discovered. The old structures had a charm difficult to find in new construction. At least, they contained a charm that was no longer cost-effective to put into new structures.

Known as the Pearl District, the once industrial part of town was now giving way to high-end retail, condominiums, and restaurants. Fortunately, in spite of the new attention, the area retained a grittiness that seemed genuine if not beautiful.

Half way between the overpass and the river was the core of the Pearl, an area not yet refined by the influx of redevelopment. Cobblestones nestled together to provide the street surface. The occasional areas that were paved contained the remnants of trolley tracks, originally used to shuttle workers to and from their homes.

Concrete and brick, supported by steel, formed the sturdy shell of nearly every building within sight. And many of these massive structures had long stood empty. It was within this context that the artists had moved into the area, converting the buildings into places to live and work. From this eccentric blend, the Angry Pear was born.

Located across the street from a large brick brewhouse, The Pear was on the corner of the block, amid several masonry warehouses. The façade retained most of its original charm; meticulous brickwork with thick mortar joints gave the building a solid yet elegant feel. And sloped window sills pushed outward, allowing prominent shadow lines. Deep window jambs punched through the thick façade, making the exterior seem almost like a shell. The large undulating brick cornice kept the original painted message – bright yellow letters boasting, *Home of PEP Plant Food*. And similar lettering ran in bands under the brick windowsills, *PEP CONCENTRATE*. Yet the entrance had been radically altered and modernized. A large steel and glass canopy, with a thin stainless steel nose, jutted out twelve feet from the doorway.

The Angry Pear now housed an art gallery on the ground floor, and a dance club on the upper levels. This unusual arrangement contributed to it being the newest 'old' hot spot in the Pearl District.

While the architect had retained much of the original building's shell, the interior had been replaced with a sleek contemporary infill. Colored lights and smooth minimalist surfaces defined the interior, and seemed thrust outward at the entrance. The original entry had been replaced with a massive brushed stainless steel door. The entire surface of the door was without detail other than a series of nine small square windows at the top. From the windows, a pale champagne-yellow light illuminated the entrance. Until dusk, the door remained closed along with stainless steel shutters over each of the windows.

On a typical night, a line of patrons would form, waiting patiently for the sun to drop and the door to open. While the sun was still in view, the throngs occupied themselves with critiques of the ensemble of fellow party-goers, and subdued gossip about whoever or whatever was enjoying their fifteen minutes. Some arrived in conservative dress, similar to Ron and myself. Others reveled in the opportunity to outrage and amuse. Bared flesh was accepted outrageous color encouraged, and a hip sensibility demanded.

Most simply came to witness the spectacle, while a select few came to be part of it. Thin, plastic skinned women with glitter applied to their faces sulked and pouted while their boyfriends spoke to one another on tiny cell phones. Scraggily hipsters in slick leather pants and straw cowboy hats pranced with mock expressions of disinterest. During the last remaining minutes of daylight, the doorstep foreshadowed the club itself. Models, dancers, poseurs, artists, and dilettantes of all sorts became part of the carnival, each trying to outdo the other in creative angst. Some simply wore black and brooded, such as myself. Others demanded attention with clothing that incorporated furs and nets in brightly saturated colors.

Simply put, it was the best show in Portland, and it happened only once a month, I rarely missed it. Despite the pretentious showiness of it all, there was an element of fun and silliness that was difficult not to enjoy. It was a spectacular play in which the audience became the actors. The drama that unfolded was staged but unpredictable, and each show always demanded an encore, to be held every thirty days.

Typically, when the door finally opened, the first act of the evening's drama ended, and the orderly mob stuffed themselves through the entrance into the gallery inside. The exhibit area itself took up most of the ground floor, containing perforated metal panels suspended by cables from the timber beams above. The cables continued to the ground where they were bolted to the floor, keeping the panels steady. Each month different shows could be mounted onto the panels.

Above the gallery was an atrium that continued all the way to the top of the building, which allowed views of the night sky through several large skylights. The club itself was contained on the two levels above the gallery, which allowed each floor to be viewed through the atrium. Skeletal, steel catwalks crisscrossed above the gallery, across the atrium, allowing voyeurs a constant feast of fashionables strutting through the air, posing while disco lights pulsed to a techno-dance-beat.

The atrium itself took up no more than a quarter of the floor area, allowing plenty of space for dancing, schmoozing, and romantic scamming. It was also slightly shifted off-center toward the back of the building, allowing easy viewing of an industrial elevator. It was a mammoth steel cage elevator, exposed on three sides, allowing passengers to be on stage for the full duration of their ride. It was nearly impossible to arrive at one of the dance floors at the Angry Pear and not make a visible entrance.

When Ron and I arrived at the Pear, the sun had just dipped below the horizon. The massive entry door had already been thrown open, and most of the crowd was inside. Regardless of how full the building was, we would not be given admittance quickly. There was a 'velvet-rope' treatment that most had to endure in order to earn admittance.

"Think it'll be a long wait?" Ron asked.

"They say they need to keep a lid on the number of people in case of fire – I think it's really just to ensure there's always a line," I said.

"There's power in a line."

From behind us, a gangly woman walked expertly on a pair of short stilts. Long striped pants nearly brushed the street as she took long strides in circles. She held hands with an small man in an expensive looking argyle bowling shirt. Head and eyebrows shaved, he wore ornate tattoos running up his neck and across the side of his face. Several people stood in line with us, indifferent toward the entertainment. Other passers by lingered, gawking at the side show.

"They get paid by the Pear, I think," said Ron. "Keeps us on the outside from rioting."

"Maybe that woman is just really tall."

Ron smirked. "Either way, this line moves way too slow. They should have a bar out here so we can order drinks while we wait."

"If you were an entrepreneur you could open a side business. Sell beer to the carnies."

We waited patiently in line while watching other street performers walk by, amping up the remainder of the crowd. I've never been a fan of street performers. I don't mind watching from a distance, but I'm always afraid I'll run into someone who isn't really a street performer – just an eccentric vagrant.

After inching closer and closer to the door, we were finally granted admittance. Once inside we meandered through the gallery, taking in the artwork. Encaustic paintings hung from the panels in the gallery, layer upon layer of lacquered paint coated each canvas. The thick paint, applied with a palette knife, revealed abstractions of faces and groupings of people. Each painting provided enough clues to suggest a human form, but never a complete figure. Always, the portraits demanded a second look to assess what was actually being depicted. They allowed the mind to fill in the blanks and provide meaning, while the paintings were, in fact, ambiguous. Each form, however, was rendered as a particular gender, never androgynous. Not that the pictures necessarily illustrated nudes, rather some revealed a distinct softness that was unmistakably feminine.

Others were drawn with determined, sculpted lines that implied male aggressiveness.

One image, colored in unsaturated hues that would have appeared nearly gray if not displayed on a neutral panel, depicted a man waiting for a bus. His body was stylized, contorted as if he were a spring. A heavy, yellowed sky pushed down on his back, forcing his head below the horizon line. The shape of his body was repeated in the inanimate objects that surrounded him; garbage cans, bushes, all forms of street furniture. The encaustic paint, with its glossy finish, made the portrait seem permanent and fixed, as though all of the energy and tension in the body would never be released, but simply held indefinitely.

Curious, I asked Ron what he thought of the painting.

"It's awfully yellow, isn't it?" Ron squinted, as if the painting were far away. "I mean, could they have used more yellow? Yellow paint, there must have been a sale somewhere."

"Honestly, do you like it?"

"Yes, I like it – or rather, I think it's well done. But so much yellow makes me anxious. I've heard that yellow is supposed to do that, that's why you see so few rooms painted in a bright yellow."

"Don't you usually bring insight to a conversation?" I wondered if Ron was punishing me for my previous indiscretion of the failed introduction.

"Look, I like to look at artwork, but I'm mulling it over; the ideas need to simmer, then I'll let them out."

I conceded his point, not with words, but with a slow nod. His very short and focused rant concluded the debate.

Ron had always been good at ranting. To really be good at a rant, it was important to start small and build. Ron's mind was naturally inclined to plan events in advance; therefore, he could construct the entire outline for his rant in his head before it was delivered. This would happen in a split-second. The specifics would be determined on the fly, but there would always be a planned destination. There had been times in school when Ron had kept the entire studio enraptured with his verbal acrobatics. First he would perform somersaults and windmills – effectively clearing his throat. It was then that he advanced to the parallel beams where his mouth and acerbic mind would circle and spin, eliciting applause and admiration from anyone within earshot.

On one such occasion, we both were studying in the architecture building. Our design studio was on the second floor of a large, modernist concrete building that held the arts and architecture department for the school. There is an unwritten rule that the architecture building must be the worst on campus. Many are surprised to learn this – after all, what better building to inspire and educate the community about design? At least, this was the logical argument. The reality, unfortunately, was that it was rare for architects to offer large endowments to the programs that taught them how to draft, design, and dress like an architect. This was due in part to middling salaries, and in part to a tradition of suffering which architectural professors eagerly pass on to students.

Ron lounged on a dilapidated sofa that shared the common space between our design studio and the next. One hand held the course-reader for our post-modern theory class, the other was clenched into a fist that he gently pounded into the sofa cushion. I sat at my desk cutting small sticks of wood for a study model.

"Why do we need to read these 'Post-Modern' essays? The professors themselves can't even articulate what they're about." Ron would usually begin a rant with a simple premise.

"I mean, sure, we need to stay in tune with current design trends, but these books are sophomoric," Ron continued. "Honestly, why are architects allowed to get their hands on typewriters? Their minds work in images not words, so they're forced to create nonsensical declarations to legitimize their work."

"Venturi can write, but he's one of the few. The worst are the philosophers who wish they were architects." I said. Ron nodded his head emphatically at my simple observation and continued with his tirade.

"*Constipated architects*, do we really need them writing and mewling about form and spatial order? Commodity, firmness, and delight have been replaced with irony – which seems to be the rationale behind most post-modern rhetoric. After all, how much better is a building if you can *explain it*. Forget about experiencing a building; first-hand experience is trivia. Give someone a good quote about design for a cocktail party and they can pretend they're a designer."

"Why do you bother reading those essays? You can pass the tests without having to trudge through it all." I referred to our weekly quizzes, dealing with 'The Post-Modern Reader'. Ron, somewhat surprised that I would interrupt him, considered my question.

"I like to read. I just don't always like what I'm reading."

"Yeah, but you let yourself get worked up about this stuff. I agree with what you say, but I just don't dwell on it." At this he seemed almost hurt. Perhaps hurt that I cut his monologue short, or more likely, hurt that I rebuked him for being a compulsive cynic. That cynicism, after all, had always been his defining characteristic. To criticize him for his jaundiced eye was to insinuate he was unneeded.

"But how can it not get to you? Look, this is going to be our profession, this is what we do. We're to design buildings and that means we need to respond to criticism written by half-wits."

"Then just don't respond."

"Example," he continued undaunted, "take the term 'Post-Modernism'. For a moment, think about how needlessly self aware and self impressed that term is. Rather than come up with a word that describes our present ideology, it simply refers back to the previous ideology, Modernism. I mean, at least Modernism was about something, it wasn't simply the next mode to follow revivalism."

"So what should it be called?"

"I don't know, and that's not the point. The same logicians would have coined the Renaissance as *Post-Romanism*. Then the Baroque might have been *Neo-Post-Romanism*, and so on," Ron said.

"What about Neo-Classicism? Doesn't that description refer back to Classicism? I mean, Post-Modernism isn't the first example of a poorly described era," I rebutted.

"Fine, perhaps not the first. But it's still a sorry description. Example - why not call the twentieth century the *post-nineteenth century*? Why call me Ron? Why not *Post-Howard Wu*, after my father?"

"You're not like your father, you should be Neo-Howard Wu."

"Good point."

"Your problem is that you actually read the essays. You'll experience less anxiety and do better on the tests by faking it. When writing essays, use collegiate words like *milieu*, *zeitgeist*, *echelon*, and *ontological*. You'll do fine."

"Nick, you read the essays?"

"No, I skim them. I don't read for understanding like you do."

Ron looked back at his book and continued to read, in silence. After I finished building my study model, I waved at Ron and left the building.

Ron and I had finished examining the paintings on the Pear's main floor. Inching through the crowded gallery, we moved in different directions, pursuing our own paths through the beautiful people. As the gallery filled, the space between revelers became tighter and tighter. Smells of perfume mixed with perspiration, as the collective body heat increased. The scent was nearly sweet, reminding me of previous summers – a smell that at any other time of year would seem unrefined, now only punctuated the sense of expectation, the excitement.

Amid the din of laughter and conversation, feeling claustrophobic, I made my way to the elevator. The cage that housed the lift was still speckled with paint, the most noticeable clue to the building's industrial past. As the lift settled back to the ground floor, the cage opened and I stepped in alongside a half dozen others, hoping to find more breathing room in one of the upstairs ballrooms.

The elevator's creaks and groans were barely audible over the crowd as we rose above the gallery. I rode all the way to the top floor and stepped out. The upper floor was also the smallest, losing floor space to the atrium and a small terrace at the back. The terrace was only large enough for a foursome, making it one of the few intimate locations in the Angry Pear. With four already occupying the terrace, I purchased a drink from the bar and hovered, waiting for the small group to disperse.

There is a special sort of awkwardness in standing by oneself at a crowded party. My first impulse is always to look nonchalant, demonstrating that *this is where I want to be – I prefer to stand by myself surveying the crowd.* Quickly, this becomes uncomfortable and I move into phase two – which is to try and appear that I'm merely waiting for others to show up at any moment. A glance at my watch adds to the charade.

I was nearly finished with phase two, when I noticed one of the bodies on the terrace waving at me, motioning me to join. I moved closer and realized it was Andrew, standing with a grin, continuing to beckon me forward.

I squeezed onto the terrace, making it a crowd of five.

"Andrew, good to see you."

"You made it, I'm glad. This is a treat to see you outside of the museum."

Andrew had a cigarette, half smoked and pinched in his right hand, while he slapped my shoulder with his left.

"The paintings are good, I've got to admit you know your stuff." I said

"Yeah, very good, I told you this was a show to see. Have you caught the black & whites?"

He referred to the photos on display, which I had not yet seen. Typically when Andrew advised I see a show, it was more about the scene than the art on display. As far as he was concerned, the two could not be separated. To him, art could not be removed from the moment – the same painting viewed alone without the crowd was an altogether different piece of art. He often gave elaborate explanations on the importance of context; viewing an artist's work as part of a series was paramount. To view one in a series of ten without the others was to miss the whole point.

I had been to shows of his where he had gone to great effort to instill a specific mood within the gallery in order to compliment his work. He had done a series of portraits that depicted violence – the walls of the gallery were painted red, except for the door, which was given a white wash. He explained that it was important that a viewer experience the emotion that was being conveyed within each portrait. To him the portraits were altogether different pieces of art when removed from the context of the red wall.

That evening at the Pear, he wanted me to see the artwork along with the throng of partygoers who inhabited the gallery - or *club* might be more accurate.

"Do you know the artist?" I asked.

"For which, the painting or the black & whites?"

"The paintings."

"Yeah, You'll meet him later tonight. Tell me what you thought."

I considered Ron's comment about having time to contemplate the art before articulating his thoughts.

"Well, they were good, I'm still sort of digesting them," I said pathetically.

"No, no – you can't think them over, you need to react."

"Just a reaction?"

"Yeah, how do you feel about them, what were the first thoughts you had when you took a look?"

I looked away and considered the first painting I had seen.

"I guess I felt a little tight, maybe even uneasy. It looked like the artist used a palette knife – so the strokes were a little choppy - maybe frenzied is the word."

"Cool, so you liked it?" His smile did not waiver as he took a drag. He turned his head, keeping his eyes focused on me, while he blew a jet of smoke into the air.

"It was well done. I also caught on to why you wanted me to see the show tonight. This crowd sort of added to my sense of claustrophobia and tightness as I looked at the paintings."

"The crowd?" he asked.

"Yeah, the context."

"Oh, sure, that's good." He nodded, clearly surprised by my comment. "I hadn't really given that any thought – I just thought it'd be cool to catch up with you."

I laughed and pointed to his cigarette.

"Got an extra?"

I lit up; he let me smoke a few puffs and then motioned to the other three on the terrace.

"I'm sorry, I'm not thinking – everybody, this is Nicholas."

I smiled. He introduced me to each of the others. Shortly after being introduced, I had forgotten two of the three names. The two guys both dressed in black pants with untucked short-sleeved shirts. One had a dark blue button down shirt that hugged his chest. The other had a loose T-shirt that depicted some Seventies television show with which I was only vaguely familiar. The T-shirt was supposed to be ironic and playful.

The third was a youngish female, Meg, who appeared unable to keep herself still. After sipping her drink, a fizzy concoction with chunks of floating fruit, she would tilt her head and shift her weight from one foot to the next. While conversing, she would allow no pause, filling sentences with a "yeah" or some other affirmation. At times she seemed self conscious, not able to sustain eye contact with either of the two men. Periodically she would glance down at her pink T-shirt & Capri pants, perhaps debating if she had managed to achieve the right affect. With only a quick appraisal, I found myself unsure if she was actually superficial, or only had that appearance. I was struck by the absurdity of that debate – trying to decide if her artificial nature was genuine or merely a ruse.

She was a slender girl with sculpted features. Uninviting breasts huddled together tucked in her shirt; and she wore little makeup, accentuating her somewhat androgynous appearance.

Without knowing, I assumed she had been a model for Andrew's paintings. Often, he used live models and the cheapest were usually other students. I tried to envision her posing as a model for Andrew, she had a distinctive look that he typically sought in his models. Next, I tried to imagine both of them going out for drinks, chatting, flirting, and falling for one another. Rather, she falling for him. Andrew never fell for anyone, so far as I knew. He was in love with the chase, but most often he was up front about that.

Andrew explained that Meg was another Art student from one of his history classes. They had been researching the emergence of Romanticism and Neo-classical thought. Their body language gave no clear indication that they were together, but it was a conclusion I was happy to jump to.

"We've been cracking the books together – trying to ace the class," she said.

Andrew picked up his glass and tapped hers.

"It's not a tough class, we'll do fine."

"Are you a painter, Meg?" I decided that I wasn't going to let the conversation degenerate into a bonding experience for the two of them.

"No, I'm an Art Historian. I actually intend to continue with historic preservation or Museum Studies. I enjoy studying art more than I do creating it."

"She should have my work study job, right?" He smiled, jabbing his glass in her direction. "Have you looked into the museum yet?"

"No," she said. She batted her eyes and then continued. "I will, but I've got too many classes this term."

"Historic preservation?" I asked, grabbing back the conversation. "Do you mean preserving art or buildings?"

"Well, I love the Neo-Gothic buildings on campus and could just see myself working with those."

"Cool – I know the buildings you're talking about, the humanities building and there's another." I couldn't think of it but we both nodded agreeing that there was in fact another Gothic building that we both knew of.

Andrew held up an empty glass and looked at both of us.

"I'm going to grab another gin n' tonic, can I bring anything else back?"

Both Meg and I were only halfway finished with our drinks, so Andrew went on a personal mission for alcohol. Being alone with Meg, I had to take the opportunity to quiz her. Not that I was typically the nosey sort, but I couldn't resist trying to determine if she was another of Andrew's flavors of the month.

"You and Andrew known each other for a while?' I decided to start small and see if she would volunteer anything.

"No, not too long." she smiled, but refused to elaborate.

"I imagine that, being an art student, you've checked out his studio – pretty nice?"

"Yeah, it's quite a setup. It's so interesting to see the works in progress. I feel like I can really get a feel for his artistic process."

"But you said that you don't paint, so you haven't ever worked in his studio." I hoped that this was a leading question without seeming too obvious.

"Have I painted in his studio? No, I told you I'm not a painter." She looked a little perturbed, as though I wasn't following the conversation and was forcing her to slow down.

It occurred to me that the quickest way to get information would be to ask directly, but if I was too blunt, I might risk messing up things for Andrew. Instead, I resorted to a different tactic.

"Do you know many other people here tonight – did you show up with a group?"

"No, and no. It doesn't seem like there are many students here period."

"Yeah, but there are a lot of young designers - seems like it's more a social event than a chance to view art."

Meg rolled her eyes and giggled. "Nick, are you for real? This is one of the biggest meat markets in the city. Please don't tell me you're this naïve."

"I'm not saying that this isn't a singles scene – I mean it is a club. I was just commenting on the crowd," I said.

"Look, I'm getting the sense that there's something you're not saying. Is there something you want to ask me?"

I was caught. I suddenly felt very awkward, not so much for being nosey, rather that I appeared to her as if I was clueless.

"Ask you? No, I'm just making conversation."

"Yes, I get it. You were going to ask me out. Why didn't you just say it?"

"Honestly, I was just making conversation."

"Either way, I'm already taken. I'll just let you know that right from the start."

"Meg, you don't understand." Now, I was put on the defensive.

"I'm not offended, relax."

"Honestly, I wasn't." I realized that further protest would be counterproductive. I had dug myself into a hole, and there I would stay. I waited, hoping that she might change the subject. Instead, we both stood looking at each other in silence. I earnestly wanted Andrew to come back with his drink and change the direction of the conversation, but he was nowhere.

"Meg, did you enjoy the paintings?" I offered.

"Sorry, I didn't see them yet." She smiled unconvincingly and looked away.

"Look," she continued, "You don't have to stand here and talk."

"No, that's fine."

"You just look really awkward. I didn't mean to be so blunt."

"No worries."

We both looked away, trying to find a subject that was safe to talk about. As I gazed away from Meg, I noticed Ron across the room amid the periphery of a large group. He was sulking over a gin and tonic. Nearly leaning against the railing that looked over the atrium, he was only distinguishable as a silhouette, most of the light coming from the lower floors. He turned in my direction, but it was impossible to read the expression on his face. I saw him gesture to the girl he was speaking with, turn, and push his way into the crowd. I tried to follow his movement but quickly lost sight of him. I had raised my hand to get his attention, but apparently he had not seen me.

It was as I was trying to locate Ron that my eye caught the ascending elevator, and my past caught up with me. The open elevator allowed full view inside, and amid the throng, I was certain I saw Angeline. Though we had not seen each other since Rome, I immediately knew that it was her. For a moment I could only stare, forgetting that I was still talking with Meg; then realizing my awkwardness, I dropped my cigarette and smashed it into the floor. Shrugging at Meg, I looked back to the elevator, still rising toward the third floor.

"Who's that?" Meg asked.

"Pardon?"

"The girl you're staring at, do you know her?"

"The girl?"

"The one riding the elevator."

"Oh, I'm not certain. She looks like someone I used to know."

I looked back as the elevator finished its ascent. The cage came to an abrupt stop as the metal door sprung open, sliding upward, gaping open like a mouth. From amid the throng stepped Angeline. She emerged, gliding between two women chatting near the front of the cage. They were adorned in brightly colored dresses, one in tangerine with matching pumps, bag, and sunglasses. Angeline paused, seeing someone she knew, and greeted him with a hug. As the crowd in front of me shifted, I lost sight of her. I turned back to Meg, not wanting to be rude, but my gaze returned to where I had last seen Angeline.

"Is that her?" Meg inquired.

"I thought so, but probably not – just someone who resembled an old friend."

I could tell that she knew I was lying, but was unlikely to call my bluff. I fell silent, trying to recall the last time I had seen Angeline. Both students in Rome, we had shared a romance, and for a time had both cared for each other. When I had met her, she had been shy, a few years younger and perhaps still uncertain of what she wanted from life. At first, it had seemed that her affection for me was serious – perhaps it had been. But, as the summer wore down, she had changed toward me. Truth was, I knew it, but didn't want to admit it. Perhaps I knew it because in my own way, I had pushed her to it. At the time, I could only speculate. What I knew to be true was that when we had first met, we had grown close, incautiously. But the mood changed abruptly. We had last seen each other in our studio classroom in Rome, at the end of classes, the summer nearly over. I had thought we would be taking the same flight back, and assumed that whatever had come between us might work itself out. However, I never saw her at the airport. I waited, realizing only at the last that she would not show up. She had left to continue her travels, already on a train, never telling me, though I should have suspected. I wasn't angry that she never showed up, only disappointed that she hadn't told me. There were a number of things I didn't know at that time, but now that I understand what had happened, I wouldn't have been upset that she didn't meet me at the airport – I wouldn't have had it any other way.

"Meg, excuse me a second, I'm going to grab another drink. Can I get you anything?"

"Thanks, maybe I'll wait."

I made my way in the general direction of the bar, taking a detour in the vicinity of where I had seen Angeline. The crowd, nearly too thick to walk through, provided too many distractions for me to spot her again.

I felt some relief in being unable to find her. In the time I had been living in Portland, I still thought about her. However, I was also aware that there was more to the summer in Rome than I knew. Pierce had more than once alluded to that, but was unwilling to offer details. For all of these reasons, I concluded that it would be easier if I simply never spoke to her. Easier still if I could convince myself that I didn't want to speak with her.

As the line crept up to the bar, the queue finally pushed me to the front, where I ordered another drink. For reasons I'll never know, I always feel pressure when ordering drinks. It's almost like a test - an opportunity to demonstrate both knowledge and taste. So a drink must be selected with care – it's not just alcohol, it's a statement of who one is. That evening I was sophisticated yet understated – I was a Manhattan.

I tipped the bartender before ordering, ensuring that the drink would be stiff. With a quick smile, he traded my cash for drink, and moved on to the next customer. As I pushed through the crowd, I saw her again. Only her face, but it was unmistakable, she was here in Portland, at the Angry Pear. This time, though, she saw me too.

7

Steering through the masses, my only goals were to keep my drink from spilling and to find a break in the crowd to provide some breathing room. It was half past ten, the crowd had reached its peak and most were done talking about the Art. The scene had shifted to a nightclub, perhaps its true identity all along. By now, I was seeking familiar faces. Andrew and Meg were nowhere to be seen and more surprising was Ron's absence. I had been depending on his presence and his cynicism as an anchor. Then, I felt a hand on my shoulder.

"Nicholas, I though it was you."

"Angeline," I smiled.

"I was told you were living in Portland, are you an architect by now?"

"You know as well as any; one doesn't become an architect. It's a condition that one never shakes."

"I shook it," she said.

She looked different than I had remembered. In Rome, she had preferred comfortable casual clothes. She was beautiful, but in an unconsidered, almost careless way. Now her beauty was calculated and deliberate. It was evident that in the time since I had seen her last, she had sought something new. She wore her dark hair long, straight and uncomplicated. She had elegant low-cut boots that matched her simple but tight skirt. Her eyelids had just a hint of blue, and her lips were painted. Though more makeup than she used to wear, it was subtle, not overdone. Her top exposed arms and shoulders, making her appear somewhat thinner than I remembered. She no longer had the girlish quality that I had observed on first meeting her years ago; she was likely to become a regular at the Pear, no stranger to the scene.

"Well, you look great – Do you live in town?" I asked.

"Yeah, I've meant to call you. Actually it doesn't seem that long ago since I moved, within the year."

"But you're through with Architecture?"

"With the profession of Architecture, yeah. I still love buildings. I'm a designer, but in branding and imaging; company logos, packaging - that sort of thing."

She held herself confidently, that had not changed, and her smile still had an unsophisticated quality, as though she didn't mean to smile, but couldn't help herself.

"Look, enough about our jobs, tell me what you've been doing? Where are you living?" I asked.

"I've got a little condo in the Pearl, in the middle of everything. It's a place to crash."

There were a hundred questions that I wanted to ask. For a moment we both paused, uncertain where to take the conversation. I looked away and held back a nervous laugh. We both looked at each other and then it was she who broke the silence.

"Nicky, it's so good to see you." She laughed and with drink in hand, wrapped her arms around me and squeezed. My drink teetered, but did not drop as I returned her squeeze. It occurred to me that I wanted to be angry with her, but was not.

"I thought that I had seen you stepping off the elevator, but I couldn't believe it would be you. You look good. A very different style than I remember, but it suits you."

"Nicky, when I saw you getting your drink, I did a double take – I wouldn't have expected to see you here."

"Oh, why's that?"

"Well, you know – is this really your crowd?"

I looked around at the menagerie and concluded that the group was so eclectic that it was not any person's crowd. Rather it was five or six people's crowds all mixed up together.

"I just remember you appreciating a more stoic scene"

She paused on the word stoic, clearly searching for, but not finding another word to use.

"I'm not stoic, I'm just reserved – laid-back maybe."

"No, Nick, *laid-back* is not the word."

She smiled and poked my shoulder to emphasize the tease.

"The Nick I remember," she continued, "needed a reason to do anything. Spontaneity was not part of your vocabulary."

"I get it, I get it," I said.

Pointing at my drink, she continued, "I bet there was some ulterior motive behind the drink you ordered." She held up her gin & tonic. "I ordered this 'cause I like gin n tonic; why did you order yours?"

"Just a spontaneous decision," I lied.

"Really? You don't have any other rationalization for your personal taste?"

"Well, I also like Manhattans."

Near a large dance floor, a determined group began setting up instruments and plugging together equipment. As more instruments were brought toward the stage, the noise of the crowd intensified. Angeline started to speak and then simply laughed as the crowd gave up a roar; someone tuned a guitar. Again she tried to speak, but was over-matched by the din. Now, only mouthing words, she finally grabbed me and pulled my face inches from hers.

"I can't hear a godamn thing, let's scoot to a place where we can actually talk."

I nodded and yelled, "Yes, let's."

Grabbing my hand, she pulled me through the crowd. Squeezing between bodies we slithered through to the perimeter and then ducked into a narrow hallway. The hall connected to various mechanical and storage areas, and at the far end emptied onto an exterior fire escape.

"It's a nice night, let's not waste it with a sweaty crowd," she said.

I looked toward the fire escape and she nodded. Pushing up the window we both ducked through and stood on a steel grate that faced out to a utilitarian courtyard between buildings. A balcony directly above allowed the hum and shouts of the crowd to spill outside, but with diminished volume.

"Ok, now I can hear myself think," Angeline said.

She set her drink down and leaned against the railing.

"So you've been in Portland working as an architect. Any buildings I might be familiar with?"

"Haven't worked on anything local. And for that matter, I haven't worked on anything notable. But I've worked on dozens of buildings you've never heard of."

"Try me."

"A branch bank, a couple discount warehouses, a shopping center. My day in the sun was working on a spec office building."

"Sounds fascinating."

"Oh, it's not as glamorous as it sounds." I said.

"Have you done any competitions in your spare time? Anything to spice things up?"

"Yeah, I've done a few; one on my own and one that I did with Ron. The entry we did together got an honorable mention. No prize money, just satisfaction."

"I miss architecture. Or, at least I miss designing buildings – the two aren't always the same thing," she said.

From the balcony above I could only see a silhouette, but I recognized the voice, it was Andrew.

"Nick, that you?"

"Yeah, just needed a little air."

64

"You're with a lady-friend, I won't disturb you." He yelled.

"We're just gabbing, come and join us," Angeline shouted back.

I looked at her as she squinted, trying to conjure up detail from Andrew's silhouette. Her posture was somewhat more relaxed, similar to the Angeline I had known years ago.

"Andrew, climb down here, we'll turn it into a party," I called up to the balcony.

Andrew handed his drink over to a friend. Then, lifting his leg over the railing, he pushed off and let himself glide several feet down to the fire escape. With a rattle, he landed on the platform. Quickly standing he bounced down the metal stairs to our landing, one floor below.

"Break any bones?" I asked.

"No breaks, smooth landing."

"So what brings you to this side of the fire escape?"

"Curiosity. You?"

"Less noise and fresh air," I said.

Andrew looked at Angeline, then back at me. "Nick, are you going to introduce me to your friend?"

"Andrew this is Angeline, Angeline, Andrew. We studied together, at least for a term. Spent our summer in Rome, worked on a competition."

Angeline looked away at the mention of our ill-fated competition. It was still a subject avoided by Ron and Pierce as well. I also deliberately omitted any mention of our previous relationship.

"And who is Andrew to you?" She inquired.

"He's an artist, a very talented painter, who is currently wasting said talents. Also a student at Portland State, nearly finished."

"Always a critic, Nick." He looked at Angeline. "You should have heard him analyzing this evening's show. If you're a friend of Nick's, you must be familiar with his verbal essays – they get longer the more he drinks."

"I was just trying to get him warmed up by asking him about being an architect," Angeline replied.

"I've heard Nick talk all day. How about you, what do you do?" Andrew asked.

"Me? I'm a professional socialite. I get my drinks for free, I dance, and I mix with artists."

"That's what I like to hear," Andrew said.

"That's not all I do, but those are the high notes."

"Well, this is the right place. No better place to mix."

"What sort of paintings are you working on?" she asked.

"I like to work with oils, mostly portraits, some still life painting. I've never been a big fan of landscapes."

"Any shows coming up?"

"There's the tricky question," I said. "Remember I told you he was talented, but determined to waste those talents? I keep pestering him about a new show."

"I'm working on it, good things take time."

"Some good things happen fast," I said. "I know the creative process can't be rushed, but there's nothing wrong with prodding it."

"Sometime, you'll have to show me what you have in the works. I'd love to take an early peak at your paintings," she said.

"Sure, but first he has to come up with some paintings."

"The paintings will be ready when they're ready. Besides," he said looking at Angeline, "You have me to thank that Nick's here at all. I had to beg him just to show up. Usually he's asleep by now."

Angeline smiled, "That's my Nicky, has to be dragged out to the scene."

"Alright, enough of the third person, I'm standing right here – or didn't you notice?"

"Just pitching you shit. That's not an apology, by the way. Just an observation," Andrew said.

"Anyway, Angeline, if you can get him to show you some new paintings, let me know. I'd like to take a look too. His last show was good, it's just been a long wait in between."

"What galleries have you had shows in?" Angeline asked Andrew.

"I've been in a few shows at the University. I had my own show here at the Pear, and some tandem shows at a handful of other galleries."

"Are you a regular at the Pear?" she asked.

"I am," he nodded absent-mindedly, "When I'm not studying art or painting."

"So, when can we see new material?"

"It's coming. I just need two things: Inspiration and discipline," he admitted.

"Andrew, I'd say it's discipline – you've always had plenty of inspiration," I offered. I wondered if Meg had gone back inside, perhaps already tired of waiting for Andrew.

"Alright then, I need the *right* inspiration."

With three people, the fire escape felt crowded. Andrew pulled out a pack of cigarettes and offered them around. Only a social smoker, I still accepted a smoke and joined in. Angeline also indulged, although she took turns between her cigarette and her drink.

"Tell me," Andrew began, "What are the two of you doing after this?"

The question gave me pause – after this? For me this was it. I would finish my visit at the Pear and then return to my apartment to sleep. Angeline regarded Andrew, but refrained from answering. I took another puff and shrugged.

"It's a school night for me, I don't know that I'll do anything else," I said.

"Tonight's no good, I've got a busy morning," Angeline said.

"You both disappoint me, I had hoped you were made of better stuff."

"Andrew, there's alcohol, dancing, and beautiful people here. Why go anywhere else?"

"I'd like to," Angeline said, "but not tonight. I'll give you a rain-check."

She cocked her head, as she said this, smiling, as if to suggest some level of indifference. Andrew regarded her while she took one last puff on her cigarette and then threw it down into the courtyard, where it bounced on the pavement below. Andrew turned back towards me.

"Nick, I thought for sure I could count on you. I've only just met Angeline so she's off the hook."

"Tell you what, you name the evening and we'll join you providing it's a Friday or Saturday," Angeline said.

"Fair enough," Andrew agreed, "I'm going to hold you to that."

"Then we're all square," She said. "Boys, I'm going to leave you two and hit the dance floor."

From inside, a drum began to thump and more cheers followed.

"Hey, don't hurt yourself in there," Andrew said.

"Thanks, I'll stretch beforehand."

She jumped up and sat on the windowsill, preparing to enter the building. Stepping toward her, I offered a hand to steady her while she brought up her feet and swiveled them through the window.

"You have time for coffee on Saturday?" I asked.

"I never start a day without it."

"Good, should we meet in the morning?"

She smiled and nodded her head as I pulled a pen from my back pocket.

"I don't have any paper; give me your number and I'll write it on my hand," I said.

"Nick, I'm in the phone book. Just look me up. Let's plan on around eleven?"

"Good enough," I said.

"Angeline," Andrew began. "Very good to meet you. I hope we'll see more of each other."

"You've got my rain-check, it's good on Fridays and Saturdays. Offer excludes major holidays."

"No pressure, but there's a weekend coming up," Andrew said.

"Is this the rain-check that we concurrently issued?" I asked.

"Yes, the three of us could meet up. Anyhow, I've got to get on that dance floor."

"How should I get in touch with you?" Andrew asked.

"Nicky will have the number." She smiled, waved, and then popped through the window and hurried down the hall.

8

Andrew took a long drag on his cigarette, tilted his head toward the sky, and puffed out two rings of smoke. The first was tight and lingered in the air, the second dissipated in an instant.

"So you've known her for a while?" He said.

"Not so long."

"But you know her well?"

"Haven't seen her in some time."

"Really? You two, out here alone, I got the idea maybe you were pretty good friends. She teases you as though you go way back."

"Yeah?"

"Are you going to join her on the dance floor?"

He took another drag from his cigarette, this time blowing it out in a long stream. I tapped the ash from mine, by now only nursing it. I watched the embers, still orange, drift down to the pavement below and then vanish.

"Maybe I'll dance next time. You?"

"Nah, not now."

"How late are you staying tonight?"

"Until I finish my last cigarette, then it'll be time to go. No watch," he said holding up his wrist for me to see. "So, I'm not on the clock. You say you studied with Angeline?"

"Something like that, yeah. It was only for a summer."

"So she's an architect as well?"

"No, she gave it up. She still designs, but not buildings. She's an interesting girl, different than I remember, though."

"She seemed interested in painting, I'll have to bring her by my studio."

"Why? You don't have any new work to show."

"Nick, are you taking on the role of my conscience? Scolding me for not working?"

"No, I'm just concerned about Angeline's safety, should she accompany you to your studio."

"There's no safer place than my painting studio."

"Safe? Is that what Meg would say?"

Andrew blinked as he nodded his head and grinned.

"You, my friend, are overly suspicious and a snoop," he said. Grinding his cigarette stub onto the top of the railing, he squinted, lost in thought, and then dropped the stub. "What time do you have?"

I glanced at my watch.

"Not so late, a little past eleven."

"You wanna' go back inside? Fire escapes are for wallflowers and dodgy encounters."

He motioned for me to follow as he ducked through the window. Still holding my own glass, I picked up Angeline's empty and followed Andrew through the window. As we made our way through the hallway, the sound of drums intensified.

"I've heard these guys before, they work the crowd, but their sound isn't very tight," Andrew said.

"They played at The Crystal Ballroom last February, I saw part of their show."

"But you didn't stay?"

"I didn't, but not because of the band. The crowd got into it, but I didn't really know their songs. It's tough to get into a live band if you haven't heard the songs before."

"Really? That's all the fun – hearing something new. For me, live music is the way to go."

"Is this about *context* again?"

Andrew smiled. "I'm not trying to get preachy here, but live music is best, because the artist creates it *in the moment.* It's not planned or scripted."

"Andrew, actually it is planned and scripted. Musicians practice songs at length before performing."

"Okay, poor choice of words on my part. What I mean is that the artist has to be able to create on stage; they can only plan so much. When several musicians take the stage together, they need to respond to each other. They can't plan each note, some of it needs to happen spontaneously."

I nodded. I admired Andrew's enthusiasm, but at times didn't know how to respond to his truisms. Some ideas, however true, simply didn't need to be stated, at least to people with like minds. I attempted to steer the conversation in a more mundane direction.

"Come to think of it, you've seen them before, with me at Berbati's. How long ago was that?" I asked.

"We saw them? No, can't be," Andrew looked at me incredulously, and then with a twinge of embarrassment. "When?"

"Don't remember the day, but you brought a lady friend, the one in your ceramics class."

"Ceramics class? I don't remember dating any girl from a ceramics class."

"Of course not, but you went out with her for at least three or four weeks. I remember her, but didn't get to know her well."

"Apparently I didn't either."

"We didn't get together much, just for music and drinks."

"Really? We always get together, even if one of us is seeing somebody."

"Yeah, you invited me to go out, but I usually said no. I couldn't stand that chick."

Andrew opened his mouth to speak, then discovered that he had nothing more to say. I shrugged my shoulders and filled the silence.

"Anyway, the band, we saw them. Their sound hasn't really gotten any better. I still enjoy a number of their songs, but in a bubble-gum kind of way."

We continued through the hallway, and then into the ballroom. Most of the crowd was pushing up toward the stage. Young hipsters, drink in hand, bobbed and swayed to the thumping drums, while couples on the fringe spun each other in circles to the music. Between choruses, the lead singer prowled the stage lifting his hands high in the air to build the frenzy of the crowd. While the mechanical pulses of drum throbbed, colored lights blinked and swept across the faces of the crowd. As the lights strobed on and off, the dancers appeared to be still motion photographs, quickly changing their poses. Andrew scanned the crowd intently.

"I don't see Angeline out there," he said.

"She's an avid dancer. She's out there somewhere for sure."

By now, I was holding two empty glasses. Looking for a table to deposit the empties, I stepped to the side. As I set down the glasses, I felt a tap on my arm. It was Ron.

"Two drinks? Must be some party," he said.

"You know me, I can never make up my mind. Say, where have you been? You disappeared fast."

"I've been over here by the bar for a while. You?"

"Outside, on the fire escape. Andrew and I were comparing notes about the band."

"So this is what the kiddies listen to nowadays," Ron quipped.

"You listen to it too - I've seen clubbing CDs by your desk at work."

"True enough, true enough. I like to think, though, that my choices in techno are a cut above what we're listening to at the moment."

I began to reply, but the noise of the crowd now intensified, and my words were drowned out. I leaned towards Ron and shouted louder.

"Did you find yourself a lady friend? Remember, that's been your goal for the evening."

Ron shrugged, "If I had been successful I wouldn't still be here talking to you."

"I know that, I'm just making conversation." I motioned toward Andrew, "Come on over, leave the bar for a second."

I retraced my steps as Ron and I found Andrew. In the short interval that I had been away, he had regrouped with Meg. With arms folded, she was scanning the ballroom; this in spite of Andrew's attempts to engage her in conversation.

"You two found each other," I said.

"How do you mean?" Meg asked.

"Didn't you both show up together?"

"Yeah, we met up before the show opened," Andrew said.

Ron looked at Andrew and then turned to look at me. His eyebrows raised, he brought up his hands as though asking for donations.

"Have you learned nothing?" Ron asked.

"I'm sorry?" Andrew asked drawing closer.

Ron stuck out his hand towards Meg and took a step forward.

"Hello, I'm Ron - good to meet you."

Meg smiled and blushed. In truth, it was too dark to see if she actually blushed, but I was pretty certain that she did.

"Thank you, Ron. I'm Meg."

"Are you and Andrew an item? I'm sorry if I'm forward, but clearly no one is going to tell me a damn thing."

"Ron, relax," I said. "I didn't realize that you didn't know Meg."

"Yeah, you did realize, but don't worry about it," Ron commented with his back toward me.

Meg looked at Andrew and raised her eyebrows as if awaiting a response. Andrew looked back at Ron, then he realized that we were waiting for him to speak.

"Didn't I say, *Meg and I got together before the show.* We met in our courses in the art department."

"Apparently, I'm just doing some modeling work for Andrew," she said.

Ron, catching on fast, offered a non-sequiter. "I'd like to take an art class. Maybe I can give up architecture and take up painting."

"Seems like you architects are always looking for some way out of the profession. Angeline used to be an architect," Andrew said, looking at Ron. "I just met your friend tonight."

"My friend? How do you mean?" Ron asked.

"Angeline, you know. You're friends with her, right? Didn't you and Nick study with her in Rome?" Andrew replied.

"Who? Point her out," Ron said.

"It's true Ron. Surprise of surprises, Angeline is here," I said. I wanted to offer a lot more, but realized that I didn't even know how to begin.

"Angeline? You mean the one from school." Ron said.

"Yeah, she's here at the Pear, and living in town. Andrew and I talked to her briefly. She's changed a bit."

"That doesn't surprise me. Too bad it's getting late, I'd like to catch up with her," Ron said.

"Wait a second," Andrew commanded, "Ron, you are friends with her, right?"

"I remember her from Rome, but I never kept in touch with her. Not like Nick. Or, I mean, *Nicky.*"

"Ron, you're playing with us," Andrew said smiling wide.

"What are saying?" Ron asked, looking at Andrew. "And why do you keep asking if we're friends? Is that what Nick told you?" Now, Ron whirled around regarding me.

"I thought you were friends because I saw you two talking earlier tonight. You just looked as though you knew each other pretty well," Andrew said.

Ron stopped and looked up at the band. He began to speak and then stopped again.

"So you've already seen her?" I asked.

"We talked. I didn't really want to bring it up."

"Yeah, apparently she didn't either," I said.

"She and I talked, but we really don't have that much to say. Mostly, we talked about the band," Ron said looking back toward the stage.

"Strange that she wouldn't mention seeing you earlier tonight when we were together," I said.

"Was I intruding on your conversation earlier?" Andrew asked.

"No, you were invited."

"Sure, but do you and she have something going?"

"A while ago, but not anymore. We haven't talked in some years," I said.

"I feel like there's a little being left unsaid tonight."

Meg put her arm on Andrew's shoulder. "So true. There's quite a bit that still needs to be said," she murmured.

Andrew stared down at his feet, now tapping at the floor. With the music still competing with the crowd noise, Andrew leaned towards Meg, but I lost his words in the din. She nodded in affirmation at whatever he had told her.

"I think we all need new drinks," Andrew offered. "Meg and I will bring you both back something."

"No, go ahead. Actually, it's getting late; past eleven," Ron began. "I'm going to head out."

I nearly said that I would stay at the Pear, but I decided to leave one more thing unsaid. Instead I just waved and nodded.

"Nick, I'll see you tomorrow at work. Lunch?"

"Yeah, that's a good idea. Either lunch or happy hour. We'll hook up tomorrow."

Andrew waved as he and Meg walked toward the bar.

"See you two later," Andrew said.

"Good to meet you both," Meg echoed.

As each person departed, I stood with my hands planted firmly in pockets. Turning toward the stage, I felt the dance lights sweep across my face as they swirled around the room. The music wasn't so bad, but I left before the band had finished their first set.

9

Once outside the Pear, the bright lights and frenzy gave way to darkness and quiet. After walking a couple blocks, I decided to be lazy and take the streetcar home. I approached a streetcar shelter underneath the overpass. Headlights above buzzed by at regular intervals, making shadows below grow and dance across the street. I sat, waiting at the shelter, only seeing two couples walk by, chattering and laughing at some late evening joke. Soon, the streetcar arrived and I stepped on, taking the brief trip to Nob Hill to return to my apartment.

The streetcar lurched forward, slowed, then became smooth and began to glide ahead. Bright, colorless light bleached the inside of the car; a few washed-out faces sat motionless on the hard plastic seats. While I was lulled by the hum of the streetcar, my phone came to life. I quickly pulled it out of my pocket, not wanting further beeps to intrude upon the calm inside the car.

"Hello, who's calling?"

"Nicholas, this is Pierce."

"You're awake - why a no show at the Pear?"

"I gave you no guarantees my friend, but I wanted to call you."

I looked around the car and turned my face to the window. Not that it mattered, but I felt self-conscious allowing the other passengers to hear my half of the conversation.

"Pierce, what did you end up doing tonight? Go anywhere?"

"Obviously, not to the Pear. I met up again with Janet; sorry we didn't catch up to you. Seems she wanted to talk a little more about her projects."

"Beauty," I said, trying to allow him to elucidate.

"Well, this involves you, and that's the reason for my late call."

"Now that you mention it, this is a late ring."

"Yes, but I knew you'd still be up. And this is sort of an important call."

"Couldn't wait, huh?"

"Actually, it's definitely a call that could wait, but I'm pretty enthused about what I have to say – so, I couldn't resist, I had to dial."

Unaccustomed to this sort of overt emotion from Pierce, I said nothing, just listened.

"Janet gave me some more information about her potential job, and she's interested in working with another designer. The plan is that I will collaborate to generate schemes to show to the client. You remember who the client is?"

"I remember his name, Harlan. Beyond that, he's Joe to me."

"This is the Joe that owns the Pear – that's his building. I coaxed a little more information from Janet, and this could be a tremendous opportunity. The project is for another gallery, very cool, no?"

"That is good news," I said. "I'm still not all together clear on what this means to me."

"The client is very adamant about working with Janet, having worked with her previously. He's told her that he is interested in working with any other designer she recommends, provided that she's involved."

"A rare situation," I said. "Are you the recommended designer?"

"Perceptive. The point, though, is that it's more than I can handle alone. Are you in?"

I paused to consider all that had been said. As I pondered, the streetcar slowed and stopped at my street. Leaving the train, I walked toward my building while listening to Pierce.

"Nicholas, did you hear me? I'd like your help on the project."

"Yes, of course I'm interested. This is just a lot to consider at midnight after an evening of Manhattans."

"Manhattans upon Lemon drops on top of cigarettes," Pierce quipped.

"Plus I have to take my headache to work tomorrow."

"You have a headache?"

"Not yet, but soon," I began. "Pierce, no question I'd like to help out, but there's a lot I still don't know about this. Is there likely to be some real design? Not dreck?"

"No dreck, I promise. Look, it's late, I apologize. Let's get together on the weekend to talk about it. You, Janet, and me."

"Yes, only not Saturday," I said. I considered my coffee with Angeline. I wasn't even certain that we'd get together. Our rendezvous had been setup on the cuff, and I knew she might change the plan or forget it entirely.

"No Saturday? What've you got going?" Pierce asked.

"I forget, I just recall that I'll be busy."

"The whole day? Work with me, Nicholas. Sunday won't work for Janet, there's got to be some time on Saturday. How about early morning?"

"I can make early work."

"Done," Pierce said. "Alright, I'm going to let you go - you're tired."

"Okay, Pierce," I stopped. "Hey, thanks, this could work out well for both of us. I'll get in touch with you tomorrow."

"Good, now rest."

I closed up my phone and continued home.

Chapter II

On Coffee, and Why We Drink It

[Summer 2001]

1

When I woke up, my head was throbbing in time to the alarm clock. It was too early to open my eyes without protest. With a groan, I stood up from the couch, then shuffled into the bedroom to shut off the alarm. The volume in my head had been dialed up, every sound demanding my attention.

Without lifting my feet from the floor, I shuffled into the bathroom. Slowly and deliberately I showered, shaved, and brushed. Today, there would be no breakfast, as there had been none the day before, and the day before that. Breakfast seemed a luxury, it was opulence. A well-trained stomach knew to expect nothing until noon. This matter had been settled long ago, and stomach had learned who was the driver and who was the passenger. Nonetheless, I would not go entirely without. After shutting my door, I made my way to the barrista across the street and stood in line.

Other patrons chatted amongst themselves while fumbling with newspapers, smart phones, and briefcases. Those not on their way to work clutched books or simply folded their arms. Most were young and lived within walking distance. Some had already completed their commute and were grabbing a quick fix before stepping into the office. In some ways, the whole morning ceremony was reminiscent of taking communion. After an evening of transgressions, we waited in line to acknowledge our sin and drink from the cup of salvation. Each waited patiently, then received the

sacrament and spoke a brief prayer, *forgive us our trespasses as we forgive those who forget to put whipped cream on our café mochas.* Some drank the blood of life, while others ate of the biscotti. And always, *Javagnostics,* were content to simply watch and drink tea.

Upon receiving the sacrament, I added milk and sugar, then proceeded to work. Inside the office, the morning progressed in slow motion. No one was standing or talking or even walking by with hand-fulls of papers. Instead of the busy hum of an animated office, the sound was reduced to a rhythmic drumming of mouse clicks. Like crickets, speaking to each other across a grassy field, intern architects clicked their mice and stroked their keys. *Click, click, stroke, click - click, click, stroke, click.* As if there was a cubicle orchestra leader with a laser pointer for a baton, each worker kept hands busy and head bowed. Each worker also maintained a well-practiced *CAD slouch*, in which the buttocks are shifted to the front of the chair, allowing the shoulders and back to rest easy against the chair-back. This also puts one's face in a direct line of sight with the computer monitor, allowing the light of truth to wash over each intern.

I spent the bulk of the morning wading through flashing details and code summaries. Without caffeine I might have fallen asleep right at my desk. Building code could be the world's cure for insomnia. Page upon page of tiny nondescript text, referring to elusive tables of abstruse data, sat lifelessly upon yellow pages. As I flipped pages and skimmed text, I discovered the quantity of toilets necessary to serve a commercial space with two levels that are both accessible to the public. Of course, I was able to reduce the number of stalls needed by replacing them with urinals in the men's room. But in order to do this, I needed to describe the meeting rooms as offices in order to reduce the number of occupants.

If the above description fostered a yawn, imagine what an entire morning of such information could do. I picked up a notepad and a pen, my prop to appear productive, and walked with purpose over to Ron's desk. I caught him in mid-staple.

"Just a second, I'm stapling," He said. "Are we grabbing lunch? It's a bit early."

"My head's numb. I'm desperate for a break."

Ron stood up to see who was still in the office.

"Okay, yeah, now works," Ron said, then looked back at me. "Hey, we all left pretty abruptly there last night."

"Well, it was late, everyone was tired."

"Tired," he agreed. "I'm still tired."

I set down my notepad prop, and we stole down the stairwell out of the office. After grabbing a bento from a street vendor, we sat on a bench amid an urban park block. It was evident that Ron had little to say, we ate our bentos quickly without conversation. Finally I offered a topic and he bit.

"I think I've got a lead on a design project, some moonlighting out of the office. I'm only now learning about the specifics, but this could be a good one."

"A design project? Doing what?"

"The same guy who owns the Pear is opening up another gallery in the Pearl. He needs someone to develop the renovation of the existing building."

"Where? Which building."

"Not sure yet, I just know it's close to the Pear."

"You're going to do an art gallery? I'm envious, you know I'm completely envious." Ron stammered. He stood up, turned in a circle and then stared at me.

"Nick, that's only the most exciting news I've heard in weeks. How'd you get it? How'd you get involved in this? This is such a better gig than looking up code. I've got to ask, though, how will you find the time?"

I hadn't even considered that issue. During the previous twelve hours, my emotions toward the project had wavered between excitement and anxiety. From talking to Ron, I began to view it as a form of salvation from endless code summaries. It had only taken one morning in the office to make me realize how much I wanted some diversion from the typical routine. An art gallery was a cake project, especially for an intern. But now, Ron had hit upon the rub, how was I to find time to work a full time job and help Pierce with the gallery?

"The time? I suppose I'll get less sleep."

"Nick, you already cheat sleep, we all do. For you, sleep is like a girlfriend you're trying to get rid of. You spend fewer and fewer hours sleeping, hoping it will get the message that it's not wanted."

"Yeah, but I've got to take the opportunity. I need to find some escape from flashing details and the banal of the office."

"Don't misunderstand," said Ron. "You *have* to take this opportunity. I'm only pointing out that it'll kill you to work two jobs. But if you have the chance to do some design, take it. You'll never get the opportunity in an architectural office."

Ron turned and dropped back to the bench. I had always believed that of the two of us, it would be Ron who would first have a chance to work on a project that was worthwhile. He was far more knowledgeable about architectural theory, and tended to mix well with a crowd that spoke *designese*. It was also Ron who was clearly the most miserable with the weekly routine of an architectural office. Neither of us had found our jobs to be what we had hoped, but it was Ron who was actively seeking some way out.

"I hardly even know anything about the project yet," I said. "I just heard about it from Pierce."

"You're working on it with Pierce? Was he at the Pear? That doesn't seem like him, the crowd was too big."

"You're right, the crowd kept him away, but I talked to him on the cell."

"It's a great opportunity, like I said, I'm envious. If you do enough jobs like this, then get your license, you could hang up your own shingle."

"I haven't even thought ahead that far," I said.

"That's the most exciting part."

"It hasn't all sunk in yet."

"Well, then it's time to start sinking – if you start your own show then forget about playing cleanup for our design principal. It could be the last time you have to mop up after his design disasters."

"Easy there, Ron. We both know you aren't a fan."

"Am I wrong? Does he understand good design? Has he ever had a brush with competence?"

"Not the point, he signs our paychecks."

"I just get tired of groveling for a buck. You've at least got an out. For me, this gig isn't satisfying, but I've no better option."

Ron had a penchant for melodrama that most lose by the time their teen years are spent. His venom, often enough, was targeted at our design principal, who owned Integrated Designs. Hard to please and often unrealistic, he dominated every conversation, even when he had nothing to say.

When not demanding attention through his words, he used his appearance to make statements and offer proof that he was hip and *in touch*. He stretched tight fitting black turtlenecks over his flabby body, giving definition to every curve and roll. Often boasting about the price of his shoes and the names on his clothing, it seemed that there was a scorecard of cool of which only he was aware. His hair, coifed in fashionable disarray, followed the most current trends, as did the thick retro frames for his glasses. I was never totally convinced that he actually needed his glasses for vision so much as vanity.

At the beginning of any project he was quick to expound on the virtues of good design. But as the project progressed, and the profit margin grew slim, his speeches tended toward the merits of efficiency and budget. Architecture is literally the art of compromise – each design being a struggle to keep within the parameters defined by the dollar. The value-engineering fairy paid frequent visits to buildings while the design was in progress.

People describe a spiritual nature to design. For our principal, that spirituality was worship of the dollar. In that respect, he was our high priest, and efficiency his greatest commandment. The prayer he taught each of us to say began:

Lord, A righteous man is judged by his time on this earth.
Firstly, let my time be efficient, as if gleaning wheat from the fields.
Secondly, let my time be abundant, as fruit on the vine.
Thirdly, let my time be well managed, that not a drop falls from my cup.
And lastly, let all my time be billable.

He could often be found blustering through the office, scurrying around his desk, where he kept tall stacks of old samples teetering on the brink of collapse. His files were in a constant state of disorganization, and smelled vaguely of cheese – likely due to forgotten sandwiches trapped under mounds of paperwork. He had been running the office longer than some had been alive, and he intended to work until he dropped.

Ron allowed me to finish my bento, while he finished his tirade.

"Nick, I don't know if I'm excited that you have this chance, or upset that it's not me. Either way, we've had lovely bento together."

2

That night, I decided to spend an easy evening at home. I mixed a gin and tonic and stepped with bare feet out to my balcony. While plopping down into my white resin chair, I noticed Carly reading on her own balcony. She was lying on her side wearing a bikini top, though the sun was now low in he sky the temperature hadn't yet cooled.

"Carly, how's the book?"

"That you, Nick? Book's fine." She squinted, bringing her face up and looking my direction.

"Mind if I come over? I can mix you a gin and tonic."

"Please, I'm just hanging out."

I brought two bottles and tried her front door, still locked. I knocked once and heard her undo the latch.

"I'm glad to see you deliver," she said.

"What are neighbors for?"

"Come join me." We walked out to her balcony and sunk down in chairs, surrounded by her healthy garden.

"Just a couple of days until we go plant shopping. Soon, my balcony will look this good."

"If I help you out, then you'll owe me. Maybe you can teach me about art or architecture."

"Sure thing, I can tell you all about my favorite artists."

"Go ahead."

"Big fan of Salvador Dali Parton."

"I thought you were going to be serious."

"Familiar with *The Persistence of Mammary?*"

"Sorry, Nick, but that's just dumb."

"You just don't like art."

I went back to her kitchen and mixed up a gin and tonic. She followed, padding behind with bare feet. As we stood talking, I tested the waters, putting my hand on her shoulder. For the moment, I was content to keep my flirtation with Carly friendly. If things didn't work out, being neighbors could prove a difficult situation. After finishing drinks, we plopped on the sofa and surfed the television. Several times through the channels, and we both started dozing off, so I excused myself. We firmed up our plans for Sunday to visit the farmer's market and then I made my way back to my own apartment.

Before retiring, I scanned the web looking through the telephone listings; only one Angeline Cardieu listed. I called, but got no answer. I've never been eager to leave messages, mostly because I can't say that I've ever left a good one. I decided to keep it brief, offering a time and place to meet, and telling her how good it would be to catch up.

3

Saturday morning came quicker than usual, and I found myself scrambling to get showered and dressed in time to meet Pierce and Janet. A pair of track pants and long sleeved T-shirt would suffice for a breakfast rendezvous. Out the door, I walked to a small breakfast diner located on the ground floor of a seasoned Victorian house. The diner was two blocks removed from the hustle and motion of 23rd Ave. Even at this early hour, at least early for a weekend, people in search of lattes' walked their dogs up and down the street. The dogs eagerly greeted one another while the owners smiled and complimented each other's animals. I was late, and the walkers only slowed me down.

As I approached the diner, I could see a group waiting for a table. It was a line of sorts, with people sharing sections of two different newspapers. A few sat in benches, a few leaned against the building. Large windows collected condensation from the patrons inside, as the sun had not yet warmed up the glass.

Not seeing any familiar faces in line, I opened the door and poked my head inside. Sitting in a far corner with mugs and a newspaper, Pierce and Janet waved for me to join.

"Been here long?" I asked, breathing harder than I should have – blaming it on the smokes I had last night rather than being out of shape.

"Nope, only for half a cup of coffee," Pierce said.

"Good to see you Nicholas. We've already ordered for you; Are you a fan of eggs, toast, and potatoes?" Janet asked.

"The standbys, good. Coffee, too?" I asked.

"On its way," Pierce began. "First, I want to apologize for ambushing you with such a late evening phone call, but I think this is pretty exciting. You're short on details, so let Janet fill you in."

Before Janet could speak, food and coffee arrived at the table. Greedily, I grabbed my mug and stirred in cream and powdered-sweetener-product. I shoveled hash browns into my mouth while looking at Janet expectantly. She was waiting with patient hands folded on the table.

"I'm listening," I mumbled.

"You want details," She began. Before continuing, she arranged her plate of eggs, plate of toast, and coffee mug, moving the toast closer to the jam and shifting the coffee to her right side. "You remember earlier, our discussion of potential projects? The potential has become reality. As I'd hoped, I've been offered a chance to prepare a design; I have a client and a project, which means billable work."

With a knife delicately clasped between fingers and thumb, Janet spread jam across her toast. She waited until the jam had been evenly spread before continuing.

"The client is interested in a conceptual design, and enough specific detail to prove that the design is feasible." She said this before lifting a piece of toast and straining her neck toward the food. Upon realizing that I was watching her eat, she blushed slightly, and smiled. I turned toward Pierce, even though I knew she was not finished speaking.

"The fact is, it's too much work for me to do alone, so I need collaborators. I assume you're interested, or you'd still be in bed."

I took a sip of coffee, waiting for her to go on.

"You remember me discussing Jack Harlan? He's developed a number of projects in the Pearl; some good, others downright awful. His best project, Nicholas, is your current hangover, the Angry Pear Gallery. Lately, his projects have slouched toward awful, so he needs a homerun; that's very good news for us." Upon saying this, she brought her coffee mug up, in front of her face as though she'd just shared a joke.

"I've decided," She continued, peeking over her coffee mug, "that Pierce is to be the lead architect. I received the invitation to submit the design proposal, so I believe it is within my right to make that choice. I have worked on galleries before, so I will handle the interiors. Pierce recommended you, and I trust his judgement, so the two of you will work together. Our design will be evaluated exclusively by Harlan. Unfortunately, he wants to get things moving fast, so we've got to wear sprinter's shoes as we design."

"I hope you don't mind my curiosity, but how do you know this individual?" I asked.

"I don't mind you asking," Janet said. "But I'm also not going to tell you the answer. Now, please keep eating while I tell you more about our project."

I shrugged and scooped up another bite of scrambled eggs.

"Although he hasn't told me, I happen to know that Harlan has contacted other designers about submitting proposals," she said. "As you can imagine, our design needs to be sexy and beautiful. I know Harlan, and I know what he likes; this is our project to lose."

"Do we know how many others are submitting designs?" I asked.

Pierce responded, "I don't know, Janet might. Regardless, Harlan likes working with Janet. So if the design is sexy-beautiful, then we are too."

"And keep in mind, Nicholas," Janet said, "If he goes with our design, then we likely get kept on the project as the lead design team. This is no small project, but one of significance; it's sure to turn some heads in town. When the gallery is built, it could be a rocket for our careers."

Janet finished, then took a sip of coffee to punctuate her words. She dabbed her mouth lightly with her napkin, then tucked it back into her lap. Thoughtfully, I began collecting another bite of eggs on my fork, but my hunger was rivaled by my curiosity. "Tell me a little about the gallery," I said.

"We've collected some photos and program information," Janet said. She lifted a large envelope from under the table and set it down. She began to pull maps, floor plans, photographs, and typed pages.

"Here is the location," she said, pointing to a map of the Pearl district. Close to the Pear, it's a nearly vacant building. I say nearly, because Harlan has set up a temporary office on the top level. As is, it's a firetrap, much like the Pear. But part of our job is to bring it up to code.

"The parameters of what the gallery is to be are quite loose; our task is to define them. We need to determine the space plan, the finishes, materials, lighting, and so on. For three people, it's a lot of work, but we will manage it."

Pierce grabbed several photographs and arranged them on the table, in between plates of toast and eggs. The first group showed the exterior of the building, a compact masonry building that sat on the corner of an industrial block, taking up approximately half. The floor plan was open, with sturdy columns evenly spaced throughout. The space inside extended the length of the block, allowing one to peer from one window all the way to the opposite street. The west façade of the building connected to a raised concrete platform, which paralleled the cobblestone street. The east façade was almost all wall, allowing only a single door and tiny punched windows to face the street. The interior of the building remained dark, with little natural light able to penetrate; a skylight would have allowed some much-needed natural light to enter the interior of the building.

The structure of the building consisted of heavy timbers that created a frame, supporting the roof and interior partitions. The exterior masonry walls had been built at a time when laid brick was common, allowing the courses to step in and out, the wythes to lean against one another.

On the east side, the sidewalk was wide enough to use as a front porch of sorts, although the street itself was scarred with potholes and the remnants of buried train tracks.

Photos of the surrounding neighborhood were also provided, showing the character and history of the Pearl District. The neighborhood had long been a warehouse district, home to trucks and loading cars. The large masonry buildings were only a short walk from the residential neighborhood, providing a quick commute for workers. There had been a time when rails connected the Pearl District to the River, allowing for easy transportation of cargo. In time, though, the area outlived its usefulness, and many of the warehouses were left empty. Eventually they became permanent canvases for architects and artists to redesign and slowly redefine the neighborhood. Now, the boutiques from Nob Hill were meandering east toward the river, populating portions of the Pearl with cafes and galleries.

After I had examined the photos, Pierce pulled a stack of pages from the envelope - permit and zoning information that he and Janet had already gathered from the city. I thumbed through the documents, sipping coffee and munching toast, all the while finding the experience strangely similar to my competition tragedy in Rome. I tried to convince myself that this design would be different than my other experience. I said nothing out loud, but contemplated the myriad number of ways in which our effort could implode. The most common cause might be a clash of egos. Another contender would simply be a lack of time to complete a thoughtful entry. Of course, even a complete and well-conceived entry would have to prove to be more compelling than any other submissions. However, in spite of some misgivings, I decided that there was too much to be gained; even if there was risk, I simply had to take it. I had agreed to become a part of the team, and I had done so understanding that every design project could be a gamble.

"Now that we're all on the same page," Pierce said, "we need to set a time to meet and develop our first scheme. We'll want to start early, so I'm nominating Monday evening."

Janet and I nodded in agreement.

"Do either of you know," I said, "if the client is looking more for a conceptual approach or a scheme that has some numbers tossed at it? You know, should this entry serve as inspiration for an approach or a scheme that is ready to be built?"

"There are no guidelines. I think we're wasting our time, though, if we offer too many specifics. We need to capture the client's imagination and show him the possibilities that his building offers," Janet said, nodding her head for emphasis.

"A strong concept is good, but we need to be confident the scheme is workable; we need to allow for a reality check," I said.

"Nicholas, we're likely not the only team providing a design for Harlan. While we're the front runner, it's not a given that he goes with our scheme. The client wants ideas, he wants to see what's possible. Now's not the time to restrict the scope of what this gallery could be," Pierce said.

"Can't we offer an inspiring concept, but carry it through with some real numbers? I mean, I want a thoughtful entry, but there are real constraints that we need to acknowledge. Don't we have a responsibility to offer a logical concept based on some precedent?" I countered.

"Nicholas, we're designers. Our first responsibility is to be artists; without an emotional basis, a design has no soul, no passion. Our concept needs to have some scx appeal. After the client has selected a design approach, then we determine how to make it work," Janet said. She articulated this with confidence, but also respect. I gathered that in spite of our differing points of view, my questions were regarded as valuable.

"I suppose my question is how far to develop the idea. Perhaps that's a question for later," I said. Rather than wait for a response, I continued, "Can you hand me the jam? I need a little more coffee, this morning came along and cracked me on the head."

After finishing breakfast, we set a time to meet on Monday. Further discussion had encouraged my appraisal of our chances to create a strong proposal. We would have an aggressive schedule, but three brains could manage the task. I was only a little bit apprehensive about finding time to work on the gallery while maintaining my typical work schedule; *more coffee, less sleep* would become my mantra.

I looked at my watch, I had a half-hour before Angeline and I had agreed to meet for coffee. With a few cups already in my system, I was awake, and could hardly keep my hands still. However, it being a weekend, I was unconcerned, and was not going to perform any high precision tasks.

I strolled to the café we had agreed upon, purchased a newspaper, and found an unoccupied table. The café was not so unusual; muted colors adorned the walls, with black and white photos framed and for sale. Large overstuffed chairs huddled around tiny tables, while racks of CDs and coffee mugs marked the path to the register; available for purchase was not just coffee, but a lifestyle. In spite of the crass commercialism, I couldn't really complain, I enjoyed the ambience. To be sure, I was paying a heavily inflated price for beans, but I was also buying atmosphere. I could make the same coffee in my own home, but I would be forced to stare at dirty clothes piled on the floor, and sit on a crappy sofa covered with a sheet.

Many cafés in the area were privately owned, and therefore had a more unique character. This one, however, was easy to find and agree upon over the phone. It also was a familiar place, which seemed important.

I hadn't really had a chance to talk to Angeline one on one at the Pear for very long. The time and distance between us since Rome, that had once seemed so vast, now felt trivial. I almost felt as though we could simply sit down and continue conversations started years ago in Italy.

Yet Angeline was clearly changed. The girl I had known was wise, but not sophisticated; she had not been so self-aware. Now, she wore her new found confidence well, but I missed her naïve quality that used to immediately set me at ease.

I had been in love with her, or at least infatuated with her. There had been a time, when I believed she had been in love with me. I felt foolish for calling her to meet now, after it had been so many years. Perhaps the only thing we could have in common would be the past; our coffee would be a chance to say, 'Remember this one?' and 'Do you recall that day?' After cycling through the better memories, and filtering out the bad, we would hug and agree to meet more often, but neither of us would mean it.

Most importantly, I knew that I would not feel comfortable asking any of the questions that I really wanted answered. The issues that had seemed so important for so long would be the eggshells to avoid walking over.

I considered how I had felt about seeing Angeline on Thursday. It had been a surprise then, but I had been given time to consider. She had no right to any more of my time or emotions, yet I sat alone in a coffee shop, twenty minutes early, waiting for Angeline.

Chapter III

Learning from Rome

[Summer 1997]

1

I n the city of generations, built layer upon layer over eras of prosperity and eras of tumult, built from marble, from stone, and from clay, I became capable of understanding beauty. I studied at arcades fashioned under the direction of Boromini. I learned from the graceful proportions designed and chiseled by Bernini and Michelangelo. And it was in Rome that I met Angeline.

In the truest sense of the word, I was a student, and the streets were my textbooks. The summer term was my last before receiving my degree in architecture. It was the culmination of an education that had spanned seven years. After receiving a Bachelors degree in Fine Art, I chose to apply my skills towards architecture, and pursued a Masters degree. Now, after a three-year tenure of study, I was beginning the final series of lessons before becoming a professional designer.

The program in Rome would last approximately twenty weeks, and involved a design competition to be judged during the final week. I believe there had been 25 students who had traveled overseas from various universities to take four separate classes, including a design studio. It was the design studio that would serve as the basis for the competition, which would be offered to students and professionals practicing in Rome.

During the spring term, before traveling to Rome, each student participated in a variety of classes intended to prepare the mind and the eye for the anticipated journey. We took courses in basic Italian, learning how to order food and ask for lavatories. Many invested hours learning how to swear properly in their newly acquired tongue. My Italian was no good, so I resigned myself to simply speaking slowly and loudly in English.

Each student also took a history course that examined the buildings and monuments of the city, while comparing this to the politics and arts of significant time periods. The class was only ten weeks, so we didn't devote time to Romulus or Remus. However, the course provided a good basis to the previously uninitiated.

Unfortunately, schedules did not allow all over-seas students to sit in the class together, so many of us arrived in Italy as strangers; though, we did all share much in common. Each of us was equally able to butcher the Italian language, and equally able to misread Italian bus and train schedules. Few things turn strangers into brethren quicker than shared adversity.

After months of preparing to travel across the ocean, the journey itself was a blur. I had put surprisingly little thought into what items I would cram into my duffel bag. At first I organized appropriate clothing, folding and then stacking it at the bottom of the bag. Then, my system of organization became increasingly unclear. I shoved books, maps, and notepads into the bag. Then, upon realizing that much of that was to be provided, I haphazardly removed some books, but not all. I assembled loose toiletry items and stuffed them into pockets and in between shirts. Soon, tapes and CDs and food joined the contents of my luggage. The longer I packed, the more unnecessary items were included. Eventually, I removed items in a frenzy and replaced them with assorted visas, passports, money belts, and lira.

The flight itself lasted hours, first crossing the continent and then crossing over the ocean. The time went by quickly, however, as it often does when enthusiasm is mixed with apprehension. Upon touching down, I was most aware of the humidity and the heat. Even with so many differences, I noticed few things so much as the sticky heat that persisted.

I made the mistake of wearing long pants on the flight, and with a bag slung over my shoulder I labored, marching toward the bus that would take me to my temporary residence. Even with windows down, the heat would not relent, and perspiration began to soak half moons under my arms. The breeze was not cooling, and dried my lips and eyes. At first, I was quick to wipe away the perspiration that rolled from forehead, to cheek, and then to chin. Soon, though, my entire body felt damp, and I resigned myself to the discomfort.

When classes began, I had learned to wear the minimum amount of clothing that was decent, sit in the shade, and keep cold beverages at hand. I also began a habit of spending free time away from class, sketching the city. I was determined to understand Rome by drawing what I observed.

My first sketching safari was at Piazza del Campidoglio, the Capitoline Hill. It was a piazza that had at one time been a gathering place for political and religious events, enfronted on two sides by palazzi.

Centuries ago, the piazza had gone into a state of disrepair, the center little more than a muddy morass. The city of Rome itself was in a similar state, disintegrating from within. The government's authority had been eroding as threats from other regions mounted; the Campidoglio served as metaphor for the dilapidated and ruinous state of sixteenth century Roman authority.

The Pope, embarrassed by the condition of the Capital, commissioned Michelangelo to renovate the building facades and repave the piazza; he accepted the challenge to devise a solution to restore the eroded seat of government, symbolizing Rome's resurgence. His solution was both a brilliant work of artistry and architecture. The piazza, at the time of his design conception, was little more than a mound of dirt and debris. It was flanked on only two sides with adjacent buildings that were at skewed angles, Palazzo dei Conservatori on the side and the Palazzo Senatorio opposite a large staircase. The new buildings retained a gesture to the traditional orders, but played with multiple scales, single story columns to the side of giant columns. It was Michelangelo's sense of scale and proportion that typified his mannerist eye.

The real stroke of brilliance, though, was in the way Michelangelo dealt with the piazza itself. His design called for a building on a third side, the Palazzo Nuovo, at a skewed angle mirroring the Conservatori. This not only created a sense of order and calm to the site plan, but also gave the piazza a funneled or trapezoid shape. The thin end of the funnel at the back played an optical illusion, forcing a sense of perspective that made the Senatorio seem larger. Within the trapezoid, the floor of the piazza was covered with patterned stone, forming an oval. And at the center of the oval sat an equestrian statue of Marcus Aralius, symbolizing the power and authority of Rome.

Michelangelo was as much an artist as an architect, and he felt that the built environment could relate the history of the people who had used the site. Therefore his design called for the oval patterned stone to rise at the center, alluding to the mounded dirt and mud that had once sat in the middle of the piazza. The concrete around the oval was raised higher than the patterned stone, creating a distinct threshold between the two. The concrete was intended to symbolize the order provided by Roman authority, while the mounded stone became a metaphor for the untamed disorder inherent in Roman society. The two forces competed against one another, demonstrating the ongoing struggle between order and chaos that had always been characteristic of Rome.

As I sat gazing at the beauty and depth of Michelangelo's design, I couldn't help smiling at the most amazing part of the piazza; it wasn't completed until centuries after Michelangelo's death. He only lived to see the completion of his design for the Campidoglio's staircase; the rest of the piazza was not completed until the seventeenth century.

I sat along a series of steps, with my sketchbook resting on top of my knees and a pencil plugged between my lips. As I observed the bodies moving through the

Piazza, Pierce approached me. We had taken classes together at the university, but no studios. I had gotten to know him by reputation before actually talking with him in a class; he had developed a small following of underclassmen that held his skills in awe. While talented, he tended to buck convention and could be accused of being at least slightly antisocial. However, we had gotten along well, and I found that even brief conversations could yield a wealth of information.

"Nicholas, sketching and scratching. What caught your eye?" he asked.

"The building facades, capturing the proportions. See the window bays, they have the same proportion as the colonnade," I said, pointing to the ground level columns. "Michelangelo had a remarkable grasp of proportion and scale, easy to see he was a sculptor."

"Can I see your drawing?" Pierce asked. He had his hair cut to a bristle by an Italian barber on the first day. His only instruction had been, '*corto, corto!*', meaning *shorter* in Italian. The barber had complied. Pierce also was one of the few students to continue wearing long pants in spite of the heat. Being light cotton, they were likely more comfortable than they appeared. He wore a loose, patterned shirt, the top two buttons left undone. He had crouched down in front of me, legs bent underneath him, in a position that I couldn't imagine was comfortable. He remained in the same position, though, as he examined my drawing. His thin fingers tracing over my sketch, he first glanced at it, then nodded his head.

I had first drawn a grid across my page as a guideline to ensure the proportions would be correct. Then, drawing the extents of the picture, I drew the massing of the building quickly, with loose faint lines. After determining the location and size of the objects, I had begun to refine the details, strictly using lines.

"Excellent line work, you've done this before," he laughed.

"I'd like to do one in ink and then watercolor over it."

"There you go, you'll have all your postcards."

"Funny man; I haven't done watercolors before, so I'm not ready to send them out for posterity."

"Watercolor can try your patience, but it's well worth it."

"You've done quite a bit of watercolor, correct?"

"Some. I'll do more this term, perhaps for my design project."

Pierce was, in fact, an accomplished artist and had a high facility with the brush. I was hoping to glean some techniques from him, but he was simply an observer today; he had brought no drawing tools. He stood up and stretched his legs, while looking at the surrounding buildings.

"The important thing to remember when working on a watercolor," he began, "is to realize that you cannot control the paint. It will flow where it wants. Work with the paint, but don't fight it."

"See, that's why I love pencils, they're predictable and precise. Most importantly, though, mistakes can be erased. Water color isn't a forgiving media," I said.

"True, but that's a positive. It means that you need to move quickly and not over think. Overworking and overthinking are the two greatest sins. Watercolor forces discipline and demands economy."

"With pencil, though, a drawing can evolve. Working a drawing leaves traces of the process, like my guidelines," I said pointing to my sketch. "Traces similar to the ones Michelangelo left in his design of the Campidoglio."

"Similar to the city of Rome itself; each building one more layer built upon the remnants of what stood before. Each stone we're sitting on speaks a fragment of that history."

"Well, these fragments are becoming painful to sit on; all agony no ecstasy."

"Should we head back for class?"

"Class, is it almost time?"

"We've a little time, but I may grab a bite first. Join me?"

I packed up my sketchbook and pencils, and we walked down the great set of stairs leading away from the Capitoline Hill. As we neared the bottom, Pierce turned around to take in the entire design.

"Quite a work, his design is emotive – his gestures difficult to put into words," Pierce said.

"That's what I hope to do. Everything I see in Rome, I want to be able to break down and analyze. I want to understand what Michelangelo was thinking, how his process worked."

Pierce smiled, "Sorry, you're going to be disappointed. Some things defy analysis; some things can only be felt. This design is intuitive and won't be cracked through analysis. You're right to sketch it; you'll see and understand, but you won't be able to put it into words."

"If I can't find the words, then I'll buy a postcard – how's that? I'm convinced that good design is rational. There's an order, a sensible pattern to how the Campidoglio evolved."

Pierce turned and walked away from the stairs, in the general direction of our studio. I adjusted my pack and hurried after him, feeling a thin dot of sweat roll down my neck.

"Nicholas, we'll have to sit down with a pitcher of beer and have this out. You understand design, but you have too much faith in reason as the means to good architecture. Intuition is powerful."

"I can make time for philosophy and beer any day. We can exchange doctrine over a few pints. What I wouldn't do to have one now."

"Tempting, but I'd fall asleep before we got to class. Professor Rice would have a fit."

"He would be a good man to include in our discussion; although one beer might put him under the table."

Edward Rice had been a professor at the University for more than two decades. This was not the first time he had been designated to teach the traveling program in Rome. Previously, he had used the same design program for each of his Italian studios. This time, however, he had discovered a design competition that coincided with our summer term of studio. It was easy to sense his enthusiasm for both the competition itself, and the variety that the new design program provided. An international design competition gave him an opportunity to show off his encyclopedic knowledge of Italian history and design. At the end of two terms, the studio would culminate in a presentation of all the final designs. The competition winner would receive a ten thousand-dollar stipend for further study and travel. A winning entry provided a rare opportunity for a young designer; and also provided an extension of study, which kept the *real world* at bay that much longer.

Pierce and I walked along the Via del Teatro di Marcello, a large well traveled street that meandered toward the Campo de' Fiori. Pedestrians hustled across at breaks in traffic, avoiding cars, and enduring horns and exhaust. We quickly crossed and lost ourselves in the confusing but less congested side streets. We had just left the center of the ancient Roman world, and were burrowing deep into the alleys and streets that linked the modern city. Small motorbikes and tourists with cameras dangling from their necks crisscrossed over stone. Soon, we left behind the hum of traffic, and found less inhabited paths. The alleys were so thin the bright sunlight could only reach the sides of the buildings, leaving our feet in shadow. Lines of clothing, drying slowly in the humid air, reached out from window to window, and old women with large purses walked slowly but with purpose. These were the living streets, the front porches of people whose families had lived in Rome for generations. Pierce and I walked quickly, leaving behind Piazza del Campidoglio; I knew the place I had come from well, but these streets all looked the same.

2

Pierce walked confidently, slowing briefly to take in his surroundings, but never hesitating to choose his path. When we spilled out into an opening, he never wavered for direction, but turned sharply with the street. To me, the roads meandered, never maintaining a straight path. They curved and kinked, loping along huddled buildings, then bursting out into piazzas. As we continued, stuccoed façade followed stuccoed façade, each building the cousin of the one that preceded it.

"This street, we've walked it before. Is this the right direction?" I said.

"Not a navigator, are you Nicholas?"

"This *is* a street we've walked before."

"No, take a look." Pierce pointed toward an open court adjacent to the thin street that had seemed so familiar to me. Inside the court, just beyond the shadow line, a fountain quietly bubbled water around a statue. Pierce looked at me, then back toward the statue, letting his finger drop once it was clear I agreed that this street was new.

"I've got to look at a map," I murmured.

We both continued walking, but detoured into the court, staying within the shadows. The small space was empty, no people sitting in the sun or walking by. There was only me, Pierce, and the statue; all standing wordlessly. A young woman, polished smooth, rose from the bubbling water. Rounded curves defined her torso, which was partly concealed by her arms. The woman seemed shy, as though she had been bathing, just before Pierce and I had walked by. However, she was a frozen moment, forever covering her nude body from passing voyeurs. I smiled at the simultaneous modesty and brashness of her posture. The manner in which she covered her body seemed to add to the provocative nature of the pose.

"You've studied this statue?" I asked.

"Not this one, no. However, the theme is familiar."

"Nude women? Yeah, I've seen a lot of that theme in Rome."

"Quite popular here, yes?" Pierce smiled.

"Do you think it will ever catch on in the States?"

Ignoring my comment, Pierce finished his thought. "Of course, I mean her emerging from the water. That was a common motif for rebirth."

"No, I think she's bathing. She's not emerging from the ocean."

"Bathing? Then we're a couple of peeping Tom's."

"True, but in Italy, that's no crime; as long as we peep in an artistic manner, I think we're okay."

"Fine, then I'm artistically ogling her breasts right now," Pierce said.

We both walked around the statue, each different angle presenting a slightly different reading of the pose. The bright sunlight emphasized the curves and volumes, adding highlights that lent drama to the woman's features.

"Not to change the subject from sex to art, but I'm not familiar with this statue."

"I'm not convinced you can separate the two, but I'd also like to know its history," he said, still circling the fountain. "Bathing or emerging. Have you got your camera?"

"Sorry, no camera. We'll have no record for posterity."

Pierce shook his head. "Not so much that. I wanted to ask Rice if he was familiar with her."

The fountain that surrounded the statue was small, scaled for the confined size of the court. The lip of the fountain was just barely large enough to be a seat, though it had cracked in places, making it seem unfit for support. The statue itself was smooth, though areas were discolored and showed small veins from cracks.

I looked at the face, the features well defined and precise. The sculptor had meticulously defined the eyes and given her rounded lips that seemed uncommon compared to other Roman statues. I considered how different this woman was compared to statues I had seen in Portland. I was used to statues that lacked detail and clarity. Often the figures were abridged or simplified; as though the point was to merely suggest a female form. The subtleties were absent, and there was less care in shaping the contours of muscles. This statue, however, was carved by a sculptor who understood every curve, every angle, and proportion of the subject. Clearly, this was not simply a carving of a woman, but of a particular woman.

I was beginning to understand that in Rome, sculpture had been woven into the city fabric over the course of centuries. So many designers had left their mark, that it was now simply commonplace. Artwork was as common in Rome as blue post drop boxes were common in Portland. An Italian, walking down this same street might find no reason to take notice. I set my backpack down, leaning it against the fountain. Opening the zipper, I pulled out my sketchbook.

"No camera no problem," I said. I flipped through the book until I came to the next blank page, then sat down with legs folded and began scratching my pencil across the paper. Pierce, without his sketchbook, walked around the statue, then behind me to view my sketch. Sitting in the direction of her gaze, I regarded the woman; her body was slightly twisted. I began by blocking out her form in a generalized way in order to understand the proportions. By first planning the sketch, I could then come back and fill in the detail. The direct sunlight made it easier to show the rounded nature of her features, creating bright highlights and dark shadows. As I quickly moved my pencil, I applied greater pressure when drawing shadows to emphasize the darker lines. I made a deliberate choice to draw a looser less polished drawing.

After reducing the statue to a series of basic shapes, I began drawing in greater detail, forming the shapes to be truer to the subject. I wanted to capture what I perceived to be her sense of surprise at being discovered. To me, her arms covering her torso seemed to provide the drama for the sculpture. Because her arms concealed her body, I found that the statue had a sense of intrigue that could not have been achieved with a more traditional nude sculpture. I couldn't help but imagine a scenario in which the sculptor had first seen his subject in secret. There was something genuine about the sense of modesty that the girl possessed. I pictured her bathing at the bank of a stream, presuming that she was alone. When discovered, she covers up. However, aware of her beauty, she allows judicious views of her legs and torso.

Imagining this scenario, I added greater emphasis to her legs and stomach. I used a kneaded eraser to lift graphite from her stomach in order to create greater contrast from a darker arm that provided shadow. I showed her front leg, slightly lifted, with fewer strokes to emphasize the simple gentle curve of her thighs and ankles.

I leaned on my pencil as I added shade and shadows. Emphasizing the shadows for greater drama, I brought out a small eraser and proceeded to pull up graphite in areas where I wanted greater hi-lights. After this, I added hatching behind the form of the girl to make her stand out from the faint background that I had drawn.

I began to work more quickly in order to avoid scrutiny, but finally Pierce spoke, "Much better than a camera, I like this sketch."

"It's a beautiful sculpture. Think Rice will recognize it?"

"Perhaps if you add a face," Pierce said pointing to my headless drawing.

This was the greatest challenge. Often, I found myself wanting to punt when drawing either a face or hands. Those were the features that really needed to be specific in order to be believable. Other areas could be faked and still look good. However, a mistake on the face or fingers would simply look like a mistake. I had shown only one of her hands, the other hidden from my viewpoint.

I had taken figure-drawing classes as an undergrad. The first time live models were discussed, I had to shake off some sophomore embarrassment. In the class prior, the professor had informed the students that we would be drawing from a model, and that we should bring a variety of different media materials so that we could practice using brushes, pencils, pastels, and anything else we could imagine. Everyone else in the class treated the announcement with such ambivalence that I decided to conceal my curiosity. I wasn't unfamiliar with the idea of a nude model, but as a sophomore in college, not yet twenty, I found myself intrigued. Particularly, I was surprised to learn that the models had been solicited through flyers distributed around campus by the art department. I considered what this might mean; in a few days one of my peers might be standing in front of me with nothing on. This notion wasn't exciting to me, so much as it was amusing. I couldn't imagine how I was going to keep a straight face.

The day of the class arrived, and I tried to appear as disinterested as possible. I walked into the studio with pads of paper and a bin filled with various brushes and pencils. As I set up my easel, I was disappointed to see, standing next to the professor, an older man wearing a bathrobe. This gentleman wasn't just older, he could have been my grandfather.   As the class began, he disrobed, folded his garment, and stood up on a platform centered in the classroom.

When the model took his stance, the professor announced, "Now, the important thing is to work quickly. Remember, we're all working to create 'gesture' drawings. You're trying to convey the feel of your subject."

Each student stood intently watching the subject, hand outstretched, making broad sweeps across their pages. At first, I held out my pencil to measure the proportions of the model; then began making tentative strokes. After a few minutes had passed the professor said, "Switch." The old man moved from his pose and crouched on top of the platform, folding his arms on his knees. In unison, the group of students flipped their pads of paper and began a new sketch. Although intent on capturing the current pose, I couldn't help but think of the absurdity of the situation. I stood, no more than five feet from a naked, crouching man, whose skin sagged in loose folds nearly ready to fall off his bones.

After a series of poses, the class, and the model, took a break. As if an actor who could not break character, the old man began walking around the studio looking at each different sketch. He had picked up a bottle of water, but had not bothered to put his robe back on. From easel to easel, he moved, grinning as he looked at the different renditions of himself.

The few students who had foolishly not left the studio for their break were forced into conversations with the naked gargoyle. He would excitedly point to drawings of his shoulder blades or hips, inquiring if he really looked like that. It was comical to see him engaging the male students, but seemed almost sordid as he cornered female art students. With one hand on his hip, the other clasped around his bottle, he followed students around, inquiring about their drawings.

It occurred to me that this was probably not an uncommon scene for figure drawing classes. In order to pose nude, I suppose it took a different mentality than was typical. This thin, gaunt man had likely been doing this for years; it was evident that he knew the professor from previous classes.

Figure drawing, I learned, could be a clinical exercise, similar to a doctor examining a patient. As I sketched, I gradually forgot that I was drawing a person, and only noticed the light and shadow. In subsequent classes, I again had the opportunity to draw this uninhibited man, but I gradually saw less and less of the comedy of the situation.

I realize now, that I should have retained some of that comedic viewpoint. I should have remembered the absurdity of staring at a naked man crouching in front of a group of strangers.

Years later, sketching the statue in front of Pierce, I was careful to get the drawing technically correct. However, I only used my drawing to document what was in front of me. I didn't use it as an opportunity to show how I felt about my subject. In that sense, a camera could have done the job of a pencil. If artwork is only a record of what one sees, then it can't matter whose hand holds the brush, or whose eye looks threw the lens. Looking back, I wonder what my sketchbook might hold if I had first filtered the subjects through my own experience.

After finishing my drawing, I handed my book and a pen to Pierce. He hesitated, then agreed, flipping to a blank page. He held the pen loosely, allowing lines to stray. He used his entire arm to generate strokes that varied in thickness. He attacked the page, leaving the guidelines used to measure his subject. As the drawing developed, the level of contrast in the sketch became increasingly pronounced, each stroke revealing the subject in more depth. As the strokes built up, the drawing became more emotive, less a literal depiction of the statue. Pierce deliberately elongated the torso, exaggerating the hips, stretching her proportions.

The drawing showed her not so much as a person, but an exaggeration of a female form. As he drew the face, he enlarged the mouth rounding the lips. The eyes and nose were drawn as tiny delicate features without detail. His depiction of the statue lacked the innocence that, it seemed to me, she possessed. The demure manner in which she covered her body was lost with the vantage-point that Pierce had chosen. His drawing revealed an angle that obscured her arms, showing more of the torso and hip. He also chose to emphasize the water bubbling in the fountain. Instead of a subtle wash, the water was shown with a spray that framed the figure of the woman. The spray served to heighten the sense of energy, and also to provide a contrast to the highlights he depicted on her body.

I examined his line work. Pierce used his pen to generate different characteristics in each line he applied. By using different amounts of pressure, he created bold confident lines. He used them to create unbroken curves that enveloped his subject. Then, by pulling up his hand at the end of the stroke, he created a thin tentative line that emphasized the feminine delicate nature of the facial features.

The drawing, while outstanding, was not intended to show the woman in an objective way. Pierce would have depicted the same statue in an entirely different manner had we returned to the same spot a day later. In fact, if we had returned each day, to draw the same sculpture, over the course of the entire term, no drawing would look alike. Each sketch would convey a different aspect of Pierce's perception of the woman he was observing.

I compared our sketches, mine entirely about the woman I saw in front of me, Pierce's entirely about how he saw the world, his subject almost incidental. As I imagined showing the sketches to professor Rice, I couldn't help but wonder how he would react to the different nature of each sketch.

"What does your watch say?"

"We're alright; still time to grab a bite and slip into class."

Pierce handed the sketchbook back to me, closing it first while I pulled out my map.

"No need, we're on track," Pierce said

"On track if our goal is to wander aimlessly. Not long 'til studio begins, I'd like to have time to stop at the market for lunch before class."

"Good that we've finished our sketches."

"One more look at our work," I said opening the sketchbook. I flipped through the pages, back to the last drawing revealing Pierce's sketch.

The idealized beauty that was present in the statue was nowhere to be found in his drawing. The proportions of the figure where pulled and elongated. The drawing still maintained a quality of beauty, but one that strayed from what was typically feminine.

"This reminds me of a Giacometi," I said, referencing a sculptor famous for his elongated depiction of figures.

"We're fifteen minutes from the market, let's start walking."

"Some people can't take a compliment."

"Hurry, and we'll still have time for lunch."

We moved ahead, once again toward the Campo; Pierce moving with purpose. I hurried, though I would have enjoyed time to take it in, time to think about what I had seen.

.

"I'd like to show the sketches to Rice. What do you think he'll say about the statue?" I asked.

"He'll no doubt comment on her supple breasts of marble."

"You're right, though I was certain I could see surgery scars."

"A pity; when will antiquity adopt a more 'waifish' look for their models?"

I considered the possibility of a Roman fountain adorned with flat-chested, ultra thin runway models; perhaps with dark circles under their eyes to portray a look more akin to a heroin addict. Instead of idealized voluptuous beauties that were the typical subject, how different The Fontana del Moro would look with lingerie models posing amid the Roman orders.

Were there women *Super Models* for Italian sculptures? Did Michelangelo sulk if he couldn't get the 1500AD "It" girl to pose for his current version of the Madonna? In that century, a nude model would more than likely be an 'It' *guy* – leading me to believe that the statue in question could be as recent as the eighteenth century. I promised myself to sit down with a history book and become educated; marble must have been the celluloid of Rome.

Despite Pierce's assurance that we did not need it, I opened my map. Even if we were close, I still needed to know where we were. I couldn't spend my entire time in Rome shambling about, uncertain of the streets. I was beginning to understand different regions in Rome and could, in a pinch, find a bus that would take me through the major roads. But on the side streets, I was hopeless. Pierce patiently allowed me to study the map. Satisfied, I folded it up and stuffed it back into my pack.

Pierce had put a cigarette in his mouth and was touching the end with a match. After a few drags, embers glowing, he tossed the lit match into the fountain, were it hissed upon impact. He looked at me, waiting for an indication that I was ready to proceed. Holding up my hand, I pulled a bottle out of my pack and filled it from the water that poured into the fountain. After the bottle was full, I capped it and put it back into my pack, while leaning over for a quick drink from the flowing water.

The water flowed from surrounding hills to the ancient Roman aqueducts, which still serviced the city. Modern plumbing had nothing on the original for clear cold water.

"I don't think Rice will recognize our lady of the fountain," I said.

"Are you commenting on the quality of our drawings?" Pierce smiled, both of us walking further up the street, toward the noise of the main road ahead.

"I don't think that statue is well known. The craftsmanship is amazing, but not the norm for classical sculptors. The woman is beautiful, but not notable; that's my guess."

"Difficult to place in any particular era, at any rate," he said after taking a drag from his cigarette.

Hugging the shaded side of the street, we strode back toward the Campo de' Fiori, the public square where our studio was located. Our first steps, slow and leisurely, were meandering. As we became synchronized with the pace of the city, however, our strides became quicker and longer. I wanted to stop and feed my curiosity. The thin, canyon like streets invited investigation with their myriad of

110

cobbles and crafted masonry buildings. But there was an energy to the city that demanded movement. We followed a small crowd and hurried behind them.

The street snaked in between buildings, the curves making it impossible to see further than twenty feet ahead. As one curve broke, another took its place, stealing away any long vistas that might otherwise be provided. Gradually, the typical buzz of the street grew louder, as we neared the Campo. After a final twist, the road spilled into the Campo, and sunlight washed across the cobblestones, which sucked in the heat.

Each day the Campo de' Fiori was filled with street vendors. Early, while the morning shadows were still long, the vendors would push huge wooden carts into the square. Lining up in the same location as the day before, they would arrange fruits, spices, and vegetables, then open up a huge umbrella to block the approaching sun. For anyone walking through the gauntlet of carts, all manner of fresh foods were available to be gathered and purchased. The sweet sticky fragrance of grapes, oranges, and pomegranates permeated the air. As the day progressed, scraps of fruit and berries, jumping from overstuffed bags, rolled onto the street to be smashed underfoot and smeared onto the stone.

I reached into my front pocket and pulled out a thin wallet with colorful bills wadded haphazardly in the fold. I knew better than to leave money in my back pocket, as Rome was a haven for pickpockets. I pushed up to the front of a cart, pointing to a basket of sweet smelling grapes. I caught the attention of the vendor and shouted, *l'uva* while holding up several lira. The basket was nearly empty, the remaining grapes soaking in small pools of sticky juice.

The sun was high, and without any shade I could feel the rays hot on my neck. I turned, feeling my shirt cling to my back, sticky perspiration gathering in the creases. It was while I stood under the noon sun, waiting for lunch, that I first saw Angeline. While I stood, dropping my crushed bills onto a small table, Angeline emerged from the crowd. Her attention was fixed on a stack of wooden palettes, each containing an array of brightly colored spices. I watched her, noticing the slightest bit of pink warming her pale skin. Though her hair was as dark as any

Italian, her marble-white skin showed that she avoided the sun. She had a ball cap with the brim pulled low to shade her face. The shadow concealed her eyes, but I could see her mouth and nose. Her face was delicate, and she was dressed casually in cargo shorts and tennis shoes. With her hair tied up, pony tail out the back of her cap, she was easy to spot as an American. At that moment, watching her walking through the Campo, though, she was nobody more than a stranger who had caught my eye.

As I stared at Angeline, the vendor poked a handful of grapes at me and laughed. I was caught. He smiled; clicking his tongue he whispered *ragazza* under his breath. I thanked him, shrugging my shoulders, and stepped back from the cart.

Angeline was walking away, nearly swallowed up by the crowd. I took a step toward her, but a steady swarm of people meandered in front of me slowly examining bananas, plumbs, and grapes. I tracked her cap moving further into the crowd, then lost her entirely.

"Still finding lunch?" Pierce said, tapping my shoulder. He had collected a bag of sweet rolls and a block of cheese wrapped in paper.

"I bought some fruit. Trade cheese for grapes?" I asked, staring past him, hoping for a parting glimpse of Angeline.

"Let's do. You lose something?"

"Me? No, just saw someone; American. Thought maybe I'd chat, but she's gone."

Pierce and I made our way across the Campo to the entrance of the Palazzo Pio Righetti. The studio for the summer program was housed in this vast Palazzo, owned by the University of Washington. A *Palazzo*, literally meaning *palace*, was originally constructed to be the home for a wealthy Italian family. In many Italian cities, there were a number of historical palazzi that had been converted to any number of new uses. The original intent had been to provide a safe and sumptuous home, surrounded by massive stone walls that allowed the wealthy to keep out the riff-raff. In addition to providing protection, the large stone structure also served to demonstrate the wealth and importance of the family who commissioned the palazzi.

Typically constructed of large rusticated stones, the buildings consisted of thick masonry walls on each side, protecting an opulent inner courtyard, often a garden, which served as the escape from the frantic city that lurked just beyond the walls. By definition, a palazzo was always built in an urban setting. Without a city to surround it, a palazzo was not a palazzo. In a sense, the building served as a stronghold, and provided an important family a presence within the city.

The urban palazzo was a product of the city streets; the main entrance often was adorned with a long bench. Those interested in borrowing money from any important family would first need to line up on the bench, waiting for an audience inside. The longer the bench, the longer the line. This was yet another way to measure the importance of the family.

The Palazzo Pio had no bench whatsoever. The Pio da Carpi family built it over the foundation of the ruined Theater of Pompey in the seventeenth century. The original theater had been completed in 55 BC, but now served as a functional location in which to cram drafting tables and a library for architecture students. The University of Oregon leased space each summer for its own program, allowing me and others to study in the heart of Rome. I hesitate to call it downtown Rome, although that's really what it was. The building had one façade that looked out into the Campo de' Fiori, though the view only allowed visibility of a portion of the Campo. During the day, umbrellas from the vendor's carts completely obstructed any view of the Campo's paving, instead making it appear like a series of small circus tents.

The building's interior had been renovated to allow multiple programs to study simultaneously, and separately, within the palazzo. Each program had been shoehorned into the building, creating a labyrinth of hallways that both connected and divided the major rooms. Upon first entering the building, I had the impression that it was far smaller than it really was. The main door was solid and plain, with no window. In fact, the entire entry had no windows, making the inside of the

113

building a complete mystery to any visitor. The only clue that this was a school was a small intercom labeled *Univerità*. The device had several small buttons, most with a faded sticker just below. The stickers listed the names of the department head for the University of Washington and for each visiting program. One sticker, still new and unfaded, simply read *Prof. Rice*, the Architectural Professor for Oregon's Rome program.

Past the main door was a small lobby, crammed with one couch, two chairs, one table, and a coat rack. Each piece of furniture, though aged, retained a regal quality that spoke of the building's past. The lamps, though they produced little light, were examples of amazing and uncommon craftsmanship. Each shade contained a mosaic of colored glass, each piece cut to shape and size to fit inside a leaded lattice. The sofa, though not comfortable, made one proud simply to sit down. The cushions were worn just enough to indicate exactly where one should plant their buttocks. Only slightly less comfortable, the chair showed little wear, and possessed a deep mustard hue that had certainly faded over the years. I had yet to see any student actually sit in the lobby, and it seemed more a museum than an entry.

Once inside, a primary hallway containing four doors distributed occupants to any one of the summer programs studying architecture within the building. My door was green. I never entered any of the other doors, only possessing a key to my own studio. Past the door, another hallway led to a set of six steps. The stairs climbed to a tall, open room that provided barely enough space for the drafting desks and two well-worn couches. These would be the desks we would use for the duration of the studio.

Carrying what was left of our lunches, Pierce and I entered through the green door and into the studio, where class had begun moments before. The students had all chosen desks, and had arranged them in a somewhat random fashion around the room. I scanned the studio for an empty desk, and stopped as my gaze fell upon the same young woman I had seen in the marketplace. She had pulled her ball cap up, revealing more of her face, and she leaned on her desk casually as the professor went through introductions. Her desk was close to the front of the room. Even if I had felt bolder, I wouldn't have been able to claim a seat next to her, those already claimed by other students. In the seat immediately to her left, sat Ron, slouching indifferently, staring at the beams above him. Pierce and I walked to the two remaining desks, adjacent to each other, next to the windows and therefore in direct sunlight.

"*Buona sera*," began Rice. "*Questo termine è il primo di due.*" He smiled, confident that we had understood his Italian. Our grasp of Italian was tenuous at best, and there was little we could do but smile and wait for him to break character. Mercifully, he did so quickly.

"You've all had some time to explore the city; now let's consider how to redesign it. In my hands I have the program and site map for your competition," he said, holding up a stack of large envelopes. In his other hand, he held a ceramic mug, nearly full with steaming coffee. I watched nervously, each of his gesticulations nearly spilling the contents of his mug.

"Today, I'd like to introduce the term's design problem," he continued. "You'll have the better part of five months to develop your solution. During the last week, in addition to receiving a grade for your design, you will also be eligible for the *Boromini Prize*; winners announced shortly after designs are presented. For that reason, I hope your travel itinerary allows you extra time in Rome after this studio is over. You'll want to be here should you win the prize, and even if you don't win, better to be here where good wine is cheap."

Edward Rice was well liked by his students. Possessing a dry sense of humor, he succeeded in putting people at ease, despite not being an easy-going person himself. His persona was never stifling, and he was able to demonstrate that he didn't expect others to exhibit the same formality that he possessed. Rice was equally capable of enthralling his students or boring them to tears. His years of experience and study gave him a uniquely broad scope of knowledge that seemed inexhaustible. With so much information swimming around in his head, he was not always able to discern the important from the trivial. This made conversations with him a little bit like prospecting for gold. There was always some priceless nugget lurking just beneath the surface, but one had to pan for it. This lent a sense of expectation to all of his lectures. Even those that seemed to meander were still filled with the possibility of providing some unique and important chunk of wisdom.

Well liked and well respected, he nonetheless was also a source of amusement. His advanced age carried with it the mannerisms and perspectives of an older era. Euphemistically, *he was getting up there.* Realistically, he was ancient. In the forest of academia, he was 'old growth'. Cut open, his rings would reveal decades of study. There were no doubt thin rings, indicating periods of intellectual drought, and thick rings demonstrating periods rich with learning. Though his long career provided him with a knowledge of architecture that was unmatched, the knowledge required translation.

He seemed an anachronism, even in Rome. Dressed in pleated pants and a colored shirt with long sleeves, he seemed unaware of the persistent heat. The only comfortable element of his wardrobe was a pair of sandals, slightly too large for his feet. No more than five and a half feet tall, his diminutive size gave him an almost gnomish quality that was heightened by his neatly trimmed graying beard.

He handed the envelopes to each student and instructed that we open them. While we opened the envelopes, he fought to stifle a grin. Sipping from his mug, he walked briskly around the studio while we read the introduction to the competition design problem.

"You'll note, from your site map, that your design will be located next to the Forum. Should provide plenty of opportunity for you to research Roman history. Wouldn't be school unless you had to learn something.".

"Is there a restriction on the size of our project?" Pierce asked.

"Of course there are restrictions. There have to be some hurdles to keep it interesting," Rice replied. "In your packet, you'll find a description for the components of the building, as well as a recommended square footage. The map shows the locations where building is allowed, and where it is restricted. As you see, your challenge is to design an embassy adjacent to the Forum. You choose the country, and your design must weave together the character of Rome with the qualities of your chosen country. An embassy, while it might seem an unusual choice, provides you with the challenge of understanding and reconciling two potentially unlike design criteria."

After a period of questions, Rice had finished his coffee, and appeared ready to fill his mug with more. As he walked from student to student, he sat down to discuss a potential direction for each design. I placed my sketchbook and pencils on my desk and began to brainstorm. Pierce had deposited his supplies in the classroom earlier in the day, and now had a roll of trace paper stretched out, his pen moving quickly.

"What do we know about the Forum?" I asked.

"Not certain what you know about it, but I don't know enough," Pierce replied.

"What do we know about an embassy?"

"Less than the Forum."

"Good thing we have twenty weeks."

"Seems like plenty of time now, though, I'm sure I'll be nervous when there's only a week left."

"No reason to be nervous," I said. "There will be many entries, but we've as good a chance as anyone. Half the fun will be to see all the entries. The other half of the fun would be to have the winning entry."

"I think you'll have plenty of fun working on the design. Great to win, but better to enjoy your twenty weeks of design."

"Happy if you win, happy if you lose? I'm skeptical that you're actually that philosophical. You're as competitive as anybody. I've seen your work in other studios. You look over your shoulder as much as me, hell, more than me."

Pierce stopped drawing and laughed. "Yes, but I'd just as soon keep it a secret. Plotting and scheming is all part of design. You'll see my design on the last week and not a day sooner."

"Maybe I won't see it right away, but I hope you don't intend to keep a closed mouth. Gabbing about our projects is a crucial part of designing," I said.

"Only if wine is involved."

"Then after dinner, we have an appointment with a bottle."

Ron, at the other end of the studio, had been talking with Angeline and another girl. Happily, I realized that Ron could be a good source of information about Angeline. I could learn something over drinks some evening; I resolved to make it a regular habit.

3

Just beyond the Campo, on a narrow side street, a small bar opened up each evening shortly after the marketplace vendors pulled their carts away. I discovered this hole in the wall nearly a week into the term, on one of the occasions when I got lost attempting to return home. After walking down the same streets, I noticed two young Italians pulling chairs and small tables out onto the street. After the tables had been arranged, they pulled a series of large potted trees out to mark the perimeter of the outdoor seating area. The street, now only wide enough for a motorcycle to pass, was transformed into a comfortable location to enjoy some conversation and wine.

A day after making my find, I invited both Pierce and Ron to meet me for beverages later in the evening. I had remained in studio for a few hours after class had finished, continuing to develop the concept for my design scheme. Before the sun had dimmed, I put away my drawings and left to join them.

"Ciao, bien venito," Ron shouted, waving a hand in the air.

"Dove' vino?" I replied.

"Sit, sit, we've ordered, and your wine is waiting for you," Ron said.

"Your glass has been lonely," Pierce added, "you'll find it an excellent companion."

I walked around a potted tree to get to the table, and picked up the glass, holding it tight to my chest. "Now that I have found you," I said to the glass, "we will make tonight special. I won't make foolish promises, only to love you until the wine dries up." I pulled out a chair and sat. "Pierce, Ron, salute!" I lifted my glass, already full, and tapped glasses to initiate our debauchery. I pulled out several Lira, not really knowing how much, and tucked it under the bottle.

Ron's habit was to try to pay the entire wine bill when no one else was paying attention. This was generous, but often resulted in his wondering, the next day, what had happened to his cash. With a grimace, he would then find the next ATM, and reload, ready for the next round. The machine, having spit out the requested lira, would then hum until a receipt appeared. While tucking the money into his pocket, Ron would crinkle up the receipt and dispose of it.

To be honest, I didn't object to someone else paying for my wine. Financing my trip to Rome had been a challenge. I had really not found a way to afford it outright, and was relying heavily on credit. My logic followed that after I landed my first job, there would be no time for travel, so this might be my only opportunity. If I had to engage in some creative debt management later, then that was a price I'd be willing to pay. Or at least, a price I was willing to defer.

There was a limit, though, to how cheap I was willing to be. Actually, let me rephrase that; there was a limit to how cheap I was willing to appear. By putting my money on the table, I at least made it clear that I had come prepared to pay my own portion of the bill.

"Either of you been to Italy before?" I asked.

"Been to Little Italy."

"I passed through years ago," Pierce said. "When I left Japan, I found work in Denmark. I'd go around on holidays, but didn't make it to Rome."

"Rumor has it that you used to be a fighter," Ron said.

119

"Fighter? Maybe."

"Nick tells me you used to punch people in your spare time. Honestly, did you used to get in the ring?"

"When I was younger I'd try anything once. I tried boxing, and couldn't stop. Adrenaline rush like nothing else."

"Were you good?"

"Not as good as I thought I was. Thing about boxing is, you can't do it unless you can fool yourself into thinking you're the best. If a person believes that they're only the second best boxer, then they fight scared. Can't do that, it's a quick way to a busted nose."

"When did you stop?" Ron asked.

"When I threw a punch that broke my hand."

"If you threw a punch like that, you must have won."

"Except he threw a punch that broke my nose. We would've called it a draw, but I was lying face down on the mat. That ended my career."

"Finished your career, but makes a great story." I lifted my glass and tossed it back. Pierce and Ron followed suit. We waited to let the wine warm our stomachs, then I looked at Pierce. "Why did you leave Japan?"

"Nothing to keep me there. My mother was no longer living."

"And your father?" Ron asked.

"Not close; we weren't close. Gave me a good excuse to travel."

"Sometimes that's all you need, a good excuse."

After speaking, Ron set down his glass and filled it. He held the bottle up, looking at each of us. We stuck out our glasses and accepted a refill.

"Nick, this is your first time in Rome; what are you interested in seeing?" Ron asked.

"I want to see the hilltowns, one of the small ones where they've kept things the same for centuries. I'd also like to see the Vatican; I've heard the Pope lives there."

"Lot's to see." Pierce said, "Pope's house is a big place."

"One other thing I'd like to see more of," I said. "Ron, that girl you sat next to in studio, what do you know about her?"

"We talked a little. Not taking classes at Oregon, some other school. I don't think she's traveled much, sort of a small town girl."

"Small town, what, like a truck stop?" I asked.

"No, somewhere in Wyoming. Small, but not tiny. Nice girl, can't wait to see more of Rome."

"Perhaps I'll find a way to show her more," I said.

"Rome is a good place to sight see, plenty of young ladies. They spend so much time in the sun, letting their skin tan. Plus they have some attitude," Ron said.

"No, it's not the attitude, it's their calves," Pierce said.

"Legs?"

"No calves. It's their calf muscles. They walk so much, they get really toned calves."

"I've never heard anyone say that but you," I said. "That's a very peculiar but candid thing to say. "What amazes me, is how slender and toned young Italian women are. But you don't see any slender, old Italian women."

"True," Ron said.

"What happens? Do the thin Italian women disappear when they turn thirty?"

"No, they eat."

"Pasta isn't health food," Pierce said.

We thought about this for only so long as it deserved. After a few moments we all took another swallow of wine.

"Either of you planning travel after the term's done?" I asked.

"I'd like to, but for better or worse, I've got a job lined up back home," Ron replied. "Last week I was excited to get that monkey off my back, but now I have my regrets. We've got almost five months here, I'd like to continue traveling after the program ends."

"Your job search is over before it began," Pierce said.

"True, but I don't know if it's the job I want. My brother gave me a good tip, it's an office that does some decent work. But they haven't built anything very sexy."

"Stay in Italy, travel," I said.

We stayed and ordered another bottle. The night seemed too hot to sleep, conversation was so much easier.

4

After several days, Rice guided the class on the first of several field trips. Along with our studio course, we also took classes in history and media techniques. This trip would take us to Orvieto, an Italian hilltown sixteen miles southwest of Rome. There, we were to document the buildings, the landscape, and the people, in watercolors or pastel. Not wanting to deal with the mess of warm pastel crayons, I brought my sketchbook and brushes.

The class, still half-asleep, was to be shuttled by van to Orvieto and released to wander until lunchtime. While the morning was still cool, we gathered near Pio, along the Via Dei Giubbonari waiting for the vans to arrive.

A puffy-eyed Ron leaned against a Palazzo and sighed. "Nick, this is too early, the market hasn't even opened."

"Go get yourself a coffee, it's not like you can't find an espresso," I said.

"No, they don't do it right here. You walk to the bar, they give you a shot in a glass and you're done. I want my coffee in mocha form. Give me a little whipped cream on top."

"Ron, this is Italy, they don't do it wrong, we do."

"Sure, the same way we do pizza wrong. Here, pizza is a piece of flat bread dredged in olive oil. Back home, pizza is peppered with four different meats and thick with cheese and tomato sauce; you tell me who has it wrong."

"Fine, but you're too tired to stand; go get yourself a shot and quit bitching."

"You make sense, hold the vans for me."

He shambled off to the nearest barrista, grumbling as he went. Standing in the shade, I found the air just a touch cool. I was dressed in shorts and a pullover, prepared for the heat that would catch up to us in the exposed hilltown. I had two bottles of water that I had stuck in the freezer the night before. Still chunks of ice, they would be perfect by the time I had spent time walking in the heat of the day.

I sat against the side of the building and shut my eyes, taking time for a quick nap before our transportation arrived. Without really being aware of it, I had dozed off, and was woken by Ron. Still groggy, I was ushered into a van, and then we departed.

The ride was uneventful, in so much as I was asleep for the duration. After we unloaded, the vans pulled away, and Rice motioned for the class to gather.

"What you see in front of you today was originally an ancient Etruscan city, until the 3rd century BC when it was annexed by the Romans. However, it was a papal possession as recently as 1860." Rice paused for effect while he drank coffee from his thermos. His skin was flush, and his hand shook just the slightest bit as he eagerly recounted the history of Orvieto. "Look around. You see stone walls, standing columns, buildings. True, the buildings aren't all proud, but look at the top of the hill. There, the duomo remains, preserved and whole."

At this Rice stuck his finger ahead, pointing to a small building that perched atop the rock-hewn town. The small city appeared carved from the large butte upon which it was situated. The buildings were built from blocks of the same volcanic *tufa* that formed the plateau. Short trees and swaths of brown grass mingled with buildings, creating a geometric garden of stones and branches. "What you probably don't know about this town is that Orvieto contains countless Etruscan ruins, and remains of the wall surrounding the city are over 2000 years old. Enjoy what you see, and paint, draw, and write. Record your thoughts in drawings and words. What you learn about history, you'll later apply to your designs."

He finished and waited. When nobody moved, he began waving for everyone to disperse. "Come on, start walking, explore. You won't learn anything sitting here listening to me."

As students dispersed, I noticed Angeline. While others had hurried off, beginning their trek to the baptistery, she walked slowly. She took her time, examining the stone gateway that was the portal into the town. She paced steps along the stone wall. Her manner was careless, her pace slow. She was in no rush to get to the baptistery. Instead, she watched her feet, noticing the earth, taking in her surroundings. Then she would lift her head to look out and down at the valley below.

After the other students left, the gate seemed strangely quiet, as though the vast expanse was swallowing up all sound. In Rome, sound reverberated off of the streets, the buildings, the monuments. There was little vegetation to muffle noise – sound had a life. But in Orvieto, sounds continued out into the rugged landscape, escaping the city.

As she made her way into the town, I stayed back, flipping through my sketchbook as if eager to begin drawing. I waited until I had lost sight of her, and then followed through the gateway. I had struggled to come up with an introduction, but without having any words to start a conversation, I let her continue toward the ruins inside Orvieto. I saw no reason to force an opportunity; the town would provide other chances and other meetings.

We passed the wall that once provided security for the city. Like all hilltowns, Orvieto was organized on a plateau and had rigid boundaries that provided protection. But the same layout of walls and buildings that kept the population safe also prevented it from changing or evolving. If a town represents the body, and the population the mind, then Orvieto's is a mind content and devoid of curiosity; familiar ideas are the only ideas. However, there is a wonderful simplicity to the harmony achieved between the walls surrounding the city, and the landscape that they push back. From a distance, it is nearly impossible to distinguish rock from building, and building from hill. The manmade structures appear to rise out of the hill itself, as if hewn from the rock upon which they sit. Walls and facades snake around and up the hill, surrounding the Baptistry, which perches at the top as if gazing out toward the surrounding hillside.

I made my way along the medieval streets of the hilltown, crossing to the shaded side of the streets. As the afternoon wore on, the sun rose higher in the sky, diminishing my shade and storing heat in the bricks and stones of Orvieto. Before lunch, I was determined to complete at least a page of sketches. With little shadow, I focused on capturing the textures of the hard materials surrounding me.

As time passed, my sketch evolved from tentative lines to bold strokes as I worked to fill in detail and emphasize contrast. Before the periphery of the drawing was filled in, I set down my pencil, deciding to keep areas undefined. As I paused, I noticed fewer people walking by, many opting for a lunch inside during the heat of the day. Opportunity, though, was on my side, as I saw Angeline standing on the street looking through her camera. It was time for me to force the issue; I waved at her, gesturing for her to come near.

Angeline walked to where I sat and looked over my shoulder, "You're working hard, breaking a sweat?" She lifted up on her toes to get a better look at my sketchbook, clutching her own sketchbook close to her chest, arms crossed.

"No, these are just warm-ups. Nicholas Black," I said holding out my hand, pencil still tucked in between two fingers. Shaking my hand, she managed to avoid the pencil.

"Angeline. Seen you in class, good to finally meet," she said.

"Glad that we've taken care of introductions, I've got plenty of shade here, you want to share?"

"It is pretty hot, I'm still getting used to all this sun." Angeline remained in the sun, her pale skin just beginning to show pink. Her face was shaded by a baseball hat that was tipped down, preventing direct sun from touching her face. She wore a thin T-shirt with rolled up sleeves and denim shorts with large pockets.

I pointed to her sketchbook. "Show me your drawings?."

"Oh, I'm a little self-conscious," she laughed.

"You're modest. Just a sketch."

"Persistent."

"I can be. You look warm, howabout take a seat in the shade and show off your drawing talent."

"Would you settle for a thousand words?"

"Nope, I want a picture."

"Hmm, " she said, amused. "Okay, I'll show you mine if you show me yours."

She sat down with legs together in front of her. Opening her book she flipped open to a drawing of the Tempietto. She had outlined the building with black pen and brushed watercolor hues insider her drawing. The color was applied with an intentionally loose hand, allowing the color to seek its own boundaries, giving the illusion of modeled light from a setting sun. She had added a slight hint of orange to the high lights and colored the shadows blue in order to emphasize the quality of light from the setting sun. The drawing omitted details in the background, leaving it rendered in a painterly manner. The painting contained no people, and the courtyard was rendered in the same painterly fashion, making it fade into the background. The Tempietto, absent of people, seemed alone. Long shadows added to the sense of melancholy, which seemed in stark contrast to Angeline's demeanor. She smiled as I studied her drawing.

"I like this, very much," I said. "Tell me what you thought about when you painted."

"Mostly that I had to finish it fast. Now you show me what you were just sketching."

"I want to know more about your painting. Are you going to make me guess?"

"Yes, but don't guess out loud. Now, your book."

Having nowhere else to go with my questions, I flipped open my sketchbook. My drawing was only half finished, showing a stone wall with a clothesline stretched in front.

"Oh, I like this," Angeline said, politely grabbing my book.

"It's only half done."

"No, no, leave it like this – this is better."

`"But the clothesline only has one shirt, it's missing a couple pairs of pants, some socks -" An unfinished drawing is always more intriguing because it allows one to fill in the blanks. However, I find that I sometimes fill in the blanks incorrectly; it's always a disappointment to look back and discover potential unrealized.

"Any other drawings?" she asked.

Perhaps if not for the sketch of the lady at the fountain, I would have agreed. When I had looked at Pierce's sketch, it had shown me as much about him as it did about the subject. I wasn't yet ready to show that much to her, so I closed my book.

"Some other drawings, but really only scribbles. Nothing as good as your watercolor. You must have spent some time developing your technique."

"My Technique? You're being funny."

"It must be the heat, it does make a man say crazy things. Or maybe it's the altitude. The air seems a bit thinner in this hilltown."

She smiled appreciatively. I considered it a good sign that she pretended to enjoy my jokes, though we both knew they weren't funny.

"Air seems fine to me, I know something about living in high elevations. I grew up in Wyoming. Men say crazy things there too."

She paused, set down her book and reached for a bottle of water I had at my feet. She looked at me while unscrewing the cap, took a short sip and placed the bottle back where she had found it.

"Nicholas Black," she said as though still mulling over the name. "You've been attending school in Oregon?" she asked.

"Yes, completing my Masters. You?"

"I'm studying in Seattle, undergrad."

"Not so far away."

"Glad that we're finally getting to chat. I only know a few people in the program; I'm trying to make friends quickly. With a two-term studio, I'm sure we'll all get to know each other."

"Perhaps very well. Your dorm, is it in the Palazzo?"

Half of the students were staying in the same building that housed the design studio, the balance were scattered around the Campo in other buildings.

"No, I've got accommodations across from the studio, just myself and another girl from the program."

"I'm sharing space with Pierce and Ron, whom I think you've met."

"Yes, he's funny. I'm looking forward to sitting next to him this studio. Now I know two people, I'm doing better already."

Even in the shade, Angeline was beginning to perspire, her forehead slightly moist. Strands of hair hung down below her hat, one just in front of her eyes. With the heat and humidity, we had given up on worrying about our appearance. I thought nothing of the creases of sweat that formed on my fingers and palms. I could feel, if not see, a thin layer of dust that had stuck to the moisture on my skin. Angeline lifted the neck of her shirt to dab at her cheek, letting it drop only after fanning herself. The thin fabric of her shirt clung tightly to her body, revealing the curves of her breasts. I felt guilt in noticing her body, having only met her. She seemed girlish. In spite of this, when she had briefly used her shirt to fan herself, I took notice of the narrow gap between her breasts, revealed in short glimpses. Guilty or no, instinct is instinct.

"Tell me how you got from Wyoming to an Italian Hilltown? That where you were born?" I asked.

She picked her sketchbook from where she set it and brought it back up to her chest, arms folded. Her easy smile was now replaced with a more serious expression. I waited for her to answer, but she remained silent, looking away to the valley below.

"You weren't born there," I began, uncertain how to regain the momentum of the conversation. "Where were you born?"

"Big city, Boston," She said.

"Bigger even than Orvieto?" I deadpanned. Angeline, though, did not acknowledge the joke. In fact, she seemed to have aged in a matter of mere moments. Her girlish demeanor had suddenly passed, revealing someone more serious and aware. Looking back, this was the Angeline that I was never able to see, but should have understood.

"Not much of a story, really. I'm more interested in where I'm going than where I was. With any luck I'll have some more traveling to do after Rome."

"You mean the competition prize? Feeling pretty lucky, I see."

Her smile returned. "Lucky? No. I'm just that good. You don't know what sort of designer you're up against."

"I'll make you a deal, as we develop our designs we can bounce ideas off one another. Shared creative inspiration."

"Time will tell, perhaps we'll end up rivals."

"Perhaps, but for a start, let's shake and be friends."

"Agreed."

We continued to chat, sharing a bottled water until it was empty. Angeline seemed a very serious student, eager to learn what she could about our hilltown. Just before she excused herself to continue exploring Orvieto, we made a hasty agreement to grab lunch later in the week.

As I sat on the stone steps of Orvieto, I recall thinking bout how pretty and naïve Angeline seemed. She was eager and confident, but not experienced. In truth, I don't think that my assessment was far off. But I was wrong to think of her as naïve, and arrogant not to realize how little I knew. I filled in the blanks to complete the picture of who I thought Angeline was.

Given the benefit of hindsight, I understand that there was much about her that I didn't see. Or perhaps what I saw was never there, but just a trick of the light.

5

Ron was seated in front of his desk, a pile of bass wood dowels in front of him. He was cutting each to size, in preparation for a schematic model that he was building for his competition entry. Upon cutting the pieces, he scored and sanded each to ensure uniformity. If there was one defining characteristic about Ron aside from being caustic, it was that he was meticulous.

Taking a break from his labor, he shook out his fingers and walked over to my desk. "I need to start contracting out this labor, my fingers are killing me," he said.

"Considered outsourcing? Perhaps you could farm out the work to the States, and have the finished model shipped back to Italy in time for judging."

"Good plan, but it's getting harder and harder to find sweat shops in the States. Back in the day, you could count on an unskilled work force to labor for pennies, but now we just can't compete with the foreign markets. Americans just won't tolerate manual labor."

Rather than allow Ron to digress into a full-blow tirade, I decided to find out what he knew about Angeline. "In Orvieto, I spent some time talking with the girl you sit next to."

"Good for you."

"Seems friendly."

"She is."

"What can you tell me about her?"

"Well, she's gorgeous – or maybe you already knew?"

"Figured that out. Look, I'm just trying to learn a little more about her. We had a good chat, I'd like to pursue things a little further."

"Don't try to tell me you're calling dibs."

"Ron, are we in junior high? Nobody's calling anything, I'm just curious."

130

"Why are you so concerned about how she really feels?" Ron asked. "I find that reality always suffers by comparison to perception."

"What are you talking about?"

"Well, I'm a big fan of the faux bits of life; reality is unpredictable and undependable. Perception, though, that's whatever you choose to make it."

"For argument's sake," I began, "let's say that I have no idea where you're going with this. And furthermore, let's say that I'm more interested in how she really feels, than in rationalizing."

"Fair enough," He said continuing to cut pieces of bass wood.

"So, you don't have any more to tell me than that."

"Nick, get to know her the old fashioned way, talk to her."

"Fine, thought you might have some insight – I won't make that mistake again."

"Honestly, we've talked a little bit, but not a lot. I haven't known her that long. Tell you what, I'm meeting Pierce for drinks this evening. Care to join? We can get drunk and talk for hours."

"It's a date."

I discovered the key to design was to create rituals that acted as catalysts for inspiration. Creativity was like a prudish woman who needed to be cajoled and prodded; hours of pleading might result in one sweet kiss of brilliance. Accordingly, a small bar near the Campo became a habitual meeting place. Libation served as lubrication for the wheels that spun our design ideas.

Pierce, Ron, and I would settle in, and begin by trying to convince the other two that it was their turn to purchase a bottle. In time, one of us would either capitulate or tire of the game, and walk to the counter to select a poison. More often than not, Ron would submit, money not being so scarce for him. On one of our sojourns, in the early weeks of the design competition, Ron trumped both Pierce and myself by forgetting his wallet.

"I'm sure they accept credit," I said.

"Or you could wash dishes, scrub, scrub," added Pierce.

"No, I wouldn't want to risk the three of us getting thrown out of our favorite bar. Especially now that they recognize us here, we've become regulars."

"All the more reason to take advantage of that fact. You could easily offer to pay tomorrow for wine we drink today." Pierce said this, knocking on the table, a sure sign that he was getting ready to cave.

"Nick, Pierce, if memory serves, I paid previously. One of you needs to be the bigger man and pay for a bigger bottle."

"Alright, you're both cheap. Not frugal, not shrewd, but cheap." Pierce got up and made his way to the counter.

Ron and I, tucked away in a dark corner as we were, must have looked like conspirators, huddled close to the votive flame at the center of the table. Evening had taken over, and there was no light coming through the tall windows at the front of the bar. Though the shutters were open wide, only the faint sound of passers by entered back to the recesses of the bar. With only a modest amount of light, none found the ceiling, leaving the top of the space a mystery. Like most Italian buildings, the bar possessed ceilings excessively tall by American standards, fifteen feet was an average.

"Nick, what will you do if you win the competition? Our chances can't be bad, there are only so many students competing. A traveling scholarship good for a year, imagine where you could go."

"How about you, you've already got a job lined up."

"If I win, then I quit my job before I even show up; it's too much to pass up."

"If I win, I'm going to travel to Scandinavia, see some of Alto's work."

"What will you study? You need a thesis for a presentation at the end of the year," Ron reasoned.

"I'll worry about that if I win."

"Here's to winning." Ron raised an imaginary glass.

Up to this point, the term in school had been dominated by researching background for our designs; only in the past few days had students began making progress on their actual design ideas. Yet, nearly all the designs were secret, no one wanting to offer an advantage to any other competitor. It seemed somewhat foreign to how we had worked in previous studios. Typically, there was a camaraderie about working on a similar design problem; I decided to test the waters with Ron.

"The model you were building earlier, when do I get to see it?"

"When it's done," Ron replied.

"Tough to get feedback unless we show our work."

"I'll talk to you about my design, but I'll not show it."

"Why so hush-hush?"

"It's what we were just talking about, a years traveling scholarship. I'm not playing the nice guy and helping other people beat me."

"Ron, I'm a trusted friend, I'll keep things in confidence. No one will hear about your design from me."

"Correct, because you'll never see it."

I feigned a pained expression, trying to look stung. Truth be told, I was a little disappointed that both Ron and Pierce had been so reticent to offer any insight into their designs. While we sat in silence, Pierce returned with a bottle and glasses.

"Gentleman, start your livers," he began.

"Thank you, our evening can begin," I said.

"I hope red is alright, I always prefer it when the night is muggy."

He poured three glasses full. No one offered a toast, we simply smiled at each other and swallowed our wine.

"Well, if each of you is intent on being so secretive about your design," I said, "then maybe I should be too."

"I'm not telling you we won't talk about it, I just prefer not to show people my work in progress," Ron said.

"Talking about the competition?" Pierce asked.

"Of course, a year to travel is hard to ignore," I said.

"I can satisfy some of your curiosity by telling you what I won't do; how's that?" Pierce said. "We've all been in Rome for a bit now, and studied it for quite some time before arriving. What's more, we all know our history. So, when in Rome, the saying goes, do as the Romans. The Romans always played off of what was already present; they had to. They had to build layer upon layer, dealing with the environment that had been built up by the generation before. What's more, they absorbed influences from countless cultures."

"All of which doesn't help us understand what you 'won't do'," Ron said.

"Just setting the stage, finish your drink, the bottle's not close to being empty," Pierce said. "I'm only saying that it would be a mistake to try to produce something of any particular era. The Romans always allowed new influences to dictate their work. Designers like Bernini and Boromini weren't restricted by tradition, but they did play off of it."

"So, let me guess," I said, "you're not going to work with any classical vocabulary; you're going to work with modernist tectonics. No stone arches when a lintel would do the trick."

"I'm not going to ignore the orders, but they're part of a dead language. Rome shouldn't be a museum, there's room for another style, another voice in the wilderness," Pierce said.

Ron, finishing the last of his wine, wiped his mouth and held out his glass. "You're both full of shit, another glass please."

"Since I've been begging you both for the scoop on your designs, I'll be the next to go," I said. "I disagree with you Pierce, I think Rome *is* a museum. True, for centuries it was a city alive and expressive of new culture, new thinking. But that's not today's city. Now, real innovation is elsewhere, look at Germany, Japan, Hong Kong. Even the States offer more that's relevant to us today. So, my idea is to treat Rome as a shell, and my new design will be infill. Think of my design as a parasite, inhabiting its Italian host."

"Lovely image," Ron said.

"Isn't it?" I asked.

Pierce laughed, "It is good, though. So your design will inhabit the ruins of the Forum?"

"Precisely. I'll leave the crumbles that are strewn about, and make my design fit within that framework."

"A design among crumbs; that only reminds me of how hungry I am. Does anyone else want food? What can we get?" Ron asked.

As the three of us considered for a moment, the flame at the table's center suddenly jumped with a gust, when the front door opened wide. From amid the clatter of the crowded street emerged Angeline, gazing back and forth, eyes adjusting to the dark. I waved twice, the first time not catching her attention.

"There's your girl," Ron said.

"She's her own girl," I replied.

"What's this, Nicholas, you have an interest in young Angeline," Pierce looked at me. I simply shrugged my shoulders, imagining I was more evasive than I actually was.

"Nicholas doesn't know if she's interested or pulling his chain," Ron said.

"Why don't you ask her," Pierce reasoned.

"Perhaps I like the thrill." I said looking at Ron.

"The thrill?"

"The thrill of the chase."

"Or the thrill of the chaste?"

"One of the two," I said, "and you two will be the last to know."

Angeline stopped at the bar, and brought a bottle of sparkling water and a glass to our table. She continued blinking, her eyes wide, adjusting to the darkness.

"Looks like you're getting low." She eyed our bottle of wine.

"Allow me," I said, standing up and pouring the last of the wine. After Pierce and Ron were back up to full, I sat down. "What no tip?"

"Service wasn't that good, don't kid yourself."

"Thanks."

"You boys keep a busy social schedule, this is the hangout?" Though smiling, Angeline held her glass close to her face, as though for protection.

"Work hard, play hard," Pierce declared. "And what brings you out this evening?"

"It's so hot out, there's no way I can sleep. If I'm to be sleepless, I might as well have fun."

"We may get no sleep at all this term, I don't think the heat is likely to let up," I said.

"Enough about the weather. You three were talking and I interrupted."

"Maybe we were talking about you," Ron offered, making it sound like a question.

Angeline blushed, or at least I think she did, it was very dark. I'm certain, though, that she smiled. "Me? Oh, God, I'm sure. Well then, go on ahead, keep talking. I'll chime in if you say anything that's not flattering."

"Really, Nick was telling us about his design for the competition," Pierce said.

"No he wasn't."

"Correct, Ron. Because I've just finished. Now why don't you tell us about your design?"

Ron, who had been leaning on the table with his head low, now sat back and looked up at the darkness. Either deep in thought, or for dramatic pause, he simply drummed his fingers on his chair, then abruptly broke his silence.

"Our site, the Forum was the center for commerce in ancient Rome."

"Also the center for politics and law," Angeline added.

"Like I said, commerce, it's really all about the money," Ron continued. "So, I will create a brand new idiom for commerce in Rome. I'll begin by razing the basilicas, the temples, the markets. Then pave them with black top and build a bold new shopping mall."

"Oh, good, will it have a food court with Thai?"

"The slogan can be 'The ruins of the Forum mean lira in your pocket," Ron said.

"That brilliant idea aside, what do you really intend to do?" I asked.

"Honestly, I haven't got it figured yet. That's why I'm starting with a model. Sometimes the only way for me to get an idea going is to begin by building."

"Sad, your Palazzo de Meg-a-Mart had promise," Pierce said.

One stop shopping for antiquity brought to mind images of teenyboppers strolling the mall, searching the Roman Banana Republic for tight fitting shirts and sarongs. Small groups of Vestal Virgins, keeping alight the flame of commerce and clumsily applied lip gloss, could guard today's Palladium that was The Gap. Perhaps pausing at the temple of Nike to grab a new pair of shoes and gossip about who Constantine might take to the prom. Few cities better embraced an anachronism than Rome, with the possible exception of Las Vegas, which has a greater resemblance to Rome than one would readily admit; the fundamental difference being that Vegas *was* built in a day.

Ron began drumming his fingers softly on the table, looking from side to side. He was clearly waiting for someone else to continue the conversation, but it was evident he had something to say.

"Ron, what are you really planning for the Forum?"

Ignoring my question he asked, "Someone else must be hungry, I haven't eaten since just before class; I'm dying."

"Honestly, tell me about your design."

"Honestly, I won't know until I build it. Look, if no one else is hungry, I'm going to order some bruschetta."

"No, not here," Angeline said, "I've had the bruschetta here and it's not so good."

"This is Italy, all the bruschetta should be good," Pierce said.

"They don't make it fresh, and there's next to no tomato. Order the Suppli, you won't be disappointed." Angeline referred to an appetizer consisting of breaded fried rice balls stuffed with mozzarella. She was thin enough to make me believe that she had never actually eaten one of these, perhaps she was going by word of mouth.

"Then suppli it is. I'll get more if anyone else is hungry."

"Order for four," Pierce said laughing as if he had told a joke.

"Wait, Ron, you said you didn't have your wallet." I said.

"Yes, I did *say* that. Are you in?"

I nodded vigorously, to indicate that the question needn't have even been asked.

Ron excused himself, and hopped over his seat to avoid stepping on feet. As he approached the bar, Pierce gestured as though he had just suddenly remembered something extremely important, and joined Ron at the bar.

"It's so hot, how can anyone be hungry?" Angeline asked.

"I'm sweating out the wine faster than I can drink it."

"I'm not used to drinking much wine. Though, here it seems okay, nobody's bothered."

"It'd be a shame to be bothered by such a thing."

"You're right, Nicholas. Do you know what?"

"What?"

"*Nicholas* is too long for you. Nicky, or Nick, that fits you. Nicholas is an old man's name, you can use the name better when you're older."

"You need to drink a little wine tonight."

"Thanks, but I'll pass for now."

"Might help you sleep."

"Too hot, can't sleep."

"Drink enough wine and you'll be sleeping under the table."

She smiled. She held her bottled water to her cheek, letting the condensation moisten her skin.

"It's hot as hell, everything I wear seems to stick to me." I picked up my napkin and dabbed at my forehead. There was little perspiration, but I couldn't escape feeling clammy, as though the air were thick and heavy. Angeline undid one button from her shirt and began fanning herself.

"What do you want to do if we stay up all night?" I asked.

"Let's go dancing."

138

"Too tired to dance."

"You just need your second wind. If you stay here, I might have to leave you behind."

"Such a comfortable bar, why would you want to leave?"

"I'm here now."

"That's no answer."

"Time will tell. Perhaps we'll just drink until we fall asleep."

It was no idle prediction; another bottle was emptied before the night was through. We did not go dancing, but the air finally cooled enough for us to sleep.

6

Day after day, the humidity lingered, as if its own great weight kept it from dissipating. The warm sticky air was like a blanket, wrapping, encircling the skin. In studio, we kept the overhead lights off and lined up fans to blow across every desk. Each drawing was taped down and anchored, ensuring the force of the blowers didn't send the drawings scattering into the air. In lieu of overhead lights, we resorted to desk lamps, which didn't give off nearly as much heat, but did attract an unending supply of tiny bugs, crawling and hopping across our tracing paper.

This afternoon, those not in the dorms taking naps were seated at their desks scribbling ideas and preparing design work. However, studio was rarely full, as even the daunting task of the competition was not enough to keep students from venturing into the city to explore and lose themselves. The explorations were occasionally related to study, but as often as not, simply an excuse to visit discos, restaurants, and drink cappuccinos.

I walked to Ron's desk and looked over his shoulder.

"Are you spying?" he asked.

"Have you done anything worth spying on?"

"Nick, I've already got the competition won, so you might as well not bother."

"Time for me to pack it in, eh?"

"I'm a lock."

I looked at the trace paper on his desk, which had numerous scribbles, a tic-tac-toe game, and a drawing of an elongated woman's torso.

"Ron, you don't have a clue about your design."

"Then quit looking if it's not worth your while," he said covering his trace paper.

I shrugged my shoulders.

Angeline had just walked into studio, and squeezed past me and Ron to get to her desk. She sat down, pulled out assorted pens and a large pad of paper that was nearly used up. The back of the pad was a collage of smeared color and dried paint; some of the color had smudged onto her thigh, leaving a chalky chartreuse residue that vaguely resembled a bruise.

"This is the most crowded I've seen studio," she said.

"We're all waiting for inspiration," I said nodding at Ron.

"Speak for yourself, my friend, I'm on my way. The prize is as good as mine."

"Oh, really? Let's see," Angeline said leaning over Ron desk. Glancing at his scribbles she rolled her eyes upwards and smiled. "Well, we are in some trouble." She laughed and pulled her ball cap off and set it on her desk.

As I thought through my archive of witty retorts, Angeline taped down her last pages of paper and put on her headphones, blocking out the murmur of fans that cooled the studio. I returned to my desk and continued to diagram some possible schemes for my project. I cycled through several bad ideas, getting them out of my system. I crumpled my first few efforts, discarding them at my feet. I noticed Ron gesturing to Angeline, commenting on her drawings. The two continued to critique each other's work, each marking up sketches before returning to their own work.

After an hour had passed, my trace paper was covered with tiny smeared bugs that had crossed my desk and been too slow. My progress became sluggish; convinced that I had reached my productive limit, I packed my pens and locked them in the desk drawer. Unable to advance my project, I instead resolved to make inroads with Angeline.

Walking by Ron's desk, I deliberately turned my head from his drawings to avoid accusations.

"Angeline, I've been sitting at my desk too long. Are you looking for an excuse to stretch your legs?"

"What's the excuse?"

"We agreed to grab a lunch together, need to step out for a bite?"

"Nick it's past four, I ate hours ago."

"Dinner?"

"Tell you what, I need to get some supplies before the art store closes, want to join?"

"Do they have food too?"

"Unlikely, we can stop on the way."

She tucked her pens into her desk, and pulled the ball cap on, pulling her hair through the back. Ron looked up from his desk, waiting for an invitation. I shook my head, trying not to draw Angeline's attention.

"Ron, you want to join us?" She asked.

He looked at me, pausing. "No, I'll just finish a couple more games of tic-tac-toe. Thanks, though – I'll join next time."

"You're a good man, Ron," I whispered as we walked past and out the door.

We stopped at the fruit vendor before continuing to the art supply shop. I pointed to grapes and one bunch was dropped into a paper bag then handed over. I smiled, passing two folded bills to the vendor. Angeline purchased an apple and still had bread wrapped up from lunch earlier in the afternoon.

"Can I grape you?" I asked.

"If not you, then nobody will, thanks," she said accepting a handful of cold wet grapes. As we ate, I turned my head to spit out the seeds. Angeline casually brought her napkin to her mouth, wiping away the seeds without comment.

"Lunch tastes better when you're walking. Mind if I have some bread?"

"Here," she said, unwrapping the remains of her lunch. Angeline pointed to the shade. "Let's stay out of the sun, heat just kills me."

"Only bothers me at night. Can't sleep."

"Some nights I don't even bother; I'd just toss and turn until morning."

"What do you do when you're not sleeping?

"Complain about the heat."

"No, what do you do when you're up all night?"

"Sometimes I go to studio and draw in the nude," she said laughing.

"I suppose that's one way to beat the heat."

"Usually, I go to one of the clubs. I went with my roommate the first few times, but lately she's been able to catch some sleep – no fair."

"You still go?"

"Sometimes, yeah."

"Fun?"

"The first time I went alone, I was a bit nervous."

"Still nervous?"

"Yes, but I still go. Sometimes being nervous is half the fun."

"To think, all these nights I've been awake unaware of all the fun I was missing."

"I'd rather just be able to get a good night's sleep."

Angeline pulled the bill of her hat lower, keeping her face shaded. Her long hair, pulled through the back of her hat, brushed against the back of her yellow T-shirt. We both dressed like Americans, making no pretenses about blending in; though, I doubted Angeline wore the same clothing when she went out to the clubs.

After twenty minutes of zigzagging away from studio, we found the art supply shop. Off of the main street, the shop was marked only by an A-frame sign pulled out to the sidewalk, pointing toward the open door. If not for the sign, I might have feared we were walking into some unsuspecting person's home. The lights were dim, the shop relying mostly on natural light, leaving the back forbidding. Simple wood shelves marched up the walls, in no particular pattern, showing off an assortment of paints, papers, brushes and assorted books. Stuccoed walls, cracked and chipped, revealed brickwork behind the crumbling veneer. Large expanses of exposed brick wore colorful scraps of yellowed paper, the remnants of posters that had been pasted up, torn down, only to be replaced by the next.

Finding art supplies was like rummaging through grandmother's attic; piles of tired brick-a-brack concealed occasional treasures hiding just out of site. I considered asking a shopkeeper for help, but none was visible. I strolled up and down the aisles, crowded with canvases and bottles, before realizing the shopkeeper was sitting behind a counter in the back. Hidden in the shadows, an old woman remained motionless, looking down at a folded newspaper - I couldn't imagine how she could see to read with so little light.

"I'm looking for pastels, see any?" Angeline asked, absentmindedly chewing on a fingernail.

"Hard to tell, I didn't bring my flashlight."

"Paper, I also need paper."

"I've seen paper, what kind?"

"Paper with some tooth – good for pastels, grab whatever you find."

I selected some thick textured paper for Angeline and grabbed a watercolor pad for myself. She continued to scan the shelves, tipping up on her toes to see the top shelf.

"Still no luck with pastels, you seen them, Nick?"

"How do you use pastels, anyway, they just get smudged up on my fingers."

"Not so messy, I learned from my grandma; she knew how to keep tidy."

"Visit her often?"

"Visit? No, I lived with her."

"She raised you?" I asked.

Angeline was rummaging through a stack of boxes of chalk. She looked intently at each box, never turning her head. After a moment, I held the paper up and shook it around.

"Oh, thanks for the paper, that will work fine," she said smiling.

"She teach you anything else?"

"Of course, lots. Anyway, it doesn't look like they have any pastels. These boxes of chalk look pretty brittle, no point really."

"You've got me intrigued - about your grandmother. Tell me about her, is she still living?"

"Yeah, she does well by herself. I send pictures since she's never been to Italy. She always wanted to visit."

"Did she turn you on to architecture?"

"No, did that myself – there's really not a lot to tell about me and grandma."

"Gramms?"

"No, grandma. Do you call yours Gramms?"

"Course not, nobody does, not really. Anyway, mine passed away before I was old enough to know them," I said. "At least, that's half true; my father's mom lived until I was sixteen. But in her last years she wasn't really herself, if you know what I mean."

"My grandmother is certainly herself. Always has been. Nothing like either of my parents."

"Tell me about them."

"Tell you? What?"

I stammered, not really expecting a counterpoint. "It's not really a trick question, I was just curious."

"Sorry, didn't mean to be on edge. I don't know my parents so very well, so it's a difficult question. Knew my Mom a little, Dad hardly."

"If you feel uncomfortable – That is, I didn't mean to pry," I said, hoping to set the conversation right again.

"Nick, not your fault. To make it a short story, My Dad was sort of a bad guy. When he wasn't drunk he was gone, my Mom and I moved to be with my grandmother to get away. It's been a long time, though, and it's no longer a big deal. Fact is that I'm in Rome right now and I'm excited about where life can take me."

144

"I'm glad; It's good to look at life forward, never backward. Angeline, the more I get to know you, the more I like you."

"Good."

"Victory grape?" I asked, holding up the rest of our stash from the market.

"I will decline your grape and take a rain check for wine."

"Really? I thought you didn't drink much wine."

"I didn't used to, but this is Italy."

"Well, good - life is best with help from the vine. A rain check, then."

We purchased the few supplies we found at the back counter and left the store. Angeline hugged the shaded side of the streets, always eager to avoid the intensity of the sunlight. Still, her skin gradually blushed under the brief exposure to the sun, and she donned a pair of large sunglasses for relief. Before putting on sunglasses, her eyes were beginning to tear from the perspiration rolling over her eyelids, mixing makeup with salty sweat and stinging her eyes. Her aversion to the heat didn't make her any less attractive, rather it created an intriguing contrast. She was both delicate and unflappable, a combination I couldn't have imagined finding in any other person.

We returned to the Campo where we had purchased our late afternoon lunch, but most of the carts had already come down, vendors retiring for the evening.

"I owe you a rain check," I said

"We'll get together for a bottle then?"

"Soon."

I leaned forward and kissed her cheek, then pulled back and smiled. "That's for luck."

Her face reddened, but she smiled. "Thank you, looking forward to our bottle.

7

As the summer wore on, we continued developing our studio projects. Our sketches and diagrams became more realized drawings as we sustained more

progressive critiques from Professor Rice. Either because of or despite his
suggestions, most of the designs became more sophisticated and better integrated
into the existing character of Rome.

Angeline and I enjoyed frequent lunches, getting to know the vendors despite
not having the ability to speak to them. We still communicated mostly through
gesture, but discovered which vendors we preferred to solicit our meals of grapes,
apples, cheeses, and bread.

The entire time that I was in Rome, I never strayed to a fast food chain, though
they could be found. I had even sat in one of the patio chairs of a McDonald's
while sketching the Pantheon. However, I did not partake of the forbidden
McChicken, or drink from the cup of the McFlurry. Looking back, there could
have been no sacrilege in enjoying the fruits of mass-production. But for that
summer, for that period of study and understanding, it was important that I believe
that I was becoming an Italian. Needless to say, it is uniquely American to believe
that eschewing McNuggets could make me Italian, but there I was.

Angeline, however, was more than willing to grab a milkshake and a burger.
Not often, but she didn't try to hide her passion for fast food and guilty pleasures.
To me, it just didn't seem right, to sit in front of the Pantheon and gobble french
fries.

"Nicky, let's go buy shoes. We're in Italy, it's time we bought some shoes,"
Angeline said.

"Shoes? I already have some."

"But you're wearing Timberlands, let's get something new."

"I like what I'm wearing."

"Not the point, let's just go. Not because we need shoes, because it just seems
fun."

"Shoes?"

"Don't talk, just follow."

I laughed and tagged along. There was no sense in looking for a pair of shoes, but any excuse to be with Angeline seemed a good one. She could buy twelve pairs of shoes, and I could nod or shake my head if an opinion was needed. We didn't need to go far before coming to a shop with the word 'Saldi' pasted over the windows; every shoe half off.

Angeline browsed the aisles, clearly enamored with the freedom of having no need for new shoes, but plenty of time to try on every pair. I suppose that life is short, so why not try on every pair and every color? But shoes are also not something that I can get crazy over, so I found myself a spectator. After a dozen trials, and a dozen errors, Angeline decided that a purchase would have to wait.

We began our walk back, but upon seeing a beveragecart, became acutely aware of how thirsty we were.

"I'm going to grab a couple bottles, need some water?" I asked.

"You're reading my mind, I'm in."

"Just one?"

"For me, and you get however many."

I handed over a few bills, and the vendor produced two bottles of cold water, chilling my hands. Condensation dripped off the bottles, rolling down my arms and soaking my sleeves. I handed Angeline one bottle, and unscrewed the cap from mine. No cool water to be found, only a solid block of ice, trapped in the plastic container.

"Nick, this won't do. You've bought ice."

"It's cold, but this is a hell of a way to get a drink."

"I'm going to die if I don't get a drink. Does he have any water?"

"This is what the guy had, great for a thirst in a half hour." I pointed to a small market at the end of the street. "There, we'll find something to drink."

We made quick progress to the market, and through the aisles. We purchased a large bottle of liquid water and one bottle of red and one of white wine. There really wasn't an occasion, we just saw the wine, and agreed that it was as good a time as any.

Sitting on the curb in front of the market, Angeline opened her bottle of water, tipped it back and drank. She then smiled peacefully and handed over the bottle. She was not wearing her hat, letting the sun strike her long dark hair and pinken her face. She proceeded to tie up her hair, to keep it off her shoulder, and find some relief from the heat. After finishing the rest of the water, I reached into our paper bag from the market and pulled the bottle of white. Without much discussion we opened that bottle too, and passed it back and forth. It was early afternoon, and though I felt conspicuous drinking outside the market, I took large gulps and then pushed it back for Angeline to follow suit. She found it funny, at first taking small sips, but soon, we had nearly finished the bottle.

We talked and people watched as groups passed by, scarcely paying us any notice. Angeline told me stories of her first impressions of Rome, and proceeded to list the names of the other cities she would travel to next. This, she confessed, was her first time abroad, but would not be the last. I listened, and related stories from Pierce about his travels and the cities deemed worthy of a return trip. After opening the second bottle, we started round two, only to knock over the first bottle, breaking it into shards. The market owner came out to chastise us and began sweeping up our mess. He didn't seem angry so much as burdened by our presence, though he managed some English, telling us to leave and not drink at his shop. I picked up the fresh bottle as we offered a hasty apology and scurried away.

"Hell of a way to finish our conversation, where can we go?" Angeline said.

"Stupid of us to break the bottle."

"Glad it was empty, though. Pity if it had been full."

"We're still one bottle up, but nowhere to drink."

"Where to?"

"Away from the market; food's good, but service is just okay."

"You're bad. We should have bought more wine."

"We're not done yet."

"No, and I'm still thirsty, and only a couple minutes from being tired. Maybe hungry too."

"Tired? It's only late afternoon."

"Afternoon is the best time for a nap. Let's finish our wine and then have a nap."

"You said you might be hungry too, what of that?"

"I can't tell yet. I have to nap first, and then I'll tell you if I'm hungry."

"Angeline, you're pretty indecisive, I need something to go on."

"You pick, I'm sleepy. Don't ask me, you need to decide. I'm going to sit until you point us in a direction."

She leaned against a wall, and slid down to seat herself. Hugging her knees to her chest she looked up and smiled, pretending to look at a non-existent watch on her wrist.

"Alight, here's what we do – There's a pensione up the street. Cheap, close, and a nap awaits."

"How far down the street?"

"I'll help you up, but I can't carry you."

I handed her the open bottle, while helping her up. We both took a sip, and made our way to the pensione. We scrounged up enough cash between us to pay for a room with two beds; Angeline insisted on paying the whole bill, but I lied about the rate and paid half.

"Angeline, we're running out," I said swallowing a gulp of the sweet red wine. I don't recall it being especially good, but we had stopped being connoisseurs half a bottle ago. We both sat on floor, in the space between the two beds, and slowly drank down the bottle.

"I'm pretty sure I *am* hungry."

"Just now made your decision?"

"Yes, too bad there's no food here. Nothing we can do."

"Nap."

"Oh, I'm looking forward to a nap, then we'll go get a lunch."

"Be dinner by then."

"Good, one can eat more at dinner." She swirled the bottle, rotating her thin wrist and laughing.

"Drink up," I said.

"Oh, do shut up, I am drinking."

"I'm not trying to rush you," I said smiling and shrugging my shoulders.

"My Dad could drink, I must get it from him."

"Wine?"

"Don't know, I only heard from stories. Hardly knew him, you see."

"Funny how wine makes you remember and makes you forget."

"Yes, funny."

"What do you remember about him?"

"Little. Sometimes a kind man. To me, not to Mom. I think I've spent a lot of time trying to find him. Not really him, you know, but finding the person I missed when growing up."

"Maybe we don't need to finish our bottle."

"Nick, we're almost there, can't stop now," she said smiling. There was no real sadness in her eyes, but perhaps a trace of seriousness. But seconds after swallowing again from the bottle, she let out a long burst of laughter. "This wine is good. Better than the first."

I tried to stand up, then noticed the walls spin, and quickly slumped back down.

"Got a Hell of a kick, I may not get up off the ground."

"Wine's almost gone."

"Pity."

"Nick, don't worry about my parents. It's not so bad to talk about. My Mom was there for me, and after she died, my Grandmother was there."

"I promise I won't worry."

"Don't."

"Shall we sleep?"

I crawled onto my bed and shut my eyes without removing shoes. I could hear Angeline set the bottle on the floor, as she sat wordlessly, not moving. After a few moments, she then crawled up onto my bed, leaving our spare empty. Curling up to my side, she flopped an arm over my chest. We were both asleep without having even turned off the lights.

Chapter 4

A Lovely Pear

[Summer 2001]

1

My mocha finished, I sat in the coffee shop looking at my watch. My appointed rendezvous with Angeline was fifteen minutes past. I had grabbed a small table and two chairs, and now felt the stares of other patrons, waiting to grab the empty seat next to me. For over a half-hour, I had been reserving a chair for Angeline, and was close to relinquishing it.

Just as I was about to crack, and let it go, my cell phone rang. Two other patrons and I reached in unison for our cell phones. Like a lounge version of a shootout, we drew our phones and lifted them to our ear. Strange, that I felt pride knowing that I was the one who had actually received the call. As though there were a wireless scoreboard that kept track of calls received. With a small amount of smugness I answered; it was Angeline.

"Nicky, sorry to be so late. Have you been waiting long?"

"I'm about a mocha ahead of you. What's your story?"

"Story is I'm busy, but I'm on my way. I apologize for not calling sooner, but lost track of time. Anyway, I'm in my car. I'm just a few minutes away."

"Driving? No, you'll never find a parking spot around here on a Saturday morning." I could feel myself turning red. In less than a minute I had gone from

'Guy who got the cell phone call' to 'Guy about to be stood up'. "Is this a bad time to meet?" I said the words and immediately wanted them back. If she was going to bail, I wanted to make her say it. However, she surprised me.

"No, this is a good time. I told you I'm almost there. I've been looking forward to this, we hardly had a chance to talk the other night and we have years to catch up on. Look, I'm not going to park, I'm just going to stop my car in front."

"A drive by coffee-run?"

"Yes, you're funny. Can you be waiting outside?"

"Where are we going?"

"It matters?"

"Well, no, but you could fill me in."

"Do we need a destination?"

"I'll tell you what, if you just want to be my chauffeur, then I'll be waiting outside."

"Good, I'm two minutes away, and Nicky - "

"Two?"

"Yeah, two - and I do have a destination. I want to show you something."

"A surprise?

"No, I'll tell you. I want to show you my office. It'll be cool, it's small but you'll like it. I'm proud, I want to show it off. Are you there?"

"Your office as in 'you own it'?"

"Yes, but it's small. Only one employee."

"Great, this'll be fun, two minutes."

"Yes, and it's quiet there on Saturdays, so we can talk. Hey, one other thing. Can you do me a favor?"

"Lay it on me."

"While you're there, can you grab me a machiato? I'd owe you one."

"I'll get one for each of us. See you in two."

2

Ten minutes later, Angeline drove by the café and stopped her car at the corner. While not a brand new car, it looked close to it, no scratches or dents. Silver exterior, black interior, the car was more than I'd be able to afford for years to come. I was happy for her, sort of. In the same way that one is happy for others at a high school reunion.

She waved as I jogged over to the car holding a cup in each hand. She opened the door, and I ducked my head and sunk into the seat. The leather seats were immaculate, but the floor was littered with wrappers, loose change, and cracked CD cases. Angeline was dressed in warm-ups, which had clearly never been used for actual exercise. The color-coordinated top and bottom fit her tightly, as though she was trying to streamline herself to match the car. Her hair was tied up in a haphazard albeit deliberate manner; this was her version of slumming on a weekend.

"Machiato," I said, passing her a cup.

She ignored the cup and reached over to give me a one-armed hug. "It's good to see you, I'm glad we can do this." A honk from behind prompted her to end the hug and accelerate. She grabbed her coffee and thanked me.

"Nice car, new?" I asked.

"No, just leasing anyway. Let me know if the music's too loud."

"No, good. So you're in business for yourself, long time?"

"Not even a year yet. Closer to half a year actually."

"Like it?"

"Yeah, but my boss is a bitch."

"Funny girl, I'm envious."

I sipped my coffee nervously; Angeline was not a good driver. I had never before had the privilege of riding passenger with her. She saw no need to use a signal, and yellow lights had no meaning. She stayed focused, always finding the quickest route, around slower cars or cutting corners through a parking lot. I imagined her driving while she had been talking to me on her phone, and cringed.

She was confident about her skills, perhaps more so than was warranted. Clearly unaware of her shortcomings, she pushed on the accelerator only to have to brake quickly to avoid a collision.

"You're working hard, are you playing hard?" I asked.

"Both, you?"

"Neither. How are you playing?"

"Again?"

"I mean, what are you doing for fun?"

"Still lots of dancing, still going out with friends. Let me see, I workout a little, trying to keep in shape. I've kept up with traveling, I love to see new places, you know."

"Ever make it back to Wyoming?"

"No, there's no reason to go back there."

"You're grandmother?"

"She passed away. I went for the funeral, but didn't stay."

I waited for Angeline to continue, knowing she had been brought up by her Grandmother. Fully expecting more emotion, I felt slightly uncomfortable when the moment passed without any.

"Seems like you knew some people at the Pear, you're a regular by now?" I asked.

"It's a good place to dance, plus lots of corners to hideaway."

"Just there with friends?"

"Oh, I met up with a few people, helps keep things fun."

"A few people, no one in particular? I mean they were all friends?"

"Friends, acquaintances, and even a few strangers. And then, there you were. Imagine, meeting at random - wasn't expecting to see you."

"Ditto."

"But you grew up here, right? I haven't seen you at the Pear before."

"I go on occasion, but apparently not as often as you. I like to go whenever they have a show, but it can be a meat market. Not really my scene."

"Oh, I just ignore that part of it."

"You mean you're not looking for a guy?"

"Looking? You're funny."

"It didn't look like you were with anyone."

"I was just making the rounds, dancing, drinking, flirting. It was also a good show downstairs; the gallery always has nice work. You seemed to like the show."

"I enjoyed it," I paused to take another sip of coffee. "Any romances conjured up from your mesmerizing dancing?"

Turning her head from the road, she looked at me and laughed, squinting her eyes in mock disbelief. "I've gone out with guys I met at the Pear, just nothing serious. I don't know that it'd be possible to be serious with anyone I met there, you know?"

I didn't comment, but I did know. The Pear was wonderful for chance encounters, romances where the excitement was real but the emotion only imaginary. I liked to believe that I was above it all, as does everyone.

"You've remained an architect, do you like it?" she asked.

"I love buildings, but not the profession. Too much paperwork, too much bureaucracy, not enough real design. Ron and I work in the same office, he keeps things humorous. Really, I get to be more creative outside of the office."

"Sketching?"

I shook my head. "I've got a project starting up, a little moonlighting. Pierce has asked me to help him work on an art gallery that might be built in the Pearl. There's an existing corner building, currently empty. We're going to draw up some plans to renovate it." I said with the slightest bit of guilt; it wasn't really my place to discuss Pierce's project with Angeline, but it seemed important that I provide some career justification.

"Wait, I know about this, she said excitedly. "This is for the same guy who owns the Pear. I've heard that he may build another gallery."

"Better if we keep it under our hat. Nobody's supposed to know. How did you get your information?"

"I told you, I'm a regular at the Angry Pear."

"Apparently more regular than I thought."

We drove east from the Pearl District toward the Burnside bridge to cross over the Willamette. I described my gallery project, Angeline listening intently.

"Do I make you nervous, Nicholas? You look a little uneasy."

"It's not you, it's just your driving."

"Beats walking. Anyhow, we're almost there." Angeline crossed the bridge and slowed as she approached the intersection. A very large and obvious sign indicated that left turns were frowned upon, but it was evident that she was not to be influenced by something so simple as a sign. Halfway into the intersection, she stopped the car, waiting for oncoming traffic to subside.

"Not to be a pest, but this really isn't a place to stop," I said. I swiveled around to see cars approaching from the rear.

"I know I'm not supposed to, but a left here is a big time saver," she said.

"Sure, just that there's traffic backing up behind us."

"Fine, I'll hurry it up." She allowed one more car to drive by, then stomped on the accelerator, narrowly missing the next rush of cars. As she completed her turn, she cut through the oncoming lane. Reaching for the wheel, I pulled us back into our own lane. Before I could peel myself from the seat, colored lights flashed from behind.

"Oh, shit, Nicholas what do I do?" She seemed unusually agitated.

"Pullover and hope he's already met his quota," I said.

Angeline steered the car into a parking lot and killed the engine. As we waited for the officer, she began biting a nail, then turned to me and shrugged.

"Let's see if we can avoid a ticket," she said.

"Looks like it's a 'he' so this is all up to you."

As the officer reached the car, Angeline rolled down the window, and blushing on queue, she smiled. I sat, a spectator, now holding both of our coffees. Angeline had a brief conversation that involved more smiling and posing. After plenty of charm, and no ticket, the officer left us with a less than stern warning.

"Well, that short cut didn't save us much time," she said.

"Are we in a hurry?"

"No, just habit. My office is just a few blocks away. I'm usually much better than this."

"Not at all, I think the way you handled the police was masterful. I firmly believe that laws are aimed toward those not charming enough to circumvent them."

We drove from the parking lot and headed north, completing our journey in a small alley with three empty parking spots.

Angeline unlocked the front door to her building. We entered a small lobby with a door on each side, leading to ground level retail areas. One, a small clothing boutique, the sort that displayed items as if they were museum exhibits. From what I could tell, there was an inverse relationship between the number of clothes for sale and the price of the actual items. Somewhere in the world, there must be a dream boutique with nothing but one pair of million dollar pants for sale. The door on the other side of the lobby lead to a specialty store that had numerous bath supplies for the well cultured lavatory. At the back of the lobby a narrow wood stair lead up to a landing and hallway just beyond. A skylight above the stair allowed a fair amount of natural light into the building, making the small space feel warm, if just a bit too tight.

A sign announced the names of three different businesses located on the upper level. Angeline said that next to her office was a small travel office that was owned by an older woman who was a worthy neighbor. The other office, at the end of the hall, was a bit more of a mystery. Apparently a realtor, Angeline claimed that she had seen him only a half dozen times, the last being two months ago. She had wondered if he had gone out of business, but periodically she would see lights turned on.

Angeline's office was remarkably small but efficient. She had designed her own space, which incorporated an open office production area with a small workroom, and a conference area. A reception area with a small desk was flanked by a few well manicured plants. Having just one full time employee, the space was more than sufficient.

The office was equipped with modern furniture. The tables and chairs were typified by clean lines and simple shapes that sat low to the ground. As she showed me around, she still seemed a little on edge from having been stopped for her traffic indiscretion. Her movements lacked the effortlessness that had been her manner at the Pear. When opening her office door she had fumbled with her keys, for the first time betraying nervousness. Up to that point, I had felt almost out of place with her, unable to keep up with her new-found sophistication. As we toured the office, however, I began to feel more at ease. More of her mannerisms and expressions seemed familiar. Though sophisticated, she had still retained the girlish quality I remembered from our evenings sharing bottles of Italian wine.

As we walked around the reception area, workstations, conference room, and work space, it was clear that this business venture was an immense sense of pride for Angeline. While in her car, I had engaged in a subtle line of questioning to determine how she had started her business. At least, I hope I was subtle. I tried to ascertain whether, in fact, the business was a success or merely got by. I wouldn't have admitted it at the time, but I struggled to see Angeline achieve such independence, when I had managed to find so little. My first suspicion had been that she had received help from some benefactor. Certainly a possibility, but impossible to determine based on the scant evidence at hand.

Most of her projects revolved around branding or identity design. Businesses that needed expertise in creating an image would work with her, eager to make their product or service stand out from the crowd; logos, brochures, along with assorted flash, pop, and zing. The identity design proved to be most intriguing. On multiple occasions she and her associate had created a number of temporary gallery installations, and did much of the work for the Pear.

J Edward Duncan

I considered the exchange that we had already had, and had some regret at having divulged the information.

"This is my home, or at least it feels that way. More than once I've worked late and fallen asleep on the couch." She pointed to the cushioned seat that sat to the side of the entry door. Two plants served to mark the ends of the seat, it having neither back nor arms.

"I finally got smart and stashed a change of clothes and even some instant breakfast," she said opening a large closet door. Inside, a skirt and assorted shirts rested on hangers. Just below the clothing, a small refrigerator hummed. The closet had a narrow counter with a sink, reminding me more of a studio than an office. On top of the counter sat a coffee maker, four martini glasses, an assortment of bottles, and a box of 'No Doz'.

"This would have been perfect to have in our studio back in Rome," I said.

"It would have made the all-nighters bearable," she said.

I pulled at the top drawer, exposing cans of coffee grounds, filters, mugs, and assorted flatware. Stashed next to the mugs there were several small glass containers, one filled with assorted wooden matches. The other containers were cloudy, one chipped with a crack running down the side. Angeline pulled at her sleeves as I pushed the top drawer back and began to reach for the second. Grabbing my wrist, she squeezed and continued the tour.

"Never mind how I pull my all-nighters, let's assume, it's all will power," she said.

"Do you sleep?"

"I dream, so I must sleep."

We walked along a short hallway, where she displayed a gallery of previous work along the walls.

"Have you gotten to know any of the artists you've worked with? Any repeat customers for your gallery displays?" I asked.

"I'm actually hired by the gallery, but yes, I do consult with the artists quite a bit. I haven't gotten to know many very well."

"Andrew is an artist, he was the one you met at the Pear."

"Yes, he should have a show pretty soon."

"He should, but he won't. Lots of talent going to waste; he won't produce."

"Not true, he's almost got a full show ready."

"Perhaps that's what he's told you, but I wouldn't believe it unless I actually saw the work. He is very good, but also slow. Or perhaps I should say methodical, that's kinder."

"You haven't been to his gallery recently, to see his new work."

I was puzzled, apparently Angeline and Andrew had spent more time talking than I had realized. "The last time I was there he had a few canvases, nothing more. You'd enjoy his studio - " I said, picking up a half emptied bottle of caffeine tablets. She looked at me and opened her mouth, then paused.

"You've already seen it," I said.

"Yes, I assumed you knew. You're friend is quite good, he has talent."

"More talent than ambition."

"More ambition than you know."

"Seems there's a lot I don't know about him. Perhaps I need to learn to be more observant of what's in front of me."

"He's not there yet, but it won't be long before he's got enough for a show. This is what we're all working toward; Andrew for his show, me for this office, and you've got a shot with you're gallery in the Pearl."

I nodded, considering the prospects of working with Pierce and making a mark with our project.

"Nicky, I want to see what you're working on. Years ago, we always shared our work. No secrets, show me your project."

"The most I can show is our site, all the rest remains to be determined. The design is waiting to find its way to trace paper."

We left her office and got into the car, to make our way back across the river. This time Angeline was the passenger. I insisted and she didn't object.

"Exciting, your own gallery to design. And I know the building must have so many possibilities." Angeline slunk low in her seat, putting on her sunglasses, two large ovals that hid the tops of her cheek bones.

"Well, really, Pierce is going to be the lead designer, but I'm still pretty excited. Maybe the three of us should get together, be a good chance to quiz you about your experience with galleries."

"Not much I can tell you that you don't already know."

"I bet there's plenty."

"Nick, I don't think so."

"Rather not?" I frowned.

"No thanks."

"I'm surprised, if nothing else I'm sure Pierce would like to see you again. Be fun for us all to get together, catch up."

Angeline remained silent.

"Just for drinks?" I asked.

"Three's a crowd; plus we can make our own drinks."

"Okay, just thought it would be fun. How long has it been since you've seen Pierce?"

"It's been a while, no need to get caught up."

We drove in silence for several minutes, Angeline cracking her window, letting the breeze fill the car. I pretended to focus on the road, making a point to smile. We journeyed back to the Pearl District, driving over the pot-holed streets common in the industrial blocks. Easing over a defunct set of box car rail tracks, I parked the car in front of the large masonry building that was to receive new life as a gallery. As Angeline examined the building, I was struck with an unexpected surge of pride. The bricks, the timbers, the broken windows would be restored by a design that I helped develop. While I offered a quick description of the project, she pulled out her cell phone and snapped several pictures.

After the tour, I let Angeline drive me back and asked to be dropped off in front of the coffee shop. We hugged, and agreed it was good to see one another. After brief discussion, Angeline suggested another rendezvous in the near future. I made a point to program her number into my cell phone, and promised that I would call soon, perhaps for a dinner.

I had the rest of the day to relax, and made a point to do nothing useful. For the Hell of it, I purchased another coffee and drank it quickly. I'm not sure that I really wanted another coffee, but it was the weekend and that's just what one is supposed to do.

3

Sunday morning I slept late, and lounged in my sweats while browsing through the newspaper. As the morning got late, I tossed on a nicer pair of sweats and made my way out the door, and down the hall to Carly's apartment. We had agreed to spend the early afternoon searching for some vegetation to brighten up my barren balcony. She had graciously agreed to guide me through a Farmer's Market safari of all things organic.

We folded the seats down in my car and covered the back with a sheet in anticipation of a bounty of plants. It took us only fifteen minutes to drive to the market. The market was a maze of tents and crates stacked up in great pillars of leafy produce. We began strolling through rows of tightly packed shrubs.

"No shortage on choices, can I just grab some potted plants and call it good?"

"Nick, our goal is not simply to grab plants, this is also your education."

"I've been through college, I thought I was done with school."

"Life is about learning, you should count yourself lucky."

"You, know, if you really want to teach me something, how about helping me get a handle on the feminine mind."

"If you've learned nothing by now, I think it's too late."

"No, but you're a female."

"I like to think so, your point?"

"Maybe you can help me," I struggled to articulate myself.

"Perhaps, but I'm not convinced that anyone could possibly help you."

"Listen, what I need is someone to candidly explain how women think."

"You're suggesting that there is a feminine collective unconscious - in sort of a Jungian sense?"

"Yes, so you understand."

"Well, one of us does." She continued walking as I considered exactly how to convey my idea. Somewhere between potted grasses and flowering annuals, she stopped. "I'm already helping you with your garden, and now you also want feminine advice? If you're asking about hygiene, you'll have to find a different girl."

"No, not hygiene," I said, making a face while picking up a pot of miniature roses. "I'm not good at this frankly."

"It's okay, miniature roses just need plenty of sunshine, you'll do fine."

"No, no. Asking for your advice."

"You're holding a pot of roses, but beating around the bush - come clean. What are you asking?"

"I think I need a coach of sorts; a romantic confidante. Perhaps if I can explain to you my romantic questions, you can offer advice."

"Again, why should I help you? I don't mean to seem cold, but this advice thing we have going is pretty one-sided."

"It's just advice, I'm not asking you to wax my car. Look, if you need man advice, I'd be more than happy to offer."

"Nick, I don't need man advice. And no offense, but I wouldn't ask you for any." She lifted a pot with tall stiff leaves and held it out to me. "This is an iron plant, very difficult to kill. Unless you run your car over this one, it won't die. Perfect for someone with no green thumbs."

To me, buying plants seemed a little like purchasing lottery tickets. There was always a faint hope that *this would be the one, this time I'd be lucky.* Yet the results were always the same, the poor little plant would die, never really having a chance. Years ago, a friend was to spend three months traveling through Europe. She packed up her belongings into storage and entrusted me with the plants. Really, the plants were gifts; there was no expectation that they would be returned. Fortunate, that, because before her trip was complete the plants were finished, carried down to the dumpster. What hurt me, were the later allegations that I had received the plants and immediately took them to the dumpster. I had been very careful to ensure that the plants were dead before they landed in the dumpster; I'm not a monster.

My lethal habits toward plants might be mistakenly chalked up to being inattentive. That's likely the most common reason why plants die in male households. My herbicides were the opposite. I couldn't stop watering the stupid things. If ever the plant looked like it wasn't thriving, I immediately assumed that it was dying for a drink. I didn't even realize that plants could become saturated. As the health of the plant would further decline, I couldn't accept that the thing would be better off if I simply let it be. So, I'd water it, figuring that some sort of action on my part might bring it back. But they never came back.

Shopping with Carly didn't give me any more reason for hope. Granted she might pick out some nice foliage, but to what end? It was like selecting virgins for the sacrifice. I actually felt a little bad picking out healthy plants; it would have been more fair to select plants already on the brink. Why not pick a plant that was sickly, one that had nothing left to live for? Then at least it would be less a tragedy. If it were possible to pick a plant that was long in the tooth, that would surely be a better solution.

My interest in shopping with Carly, though, was not really about selecting plants. She was attractive but safe. For whatever reason, it was easy for me to view her as a friend. Perhaps because we were neighbors, more likely because she had been in an 'on again, off again' relationship for most of the time I had known her. Without intending to, I had accepted our acquaintance as a safe and comfortable friendship. More importantly, I believe that Carly saw it in the same terms. Ironic, that it was Ron who caused me to reconsider my viewpoint. For whatever reason, I was slow to acknowledge the possibility that there might ever be more than friendship between us.

Perhaps I'll never completely grasp why some girls seem like chums and others chicks. Clearly, beauty is key, but there's something beyond even that. Perhaps it's as simple as expectations. With Carly, I never expected that we should be anything but neighbors. I recall girls at school who shared my study groups. We met for a common goal, scholastic-survival. Beyond that, it didn't occur to me to look for romance. It took all my energy just to remember material for the next test. A pity that I was such a determined student; I likely missed out on a hell of a lot of fun.

But I think that there is something deeper still. For many males, there is a myth that stifles romance. It is a myth that we hold deep in our hearts, and perhaps never quite give up. It is an idea that is formed early in the pre-adolescent mind, and takes hold before there have been any kisses or caresses. It is a myth that prevents true romance, but heightens desire, feeds longing, and drives nails into a man's heart; it is the Myth of the Perfect Woman.

Somewhere, hidden between the folds and bumps of each male's brain is the notion, that there is *the* woman. Understand, when I say *the* woman, I don't mean *the right* woman. Rather, I mean that somewhere there is a woman who matches the ideal that has been conjured in the mind. She not only matches the criteria compiled in some woman-wish-list, but she is so perfect that she renders all of life's other problems moot. This woman isn't simply flawless, she actually has the power to transform a man's own iniquities into meaningless trivia. She somehow, *makes everything all right*. Many has been the man who, with perceived sincerity, has asked God to send this woman into his life. As though the single missing ingredient in a life more fruitful is a sensual minx who can cook and laugh at your jokes. I'm not denying that it's a flawed theory, but it does explain a great deal.

More to the point, it's not unusual for a man to be so infatuated with this ideal woman, that reality never stands a chance. The search for the perfect woman who will *make everything all right* is a search for a Grail that never was.

"Describe your balcony, what do you want it to be?" she asked.

"I don't want it too complicated. I'm not into that, the rest of my apartment is clutter free."

"Fine, a balcony without clutter. Do you like color?"

"I'm content with color. Color suits me."

"Oh, God, Nick – You're a designer. I thought you did this sort of thing for a living. I need something more to work with. For example, are there particular colors that suit you?"

"Yes, I'm a designer, but plants are not my forte, be patient."

"Typical male. Here take a look at this," she said holding up a pot filled with tiny blossoms. She told me the name, but it escapes me.

"That looks nice, but maybe a little too feminine. I'm looking for man plants."

"So, I'm hearing that color is fine as long as it's green?"

I nodded my head .

"How about this, it's a fichus. Tough as nails, but still adds warmth and charm."

"It's a keeper. Okay, we've got two," I said. "Tell me, how was your evening out the other night? You should join us at the Pear some time."

"Evening was fine, enjoyed a nice dinner. New restaurant that serves Peruvian food."

"The food?"

"Good, lots of corn," she said.

"The company?"

"Fine, not magic, but fun."

"Fun is good."

"Did I miss anything at the Pear?"

"Lots of artists, architects, poseurs, and a lush or two."

"What's the attraction?"

"Architects need a place to hang out."

"Why did you become an architect? Are you interested in the technical side, problem solving? Is it the creative side that interests you? You always describe yourself as a designer, what do you like to design?" She asked.

"Mostly I've been working on commercial projects, offices and whatnot."

"Do you like designing whatnot?"

"Well, I'm generally not the one who actually does the designing. I'm still a CAD monkey, so I'm in charge of documenting."

"Monkey?"

"The CAD monkey," I began, "is a species of primate found domesticated in farms - cube farms. A close relative to the draftesaurus, the CAD monkey subsists on a diet of coffee and muffins. Needing virtually no exercise or mental stimulation, this primate spends hours drawing floor plans and researching code. While other monkeys can be found flinging excrement, this one is more likely to be found shoveling it. CAD, of course, refers to Computer Aided Design. It is the umbilical chord of architecture, binding us while simultaneously providing nourishment. Ask any intern about CAD, and you'll be exposed to a litany of curses. All curses aside, it does speed up drafting, but also constricts the soul. Besides," I continued, "I can't actually call myself an architect yet, not until licensed. Well, let me clarify. At cocktail parties, I am permitted to call myself an architect, but until certified, I have to say I'm a designer."

"What's wrong with being a designer?"

"Nothing, I love designing. I just get tired of documenting. I'm looking forward to doing design work, but it's just slow to happen in an office."

"So for now, you're a monkey?"

I realized that I was quickly losing face. Carly didn't know other architects, so she was unprepared for the diatribe of self loathing that I was about to embark upon. So, I tried a different tact.

"I'm about to get my chance to design. Not in my office, I'll never get a chance there. Rather, I have an opportunity to assist with the design of a gallery. This is a moonlighting opportunity, really it's the best thing to happen to my career yet."

"A gallery, fun – tell me more."

"A friend of mine has gotten a commission for an art gallery in the Pearl district. It's more work than he can do alone, so he's asked for my help. If it goes well, it could provide an opportunity for more projects."

"Now you're sounding more like a designer. I suppose designing a garden isn't quite as exciting as a gallery. What are your ideas for the gallery?" She asked.

I went through my speech about the location of the building and the possibilities of the design. Carly seemed sufficiently impressed. I even found that I was becoming even more intrigued with the possibilities for the gallery.

"This is a different Nick I'm hearing. My often stoic neighbor can't contain his emotion. You talk about your design as if it were alive."

I smiled at having been caught. She could see me more clearly than I could see myself. It was true, though. The design opportunity had shaken me out of my doldrums. This project presented a chance to be expressive, a chance to enjoy the profession of architecture.

After loading the assorted pots and foliage into my car, Carly and I strolled through the farmer's market. We passed by organically grown corn and tomatoes untouched by herbicides, both of which were guaranteed to be chemical free. I noted the blackened pinpoints in the tomatoes. Chemical free, but not pest free, so I passed. Carly purchased some mint leaves and cilantro. Given the choice, I prefer eating chemicals to pests. I gather that an overabundance of chemicals does a body no good. That is, unless those chemicals prevent one from ingesting various flies, weevils, and insect eggs.

Being a product of this consumer age, I've grown accustomed to the chemicals. In fact, I even prefer the taste of chemicals to actual food. For example, the chemical simulation of *beef flavor* used in fast food restaurants is quite a bit more satisfying than actual beef. Natural flavors rarely have the punch that can be manufactured in a lab. And the best part of artificial flavors is that they are pest free. Of course, many also lack the actual food they are intended to simulate.

So, after Carly had purchased her bounty of the fields, I grabbed an elephant ear. I did appreciate the actual butter used on the pastry. Some things just can't be faked.

"Nick, when do you begin your design?"

"Early this week. I'm working with a couple other designers, Pierce and Janet. We'll meet to discuss design strategy. Only Janet's met the client, so we have to determine how to present our ideas. For that matter, we also need to generate our ideas."

"What's your first step, how do you kick off a design?" She asked.

I finished a bite of elephant ear and replied. "First we have to examine the site and program. They say form follows function, so we'll let the program shape the design."

"That, and you'll have your muse."

"How's that?"

"Your lady friend, your muse."

"Well, there's no lady friend. No muse, I'll just have to rely on creativity."

"After all of our talk about romantic advice, I'd thought you were seeking a muse for your project. You know, your passion for one fuels the other."

"You make it sound like I'm infatuated. I think that's a little too extreme." I had overstated my case to Carly, that or she was quick to jump to conclusions. I was fond of Angeline, mostly because of our history. But I didn't want to admit my emotions went any further than that.

"Does architecture require a muse?" She asked.

"In some ways a design project is like a woman, so it is its own muse. It's been some time since I did design work, so I'm trying to remember how to do it."

"Oh, the melodrama - when did you last design?"

" It hasn't been since I was a student in Rome. Then it was easy to be passionate about designs."

"Well then designing foliage for your balcony can be a good warm-up."

"Warm-up or crescendo; I hope I still know how to do it."

"Nick, I swear, you need a good romance to drive you. Find yourself a muse."

"Fine to say, but a muse does not always assist a designer. I've a friend who paints – quite often his muse of choice becomes a distraction."

"You've asked for my romantic advice and I've tried to give it to you. It's your choice if you won't listen."

"I'm listening, I just need time to digest the advice."

"Digest quickly."

"I had no idea you would be such a harsh task-mistress."

We continued walking, me chewing on my elephant ear. I dropped a sticky napkin into the waste can. Carly started to speak, but I held up one hand while licking my fingers on the other. After I had cleaned most of the sugar and butter from my hands, I waved her back on.

"Ready now? Finished grooming?"

"Yes, washing up never tasted so good."

"Maybe you could use food for inspiration."

"No. Good design is more like romance than lunch."

"So what makes the difference between good design and bad?"

"That's a long conversation."

"Right, I don't believe you'd tell me it was simply a matter of opinion. Though, to me it seems subjective; your balcony for example - "

"No, my balcony, objectively, is bad design. I think some design issues are objective. For example, good design responds to context. Before designing a building, an architect needs to take stock of what he's working with. I would design a completely different gallery in an urban context than in a rural setting. A gallery in a city focuses on the street and reflects what is in its immediate vicinity. In a rural setting with expansive views, you respond to what may be far away."

"You describe it so analytically. Don't tell me it has to be that way?"

"No," I said, although I thought, perhaps it did need to be that way.

We continued to walk among the stands at the farmer's market. The sun was just beginning to heat up the day, causing vendors to raise canopies for shade. The crowd was becoming thick, slowing our pace. I finished the last of my pastry, cleaning the remnants of cinnamon and sugar from my fingertips. Still feeling sticky, I pointed to a drinking fountain and we steered our way over.

While I washed my fingers, Carly pulled off her sweatshirt and tied it around her waist. Now, wearing a tight T-shirt and shorts, she looked ready for a walk on the beach. Removing her shoes, she spread her toes in the grass.

"You think I take design too seriously?" I asked.

"No, I enjoy talking with people who are really interested in something. You have strong opinions, it prevents you from being dull."

"That, and my affinity for horticulture."

"Tell me about Rome," she asked. "You talk about it an awful lot. Are you going to go back?"

"I'd love to."

"Do you want to live there?"

"No, it's enough to travel. I'll always want to visit, but it's not home. Rome is a place to be inspired, but this is where I belong. Go to Italy, and you'll see history, you'll understand where you came from. But sometimes, the cities feel like museums."

"Do Italians feel that way? How do they see their cities?"

"Proud. To them the cities are not museums - the cities are alive."

"You prefer it here?"

"Most of the time."

"You like it here, because of the elephant ears?"

"I like it here because we build new buildings. New buildings say something about the identity of a society and what it values."

"So, if a design says something about what one values, what will your design say about you?"

"It'll say that I value a good drink."

"Nick, its not even noon."

"I'm not drinking yet, just thinking about it."

4

The weekend passed, initiating a brand new workweek. There's always something so tragic about Sunday evening. It's a beautiful sunset that ushers in a long darkness. I'm always reluctant to go to bed Sunday. The sooner I go to sleep, the sooner the weekend comes to an end.

I also can't shake the feeling that I did something wrong by not finding a way to extend the weekend. As I pass though my early adult life, I realize that free time is my most valuable commodity; and each weekend, though I cling to it desperately, always slips through my fingers.

Then I wake up - suddenly Monday.

This Monday, though, I didn't mind the early start once I got going. The air was cool, but I left my jacket inside, knowing that the day would soon heat up.

I got into work early, dropped my things on top of my desk and met Ron. He had logged in and had already gone through his emails and was busy with a web browser.

"Had enough? Need some coffee?" I asked.

"You had me with 'Had enough', let's go."

The office was already busy, though the morning had hardly started. Most workers showed up slightly earlier each day, hoping to get ahead or at least stay afloat. I turned on my computer and we each deposited a fresh mug of office coffee on our desks. Fresh coffee is analogous to productivity. We then took the elevator down to the street, already moving with people traveling to work. Making our way quickly, we gave way to those walking even faster, clearly more determined than ourselves. We skittered across the street toward the coffee shop, and promptly waited in line.

The familiar hiss of the cappuccino machine nearly drowned out the soft rhythm of vaguely Latin lounge music coming from the speakers. After placing our orders, demanding they be 'extra-hot', we waited some more. Ron's drink popped up first, and he grabbed his drink and traveled to the café's living room. In time, mine followed and I joined him. Ron sat in an oversized chair, slouched, one arm dropped over the chair. He was wearing his best Monday black - shirt, shoes, and pants. Holding a bright ceramic mug, steaming, he sipped his machiato, still extra hot. He waved and I made my way past shelves of holiday mugs and assorted boxes of pre-packaged cool to the empty chair beside him.

"Ready for another week?"

"Coffees hot," he said.

I sat down next to Ron, swallowing a bite of scone. "How's the early bird special?" I asked.

"Never better, full bodied, yet robust."

"I met Angeline for coffee this weekend," I said.

"You going to meet her again?"

"We've talked, maybe later in the week."

"I didn't talk with her long at the Pear. Did she say how long she's been in town?"

"Hasn't been back for long, but she's already got her own business."

"Designing?"

"Yes, but not architecture. She's done with that."

"Dropped it? She had some talent."

"I think she got smart. Good to see her."

"I'm surprised to hear you say that. You two didn't part on great terms."

"Time has passed."

"Nick, you used to adore her, why go down this road again?"

"I'm not going down any road. Tell you what, how about the three of us get together?"

"I haven't seen her in years. There's really nothing for me to say to her."

"But you have to admit the coincidence." I said.

"What's that?"

"I met Angeline again, the same week that this design opportunity lands in my lap."

"That's you, always thinking of your lap."

"I'm just saying it's a coincidence, the two opportunities surfacing in the same week." I said.

"Nick, focus on your design, forget about Angeline."

"I'm not focusing on anyone, it's a kick to see her again, but so what?"

"Then what are you asking me? You say she means nothing, and then you want me to compare meeting her again to your design opportunity."

"Hey, I'm just trying to have some fun, no big deal."

"Well, my short answer is that, no, the three of us shouldn't get together."

We sat in silence, drinking coffee. Then Ron spoke.

"Tell me a little more about your neighbor," he said. "Maybe the three of us should get together."

"Maybe I don't want you to meet her. You know, Ron, you should focus on your machiato, forget Carly."

"Nick, if you were a good friend, you'd set me up with her."

"Clearly, I'm not a good friend."

"You'll get no argument from me."

"Ron, you ever think that maybe I'm already seeing Carly?"

He took a sip of coffee.

"Serious?" He asked.

"Have you ever considered it?"

"Congratulations, I didn't know."

"I'm not seeing her, I'm just asking you if you considered it."

"No, I hadn't considered it because you seemed hung up on Angeline again."

"More coffee, less talking," I said. "Not that you care, but it was Carly who noticed the connection."

"Which connection?"

"My design opportunity and being reacquainted with Angeline."

"So, you are hung up on her."

"No, I'm not interested in her, but I'm saying that I'm getting a second chance. This design project is the first opportunity I've had since losing the competition in Rome."

"Let's forget about it," Ron said.

"Forget about which, we're talking about twelve different things."

"Nick, there are just two things for us to talk about – me meeting Carly and your gallery design. Let's forget the rest. You do have a good opportunity there, the rest is trivia."

"And Carly?"

"Just arrange a chance for me to meet her, be a friend."

"Every man for himself."

"Look, you're seeing her or you're not. If you are, I'll back off. If you're not, you should help me out."

This subject had long since been a sore one with me. To listen to Ron, it would appear that it was my duty to facilitate his romantic encounters. Not that he had ever reciprocated. If he were pursuing an attractive girl, who had an unattractive friend, Ron would attempt to set me up with the friend. The worst part was that he would present the opportunity as if he were doing me a favor. I don't know which was worse, the unwelcome romance or the insincerity of his attempt. Regardless, these feigned attempts became part of his scorecard that suggested *I owed him one*.

In fairness, he was capable of some real decency. At a time when he had been involved in a somewhat serious relationship, he had set me up a few times. After his own needs were taken care of, he could display some genuine altruism. However, it had been some time since his relationship dissolved. I say that it dissolved in the same way that an antacid tablet disintegrates in water, fizzing, bubbling, and finally gone. There was nothing sudden about the break-up; everyone who was paying attention saw it coming.

They had been good for each other, but I believe that it was a case of insurmountable baggage. Baggage, of course, meaning the vast amount of assumptions and predisposition that each person builds over time. Ron and his ex had a habit of setting up tests for each other. Of course, the nature of a test is never to reward those who pass. Rather it is a chance to say, "Ah, ha – see I was right!"

"Perhaps I can arrange for you and Carly to meet. We went to the Farmer's Market this weekend; she's a fun girl. I don't know if she's your type, though."

"She's not my type because she's fun?"

"No, because she's not bitter."

"You don't have to set us up, but don't think I won't ask every time we go out for coffee."

"Ask. Answer will be the same."

"New topic, tell me where your gallery design is headed."

"I'll be meeting with Pierce and Janet to gameplan later this week. We need to prepare something to show the client."

"What's the client like?" Ron asked.

"Don't know, haven't met."

"Mystery client?"

"No, just haven't met. We need to prepare some of our preliminary research, then meet with the client."

"For your sake, I hope he's not a constipated designer."

"Sorry?"

"You know, a repressed designer who takes control and dumbs down your good ideas."

"Ron, the client isn't the enemy. Also, we don't have good ideas yet – soon."

We finished our coffee and returned to work. The day progressed from email to CAD, and it was exhausting.

5

If the design process is analogous to a journey, the first step is to decide which way to hold the map; a good portion of the process is devoted to understanding which direction to choose. In Rome, my design direction had been sound, but I had suffered a myopia that ruined my effort. They say that when one window opens, another closes; in my case, by leaving one window open I had slammed shut a greater window. I had literally destroyed my own competition entry, and in the process, lost something much more important. The gallery project was as much about redemption as design, and with three navigators, I had reason to hope for a better end.

Though Janet and Pierce would plot the course as a team, it was Pierce who held the compass. This was due, in part because Janet needed an architect for her project and she trusted Pierce. I didn't sense that she trusted me, although I couldn't account for it. Perhaps she was the sort who naturally distrusts a person until they prove themselves worthy.

As a designer, Pierce had always quickly earned the trust of every other architect he met; he had ability and was articulate. The problem was that he was uncompromising. So uncompromising that he refused to work in any architectural office in Portland. I admired his stance, though it was one that I would never take myself. Pierce, instead, would only take free-lance projects where he could choose the client. Consequently, Pierce didn't get very much work. As talented as he was, there were few clients interested in an uncompromising vision. Most of his income came from teaching classes in drawing and design. Some of his classes occurred in schools, others he simply taught from his apartment. As one might imagine, this produced a meager existence. I didn't enjoy visiting Pierce at his apartment; rather,

I found it depressing. He had more talent than anyone I had ever met, and it had earned him a single room apartment in a house with a shared kitchen and bath.

I stood three blocks from my apartment, waiting for a streetcar to take me to Pierce's home. Tonight, he, Janet, and I were to determine our design direction. Happily, we would not stay at Pierce's home. Instead we would meet there, and then adjourn for some dinner to provide fuel for thought.

The streetcar, though comfortable, did not provide efficient transportation. It ran only within the downtown area, and was so intermittent that it was usually quicker to walk. Feeling lazy, I decided that I would rather sit, and continued to wait.

The streetcar arrived, a sleek and colorful addition to the downtown. Bright orange wrapped from one side around the front, then transitioned abruptly to metallic blue which chased the orange. The streetcar became a kaleidoscope with each corner, turning in stutters on its rails. I suppose, part of the reason I rode the streetcar was that I *wanted* it to work. I really wanted it to be efficient transportation, but it wasn't.

When I thought about riding it, I pictured the bustle of a subway, the energy of an Italian train, the classic poetry of a trolley. Instead, the reality was a comfortable but slow method of getting from point A, to point ten-blocks-away-from-A. That was the Portland streetcar.

I had a ticket in my wallet from the spring and considered validating it. However, seeing no fare inspector, I decided to save it for a rainy day.

The train sped away from my stop, two blocks to the next stoplight and then promptly stopped. This, sadly, was too often an appropriate analogy for my design process.

I got out at a stop several blocks away from Pierce's apartment. His apartment was a single room in a large house, not far from the University. There had been a time when the house sat in a residential neighborhood. However, after some zoning changes, the house was now in a semi-commercial area next to the overpass. Proximity to the University was the carrot that allowed him to accept the constant rumble of passing cars. That, and the low rent for a single room in a fairly unappealing house. The house had a spacious ground floor, inhabited by the landlord. The upper floors accommodated three separate bedrooms, but only one bathroom.

Pierce's car, an Escort with green paint giving way to rust, hugged a curb close to his home. Another advantage of the shared home was the parking permit that it afforded him. Several other cars without permits were jammed along the curb.

I knocked on the door, waited, then let myself in. The landlord was gone, but the ground floor was crowded with people. Pierce was finishing one of his drawing classes, teaching anyone who was motivated and who could pay ten dollars a lesson. It was never clear to me whether the landlord condoned these impromptu classes, or if he simply never knew, and therefore could not object.

Most of the students were packing away pencils and chalk, stuffing pads of paper into backpacks. A few easels were being folded up, to return to a closet in Pierce's bedroom. Judging by the young faces, most of the kids were students at the University. Many had taken architecture classes from Pierce, and wanted to glean yet more from their sensei. From the way some students revered him, I half expected him to finish his class by breaking loaves and fishes; instead, he offered some parting observations on sketching techniques, and handed out homework.

Pierce possessed an unusual combination of agility and power with his hands. Perhaps he retained some of the intensity he had displayed as a boxer, but translated it through the tip of his pencil. To watch him sketch, it would come as no shock that he could be forceful, his expression compressing and then releasing as his hands worked over a drawing. The linework possessed depth, ranging from faint wisps of graphite to dark gouges that cut across the page. The artwork sprung as much from his body as it did his mind.

I saw Janet waiting in the kitchen, so I sneaked away to join her.

"Is he done?" She asked.

"He's offering parting words to his acolytes. Seems to have a dedicated following."

"When he's done, we'll take a car to the Pear. Shouldn't be crowded on a Monday night, so we'll have a table and some quiet." Janet smiled while she spoke, but I sensed little warmth.

"No crowd on a Monday?" I asked.

"Thursdays, Fridays, Saturdays are the loud nights. We'll get a table off to the side, one of the alcoves. Tonight, food and drink will be our catalyst; we need ideas. We'll meet with the client soon for a preliminary schematic pitch. We don't need to resolve anything tonight, but we do need to determine a solid concept."

"Tell me about the client, what will he expect?"

"He appreciates good design, more importantly good designers. Aside from that, what we present will need to pencil out for his pocketbook."

"Alright, let me rephrase; do *you* have expectations for the concept?"

"Of course," she said tugging at her shirtsleeve. She offered a wry but awkward smile and continued. "First of all, can we agree that useless bullshit has no place in this design? I'm not interested in Post-Modern quotations or irony. I asked Pierce up front if you were into that; he said no, so I think we're good there. This design needs to be simple, but it needs to grab people. Think Modern, think minimalist, think bold. This design needs to get noticed, but not be kitschy. Kitsch is great for Elvis clocks and retro-diners, but not for art galleries. I want the concept to be direct, and I want it to be an extension of the urban fabric.

"I'll be designing the interiors, and I intend to use stark materials and clean lines. On this design, you won't see curtains or throw pillows; ornament may not be crime, but it will be scarce. I'm not afraid of color, and I don't define beige as a color. Beige is a shade.

"The interior of this gallery will be no stranger to natural light. Being a corner building, bringing in natural light won't be a chore; you and Pierce should have no trouble. You'll be working primarily on the shell of the building, but I want input for the interior. Pierce says you can draw and build models; good, we'll need both for our presentation."

When she was done she folded her arms expectantly.

"The presentation is going to come quickly. We'll have to scramble, but we can be ready," I said.

"We *have* to be ready," Janet continued. "It's important we demonstrate an ability to produce work quickly; clients like that. After tonight, we'll have a direction. The model needs to reflect our basic idea, no more than that."

"Then you're looking for an emotive model? Something that depicts an attitude toward the design."

"No, forget about emotive. This client tends to take ideas literally. Whatever we show, that's how he perceives the design."

"What about in-house work? When we're developing ideas, brainstorming, we'll need something less literal," I countered.

"Why?"

"That's how I think."

"Do what works, but don't waste your time. Remember my no-bullshit rule. We won't have time to pursue dead ends."

"No dead ends, just concept models."

The last student finally left. Pierce grabbed his sketching pens and the three of us left for the Pear. With Pierce at the wheel, the ride across town was mercifully short. He drove his car carelessly, as though he knew it might break down at any moment; stoplights were there to be challenged, not to impede progress. Traffic was a slow moving nuisance to be overtaken, not followed. While we certainly made good time, there was no peace to be found in the shotgun seat of his Escort.

Street parking was easy to find, offering a clue to the small crowd inside the restaurant. After a tense demonstration of parallel parking, we got out of the car. I gratefully considered that I was close enough to walk home, and avoid another ride. Small choices can provide a lifetime of impact; I couldn't have understood then, how different things would have been had I agreed to a ride home. My resolution to stay out of the back seat changed more fortunes than I could know.

The three of us opened the large stainless steel door to the Pear and walked in. We sat in an alcove that wrapped around a small table. A simple sconce on the wall provided light to bolster a candle that sat near the center of the table, which was adorned with a white butcher paper serving as a tablecloth. Crayons sat in a glass at the center of the table, an encouragement to turn the tablecloth into a montage of scribbles and anecdotes.

Pierce sat down and dropped a pack of cigarettes on the table. During a brainstorming session such as this, it was assumed that any vice was sanctioned. Nevertheless, I decided to hold to my semi-smokeless tradition and decline on this occasion. Instead, I grabbed at the crayons, holding them as if ready to light up.

Pierce gave us each a set of photocopied drawings showing the as-built conditions of the existing building. The dimensions would have to be verified later by rolling up our sleeves and walking the building with a tape measure. For schematic design, however, these drawings would suffice. We cleared space at the table's center to use the tablecloth as our canvas.

Pierce began by grabbing a worn piece of charcoal from his small case and drew thick lines to represent the existing walls of the building. Then, using the edge of the charcoal, he drew thin lines to represent panels for the new design.

"We're here for drinks and ideas. One idea is to use the panels to direct movement through the gallery and allow the existing shell to define space. I like that as a theme, but it doesn't provide us with a very meaty concept to design from," he said.

"I like that as a motif, but you're right; we need more."

"We need drinks," he said, motioning to the waitress.

We placed orders and quickly had our aperitifs.

"Should the gallery bring the urban environment inside, or be an oasis?" I asked.

"It needs to bring in the city's character. The client is very interested in this being an urban gallery. From inside the gallery one needs to be aware of the context," Janet said.

"However, we don't want the artwork exposed to much natural light. The windows become an opportunity and a problem." Pierce drew a small plan of the building on the tablecloth, showing the small amount of street frontage available.

"Do we want to open up the façade? Perhaps the major gallery areas can have views out to the street," I offered.

"Is this building on the Historic Register? If so, we'll have limitations on what we can do to the façade," Pierce added.

"Register? I believe so," Janet said.

I grabbed an orange crayon from the table's center and drew a cartoon version of the building façade. The sketch showed the small windows; perhaps too small to allow much light into the back of the building. It would be difficult to offer clues as to the urban quality outside without altering the building façade.

"Can we appeal if the building is on the Register? Perhaps an exception can be made?" I asked.

"Tough to appeal if the building is on the Historic Register, and I think it's a good bet that it is." Pierce said.

I drew the building from the side, a section cutting through the building and adjacent street, showing the distance between the two. I drew the window openings to scale; shading with a yellow crayon to demonstrate how deep light might penetrate. Ideally, we needed to keep direct light out of the gallery space itself; this meant no visibility of streetscape from the building's interior. This presented a real problem if we were to satisfy the client's desire to have the building relate to the street. Each of us mulled the problem silently. I set down my crayon in favor of my glass of bourbon.

Since each of us was an introvert and more inclined to problem solve silently, it was unclear how much would come of our brainstorming session. I noticed that as Janet and I discussed the building, Pierce withdrew, no doubt considering the problem. He continued to silently sketch on the tablecloth with his charcoal. At first he sketched tiny diagrams, only to scribble them out in frustration. Janet finally broke the silence. Using my orange crayon, she sketched on my building section, drawing more detail for the windows.

"See this, what if we add interior light shelves to the windows. The natural light could bounce off the shelves and penetrate deeper into the building."

"The building's going to get most of its use in the evening, so we won't get much light," I added. "Good thing to keep direct light out of the gallery space. Best to control the type of light that falls on the artwork."

"You both are the architects, I'll let you figure that out," Janet said, grabbing a cigarette. Without looking up from his sketch, Pierce pulled out his lighter and obliged Janet's habit.

Dozens of scribbles littered the tablecloth in front of us; I pushed the candle close to his sketches.

"Mind if we take a peek?"

Most of Pierce's sketches showed simple cartoons of the building, demonstrating all the ways we could get light inside. His drawings were gestural, communicating a single idea with each drawing. He pointed at my building sketch with his pen.

"The front façade you've shown here," he said pointing, "the Historic Register is pretty strict and they're not going to make an exception for us. However, here's what we can do."

He drew a thick line designating an opening through the roof plane. A shaft continued from the roof opening, cutting down through each level of the building.

"We can change the roof of any historic building since the roof isn't visible from the street," Pierce began. " We can let in as much light as we want through the top of the building; that way, we can bring natural light into the center.

"If we think of organizing the gallery vertically, we could create a circulation atrium in the center to gather the natural light. Separate rooms with controlled light could be adjacent to the atrium. Here's the trick, though, we're not just going to collect natural light, we're also going to collect artificial light. I want light from street lamps, stop lights, neon signs – at night the artificial light from the streets will permeate the atrium. During the day, the atrium will reflect the light from the sun, at night it will be a reflection of the streetscape."

Pierce scribbled a drawing of a large sign above the building section drawing. He drew several arrows to indicate light from the sign entering the building's atrium from the roof. I imagined the crowd from the Angry Pear congregating in the atrium of our gallery – neon lights blinking from above, providing our desired connection to the outdoors. There wouldn't be a direct visual connection, but the light reflecting from above would provide the link.

"I like the idea, Pierce. We don't need a direct light, just a suggestion." Janet said.

"But will we get enough light to come into the building at night?" I asked.

"There's enough light from the streets, we just need to provide the right opportunity," Pierce said.

"I've got to ask, are we creating an Art Gallery or a night club?" Janet asked.

"Janet, the gallery part is your job. Nick and I need to chew on the shell of the building."

"If we follow the model of the Pear, then art gallery and night club are nearly synonymous. Perhaps a wet bar with accent lighting could become the first display. Could we have the first show a series of modernist martini shakers? Perhaps some Art-Deco shot glasses?" Janet asked.

"Always the purist. You'll get no disagreement from Nick and me, but we all know what people's expectations are; we're creating an environment for people to see and be seen. If people can't demonstrate that they understand art, then it hardly counts."

My mouth full of bourbon, I nodded agreement to Pierce's words.

"We're making progress, No?" Pierce posed his question for Janet's sake. She took a drag from her cigarette and blew out a thin stream of smoke.

186

"Great progress as long as we can take our table cloth home," she said. Each of us had an array of diagrams and scribbles in front of us. "We've got a good idea to work with, but only a short time for presentation. We still need a scheme for the space plan."

"You've got one drawn between your martini glass and the ashtray. Can you develop that?" I asked.

"No, it doesn't lend itself to an atrium scheme. I'll need a plan where the gallery spaces connect to a central space. I can do it, but first another drink."

Pierce flagged down the waitress. Young enough that I was surprised she could legally serve drinks, our ultra-thin waitress gave a disinterested look as she listened to our order. That was the typical disregard offered by all the wait-staff at the Pear. I had come to realize that I shouldn't take it personally. It was an attitude encouraged by management, to create the correct amount of indifference necessary for any hip establishment. The moment a patron realizes that an establishment appreciates their business, all cool has worn off. Any club that doesn't turn some people away is hardly worth it's salt.

Our waitress looked away while the three of us looked at each other, waiting for someone to flinch and order first. Pierce finally spoke and ordered a drink for himself and Janet; the same ones they had ordered before. The waitress turned to me and asked if I wanted another bourbon. She gazed at me with painted lids and lashes of chunky mascara. I wanted beer, but asked for bourbon.

We worked long enough to order a few more rounds and a stack of appetizer plates. Somewhere on the tablecloth were the initial pieces of a space plan that we would show to a client that only Janet had met.

"We've taken our first step toward our design scheme. Where do we go from here?" I asked.

"We'll need some sexy drawings to sell our idea. It's not critical that we dot our 'i's; rather let's get the client excited about our concept," Janet said. "Right now, we've really only got half a concept. Bringing in light to describe the urban context is good, but we need some more punch."

"Next step is a series of design boards that show the building as a diagram. We can present the concept in rock n roll splendor, then get as-built measurements later."

Pierce looked at his glass. "Let's not brainstorm anymore until we refuel. All work and no play."

"Janet, what do you do for play?" I asked.

"Why so curious?"

"Just idle chat, what do you do when not sketching designs at the Pear? Is career everything?"

Janet dragged on her cigarette and shook her head. "Career consumes a lot of my time now. My man's abroad so I've few distractions."

"Life's all about distractions, Janet," Pierce said.

"The distractions are the fun part, I give you no argument there."

"Interesting, I wondered why there wasn't anything between you two. If you've got a man abroad that explains it," I said.

"Nicholas, tact isn't really your strong suite is it? How about you, what romantic escapades are you involved in?" Janet asked.

"Escapades? Not for me." I considered relating my recent rendezvous with Angeline. However, when I had broached the subject with Ron, the conversation had grown awkward quickly. Pierce had been closer to Angeline than Ron, so it seemed unlikely this new conversation would go any better. Instead I chose a smokescreen.

"I've got a neighbor, we see each other on occasion," I said.

"Names, names – don't even start unless you're prepared to offer details." Pierce said with a laugh.

"Doesn't matter."

"Of course it does. Now you're suddenly not so bold," Janet said with a smug expression.

"Carly. But there really isn't anything going on. In fact, Ron may make a move."

"Nicholas, don't concede anything to him. Look out for your own interests, you don't do that enough. You're too trusting; don't assume that anyone else is looking out for you but you," Pierce said between drags.

"Trust isn't a four letter word, Pierce."

"Just don't let it be blind."

"I trust you," I said.

"I'll say it once more, don't be blind. Pay attention to what's in front of you," he chided.

I looked down at my bourbon. After paying it some attention, we paid our bill and walked out of the Pear.

I was surprised at the quiet that confronted us outside. The streets were empty, and only a few lamps lit the Pear's entry. Early in the week, the Pear was slow, emphasizing the quiet of the Industrial neighborhood. There were few apartment buildings nearby, few retailers or restaurants; just warehouses and a few commercial buildings.

Pierce motioned to his car, but I declined.

"It's a short walk back to my place. You two go ahead. We'll meet again tomorrow night to work on our presentation."

"You're welcome to ride, but I'll only ask once. It's a lonely walk in the dark to reach your apartment," Pierce said.

"It's a walk I know well, see you both tomorrow."

They both waved wordlessly and I turned to walk home.

6

Nearly home, I was drawn into the coffee shop across the street from my building. The promise of a warm cup of something was too much to pass up, and I still felt restless. I planned the upcoming week in my head, realizing that all my free time would need to be devoted to the presentation. With my full time job and the extra moonlighting, there would be little time for food or sleep. I soon abandoned my time-management concerns, in favor of contemplating where this design opportunity might lead.

The gallery represented my first real chance to design since I had been a student in Rome. I had nearly abandoned the notion that architecture could imitate art. Perhaps best of all, this opportunity was one that wouldn't go unnoticed. The gallery would certainly get some attention. One can't create art in a vacuum; there seems little point in exploring artistic ideas without an audience. The audience already existed for an art gallery in the Pearl.

I imagined the design developing, and becoming real. I could envision it moving from sketches, to brick and steel and glass. There was more to think about than just one gallery. Through this collaboration, it could mean a chance to start a new office with Janet and Pierce. I might even reinvigorate my passion for design. I felt I might have already gained admiration from Angeline, envy from Ron, and perhaps freedom from my stifling job.

All of these possibilities swirled around in my cup of medium roast coffee with room for cream. I added sugar and stirred. Few things compliment a fantasy so well as refined sugar. The barrista stood at the other side of the coffee counter, and refilled the stainless steel pitchers with nonfat, two percent, and whole milk.

"Pardon me," he said refilling the napkin dispenser.

"Certainly. Hey, is it always busy late at night? Most coffee shops close down by now," I said.

"Yeah, most close, but we've got a lot of night owls." He gestured to the remaining patrons.

"Surprises me that so many people need a fix late at night. I usually take mine in the morning, sensible way to start the day."

"Sensible way to end the day, and least for some of the creative types. Lot of the musicians come here after a gig, to chill out."

"They can't cool down. Must be an exciting life to feel that passionately about something."

"I think most feel that way when they're young. Wait till they've been at it a while." He winked and finished wiping down the counters. "I'm locking up pretty quick, but stay as long as you like."

The number of patrons had dwindled, and I was done nursing my coffee. Flipping my cup into the trash, I pushed open the door walking past a row of tables arranged along the sidewalk.

My apartment was a short stagger away, and I made it back quickly. I was tired, but had been trying to extend the night. I suppose I was trying to make the moment last. I wanted to capture the brief time when a project first begins and is all about possibilities. The next steps in the process would turn possibilities into certainties. It would be a short time before we were all out of *maybes*.

I opened the door to my apartment, and sighed, thinking of the work that lay ahead to complete our presentation.

I walked in, not bothering to flip the switch. Secondhand light from the street lamps below provided enough for me to see. On my kitchen counter, a single blinking red light pulsed with steady rhythm. Kicking off my shoes, I walked to my phone, switched it to speaker, and dialed voicemail. There was a single message. It was Janet, her voice distressed.

"Nick, Janet. This is important. If you're there, pick up." She paused. "Driving back from the Pear, we got in a wreck. Are you there? The car wrecked, I'm okay, but Pierce is hurt. Meet us at Good Samaritan. That's where we're at now. Please pick up – okay, hope you get this soon."

I put my shoes back on and ran out the door. The hospital was close, several blocks from my apartment. But it seemed I had never run so far.

Good Samaritan was on 23rd Avenue, North of my apartment. After checking at the desk, I was told that I would not be able to see Pierce that evening, his injuries potentially life threatening. However, Janet had already been released, suffering only minor injuries; she was waiting for me. I approached and hesitated, wanting to give her a reassuring hug, but uncertain if it would be welcome. I compromised and put my hand on her shoulder. She seemed tired, and spoke softy, relating the important details of Pierce's injury. The car had been struck on the driver's side, crushing his hand and knee. The force from the other car had shattered Pierce's window and windshield, rocking him forward, then pinning his hand between vehicles. As the two cars spun in place, Pierce's fingers had been smashed but not severed, leaving his arm a mass of skin and broken glass.

Despite the severity of his injury, he had been lucky in a fashion. The crash had occurred close to the hospital, allowing the ambulance to arrive before he had lost too much blood. He had remained conscious, though disoriented, perhaps still not grasping the severity of his injury.

Janet and I sat for several minutes after the story had been told. There was really no reason to wait. We simply sat, unsure of what we were supposed to do next. There was no action to take, but we felt a desperate need to do something, to find some way to help our friend. After the silence became too much, we assured each other that everything would be alright, and stood up. We would learn nothing new that evening, so I got a cab for Janet and walked home. Exhausted, I fell asleep moments after hitting my bed.

7

The next day at work was a struggle; I had no ability to focus. My attention was never where it was supposed to be, so I took an early lunch. Having no appetite, however, I proceeded listlessly toward the Art Museum. I wanted to be in a place where I could lose myself, a place where I could forget. Walking into the museum, I flashed my member's card and passed through the vestibule leading toward the gallery of modern art.

Andrew stood by the entrance, wearing a blue blazer, hands clasped in front of him.

"How long have you been on duty?" I asked.

"Been here all day. You're becoming a regular."

"Call me an aficionado."

"Sure, I don't even know what that is. Don't bother telling me, I won't remember."

"Good enough, as long as you let me in."

"Sure thing, something wrong?"

I nodded.

"Sorry to hear it, hope it's nothing that won't pass," he said. "Is there really a problem, or are you just being melancholy Nick?"

"Friend got hurt last night, in a car. You remember Pierce?"

"He's your friend who teaches?"

Again, I nodded.

"Hurt bad?" Andrew asked.

"Yeah, still in the hospital. Just happened last night."

"Sorry to hear it, want to tell me about it?"

"Honestly, no – I'm here for escape. Can you offer any?"

"Escape? Sure, plenty of food for thought hung from the walls."

"Good, I need to get my mind on other things."

"Take your time, the paintings won't go anywhere, " he said gesturing toward the gallery. "Again, sorry to hear about your friend. Sounds like it was quite a wreck."

"From what I hear, yes. Unclear how he's going to come out of it. I can't get my mind off of it, so here I am."

"Spend some time with the paintings, clear your mind."

"Rumor has it that you've been painting and have a show that may be ready soon."

"Why do you want to know about my paintings? There's plenty of other people's art to look at. Besides, I'm trying to keep it under wraps until I'm almost ready. Superstitious."

"What can you tell me about the show?" I asked.

This wasn't the first time Andrew became tight-mouthed about his work as it neared completion. Perhaps he was superstitious.

"I've been painting, very inspired, lots of color," he said.

"Very inspired - does that mean that you've had a muse? Is your work inspired, or are you inspiring your work?"

"You're right, I've been working on figure paintings. You should come by my studio, see them in the flesh."

"A pleasure I'm sure. Would I experience déjà vu?"

"Sorry, how's that?"

"Have I seen them before? Not the paintings, the ladies of the hour. Look, I'm asking if I know your models. Have you painted Meg, the girl you were with at the Pear?" I knew I was being nosy, but it wasn't really Meg that I was curious about. I was probing to see how much time Angeline had spent at his studio.

"Meg's a nice girl."

"Your model or your latest fling?"

Andrew smiled and nodded.

"So, she's both?"

"In a sense," he said.

"In what sense?"

"Perhaps I should say in a tense."

"Tense?"

"Past tense."

"She was both a model and a fling in the past tense."

"What is she now? One or neither."

"Well, deep in my heart, she'll always be both, but in the here and now, she's neither."

194

"I have to confess, I'm glad that fling is flung. She was pretty, but a little cold."

"Cold? No, I don't remember her that way. She was quite warm."

"No, I mean her demeanor. She was cold to me," I said.

"Well, Nick. You kind of freaked her out. I know you're a good guy because we've been friends for a while, but to a stranger you sometimes seem a bit stiff."

"So, you're taking her side?"

An elderly couple walked up to Andrew and handed him tickets. I stepped aside to let them through. Seeing the museum begin to fill, I lowered my voice.

"Why am I a bit stiff? She was really awful. Didn't put me at ease in the slightest," I said.

"Well, hate to bring bad news, but that's not her job. Look, it doesn't matter, she's old news. We broke up. We were on the outs even before Thursday at the Pear."

"Good."

"Yes, but we're not mad at each other, she's still a friend," he said.

"Still a model of yours?"

"No, no longer a model. But I'm sure she'd be happy to model again, I think she enjoyed it."

"You think they all enjoy it, but then why do they leave?"

"You see - Nick, not all romance is meant to be. There's nothing wrong with a brief fling. It's fun, it's good for you."

"What, like Vitamin C?"

"Yes, it's a vitamin. Taken daily, it's good for all sorts of things."

"We've been here before," I said. "But don't you get tired of romance never developing into anything meaningful?"

"No."

"No? Let me ask, do you date all your models?"

"It's the other way around, all the women I date become models. They want to sit for one of my paintings."

"Do they sit or lay?" I asked.

"Either, they do so willingly."

I looked at my watch. Our conversation was eating into my sketching time.

"Nick, I can tell that you're a little tense. I don't mind, I understand you're worried about your friend in the hospital."

"I realize I'm being nosey," I said. "I suppose the wreck has disrupted me a bit. Not that I'm going to apologize for being nosey, however."

"Not asking for one."

"Look, I am curious, though. You said you were close to having enough work for a show. This means you're still working. How many canvases do you need?"

"I'm three quarters done. Close, but not there."

"So it seems that you've dismissed your model too soon. Without a model are you going to paint landscapes?"

"No landscapes, another model; a new muse."

"Another willing accomplice?" I asked.

"Well, I haven't asked her yet, but I've a strong feeling she'll be interested."

"Any details? I've got a whole lunch hour to listen to you spill."

"No. Sorry, you'll have to wait until there are details to reveal."

"How do you know? Why so sure that she'll agree? Don't you get nervous that you'll be slapped for asking someone to sit nude while you paint them?"

"First of all, I don't ask them, they ask me. Keep in mind that I really am a talented artist; my paintings are good. It's no burden to pose nude while I paint." Andrew lowered his voice, as though just remembering that he was a docent at the Portland Art Museum. "Really, though, I look for a lady that is interested in art. Not just the product, but the process. Art shouldn't just be something to appreciate on a lunch hour, it's an approach to life."

"Sure, I'd like to be able to do more than just appreciate art at lunch, but I've got a job that occupies my time, unlike you," I retorted. "Just give me details on your new lady when there's more to tell."

"There will be more to tell, I'm betting that she's interested," he said. "She's beautiful, and very keen on my work.

"Can you tell me more?" I asked.

"Yes, I can, but I won't. Keep in mind, you could be an artist, you've talent. But you insist on being such a sensible person. You never want to take any sort of risk. If you were willing to spend even a little time struggling, it would pay off."

"I take it that your models buy into your sophistry. You seek ladies you can brain-wash in order to get them out of their clothes."

"What is sophistry?" He asked.

"Nevermind. Would it surprise you to learn that I *am* taking a risk? I'm working on a moonlighting project; some design on the side. However, I'm not interested in the struggling artist part of it. So, I'm working on my side project in addition to my nine to five. While you're sleeping with your miss, I'm missing my sleep. I'm working on an art gallery."

"Nick, that's great news, happy to hear it. When you're ready, you'll have to show me your design. And take my advice, find yourself a muse, it will improve your demeanor remarkably.

"Thanks. Look, my lunch hour is half done, I'm going to run through the gallery. Good to talk and forget about car wrecks. Meet you this evening for a drink?"

Andrew shrugged as if embarrassed. "Sorry, wish I could, but I'm booked. Rain check?"

"Rain check," I said.

"When should we get together?" He asked.

"We'll figure it out, I'll be back later this week. See you around lunch time."

I waved while walking into the museum. I ended up just looking at the art, not feeling inspired to draw.

8

Later in the week, Janet and I agreed to meet at the gallery building to walk through and prepare for our presentation. I brought my camera, a pad of paper, and a tape measure to document existing conditions. We parked haphazardly, knowing there would be little traffic passing by the old industrial building. Janet had borrowed the key from Harlan, and let us in through the back door, adjacent to the loading dock. We toured through the old building, Janet scribbling notes, me snapping pictures of the old timber beams and discolored bricks. We walked around the ground floor, then creaked up the stairs to explore every level. The building was old enough that we hesitated to turn on the lights, fearing the outdated wiring a hazard. Instead, we stayed close to the perimeter, relying on natural light.

"If we're lucky, these pictures might turn out," I said.

"So far, we've been short on luck."

"Have you talked to Pierce?"

"I visited yesterday, you?"

"Not yet. I know that I should, but I haven't been able to bring myself to do it."

"I think he could use a lift, you should visit."

"I've meant to. I'm a little apprehensive."

Janet looked at me as if waiting for me to explain, but I shrugged my shoulders without elaborating.

"I think it could help him to see his friends. That's why I've gone back."

"Janet, I know I should go. I'll be honest, I'm half afraid of what I'll see. There's something about hospitals that I just don't like."

"Do what you like, I'm just telling you how you could help your friend."

"I'll visit. I know you're right, I'll go in."

"Good. You should." Janet forced a smile, then looked out the window. "Our gallery needs to have a smoking section, I'm getting ready to take a break."

We walked outside. Janet fumbled through her purse, found a pack of cigarettes, and gingerly pulled one free. She gave me a glance, I nodded my head. We both lit up and silently smoked, standing by the curb. I understood the appeal of acquiring an addictive habit; it's not so much the habit itself, but the ritual. The repetition, the subtleties to the ceremony, and the unspoken membership, all create a sense of comfort. No matter where one is, and no matter the walk of life, the cigarette is always the same - the cup of coffee, the bottle, or the syringe is always the same. It's portable comfort; it's compact piece of mind that can be hidden in a pocket. I couldn't help but wonder if the social rituals were a crutch or a fire-cracker. I liked to believe that I didn't need them, I simply *enjoyed* them. But Janet seemed to need her cigarette. Did I need my addictions, or were they simply pleasures? I couldn't blame Janet. In part, I'm a product of my generation - which has made anathema the concept of judging or discriminating. Moreover, I understood that the cigarette was also a ceremony that reminded her of her man abroad. She smoked with Pierce, she had smoked with her distant boyfriend, and now she smoked alone. I was with her, but only incidentally, so I believed she was smoking alone.

"This is going to be difficult without Pierce. Still feel comfortable working with me, with him gone?" I asked.

"I never said I don't feel comfortable with you."

"Is that a denial?"

"We don't know each other. How do you expect me to behave toward you?"

"No expectations."

I waited, anticipating some encouragement or effort to reassure. She offered none. I've never been able to tell the difference between dislike and indifference. Janet simply offered few outward clues that might express her attitude toward me. I wanted to believe she was simply indifferent; but even indifference is a version of dislike. She stood with arms crossed, nearly motionless, a perfect statue.

"Do you understand what I mean when I say that we don't know each other? I'm not willing to pretend that we're chums. Don't be offended; or be offended if it helps. But it has little to do with you."

I continued smoking, no point in responding. Instead of acknowledging, I simply changed the subject.

"You're still working in an office. When will you go it on your own?" I asked.

"If this presentation goes well, and Harlan wants us to complete drawings, I'll give notice. I have enough potential work that I can make the jump. More importantly, I wouldn't be able to manage a full time job and all the moonlighting work."

"Am I wearing my envy?" I asked.

"I'm not certain I get you."

"I wish I was in your position, leaving my office."

"You are in my position. Aren't you working on the same project?"

"Yes, the same, but I don't have anything else coming in. For me this can be a start, but only that."

"Then yes, you're wearing your envy."

The sun was beginning to sink, a dusky pink settling low in the sky. We stubbed out our cigarettes and left them crushed in the gravel that surrounded our gallery. I took one last look at the old brick shell and took a photo of the façade. We climbed into the car, making the quick drive back toward 21st Avenue. Before dropping me at my apartment, Janet asked if I was going to visit the hospital. I told her I would, a promise I intended to keep.

9

After having let several days pass since I had seen Angeline for coffee, I reasoned that I could phone her without seeming needy. For the past several days, I had devoted my free time to developing schematic drawings for the gallery. I had several failed efforts crumpled on the floor below my desk, and thought a break might recharge my brain. I picked up my cell and scanned until I found her number.

The phone rang once, then she answered.

"Hello, Nicky. Caller ID, I saw your number. How are you?"

"Doing well, yourself?"

"Good, very good," she said.

It occurred to me that I really didn't have any reason to call. For an agonizing moment, Angeline waited for me to continue, but I could think of nothing to say.

"Good, I'm glad that things are going well," I said. "Are you busy, is this a good time to talk?"

"Yes, I mean, I'm not busy. It is a good time. I'm just watching some television. What are you up to?"

"I'm taking a break from my moonlighting project. There's a ton to do, but I just can't seem to make progress. Honestly, I didn't call with anything to say, just to talk."

"I'll ignore the obvious contradiction. You're going to have to take the lead here, you can't call and expect me to supply a topic."

"A topic? How about why I'm having such trouble designing. I used to think I was good at this, but now I can't be so sure."

"This isn't the same Nick I remember from school. Weren't you always self-assured? It's strange to have you calling me for design advice."

"I'm not really calling you for advice, I just want to talk. Need a break from my project."

"Yes, yes. I gathered. So, you don't want to talk about your design – what do you want to talk about? Perhaps television? Politics? The weather?"

"The weather. I heard there's a good chance that we'll have some tomorrow."

"What?"

"Weather."

"Good, now I know what to wear. I've an idea; even though you don't want advice, let's talk about your design," she said.

"I'm working on schematics; every iteration I've come up with seems straightforward. When I say straightforward, I mean predictable. What I've done makes sense, but doesn't seem very inspired. I'm so used to working through practical solutions for the commercial projects I work on – it's as though I've lost my creative bone. Do they bottle inspiration?"

"Of course they do, that's why I've got a mini bar at my office. Have you tried simply getting drunk?"

"No, not yet."

"How about drunk and naked?" She laughed. "I bet you'd create something uncommon that way."

"I've got my shoes off, you'd think that might be a start." I didn't really have my shoes off, I only said that for effect.

"You just need to take a break and have some fun. Your design will go nowhere if you stare at it. Give your mind a little energy; work hard and play hard. Let's the two of us go out and enjoy life."

"The end of the week good for you, Friday?"

"Friday's out, but Saturday, let's get together Saturday."

"Then Saturday. Sun will be out, want to get some fresh air? Perhaps some tennis, I'll pick you up."

"Shall we say noon?"

"My calendar is officially booked."

I considered my schedule. Janet had spoken with Harlan about the injury to Pierce, and he was sympathetic enough to give us extra time. However, now Janet and I would have to complete the presentation without Pierce. No matter how I arranged the calendar in my head, I would be working every night to complete the drawings. Without a break, however, Angeline was right, the design would go nowhere. Having already agreed to a rendezvous, I had convinced myself that it would fit into my now demanding schedule. I also felt that after having bent Angeline's ear, it might be rude to put her off on getting together.

Strange too, how I didn't feel anxiety about finishing my work. There was still plenty to do, but it seemed manageable. The weeknights would be for working, and then I had a study-break at the end of the week. This wasn't so dissimilar to how I had worked when a student. Long, laborious sessions at my desk were interspersed with late night romps; release at the end of a mental wrestling match with my drawings.

After hanging up the phone, I wondered to myself if I was asking Angeline out for a date. We had already gotten together for the obligatory friend-hookup, chatting about the past few years and getting up to speed. We certainly didn't owe each other anymore time out of politeness. Seeing her on the weekend could become a habit. I couldn't shake a guilty feeling, however. I would have felt embarrassed had anyone else been listening to our conversation. Embarrassed that I could be so predictable.

Upon returning to my desk, I kicked off my shoes and unrolled a long strip of yellow tracing paper. With a soft pencil in hand, I quickly worked over my drawings of the gallery. This time, I ignored imprecisions and allowed details to remain undefined. My eraser untouched, I simply re-worked and sketched over changing ideas. I moved from section to plan to diagram, going back and forth as the concepts evolved. Areas of the drawing became thick with layer upon layer of graphite, my pencil worn down to a rounded nub.

As the hour became later, I turned my clock to the wall. Tearing off new sheets of tracing paper, I created layers of drawings that sat on top of each other, taped together. Each new iteration, I pinned to the wall, until my light table was surrounded by a wallpaper of smudged drawings and notes. As my hands gradually began to slow, I pinned up my last sheet of tracing paper. Dark graphite covered my palm and arm, betraying my method of laying across drawings while at work.

I didn't step back to examine all that I had drawn. I didn't need to, it was good and I knew it.

10

The next few days seemed indistinguishable from one another. My days consisted of routine coffee breaks interspersed with work and quick meals, until I arrived at home to continue drafting the design presentation. I had once met with Janet to compare drawings and coordinate design boards. Quickly thereafter, I had difficulty remembering if we had met on Tuesday or Wednesday. She had done the line work for perspective drawings of the Atrium. Not having determined the interior finishes yet, her drawings relied on large fields of color rather than trying to depict specific materials. This enhanced the drawing's depiction of the light coming from above, and would work to our advantage.

Our collaboration was businesslike, I found that talking to Janet was like renewing my license at the DMV; there was plenty of waiting and over-polite dialogue. With Pierce missing, there was little levity between us. Still, the days when we didn't meet to review drawings, we checked in over the phone. Our fates were tied too closely together to permit personality clashes. We also had a shared sympathy for Pierce, that seemed to provide some common ground.

Friday, I came home, worked for two hours, and concluded that I needed to get out of my apartment. Having promised Pierce earlier that I would visit him at the hospital, I decided to venture to Good Samaritan.

I stopped in the gift shop and purchased a glass vase containing a brightly colored plastic floral arrangement. For whatever reason, I found it remarkable that plastic flowers were more expensive than the kind that grow. Easier to maintain, I suppose, which gave me ideas for my balcony. Regardless of the merits of flowers that have a life-cycle, no organic foliage was allowed in Pierce's room. I also picked up an electronic Yatzee game, reasoning that it could be played with one hand.

'What is the sound of one hand clapping?' I couldn't help but meditate on the famous polemic. Pierce had emerged from the wreck alive, but had lost the use of his hand. His pencils and pens, which had once been magnificent tools, would now uselessly linger on his shelves. Despite the seriousness of the situation, my mind soon gave way to my unfortunate sophomoric nature. 'One hand clapping' seemed more appropriate as a Confucian euphemism for masturbation. Pierce, being clever as he was, had no doubt already considered this *single* entendre; no reason for me to mention it. I briefly wondered if such humor would strike him as worth a dark laugh. Best to gauge his mood first, I reasoned. Best to begin with my offerings of plastic and Yatzee.

That Friday saw fewer visitors than a weeknight, so with only a little charm I was able to convince Pierce's nurse that I should be able to pay a quick visit. Pierce had been in intensive care for a second day after surgery. Doctors had spent approximately an hour cleaning his wounds and picking out debris from his hand and forearm. The first night had been the only real scare, with the ambulance drivers finding Pierce nearly passed out from blood loss. After being admitted to the hospital emergency room, Pierce had gone into surgery to replace blood and sew his wounds. This being done, his process of recovery could begin. He had since gone through the second of what would be several surgeries to repair his mutilated fingers.

Walking to Pierce's room, I quickly became aware that in a hospital, dignity takes a holiday. I passed by an elderly man, head propped up, laying on a gurney, waiting for some green frocked Godot to wheel him back to his room. Another man paced with a drip bag strapped to a mobile walker. His gown, narrowly covering his backside, was clumsily tied in back, allowing him an opportunity to get only the most rudimentary exercise that his condition would allow. There can be no such thing as modesty when wearing a hospital gown.

I pushed open the door to Pierce's ICU. The room, compact to the point of claustrophobia, barely allowed me to squeeze between his bed and a large piece of equipment. I cautiously wheeled the equipment to allow my passage, while offering a greeting to Pierce.

"Pierce, good to see you," I said, extending my gifts as though they were a toll for entering the ICU. Pierce lifted his head from his pillow and smiled. With his right hand, he grabbed a chorded controller, and adjusted his bed to raise his torso upright.

"Nicholas, It's very good to see you. You brought gifts; better than Christmas. Did you bring cigarettes? Not certain if it's allowed in here, but what would they do? Kick me out?"

"I think you picked an elaborate way to quit smoking. I should have brought you gum. Glad to see that you're alert, I didn't know if you'd be asleep," I said.

"The two entertainment options in the hospital are television and sleep. Actually, having blood drawn is a third."

I looked at his good arm, peppered with small pieces of tape and cotton, revealing a map of his blood-work. In general, he was somewhat more pale, but that could have been the light. His hair was matted down and limp, but not unkempt. A faint odor betrayed the reality that Pierce, unable to shower, had been resorting to sponge baths, never effective or particularly clean.

"You gave us all quite a shock. I came to see you the night of the accident. Of course, they wouldn't let me in."

"Turned you away at the door, did they? Tough to get in here without either ticket or trauma. I chose trauma. I'm very glad you stopped by again; I just finished dinner, otherwise I'd offer you something." He waved his hand at a tray standing next to his bed. An assortment of canned juices was stacked on top of books, magazines, and a box of tissue. Layered within the strata were various cards, a plastic drinking bottle, a notepad, and a remote control. Pierce took the plastic plant with his right hand; using it to push a stack of books he cleared space and set it down. Then I handed him the game, which he set on top of his books.

"I've got some living plants in my other room, they won't let me have them in the ICU. This one will be easier to manage. No watering, no fuss."

"It really brightens up the place," I said with mock sincerity, glancing around at the sterility that surrounded me.

"Well if you would have called ahead I might have had time to straighten up."

"No, no, I like what you've done with the place. That bedpan is quite artistic in a Duchamp sort of way." I pointed at the metal container that rested on the room's only chair.

"You poke fun because you care, I know it," Pierce said.

"How long will you be in this room?"

"I'll be moved out of ICU tomorrow, into a shared room. I've gotten used to my own space, not certain that I want to give it up. There will be additional surgeries after this one, however. So, I know I'll be back."

"How long will you be in the hospital?"

"Couple weeks? I don't know how many."

"Pierce, I'm so sorry this had to happen. I don't even know what to say."

"What *can* one say? I won't pretend to be upbeat, I won't pretend to take this in stride. Not yet anyway. I just don't understand it." He moved his left arm the small degree that he could, though it was heavily taped and secured to restrict movement. Shaking his head, he stared at the web of tape wrapped around his mangled hand. "Nicholas, what do I do with this? What do I do with it? I can't move my fingers; I can hardly even rotate my wrist. What can I do?"

"My friend, I don't know what to say."

"I was an artist. I depended on this hand, I was sure of what it could do. Now it's crippled, the fingers useless."

"I'm so sorry this had to happen."

"Didn't *have* to happen, but did happen," he paused, lowering his voice. "Nicholas, you know I should be happy to be alive. I should be happy that Janet didn't get hurt. And I am, I'm happy for those things. I just wish it could have been my other hand. Let that hand be wrapped in tape and mangled. Let me keep the one that could draw."

There are some situations where one can only sit back and watch; there is no action to take. Pierce was alive, but crippled. I could offer little more than sympathy for my friend. But I'm ashamed to admit that I felt another emotion. As I stood listening to Pierce, I was struck by a strange gratitude. It was Pierce who had lost his hand, and not me. I like to believe that everyone thinks the way I do. I like to think that in the back of each person's mind, they derive satisfaction from not being the one in the ambulance, the one on the gurney, or worse. If everyone thinks it, then it must be innocent, human nature. Yet on that night, I felt shame for seeing my friend, and being grateful.

"If there's anything I can do," I said.

"You're here."

"Pierce," I paused, knowing that I was about to sound trite, "I'm glad, though, that it wasn't worse. You're alive. That first night, we didn't know."

"Thanks. In time, I'll be glad it wasn't worse. I realize it even now, but need some time to be angry. The first night I was afraid, and that passed. So will this."

I simply nodded.

"I've talked to Janet, she told me you've been given an extension on your presentation," he said.

"Yes, a reprieve. We're going to develop the idea that the three of us discussed. I've got our tablecloth pinned up by my drafting desk. You're still a part of this project."

"Nonsense."

"This is still a three person team." The truth was that I had the tablecloth folded up in a notebook. However, I wanted to find a way to keep Pierce involved, at least in spirit. It was no secret that he would be unable to participate in any meaningful way. After his recovery in the hospital, he would still be too weak to invest energy into a project. At the very least, that was not a decision that I would make.

"You and Janet will do a great job with the design," he said.

"It's your gallery."

"It's a great opportunity, but no longer mine. I'm disappointed, but it wasn't meant to be, not this time."

This wasn't the conversation that I wanted to have with Pierce. I wanted to talk about design, and learn from him. I tried to steer the conversation.

"There's been some progress with the design. I had been struggling, couldn't really find a direction. It's been smoother, though. I'm starting to feel confident."

"I doubt that you struggled for long."

"I had hit a wall with the design. Pierce, I've got to confess, for a time I forgot how to design. It's been so long since I really felt passionately about design, I could only look at the design in terms of code, budget, regulations. I forgot how to consider what the building ought to be."

"But when you sat down at your desk and started to sketch, you remembered. You didn't have to be told, you remembered."

"Well, no, I didn't remember. I just stared at my blank tracing paper. It just made me sad, I took a break, I had to talk through it."

"You talked to Janet?"

"No."

"You didn't talk to Ron, I think you trust him too much."

"You remember Angeline?"

"Does she live in Portland?"

"Recently moved here."

"Nicholas, why would you talk to her?"

"Pierce, there was a time when I trusted my design ability. She reminds me of that time. Talking to her made me remember what it was like to feel confident."

"Confident? I'd think she'd be the last person capable of making you feel that way."

"That was a long time ago. We were both younger."

"She broke your heart, and worse if you want to know the truth."

"Relationships end, that's no crime. I'm mature enough to deal with disappointment. I haven't seen her since Rome; we've both gone and lived our lives. No reason to keep score."

"I'm not asking you to keep score, I'm asking you to be smart. She's bad news. Nicholas, this isn't my business, but more happened than you know. It's not your break up with her that bothers me, it's the reason behind it."

I waited to hear if he had more to say. I understood that he was choosing his words carefully, not wanting to offend me or bring up unfortunate memories.

Perhaps I also trusted his sensibilities more than my own. But I also believed that he seldom risked himself emotionally; naturally he would champion a cautious approach. Now, when I reflect on our conversation, I wish that I had pressed him further. I wish that I had not let so much time pass before demanding that he speak more candidly. Perhaps I was also willfully blind, and no amount of convincing could make me see with clarity.

"Nicholas, you trust the wrong people. Now's a good time to be more discriminating."

"I know you mean well," I said.

"Good, I do. Just remember, you adored her, and she knew it. Let a dead relationship rest, don't dig it back up."

"Pierce, I haven't yet decided what I'll do."

Pierce and I talked briefly before switching on the television and splitting a can of *Boost*. I lingered, though there seemed little more to say. It's always so difficult to know how long to stay for a hospital visit. When the nurse arrived to do more bloodwork, I took that as my cue and excused myself.

11

Janet and I spent our evenings collaborating on the design, negotiating what each of us would prepare for Harlan. We had worked together during the early part of the week, and had then agreed to develop different parts of the scheme on our own. The presentation was quickly approaching, so we had decided to reconvene to weave our ideas into one design.

I let Janet pick the venue, as she had explained that being couped up in her apartment was driving her mad, and she needed new surroundings to get her head in order. She decided on a rendezvous at what had once been Seafood Mama's, the restaurant where we had been introduced. Thursday through Saturday, Seafood Mama's doubled as a jazz club in the evening. We arrived a few hours before the music was to start so we could eat and go over our work. Neither of us could think

210

straight on an empty stomach, so we idled with small talk until some appetizers arrived. I've always found it curious how much of my thought is keyed off of appetite. I think differently when hungry, the brain so keenly aware of what the body is lacking. An appetite provides a purpose, and I wonder if there can be creativity without appetite. I pondered this for only so long as it took to thank the waiter for the warm plate of calamari and then began to eat.

Janet's short hair was hidden under a tightly fitted cap. Her shirt was dark, blending in with the back of her seat. She scooped up pieces of calamari and ate them gingerly, as though each piece might have a flavor different than the last. Between pieces, she would smile, adjust her thin glasses, and scribble notes on a pad by her side. We ordered drinks and more appetizers, deciding that we would dine on sampler plates for the evening's meal. At first we ate with only a small amount of discussion, this made even more awkward because ours was the only occupied table. Gradually, we began discussing the design, becoming more engaged in conversation than eating. More people arrived as the evening got later, and closer to when the music would start. Without realizing it, we had spent two hours engrossed in our design, and all the tables had been taken over with spectators.

Musicians had begun setting up their instruments on the small stage at the back of the restaurant. They spoke quietly to each other and laughed. Cases were unpacked, and chords and stands were shuffled around the stage.

"The band," I said, "You've heard them before?"

"Of course, they play every week. Really good, you're in for a good show."

"Crowd showed up all of a sudden."

"Best jazz in the city. What music do you listen to?"

"Don't really have a favorite style," I said. Truth was that I listened to alternative, classical, and country when no one else was around. But it's easier to offer a vague-fuzzy answer.

"I love live music," Janet said. "When a musician steps on stage, every time, it's something unique." She sipped her drink and continued, nodding toward the stage. "Here, the music is always first rate. But any live show is worth a listen."

"Why live?"

"It's immediate, there's no pause button."

"I get that. Now, why Jazz?"

She took another sip of her drink, and puckered when she got to the pulp of her lemon drop. "There's a logic to the notes, a structure to the rhythm," she said. "That's what I love about the music, the way the artist creates within the structure that is set up; the way they talk back and forth." Janet pointed to the horn player. He sat on a stool unpacking his trumpet from its case. The metal caught the light, but was too worn to shine, to cloudy to brighten the instrument. Instead, the light simply warmed the metal, changing the color, enhancing the yellow and orange hues.

"He's good," she said. "Watch the way he feels the music. He's the band leader, keeps everyone else in shape, keeps them together."

We watched the rest of the musicians set up their instruments, but Janet fell silent.

"How's your lemon drop?" I asked.

She looked at me and nodded her head wordlessly. It was harder to talk to Janet without Pierce. She seemed deflated.

"Talked with Pierce recently?" I asked.

"Saw him yesterday. He's been raving about the food," she said deadpan.

"Food's probably as good as the entertainment. Did you talk to him about the project?"

"I showed him some drawings. At first, there was no way to get him to talk about it. Then, he couldn't help it. We went through dozens of different versions of the scheme."

"Wish he were here now," I said.

212

"Music's about to start."

The bandleader stood up and introduced each musician, all standing, playing their instruments with a flourish, then sitting back down. The first song began, drums building, and base following. The base player stood facing the drummer while they nodded and swayed, gesturing signs to speed or slow the rhythm.

The guitar player stood up, following the rhythm, then playing rapid notes within the structure. He moved his mouth, lip synching the notes that scurried from his guitar. His hands had their own memory, jumping effortlessly into position. Forming the combinations was instinct, like breathing. Playing notes was as basic as forming syllables, each musician had learned a language. They could speak it as easily as I could recite my phone number. On stage, the musicians simply talked. They told stories; the way they played music was analogous to old men sitting down at the barbershop, each taking a turn boasting while the others howled approval in the background.

I was envious. What they did wasn't work, it was play. I couldn't help but imagine a time or place where learning music was like learning to spell. Everyone did it, it was expected. Not being able to play music was like not being able to speak, not being able to introduce one's self. These men introduced themselves every time they played. They explained who they were, they displayed their emotions as they felt them. No one told a story of how they felt yesterday – every expression was in the moment. If they were happy, the emotion could be heard with every note. If they were unhappy or lonely, each note betrayed their melancholy. Each note could sound on its own, discordant and distant. If they were happy, the notes became melodies, then joined to form harmonies. There was never any secret about their temperament, they had the luxury of never having to conceal sadness or joy. The only sentiment they weren't allowed to express was boredom. I suspected, though, that they didn't even know what that was.

To watch their fingers, to read their eyes, to see their wide expectant mouths silently counting time and singing notes, I had to believe that they only knew exhilaration. If life began to get too dull, they simply blew on a reed or plucked a string, and life was again new and exciting.

The band continued their conversation, taking turns performing solos or providing rhythm for the others. Toward the end of the first set, the drummer took over and began his a solo by playing a drum roll that became quieter and quieter until it was nearly inaudible. The other musicians stopped playing, and the audience quieted to mere whispers as the staccato of the drums fell silent, then grew. The drummer's arms were fluid, their movement flowing and steady. Almost a wave that rose and fell without thought, without consideration, his hands simply buzzed. The sticks worked together, organizing time with each thump and every pow. As the sound grew in intensity, the rhythm also became more complex, but still retaining the seed of the original idea.

I looked across the table at Janet. She tapped her fingers on the table while cradling her head in her other hand. She was aware only of the music. I could have gotten up and walked away and she wouldn't have even noticed. Her chin swayed on her hand, the music rocking her side to side. Her body listened to the music, as though the drummer depended on her to keep the time, and the trumpet player watched her mouth to learn the melody.

Her expression was easy and relaxed. No muscle was strained, just moving steady with the music. This was communication without any filters, no one had to explain the horn, no one had to translate the drums; their message was simple. I understood Janet's fascination with these Jazz musicians, even her envy. They could communicate and express themselves simply without pretenses. The music was nothing more than what I could hear. As simple or complicated as I was willing to understand it to be.

I wondered if art could ever be that way for me. Would budgets and clients compromise every creative effort? I wondered if my creative efforts might always stumble from a need to make them important, when all they really needed to be was genuine. I understood Janet's love of the music. More than that, I understood the joy she took from the music. She was capable of analyzing the music, but not a slave to the analysis.

12

Angeline and I stepped on the court, the surface cracked and worn. The tennis courts were connected to the city-owned rose gardens by a series of long steps that cut through groves of trees. From the courts, the roses were hardly visible, but the panorama of the city below was immediate. By virtue of proximity to the roses, the tennis courts took on a quality of the old game of tennis, played in whites by the upper class. I almost felt embarrassed by breaking a sweat; as though the game was not about getting exercise. Rather, it was an excuse to go outside and change clothes for another activity.

Angeline set her gym bag on a bench. Unzipping her sweat pants at each ankle, she pulled them down and stepped out. She was wearing a tight pair of black shorts underneath. She pulled off her sweatshirt, revealing a short sleeve shirt that matched her shorts. She was slightly thinner than I remembered, and her clothing more revealing.

Earlier, I had driven to her condo at noon, as promised. When I buzzed her door, she explained she'd be down in five minutes, and that I should grab a coffee. Fifteen minutes later, she arrived downstairs and I handed over a coffee. Her warm ups were predictably new, free from wear, but her racket cover seemed to have taken some abuse over the years.

"Thanks for picking me up," she said.

"Sure, how's your Saturday shaping up?"

"I woke up a little late, the afternoon sneaked up on me. You?"

"Relaxing; cooked breakfast, watched a little television."

"Anything interesting?"

"For breakfast?"

"Sure. What were you watching?"

"Reality television."

"Good, improving your mind," Angeline said, smiling and nodding.

"Faux reality is so much more compelling than genuine reality. I'm convinced that my life would make for horrible television."

"Not true; a good editor can make doing a load of laundry better than Ben Hur."

"Still, there's something about staged real events that just seem extra meaningful. I've got a choice, I can live a boring version of reality out on the street, or I can view an inspired re-creation of actual events on my couch; and the couch allows for bathroom breaks."

"You make it sound as though there's something wrong with living a life that's undocumented. Or worse, living a life without a script," she said.

"There's no script for reality television, that's the excitement, anything can happen."

"Please. No script? Those shows are every bit as scripted as any sitcom."

"Don't burst my bubble."

"Too late, your bubble's bursted. We're going to live genuine reality on the tennis courts."

"Thanks, but I've had my fill of genuine reality – it's hard to keep up. Lately things have been too busy."

"Because of your gallery project?"

"Hard to fit it all in. There's a big presentation for the client looming ahead. Not much time."

"It'll come together; what are you presenting?"

"Janet and I will be presenting the design scheme to the client. Just conceptual, but we need to provide full color renderings. If he likes what he sees, then we'll proceed to construction documents. The presentation is coming up quickly, though."

"Thought it was a three person team."

216

"It was." I stopped, considering the gravity of Pierce's injury. "Pierce, well, he's in the hospital."

"Hospital – how?"

"He was driving home, and collided with another car. The wreck was pretty bad, he lost a lot of blood."

"That's horrible, will he be alright?"

I shook my head and shrugged my shoulders. "Depends on what you mean by alright. He's not in good shape."

"Nick, I'm so sorry."

"I saw him just minutes before it happened."

"I know you two are good friends; that's just such a shock."

We both sat in silence, finding it difficult to continue with our glib chitchat after the conversation had taken so serious a turn. She sipped her coffee, and rolled down the window as we drove to the tennis courts. I drank my coffee while driving, and was able to avoid spilling - not much of a sports drink, but it gave me some fuel.

We began hitting the ball for warm-ups, not keeping score. Angeline was considerably better at the game than I had anticipated. Though she displayed little power, she was quick to get to the ball and put it back in play. I resisted an urge to drive the ball back to her, deciding to allow warm-ups to progress at a more leisurely pace.

"You're not bad, practice much?" I asked. I retrieved several balls from the corner of the court and hit one back to her side.

"Not anymore, I used to play, in a former life."

"What do you do in the summer for fun?"

"Much the same as in the winter," she paused to lob a ball in my direction. "I don't sit around outside much, my skin can't take it."

"So, no hiking, no swimming, no sunbathing?"

"I just don't go out during the day when the sun's too hot. In the evening, it cools off, that's when I go out."

It was no coincidence that we had picked a tennis court that enjoyed the shade of several large evergreen trees.

"For exercise I like running; I've found running trails through Forest Park. Plenty of good shade, and cooler than jogging on the street."

Angeline presented an interesting conundrum; she had an apparent abhorrence for the outdoors, yet had acquired an athletic appearance, and interest in fitness. It seemed that she was content to engage in outdoor activities that were shade-exclusive and free from bugs.

"So your workout regimen consists of running, clubbing, and sit ups at Starbucks?" I asked.

"You guessed it, three reps of clubbing minimum," She said smiling.

"Nicky, what about you, how do you fill your evenings? I saw you talking with a girl at the Pear; is that your hobby?"

"No, no," I assumed she was referring to Meg, the former muse-du-jour of Andrew. "She's been seeing Andrew; I'm currently reviewing my options."

Angeline paused, and waited for me to continue. She squinted, then looked away for a moment, as though confused. I started to speak, but she looked back at me and simply nodded her head.

"So what does that mean?" she asked.

"Nobody serious right now. Architecture is my mistress."

"Oh, don't be melodramatic," she laughed. "I'll be your mistress until someone else comes along." She adopted a campy pose.

"That would be quite charitable of you. Would that be a fulltime position?"

"No, no. mistresses work part time and they always temp. I'm surprised you don't have someone serious."

"It just doesn't seem to be something that people do anymore," I said.

"Perhaps people expect too much."

"Or too little. Either way, a relationship can be work. It's a fulltime job. Who has time for two jobs? How about you, do you find time for relationships?"

"Yes, but not anything serious. I'm not ready for that yet; someday."

"Someday? What's going to change to make you ready for a long-term relationship? Are you waiting to meet the right guy?"

"No, I'm not really waiting for anything. A long-term relationship simply isn't appealing right now. Life is too interesting to settle down."

"Settle down or settle?"

"There's a difference?"

I smacked the ball, slapping it at the top of the net where it spun up in the air, had a brief moment of indecision, then fell over on Angeline's side. I gestured to the bench, and we both took a break and some water.

"If you were my mistress - or I should say one of my mistresses - we could escape for the weekend," I said.

"You'd have to promise not to tell anyone."

"I'm very discreet."

"Good, that's what's important in a relationship is discretion. So, where to escape too? Someplace relaxing?"

"Mexico."

"No, too much sunshine. Let's go to the coast. See the ocean, perhaps the Atlantic. We could go to Maine and eat chowder, escape from work and crowds," she said.

"I thought you liked crowds?"

"No, not crowds, I like the way you can get lost in a crowd. We could escape to a quiet town, relax by the beach under some shade, then in the evening escape for a quiet meal."

"So if you were my mistress, you'd want it secret; fake names, only spend cash. You prefer it be incognito," I said.

"It would be fun," she said. "People must do that all the time, just escape for days and never tell. Does everyone have an adventure, a story to tell of some secret romance?"

"Do you?"

"Nick, the whole point of having secrets is to keep them secret. If I did slip away with someone, I'd never tell. It would be between me, them, and the breeze."

"Angeline, I know we're acting, but the truth is, I do want to escape. I do want to slip away. But I've never been one to keep secrets. I don't think I could ever just slip away because I'd have to tell someone. For me, it wouldn't be real until I told someone."

"You're supposed to just enjoy it, you don't need to make it something real, simply enjoy it." She scrutinized my face before continuing. "We were having fun, and now you look a little down."

"I'm not content to just experience something, I want to keep it. We can imagine getting away, you and me. But if I did escape somewhere, I'd have to tell. Besides, my face would tell the story."

"That's fine, there's no harm in imagining."

"But to actually escape?"

"Nick, you're sweet," she leaned over and kissed my cheek, lingering for a moment. I turned my head, keeping my eyes closed I brushed my lips against her mouth. After a moment, I pulled back, keeping my eyes closed. Kissing Angeline again, I felt a jolt of adrenaline. I wanted to ask her questions, I wanted to know what she felt. But I understood that I could kiss her, but not talk about it. When I opened my eyes hers were still closed. She was smiling. She picked up her racket and walked back onto the court, motioning for me to resume play.

The only reminder of our kiss was in her eyes and smile, but we didn't discuss it. I realize there was little to discuss; it kept in the spirit of the game we played. And now I realize that we had been playing the game longer than I knew.

We played until our hour was up, then walked back to the car. Neither of us had eaten lunch, so we agreed to stop at a small market halfway between my apartment and her condo. The market featured an extensive selection of wines, cheeses, seafood, and produce, but had little of the assorted extras found in larger supermarkets. Amid rows of plump pears, shiny apples, and speckled bananas, I strolled slowly listening to Angeline describe appropriate methods for divining the sweetest fruit. Some fruit, she explained, demanded to be thumped with a finger, others require a visual inspection. There's really no limit to the number of methods. Each, however, has the intent of clarifying the condition of the fruit on the inside after the peel has been discarded.

"Nicky, don't you have any methods for picking fruit? You don't just reach for the first one do you?"

"I don't eat fruit. I'm not certain that unprocessed food is healthy."

"That's not smart. Funny, but not smart," she said.

"Not everyone's smart; God had to draw the line somewhere."

"You should take care of yourself, someday you'll be an old man."

"God willing; in the meantime no clean living, it makes the time go by too slowly."

"Here, take an orange, peel it, eat it," she said smiling as she handed me a piece of fruit.

"You haven't become health conscious on me have you? Do you still eat meat?"

"Some, when it suits me."

"Good to hear you're not a Vegan. I'd have to give you hell for your leather shoes."

Angeline's tennis shoes were still clean, nearly free from blemishes, though she was slumming in her sweats. Her hair was tied back in a manner that seemed effortless, in spite of the fact that she had no doubt spent considerable time to achieve a look so spectacularly casual. Carrying her basket as though the pears, oranges, and grapes were made of glass, she elevated her elbow slightly while she

221

strolled the aisles. More a boutique than grocery, I wondered if the food was intended for consumption or simply to be admired.

Because the market had such a convenient location, the proprietors had the luxury of nearly doubling the price of everyday items. While this didn't sit well with my frugal sensibilities, I did have to admire the dramatic manner in which the fruit was displayed. Tall pyramids of ripe produce rose up as far as could be reached. The funerary temples of Egypt had nothing on the engineering wonders that were constructed every day at the 21st Avenue market. The pears were even wrapped in white tissue paper, as though being shrouded for some purpose greater than lunch.

After a meandering stroll through the store, we had assembled a lunch in our basket and moved to the line. Instead of gossip magazines and tabloids, the check out counter displayed brochures on green living and vague urban politics. Angeline seemed strangely quiet as we waited. Her body seemed tense, and her breathing became slow and deliberate. Abruptly, she furrowed her brow and grabbed onto my shoulder for support.

"Nicky, I don't feel so well. I don't think I got any sleep last night."

"Are you okay?"

"God, what the hell is wrong with me? I just feel nauseous."

"It's all this organically grown fruit. Seriously, you need additives, they're like vitamins."

"I really don't feel well."

"Do you need something to eat? Maybe low blood sugar?"

"No, I need fresh air."

"Here, I'll do you a favor. Let me get your produce, you go outside and sit. There's a bench out front."

"Thanks," she said, taking a breath.

"Go sit, you're very pale."

She handed me her basket and walked outside. Her gate was cautious, taking each step slowly, with purpose. I waited for my turn in line, the people ahead of me seemed to be in no great hurry. I paid cash, and bagged my own groceries while the clerk counted out my change. I made my way from the dimly lit store into the bright sunlight and blinked to adjust my eyes. Angeline was sitting on the bench, seemingly in better spirits.

"You look a little better, how do you feel?" I asked.

"Better, I just had this horrible headache. Like my skull was being pounded. We should go for a drive. You wouldn't mind would you?"

We walked several blocks to the car, and then drove without any real destination. We ate our lunch while in the car, Angeline handing me small portions so I could eat with one hand and drive with the other. We drove up to the Forest Park trail, then back to her condo. Our lunch now reduced to stems and tissue paper, Angeline smiled.

"Thanks for taking me for a spin, Nick. I feel better now."

"You'll be fine?"

"Yes, much better." She kissed my cheek, then waved as she got out of the car.

"Dinner next time?" I asked.

"Can't wait. Someplace nice, we can do better than fruit in your front seat."

I waited until she was inside her building, then drove home.

13

Spaghettios and fruit cocktail. Those became my staples throughout the week. Not merely for dinner, but also breakfast. For lunch, I ran down to the burrito cart a block away from the office. A quick jog to the cart, then back up to my desk, where I balanced burrito in one hand and deftly maneuvered the mouse in the other. Time was short, I made the most of it; economizing where I could, multi-tasking and taking any short-cut that presented itself. As the week progressed, I left the office earlier each night, giving myself as much time as possible to work on presentation drawings. Janet and I were in the final stretch before presenting the scheme to Harlan, and it seemed dubious that we could finish.

Once home, I rushed to my light table and returned to the drawings, completing linework, then adding color and shadows. I kept copies of Janet's renderings so I could copy her style, giving the presentation the appearance that it was drawn with one hand. Time passed quickly, too quickly, and I found the evening getting late without enough progress being made. Janet and I called each other regularly to check in, she asking how many drawings I had rendered, and me counting the few days left until we presented. Halfway through the week, we each took a break, meeting at a coffee house a few blocks away. The café stayed open until midnight, so we were still able to get in, each still planning on a couple more hours of work before sleep. She seemed nervous, something I hadn't seen from her. Her conversation ambled, a departure from her usually punchy and pointed observations.

"Friday's going to come too soon," she said.

"Drink some more coffee, relax."

"This was a three person job, we took on too much."

"Drink," I commanded, pointing to her cup.

"Do you have your boards done, are you close?"

"I've got the same number done now as I did ten minutes ago. Haven't finished any more while we've been drinking coffee."

"Three done, two to go?" She looked at me for reassurance; I nodded.

"What's the worst that can happen?"

"The worst is that Harlan pulls the job from us. He's investing money in this project. If he suspects we can't pull it off, we're done."

I stirred my coffee, leaving the lid off so I could get a blast of coffee aroma. I was planning on drinking little, but loved the smell and the feel of the warm cup in my hands. More than anything, I needed a mental break, but more caffeine wouldn't steady my hand while drawing. Janet stared at two young women in a booth, laughing and clutching mugs. She sighed, then turned back toward me and forced a smile. Her shoulders were hunched, as she looked down at her hands and stretched her fingers. We had one more full day to work before bringing all of our boards to Harlan's office. I could finish half my remaining board before going to sleep, Thursday I might get none. I silently questioned the logic of burning our minds on an all-nighter the day before presenting, but realized we had little choice. With any luck, if we finished early, there would be time for rest.

I blinked. My eyes felt raw, not just tired but sore. Muscles behind the eyes felt heavy and in need of a break. I looked to the side and rolled my eyes clockwise and back, trying to stretch and keep energized.

We talked long enough for Janet to finish her drink, the barista locking the door just after we left. I ambled back to my apartment, sat back down at my desk, and completed another hour of work before cradling my head on the desk and napping. At that point, I decided I was done, turned off all the lights and crashed down in bed. The next night was more of the same, except Janet and I simply talked on the phone rather than meeting. I had one more board to complete, and she had the same. We talked once at 10:00, again at 12:30, and a last time at 3:00. By the time I finished putting the last splash of color on my portion of the presentation, the sun was about to come back. Rather than try to get a little sleep, I locked my apartment and took a stroll around the neighborhood.

The air was cool, and the streets nearly empty, save an occasional early bird car. After my walk, I showered, shaved, and squirted drops in my eyes. At work, I started strong, then crashed mid morning. After a few hours, I complained of a stomachache and returned home where I got some much-needed sleep. Janet and I would meet with Harlan later that evening, and I needed to clear my head and shut my eyes.

I remained cocooned in the covers fifteen minutes after my alarm went off. It was 5:00, and I was to meet Janet in a half hour. Our plan was to meet at the hospital and see Pierce before continuing to Harlan's office. This would give us a chance to regroup, and would hopefully earn us some karma points. I don't know how many points a hospital visit is worth, but I hoped it was enough to push us over the edge. Janet was waiting at the lobby of Good Samaritan Hospital. She wore large dark sunglasses, making it impossible for me to tell if her eyes were as tired, red, and raw as mine felt.

"Janet, do I look tired?"

"Yes, but not more than usual."

"Do you have a pep talk for our little meeting with Harlan?"

"Pierce is in charge of that. I told him to gather as many compliments as he could, and unload them on us when we visited."

We checked in, then made our way to Pierce's room. He had been moved to a different room, though I couldn't tell any difference from his old room. I couldn't tell if it was a sign of progress, or if it meant he still needed close monitoring. He seemed in decent spirits when we walked in.

"Pierce, we were hoping you might offer some words before we give our presentation," I said.

"No speech prepared. My only advice is not to combine pain killer with a protein drink." Pierce said, nodding toward a tray that sat by his bed. His hand was wrapped with a blue cover that surrounded his dressing. He appeared to have lost some weight, but looked cleaned; he was now allowed to shower himself. He would undergo another surgery before beginning the bulk of his rehabilitation. However, Janet had confessed to me that Pierce knew that he would never use his hand again. He sat up in his bed, still wearing his gown, with a stack of books and magazines placed on a tray just left of his bed. The remote control was nowhere to be found.

"With a good pitch today, we'll carry the design through construction documents," Janet said.

"You have a strong design, sell it. Where will you be meeting him?" Pierce asked.

"He has a temporary office set up in the top level of the building that'll be used for the gallery. We'll display our design boards there and make the pitch," Janet said.

226

"He's set up an office there?" I asked. The building was a few blocks off the beaten path, as well as in need of the TLC of our design. It seemed an odd choice for a man who could afford market rate office space. Yet Janet saw nothing unusual about this, even adding that it was typical of Harlan's pattern, to 'nest' in his buildings before work began. Part of his success came from understanding the areas that he was developing. The best way to get a feel for the Pearl District was to live in a portion that was still industrial. Though, strictly speaking, he lived in a house somewhere high in the west hills, and simply slummed in the Pearl.

"Is he going in blind?" Pierce asked.

"Harlan? Not certain I follow," Janet said.

"Is he up to speed on the concept? Have you given him any hints, or is this his first hit?"

"First hit, I think that's best, don't you?"

"Absolutely," Pierce nodded sagely.

"I don't know him the way you do, but I believe that the concept is strongest the first time around. During the pitch, he'll be swept up in the poetry of the idea. Light - gathering people around the light. Bringing elements of the streetscape into the atrium. Those are powerful ideas. But after he's heard the idea enough, he'll take it for granted. Just remember to save some of the sexy for later."

"You should be there," Janet said absentmindedly.

"No. This is the Nick and Janet show now. Someday there'll be another shot for me."

"Pierce, there's still a long haul in front of us. You rest up, we can use your help."

He laughed and raised his hand, wrapped in tape and bandages, it had become a club, heavy and clumsy. Though I had no reason to feel guilty, I couldn't shake the sense that I had done something wrong. This wasn't supposed to be my opportunity, it had landed in my lap. Anyone else might simply have felt grateful and accepted the roles that fate had assigned me and Pierce. It was the same feeling that surfaces when I watch the news, catching glimpses of nations strangled by famine, and I feel guilty for my food. As though anyone is better off for me eating every Cheeto in the bag. As if the world could be a better place because I re-heat my Chinese food for lunch, rather than throwing out the last of the Kung Pao. Yet this sentiment was silly, it was naïve. Pierce didn't benefit from my guilt, and his condition was not my doing. My happiness was no crime, though I couldn't resist the sense that happiness under these circumstances was a betrayal. I had been friends with Pierce for years, and I always thought that I had gotten the better end of the deal; he was trustworthy, a talented mentor, and always supportive. The way that I re-paid him was by waving goodbye as he lay in his hospital bed.

Before Janet and I left, I made some idle promises about the three of us seeing the project through, about the team having room for him when he recovered. He indulged my foolishness, and I felt like an ass for saying what we all knew was a lie. It eased my guilt, though none of us were better off for my saying it.

Janet and I left Pierce's room. We stopped at my car to grab the design boards, loading the entire presentation into Janet's car. She drove an old Saab that had been vigorously maintained. The paint, the interior, and the engine, all had been babied by the previous owner. However, the style and technology where fifteen years out of date. The doors were adorned with chrome ornament, thin lines that ran from back bumper, across the door, to the front blinker light. The paint was free from chips, but had dulled over time, fading into a dark velvety green that looked black in the right light. Our design boards were stacked in a black portfolio, propped up in the back seat. So many hours of work, all zipped up in a thin vinyl container, ready to do or die in front of the client.

"After we present, then what happens?" I asked.

Janet smiled. At first she kept driving, head looking straight ahead at the road. I couldn't see her eyes, the sunglasses concealing her from eyebrow to cheekbone.

"Depends."

"Right, let's assume he likes what he sees."

"First question is does he like our idea. If not, he'll drop us like a rock; but our idea is good."

"You like our chances?"

"I'm nervous, but if I didn't like our design I wouldn't bother driving to his office."

"So if he agrees, if he likes it?"

"We push our schematic ideas and produce construction documents. Although, in the past he's always tinkered with the scheme."

"Tinkered? Doesn't sound so great. Does he know anything about design?" I asked.

"Point is, our goal is to walk away with as much of the design idea intact as we can."

"It's a simple idea, how much can it be changed without ruining the idea?"

"I'm only saying that we need a strong presentation in order to keep this thing ours. I've gone in with good ideas before and had them stripped." She kept her eyes straight ahead, not turning to look at me.

I rolled down my window, the chrome crank sticking as I forced it around. I looked outside, feigning interest in the neighborhood, until finally deciding that we needed to get our minds off of what we were about to do.

"Janet, this gallery has been work, but it's going to be built. We have months ahead of us, completing more drawings. But think about opening day. Imagine the gallery inaugural, the people, the wine, the buzz."

"That's a long way down the road," she said.

"Your boyfriend going to visit when this thing gets built? I'd like to meet him."

"Maybe not right away."

"How long have you two been living apart?"

"A while," she said.

"I imagine that's difficult. How did the two of you meet?"

"It doesn't' make for an interesting story."

"Sure, sorry. It isn't really my business."

"Don't worry."

"I guess I ask, because I just can't help but notice that you and Pierce are very close. I mean, clearly you get on very well."

Finally, she turned to look at me and smirked. Had her sunglasses not been so large, I'm convinced I would have seen her eyebrow raise, questioning my motives.

"I've known Pierce for some years, he's a good friend."

"Okay, again, not my business. That's really all I had to say. I just respect Pierce a lot and, well, he always looks out for me. So, I want to do the same for him. I've never met your boyfriend, so I didn't have any sense about how close the two of you were."

"But you thought you'd stick your nose where it needn't be."

"Yes, I did. But I didn't stick it far, and it wasn't there for very long."

"Nick, there's plenty you don't know about me. Plenty we don't know about each other. You learn a lot by working with someone, but there's even more that you miss."

"Do you trust me a little more than when we first met."

"Do you feel like I don't trust you?"

"Sometimes."

"Well, Nick, I guess I trust you just enough. How's that?"

I decided that it was at least a step in the right direction.

We parked, pulling out all of our design boards, along with several foldable easels that I had grabbed from my office.

"Ready to do this?"

"Nervous, but ready," I said.

"No nerves, it'll be just like we're musicians giving a performance. We've done all of our prep ahead of time, now we just go out there and play."

"A duet, then."

14

"Set you boards down, I'll be ready shortly," Harlan said, pointing at our stack of design drawings.

Janet took off her sunglasses. "Good to see you Harlan. Do you need to see our design, or should we just assume it's good to go?"

He smiled. "No, Janet, I'll need to take a look."

Harlan sat by two tables that had been lined up end to end. He had stacks of papers organized into rows and was reading through a large document in a binder. His office space was informal, but neat. He had set up shop in a large open space of what would be the gallery. The tables were pushed close to the windows, allowing the evening sunlight to spill over a portion of top surface, the other half protected by a newly installed blind. Several tall shelves defined the room, the space being overly spacious for conferences.

Resting by the edge of the table near his open briefcase was a chipped ceramic dish, cigarette still smoldering on top. The smoke rose up, weaving and folding over itself in thin sheets. Harlan picked it up and took a deep drag, then set the cigarette back down before allowing himself to exhale. His hair had grayed, but his movements and speech were energetic, making him seem more youthful than his years should have allowed.

I sat down, waiting for him to finish reading, uncertain if he was actually in the middle of something, or if he just was intent on making us wait. Janet remained standing, though she appeared relaxed. I didn't really believe she was relaxed, but assumed she had deliberately undergone a transformation in order to deliver the presentation with confidence. At this point, I simply wanted the presentation to be finished, good result or bad, I just wanted to be done with it.

After several minutes had passed, Harlan stood up and walked over to our stack of design boards. Wordlessly, he flipped through them, reviewing the plans and renderings.

Looking toward Janet, he said, "You draw these?"

J Edward Duncan

"Those? Oh, just some scribbles. Want to talk them over?"

He smiled. "Sure, I've got some time, why don't you set up and let's talk."

We organized our boards on the easels, and Janet laid a gathering of finishes and materials on the table in front. She had assembled samples of blonde woods and dark stones, with a simple but deep palette of colors.

"Excellent effort," Harlan said. "I like it already." He walked back and forth eyeing each of the boards, while tilting his head to view the drawings from the bottom of his bifocal lens.

"You've hardly looked at them yet, let us tell you about the idea before you heap on the praise," Janet said playfully.

"I'm just trying to make you feel good before I pile on the criticism."

"Exactly, I saw right through you. Now, let's start by talking about why people gather to look at art.

Janet began describing our approach to the design, and the importance of retaining the urban feel within the gallery itself. She had memorized a brief outline, and was hitting each point while walking from board to board. She addressed the palette of materials, tying each in with our renderings. She then nodded toward me, and I explained how we brought light into the atrium, and how both daylight and streetlights would fill the gathering space, creating an urban plaza within the building itself. Our final boards were awash with color, demonstrating the way light would reflect and bounce around the central space, washing down the stairs and playing off of the smooth shined stone surfaces.

"Thank you both, lots to think about there. Lots to think about," he said, nodding with his arms folded.

"You were looking for a place for people, a place that would draw them into the gallery," Janet said.

"Sure, I want that. The more people, the better, I want this place to be filled with people. I want art to be an excuse for people to get together, and once they're here, I want them to stay. I want a club atmosphere, I want there to be a place for people to park, soak up drinks, do whatever they do." He waved his hands, framing

232

a picture in the air. "Something with some sex appeal, to pack people in. Give them a reason to show up, then plenty of tables, keep them in the seats. The Pear is a great excuse for people to mosey around the artwork, then run upstairs for shots and smokes."

"Does this work?" Janet asked, gesturing towards our boards.

"Course it works. We'll make some changes, simplify things a little. Isn't that what you designers say *keep it simple*?"

"It's supposed to be *simplify, simplify*," I corrected.

"Then why'd you say it twice? Seems to complicate it. Regardless, we'll keep the nucleus of your idea, just get rid of some of the unneeded appendages."

My head was spinning, trying to track his mixed metaphors. Harlan remained standing, and motioned for Janet to sit down next to me. He paced side to side, pointing to various boards, identifying pieces to keep and pieces to delete.

"This atrium works, I like that. That part we keep. I'm not sold on the skylight above the atrium, though. Seems to clutter things while driving up expense."

"You wanted a place for people to gather, a reason to draw them in from the street," Janet said.

"True, I certainly like that in concept. However, I'm not sold on the notion of *borrowed light*. The idea of people gathering in the center, though, is exactly what I'm looking for."

"But, the borrowed light is the whole reason for people to gather in the center. Without that, there's nothing to hold the rest of the design together," I said standing up from my chair.

Janet turned toward me calmly, fixing her eyes directly at me. She didn't turn or blink until I sat back down.

"No, I think the idea is sound, the light is intriguing, but I bet we can accomplish the scheme in another way," he said.

I looked to Janet for a sign, some clue about how far we could press our argument. She continued to regard Harlan.

"What parts of the scheme do you want to keep?" Janet asked.

"Oh, we'll keep most of your ideas. We'll keep the gathering space, it just doesn't have to be dead center in the building. Perhaps we'll shift it to the front, we can gain some space by pushing the stairs back." He nodded. "Yes, this will do nicely."

"Why move the stairs back? I think it's important to keep the vertical circulation linked to the main space," Janet said.

"I agree, she's right. If the main space is too close to the entrance, it compromises the experience of approaching the atrium," I said.

"No, no – there's sort of a nice Feng Shui about putting all the people close to the entrance. From the exterior, the gallery will always seem crowded, always lots of buzz," he said.

"Near the exterior?" I asked.

"Yes, don't you designers always say *form follows feng shui ?*" he asked.

"Well, that's a little bit of a paraphrase," I said.

"Harlan, you can bring people into the gallery by creating some mystery, and drawing them in. We hoped to create an entry sequence that builds up to the main atrium space, awash in light. The space is most powerful when we build expectation. Are you sure it's best to throw a big lounge right at the entrance?" Janet asked.

"Course, yes I'm sure. That's how I've imagined it from the start. That's what we'll do." He picked up his cigarette and drew deep, opening his mouth to let the smoke creep out in a thick tentacle. He held up his cigarette, tapped it, letting the ash drop down to the worn carpet where he quickly ground it in. "The important thing, Janet, is that I like your scheme and I want you to proceed to construction documents. We'll spend a little more time talking about changes, but I want you both to work up the drawings."

"There are parts of the design that will need to be worked out, but we have a place to start," Janet said. "Perhaps we could find a way to incorporate light even if it differs from the exact way it's depicted here."

"I agree, let's discuss some changes. Let me mark up your design boards," he said, pointing toward our easels. "When we're done here, how long do you think it will take for you to turn things into construction documents?"

I couldn't help but wonder if we could salvage any portion of our design idea, or if it was now little more than scrap. It was a victory of sorts that we were on board to complete documents, although it was hardly our idea anymore. We had been reduced to little more than drafters. The miniscule fee we were receiving for our efforts was hardly enough to justify the late nights and sleep depravation; without some sort of design satisfaction, the effort was likely to become all burden, no thrill.

Architecture is too often a type of uninformed masochism. Designers strain and struggle to realize their ideas, disregarding any business sense, or even common sense. Always, the architect holds onto the design process as their prize, rationalizing that the chance to create is compensation enough for any sort of work and turmoil. Yet, in the end, even the design and art is stripped from the process, leaving the architect with a bruised and bitter ego.

Janet and I remained with Harlan for another two hours, drawing over our boards with markers and taping tracing paper over the top, adding more sketches and diagrams. Harlan herded us toward his original vision, cherry-picking our design for scraps he found appealing, while mixing and mashing them with his own notions. When finished, we had a Frankenstein of half-resolved ideas and sewn on concepts. I let Janet do most of the talking, uncertain how my protests might be construed.

"What's the next step?" I asked Janet as we loaded the presentation back into her car.

"Documents."

"What's our direction? I don't recognize the design anymore."

"We're still on board, the project is ours. That's a victory."

"Of sorts."

"Don't be too upset."

"Aren't you?"

"No, not upset."

"Disappointed?"

"Sure, I liked our idea."

"There's none of it left. Seems like a lot of work for nothing."

"We did keep the job."

"Why didn't he just tell us from the start what he wanted? Why didn't he just draw up some plans and tell us the design was locked?"

"Maybe he did."

"Did he?"

"Sure, he always does."

"Janet, we've wasted a lot of time designing something you knew was dead from the start."

"That wasn't a waste."

"The atrium is gone, there's no light being brought into the building, the staircase is tucked in the back – this isn't our design."

"Nick, the project isn't finished. I know you're disappointed."

"Isn't it finished? Seemed pretty clear what he wanted, he drew it for us."

"Use some imagination."

"Let's get a drink instead."

Janet, clearly exasperated, got into the car and started up the engine. She looked at me, waiting for me to follow suit and get it. With little reason to care, I simply got in and slouched in the seat. Harlan hadn't really cared about the design we submitted, he had hired cheap labor to draft up the project he had wanted from the start. I couldn't help but wonder if things might have been different if Pierce had still been part of our team. He was used to being uncompromising; perhaps he would have put up more of a fight. I couldn't help but imagine him explaining to Harlan why the gallery needed to be built the way we had drawn it. I had simply assumed that Janet had the same conviction and resolve as Pierce. Perhaps, though, I was no better. I had been at the same meeting, and had kept silent when I thought it was my turn to do so. I had willingly let the design be carved up, believing it better to keep the job even if it meant sacrificing our idea.

"Nick, if we did this all over, I'd still do things the same. No changes, we did it right."

"No changes?"

"None."

"He ordered a hamburger and we brought him sushi."

"Regardless of what he ordered, he didn't know what he wanted. He ordered a hamburger because that's what he's always eaten; that's all he knows."

"Maybe we should have brought him what he ordered."

"Why? He still doesn't know what he wants."

"Did he know we would bring him that design, or some design other than what he expected?"

"Yes, or he wouldn't have hired me."

"You or us?"

"Nick, you did a great job, but he knows me, he knows what I'm going to bring. He asked for a project that was familiar, that he could predict. He did that because he knows what he likes. But it's our job to show him something different, our job to show him that there's more possible than what he could see."

"It's too bad we couldn't do that."

"I think we did."

"I'd believe that if there was some piece of our idea that was kept."

"Nick, the road is long, this project isn't done. We simply need to reintroduce our ideas as we develop documents."

"And when he sees these new ideas being introduced?"

"We convince him that they were his ideas all along."

"That's how it's gone on your previous jobs with him?"

"Sometimes."

"Sometimes?"

"Some of the time, I've been able to push back and get ideas back in the project. Other times I've pushed, but there's been no give."

We sat in silence the rest of the drive back. Janet dropped me off at my car, and I loaded my half of the boards to bring home. The late summer evening had turned dusky, most of the daylight spent.

"So, what's the next step?" I asked.

"Documents."

"And our direction?"

"We provide Harlan with the design he needs. People don't always know what they need."

"But how much of the design should be what he wants, and how much should be what we he needs?"

"We'll push a little."

"How much is a little?"

"Go back to your desk, look at your drawings."

"And?"

"And, decide how much you think we should push."

15

I stared into my closet. My choice for shirts was identical to the choice I had last week and the week before that. Yet, I still pondered, as though if I looked hard enough, new shirts would appear.

I had offered to pick up Angeline and take her out to dinner. I still wanted to ask the obvious question; it would have been so much easier if she was sixteen, and I had to meet her father before picking her up. Then, at least he could ask the obligatory questions and there would be no pretenses about my motives. As it stood, though, our evening out had no label. Angeline seldom offered discernable clues to be read and understood. I recall a girl I knew once telling me that if a man has to wonder if he's in a relationship, then he isn't. Did the same hold true for women? I suspected that it did not. Males, being acutely poor communicators, may never understand the signals they're sending, and those they are not. Women, however, have a whole language, cultivated and exact, to make their intentions understood.

In truth, though, there is a flaw in my rationale. No matter how well conceived a language, the truth is that not everyone who speaks it intends to be understood. If ever the point were to communicate clearly, gender-speak could be translated with ease. But ambiguity has value, and there is flexibility in confusion. When one is perfectly clear it is so difficult to back-peddle, so difficult to pick plan 'B', and so difficult to make proper apologies - Confusion keeps one's options open.

I was dressed and showered early, not really knowing what to do with myself for most of the day. I sat in front of my television, flipping through channels, with the volume turned down to zero. I simply watched faces flicker across the screen. Colors and motion faded and spun as channel succeeded channel. Without sound or continuity the images could tell no narrative, instead they only provided snapshots of emotion or sex or conflict. Countless nearly nude models paraded across the screen regardless of what channel I found. Then, I took a brief detour of men in suits and women who looked like men in suits as I passed through the news channels. Then back to models selling, models reliving their reality television experience, and more models. Occasionally the screen contained only superimposed graphics and letters floating across the screen. Without sound it was all collage, without any meaning that I could grab onto.

Twenty minutes before I needed to leave, I walked downstairs to the street. In front of my grocery was a florist stand. It was the sort that unrolls in the morning, spreading tubs of flowers out like tentacles, enfronting the storefront windows of the grocery. A path of bright colors defined the way to the *specials on eggs and low-low prices every day!* As though preparing the way for a parade of shopping carts and hand waving floral princesses, the flowers created a uniquely overdone reception for those with coupons in hand waiting for milk, cheese, and butter.

Then, after 5pm the entire arcade of rose petals and opening buds would get rolled up and stuffed back into the large kiosk adjacent to the building's entrance. Then, with the flowers gone, the grocery once again would become merely a place to push a shopping cart.

I walked the gauntlet and stopped in front of the Gerber Daisies. Dipping my head, I sniffed for fragrance, but could only detect the sweetness of the stems. I could buy five for twelve dollars. I decided against the purchase and continued to the ATM. The flowers would just be more baggage to carry.

My car was parked several blocks from the grocery on a side street. Living in Northwest Portland, one quickly learns where and when to find parking. Close proximity to one's apartment is the Holy Grail, but a more realistic goal is simply to find legal parking.

I didn't have far to drive to find Angeline's home. She lived in a condominium in the rehabilitated portion of the Pearl District. Her building was brand new, built only two years prior, but was set amid blocks of old warehouse construction that was being renovated. Her street was not one of the desolate industrial Pearl streets, rather it had constant activity; groups of people herded from street to the coffee shops and art galleries that adorned the ground level. Her street saw a surprising amount of car traffic, owing primarily to the abundant retail on the ground level. The street was also the main thoroughfare that connected the Pearl District to Northwest Portland, with convenient access to the freeway in between. Typically, the street received countless tourists on First Thursday Art walks. Many come for the event; some even come to see the art. But they all stayed for high priced cocktails and coffee. I shuddered at the thought of Ron bearing witness to such a scene, as it attracted a mix of the ultra-hip, nouveau-cool as well as aging Baby Boomers beset with denial about their now defunct role of trend-setter.

I found an open metered spot and left my car. This would be the first time I would see the inside of Angeline's condo, but I was already comparing our homes and our lives. I had left my shabby cramped apartment and traveled perhaps fifteen blocks to Angeline's brand new building where she owned her own home. After being buzzed in I took the elevator up three flights, and knocked on her door.

The sound of her shoes clicking on the floor preceded her voice, announcing she was coming to the door. After a brief wait, the door opened. Angeline smiled, beckoning me to come inside. She wore a black dress and high-heeled shoes that exposed her toes. The nails had been painted, but were chipped. I followed her into the condo, her perfume fading slightly as we left the entry, and continued into her main room.

"You've been here, right?" she asked.

"No, never. Remember, I asked for directions."

"Right. Well, this is my place. Have a seat."

Stylish furniture sat beneath assorted cereal bowls and glasses. Her main room was adorned with modern furniture, begging for an uncluttered home. The clutter was not precisely dirty; in fact the glasses looked washed and ready for use, simply not put away. Angeline was clearly not bothered by the state of her home. She smiled and offered to make me a drink, while I made myself at home. The couch was uncluttered, perhaps new, but the coffee table in front of it was supporting a precarious load of magazines and dinnerware.

She returned with two drinks, ice rattling and glass sweating. I moved several magazines to find a place to set the glass.

"Don't bother," she said, waving her hand.

She said it as if she were doing me a favor; however I now had to search to find a place for my glass. Coming up empty, I simply held onto it, figuring I would see her set down her glass and could then follow suit. She sat down, smoothing her dress, and then crossing her legs.

"How do you like living in the city?" I asked.

"Wonderful, suits me. Perhaps when I'm older I'll want a house with a yard and trees, but not now. I like being young."

"You'll have to tell me what it's like; someday I hope to be young."

"You live in the city too, how do you like your place?" She asked.

"It's fine, sometimes gets a bit small. But I like the neighborhood. I think I'm really paying for the neighborhood, not the apartment."

"Realtors say, *location, location, location* - architects would amend that to, *context, context, context.*"

I smiled and nodded my head. Though she had chosen a different direction for her career, she had retained some of her old identity. I sipped from my glass and finally decided to set it on the floor; Angeline didn't flinch.

"I get the sense that your home is more of a place to crash in between events, you're not much of a homebody," I said.

"I spend a lot of time in my office. As you could tell, sometimes even sleep there. That's why I finally got smart and left a change of clothes and breakfast. But I like my home. It's nice to have a place that's just for me."

"I saw the breakfast you kept in your office, looked like it was all bottled. I hope you add plenty of olives."

"Stop, I'm not that bad. If you want to give me a hard time, forget the alcohol; it's the coffee I need to avoid."

"What would life be without our substances of choice?" I lifted my glass and took another sip.

"Drink up, this is a special occasion, I don't play host to many people." She swirled her glass, taking a small drink of her lemon drop.

In my peripheral vision, I could have sworn I saw some of the clutter move. A stack of magazines swayed against the side of the couch, rocking slightly but remaining upright. Papers rustled underneath me, sounding as if someone where sorting their mail under my seat. I leaned down, seeing a tiny swipe at the back of my leg.

Angeline smiled, "Have you met Horatio? He's a bit shy."

I reached down, the cat remaining still while I picked him up. Upon bringing the cat onto my lap he squirmed, slipping out of my grasp.

"He is shy, seemed friendly, then wasn't so sure. Maybe he saw a mouse," I said.

"He won't be back. He's always been shy before, but he's been losing his sight."

"Blind? A cat? That doesn't seem right. How does he mouse?"

"Mouse? He's a city cat, not much of a hunter. He can still find a bowl of Friskies, though."

"Is he completely blind? It doesn't seem that a cat can get by without sight," I said.

"He's an old cat. It's only a matter of time."

"How long have you had him?"

"Got him when I lived with my grandmother. Horatio was good company."

Angeline leaned to the side in her chair, legs crossed, shoe slipped off her foot and balancing on her toe. I described the recent gallery presentation, focusing mostly on keeping the job, and less on the uncertainty of the design. She was upbeat, encouraging me as I got deeper and deeper into my story. I hadn't really planned to draw it out as far as I did, but she seemed interested. As she questioned me about the design, I recounted our initial idea, rather than explaining that the idea was on life support. After finishing my story, I decided to steer the conversation clear of the gallery, not wanting to dive too deep into my uncertainty about where the design would go next.

I pointed to her window, admiring the view. She kicked off her other shoe, and motioned for me to join her for a look out. She pulled the drape further back, tying it at the jamb.

"Look," she said, pointing. "My favorite part of the condo is the view. I can see to the river and across. Look at how many bridges you can see. The Steel Bridge, the Broadway - if you lean you can see the Fremont."

"Must be great view when the sun goes down."

"So many lights, I love watching the city." She put her hand on my shoulder, and continued to point. I followed her gesture, then watched her.

"You look beautiful," I said.

"I always liked the way you made me feel, Nick."

"Still? After years?"

"I haven't forgotten."

"There's a lot you never told me, why you broke things off."

"No, let's not." She brushed my hair and smiled. "You look good, Nicholas."

As I leaned toward her, she stood up on her toes, turning her head. I pressed my lips to her mouth, putting my arms around her to draw her closer. As we kissed, she let her body lean against mine, her weight pressed into my chest.

I didn't know if I was in love with Angeline or in love with the memory. When I met her years ago, I hadn't yet been in love, I was young enough that I interpreted any feeling of longing as love. But when I held her, I had the same feelings; memories of the past were indistinguishable from the moment.

She lingered, pressing her lips to my mouth, her perfume strong now with her closeness. I felt her chest rise, then relax.

I enjoyed the kiss - her warmth, the flavor of the sweet lemony drink that was still on her lips. But before the kiss was finished, I thought about it, analyzed it. This aspect of my nature, my need to understand rather than to simply enjoy, I desperately wanted to lose and bury. For me, the kiss had to mean something, every kiss needed to mean something. While I still held Angeline, I was already wondering what she was thinking, wondering what the kiss meant to her. I realized that Angeline didn't need to attach meaning to the kiss. She simply enjoyed the excitement, the passion of kissing. Perhaps she loved me, perhaps she didn't; it wouldn't have mattered. She would have wanted to kiss me either way. I envied that. I envied her ability to enjoy the moment without needing to wonder what might come next.

But for me, the moment was all about what came next. I felt passion when I kissed Angeline, but didn't kiss her to enjoy the sensation. I kissed her because I wanted her to be in love with me. I felt passion, but it was a sensible passion. We stood together in front of her window, she enjoying the moment, me wondering what it meant.

Angeline gave me a quick tour of her place before we left for dinner, a trendy restaurant on 21st that had opened a few months prior. While waiting for our table, Angeline fussed with her dress. She seemed unable to keep her hands still, finding creases to smooth out, folds to pull tight. Her lips were pulled back in a wide, close-lipped smile; she looked at me, then back at her dress. After tugging at a strap, she laughed. "It's so much easier for men. You just step into a pair of slacks and go. Everything already fits, there's no adjusting."

"Wearing a tie is no picnic, there's plenty of adjusting there."

"Sure, but you're not wearing a tie, are you? I've got straps and wires to deal with. Look at my shoes." She looked down at her feet, pointing to the red straps that crisscrossed over her feet. She had tall heels, but appeared to be practiced at wearing them.

"Your shoes are pretty."

"Not comfortable. Women's clothes are all about discomfort."

"That's what I'm told, never tried 'em on, though," I said

"If the clothes aren't constricting, they're chafing, or straining. Every man should dress in women's clothing just once, to know what women go through for men."

"By choice, you always have the choice."

"Incorrect. The consequences are too severe. A bra isn't comfortable, but the alternative cannot be endured."

"The alternative? Is that no bra or small tits?"

Angeline raised her eyebrows in shock, and then burst out in laughter. Had we not already been on good terms, I likely wouldn't have made a tit joke on the first date.

"Nicky, that's crude. You're not supposed to say that. You don't know who you'll offend."

"The only one to be offended would be a poorly endowed woman; that describes neither of us, so I've no one to apologize to."

"Just keep you voice down, there are people here that I know. Besides, uncomfortable clothing is nothing to laugh about. Women torture themselves to look appealing to men, and then we have to put up with jokes about breasts."

"It's a two way street; men put up with quite a bit too," I said.

"Like what?"

"We constantly have to compete for a woman's attention. A man invests time with some good lines, spends time listening; he drops a bunch of cash to impress. Then just when a guy thinks he's made some progress, *bam*, some other guy shows up in a nicer car and steals her away."

"Oh, listen to you. You're lucky I don't take you seriously. I'd hate to meet the type of women you've dated."

"Don't forget, you're one of them."

"Touché, but how many years ago was that?"

"Why, is there a statute of limitations?"

"No," she said, "but we were both different people then."

"Do I seem different?"

"Older, but no wiser; actually, no *you* haven't changed much. You're still the same Nicholas I remember from Italy," she said.

"So it's you that's a different person?"

"More than you know."

I waited for her to continue, but she simply raised her eyebrows. It was difficult to know when she said something for effect, and when she wanted me to draw her out. I had the idea that her statement was thrown out as bait, and I was expected to obligingly step up and jump at it.

"Are you going to elaborate?" I asked.

"Let's get a drink."

"Wait, I want to know how you're a different person."

"You can see; I dress differently, I'm more experienced, not as quaint. I've shed some of the small-town naiveté."

"You were never quaint, though you may have thought you were. There was never anything unappealing about your small town sensibilities."

I knew that her childhood had been riddled with instability. When she was very young it had been tumultuous for her, and also for those around her. She had loved her father; this was sentiment she had reiterated to me on more than one occasion. However, from what I could gather, he had done little to earn her affection.

"What you've described is mostly on the surface, you said you'd changed in ways I could only guess at."

"I never said that," she exclaimed.

"Alright, however you want it. Let's get a drink; we can wait in the bar until our table is ready."

I wished I had made reservations; waiting for the table seemed to be a move right out of the playbook for Junior High School dating. At least I had remembered to bring cash. There were rules, and I needed to pay attention to what I ordered, how I ordered it, how the check was paid, and who paid it. Splitting a tab is one of the surest known forms of birth control on the market.

We pushed up to the bar and ordered drinks. Angeline looked around the bar, occasionally waving to people she knew. Apparently this wasn't her first time.

"Hi, Peter. How are you?" She said, waving her fingers. A young man with overly tan skin walked forward and embraced Angeline. Wrapping both arms around her, he kissed her cheek and then stepped back. She blushed, just slightly.

"Angeline, you look great, how've you been?"

"Well. I've been well. Peter, this is my friend, Nicholas Black. Nicholas, Peter."

"Peter, good to meet you," I said.

"A pleasure," he replied. Peter had the slightest hint of dark liner around his lower lashes. Combined with his brown skin, it accentuated the whites of his eyes, making him always appear slightly surprised. He had long sideburns that grew down to a thin, immaculately trimmed beard. From a distance it might have looked like it was drawn on his face. We both looked at each other. He was wearing as much black as I was; perhaps even more, his shirtsleeves being longer.

Angeline was only willing to allow just so much silence. "Peter and I used to go running together on the trail by Leif Erikson Avenue. Do you still run, Peter?"

"I've stopped, but am looking for an excuse to get back into it. We should start up again."

"I've kept up with it," she said.

"Good, then you can help motivate me."

"Sorry, you've got to motivate yourself."

"So how do you two know each other?" Peter asked.

"Went to school together, studied abroad," I said.

"You studied abroad?" he looked at Angeline. "When did you move to London?"

"Right after. After finishing classes in Italy, I continued traveling and ended up in London. Hell of a good time, but expensive. It was all I could do to afford a tiny little flat."

"They call them 'flats' in England." Peter confided, looking directly at me. Apparently, he assumed that there was no way word might have gotten back to me that words were used differently across the Atlantic. Perhaps he would whisper that they road up to their flats in lifts and it was *brilliant.*

"Exciting place, though. Will you ever go back?" he asked.

"Someday, yeah. Maybe not to live, but to visit. Really I want to go back long enough to pick up a decent accent." She laughed.

"You must have been there for a few years. Why'd you decide to come back?" I asked.

"It was time, you know. A place can only stay friendly for so long, and then it's time."

"Well, I haven't seen you in a while, thought you had dropped off the map." Peter said.

"Hasn't been that long."

"Have you been busy?"

"Always, that never changes."

"Well if you get too busy and need something to keep you going, just give me a call."

"No, no thanks. I'm trying to give up on that kind of motivation."

"Really? You know I can always get some more. Plenty available."

"I'm sorry," I said. "I'm not quite following."

"Nothing, it isn't anything," Angeline said.

As if on cue, a waitress walked up to us. "Nicholas, you're table is ready."

"Thanks."

"Let's grab our table," she said.

"Sure, I'm just on the outside of the conversation, seems you two have a lot of history."

"Sorry, didn't want to create a fuss," he said. "Why don't the both of you enjoy your dinner. I've got a group to meet." He excused himself while Angeline and I followed the waitress to our table.

"Nick, don't mind him, he's a goof. Means well, but you can't take him seriously."

"I didn't."

"Good thing."

"I keep learning new things about you. You haven't told me much about London. Sounds like it was a kick."

"You should go, you'd love it. There's a ton to see, it's a city that never gets old."

"I also didn't know you were a runner."

"I'm not much of one. Just enough to keep in shape."

"You like the trail?"

"Lots of shade, keeps me out of the sun."

"Hasn't kept Peter out of the sun."

"He does tan a bit, doesn't he?"

"I've seen saddles that weren't that tan."

"Oh, stop," she laughed.

"Anyway, I get up to the trail sometimes. Maybe I'll run into you."

"How often?"

"Pretty regularly, once every three or four months – just like clockwork. Rain or shine, I'm out there at least once a season."

"Get into a good habit now," she said. "It's so much harder to keep a good habit going than to break a bad one."

We sat at a small table, tucked in a corner next to a glass wall sconce. In it was a large candle with wax building up around the glass. The waitress gave us a quick run down of items not on the menu and told us she would return with our drink orders. Angeline ordered something with color and fruit in a large bowl shaped glass. I got a simple bourbon.

"Does it seem like drinks have gotten too cute?" I asked. "I mean, I half expect to see a fish swimming around in your drink."

"I told them to hold the fish," Angeline said after pulling her lips from her straw. "It's fun. I like getting drinks I've never even heard of before."

"Nothing beats the classics. I'm a fan of simplicity."

"Like a glass of vino?"

"Yes. A good Italian bottle of wine. You don't even really need food to go with, just leave the bottle," I said.

"Just like old times, you and I," she said.

I smiled. There were questions I wanted to ask Angeline. I realized how much there was about her that had changed, how much I didn't know. Before running into her at the Pear, we had last seen each other at studio in Rome. We hadn't ever really said a proper goodbye; I had believed that she would meet me at the airport. Angeline, though, had known that we wouldn't see each other again, yet she had said nothing, had simply let the moment pass. She had likely already purchased her tickets for the train, to take her on the rest of her travels, where she would finally land in London.

While she hadn't told me directly why she had left, I believe that I knew. In fact, I should have predicted it before it happened. Funny how easy it is to ignore what one doesn't want to accept.

Very recently, Pierce had warned me to be smart with my emotions and not to trust too much. The advice seemed sensible, yet how can a person treat emotions like dollars and spend them wisely? There was nothing sensible about taking an emotional risk, but life demanded it. Angeline was beautiful, and there had been a time when we had something together. Though she was now a different person, she would always have her history of being a girl from a small town, somewhat shy, but curious. While anybody can change who they are, nobody can ever change who they were. And maybe, it wasn't that she had changed so much, rather that I had changed so little.

The lights in the restaurant had been dimmed twice since we sat down. A candle illuminated each table, making every one a tiny stage where some drama was played out over plates of ravioli di asparagi and trota grigliate, with only the faces visible. Angeline pulled a small stainless steel case from her purse, opened it and offered me a cigarette. I declined, but didn't object as she smoked, both of us waiting for our food.

"Seems you know a few people here," I said.

"We're young, might as well get out and enjoy life."

"Do anything exciting last night?"

"I got out, but stayed away from the crowds."

"Where'd you go? Any place you'd recommend?" I asked.

"Oh, not really a restaurant, seemed a good night to be mellow."

"Where do you go to get out and be mellow? Any place I might know?"

"Nick, I hardly know all the places you've been." She tapped on her cigarette and looked away. She had been intense and energetic, but this was the first example of nervous energy I had detected.

"So, you don't want to tell me, the secret makes me all the more curious. No worries, though, I don't want to pry. I don't suppose it's my business either way."

She placed her cigarette on the edge of the ash tray and picked up a book of matches. She lit one and watched it burn down to her fingers, then dropped it suddenly and laughed abruptly, watching it fall to the table.

"Careful," I said.

"Nick, I feel silly, but I felt nervous about telling you where I was. It shouldn't be a big deal, but I felt nervous."

"Nervous? Why, this sounds like true confessions. Where were you?"

"I was with your friend, Andrew. It's no big deal, I know that, but I felt funny telling you."

"Did you bump into him again at the Pear?"

"No, we didn't bump into each other; he invited me to see his studio. He's really quite an artist, very talented."

"Yes, he is," I said.

"Look, it doesn't matter, here comes our food."

The waitress jockeyed through a small group of people mingling in the aisle, then set my meal in front of Angeline and hers in front of me. I raised no protest, deciding it easier to switch after she left than explain; sometimes it's easier to say nothing.

"Can I get anything else for you, perhaps a refill on your drink?" She directed the comment at me, as I had just drained my glass.

"The same."

"Very good, and for you?" she asked Angeline.

"Yes, the same."

The waitress smiled, nodded, and vanished.

"He invited you to his studio? You were just there to look, you didn't pose?"

"I'm sorry?"

"He's not going to paint you, right? It's just that he paints a lot of girls – his muses, as he calls them. I'm just curious, being a friend and all."

"He invited me to show off some of his paintings; we went out to grab a bite beforehand, and I wanted to see his paintings."

"So, this was a planned thing, was it like a date?"

"See, this is why I felt nervous."

"No, no – why would you feel nervous?"

"I don't have to say it?"

"It depends on what you have to say."

"Alright, yes – It was like a date. Big deal."

"That's what I say, big deal."

We sat, wordlessly, watching the other patrons. Abruptly, the waitress reappeared with fresh drinks, bringing them to the table like supplies being dropped from an airplane. Angeline grabbed her drink and took a sip after discarding the straw.

"But I'm still curious," I said.

"I told you, I was at his studio."

"No, I'm curious about why you wouldn't want to tell me."

"Nick, it's no big deal."

"Fine, but what's this?"

"This? What 'this'?"

"This," I said, opening up my palms and motioning around the table. She stared at me. "Better if we drink," I said.

"Look, let's not be cross, we're having a good time. I'm not serious about anybody right now, we can go out."

"True, I'm glad we got together – it's good to be with you."

"We always had such wonderful times together; hell of a lot of fun, didn't we?" she said.

"Fun, yes," I said. I watched her while I drank.

"Honestly, when you're in the middle of a really good time, you don't even think about it, just enjoy it. Then you look back and realize."

"Realize?"

"We were young, so much we didn't know."

I continued to drink.

"You were sweet to me, Nick, I'll never forget that. Were you in love?"

"That's a hell of a question."

"I was. I really was. I was young, but not too young."

"I thought it might last. Some things do you know."

"I didn't leave because I stopped caring about you, that wasn't it. Don't look at me like that, you weren't so naïve."

"You should have told me you were going to leave, that's all. I thought you were going to be at the airport; I waited."

"I'm sorry, I really am. Here, we both need a smoke."

"It's that you just left without saying anything."

"Here." She brought out two cigarettes and stuck them both just above the candle flame. We smoked.

"You could have told me you wouldn't be there."

"Nick, you pretend that you were the only one that got hurt. It's been years now, so it doesn't matter any more, but you're not a martyr."

"No, but I would have told you."

"Would you?"

"Why not?"

"You may not want to say it, but I was in love. You won't say it now and you wouldn't say it then. We're older now, it doesn't matter, there's no score," she said.

"You know how I felt about you."

"Not then. I know it now."

"You must have known then. We were together all the time."

"You should have said more. Look, maybe we should get drunk."

Angeline lifted her hand, flagging down the waitress. We both ordered more of the same. Angeline's elbows were planted on the table, as though she was holding herself up. Her fingers still wrapped around her empty glass as she eyed her cigarette, still burning in the ashtray. It was as though she was making a choice, the drink or the smoke. I grabbed the cigarette and brought it to her lips. The corners of her mouth raised in gratitude.

"How do you feel now?" I asked.

"I feel relaxed, the cocktails have kicked in, and a smoke helps me mellow."

"No, how do you feel about me?"

"Nicky, let's not spoil a perfectly good evening with chatter. I'm happy to be here with you now." Raising her eyebrows, she said, "I've got more cigarettes."

I let the moment be, and smoked.

16

The evening grew late, and I took Angeline home. I had probably had too much to get behind the wheel, but didn't crash and didn't get caught. Sometimes, you just get lucky. Upon returning to my apartment, sleep was elusive. Not bothering to turn on my lights, I found the remote control, guided only by the bright moonlight. I flipped on the television and hit mute, illuminating my walls with a pale blue flicker. There was nothing I wanted to watch, I just wanted noise. Nothing coherent, just chatter.

I sat at my light table considering the design Janet and I had presented to Harlan. Our presentation boards had been stacked neatly on top of my table. I grabbed the first two and leaned them up against the wall. The design as conceived was dead; Harlan had been unwilling to even consider using the atrium to borrow outside light. The entire concept, the metaphor for allowing the urban fabric into the building, was diluted and rendered meaningless. It almost made it worse that he had offered to retain some trivial vestige of the idea. Better to simply let the idea die and maintain some simple dignity.

I pulled out a roll of trace paper and taped it on top of my light table. With pen in hand, I continued to consider the blank sheet. Janet and I had scored a hollow victory when Harlan had agreed to let us carry our idea through to construction documents. It seemed foolish - with no idea to carry I tried to begin something simple that might still provide a creative solution.

There is excitement in chasing down an idea; an unresolved design begs the designer to continue and realize it, make it something others can see. But I felt no excitement, I only felt tired.

I walked out to my balcony and watered my plants. Too tired to go to bed, I fell asleep outside in a chair, surrounded by my reluctant garden.

Chapter V

In Search of Nolli

[Summer 1997]

1

One map of Rome depicts only the streets and open spaces; the built
environment fades into background. The homes, the shops, the places
of business are all shown indifferently as gray shapes in a centuries old
puzzle. Only the most significant buildings are given any identity, but even these
are portrayed with little substance. It is the streets that become celebrity; the
winding interlace of thin strands that hold the city together. The map appears as
one asymmetrical web, defined by the shape of the river, the surrounding landscape,
and the gradual development of the evolving city. The buildings themselves
become unimportant. It is the city itself that takes center stage and retains an
identity.

Giambattista Nolli etched this map, pianta di Roma, in the eighteenth century,
carefully scaling every bend and curve of the streets. The mass of separate but
linked paths mingle together in Rome's center, then disperse outward into the
landscape of what had been agricultural land. The map is a snapshot, but it captures
something living. The substance of the city, preserved as etchings on a series of
plates, chronicle the development of Rome. The streets tell the story of ancient
Rome, forming around the River Tiber a thousand years before the birth of Christ.
From a small village, the city grew to become the center for civilization, dominating

the known world for centuries. These streets stretch out to show the development of the Roman Empire,

stretching outward to link not just Rome, but Italy, the Mediterranean, and beyond Europe. They have carried Popes and Caesars and were the roads that brought in the plagues and barbarians. They show a progression from Roman dominance to decline. Though, part of the story can only be inferred from the map. Rome didn't decline so much as it succumbed to cancer. The Visigoths only overran the streets when apathetic citizens opened the gates.

Nolli's map was a truer portrait of Rome than I could find in my travel guides, but it still had no notes about the people I saw riding in vespas or walking the markets in the Campo. There was no way to read the modern Rome that had grown and changed since his map was drawn. No train station, no bus lines, and no helicopters bringing gilded statues to the Vatican or pilots stopping to ogle sunbathers on rooftops. The map offered no notes leading to McDonalds, and no references to the shops pushing replicas of the David to the burgeoning population of tourists. The map also omits any mention of the EUR, hosting the Olympics, the World Cup, or the growth of Rome's suburbs; there isn't even a proper list of places to purchase Italian clothes or cappuccinos. Still, there has yet to be produced a better and more accurate portrait of what Rome is and will always be.

Chapter VI

Lunch in the Forum

[Summer 1997]

1

I t was August, and summer's heat had simply built up, making even the evenings uncomfortable. The night sky provided no relief, but seemed to hold it all in, as though the streets had soaked in the sun, slowly releasing heat after the daylight was spent.

Angeline and I had made a habit of spending such nights languishing in a small hole in the wall restaurant, drinking wine, trying to tire ourselves out for sleep. *La buca* was a small restaurant, with little menu. There were few choices, but the food tasted fine and was inexpensive. The wine was cheap. Angeline and I sat, leaning back in our chairs, finishing our meal. She held her glass slightly, letting it tip and rotate, laughing as the wine crept close to the rim, never spilling, only teasing.

"Nicky, this is fun. We need to drink wine together more often. Red wine, white wine - Vino rouge, vino blanc." She laughed as if she had just made a stunning joke, then brought her hand up to her mouth as though the laugh should be shared only between the two of us. Finishing her wine, she set her glass firmly on the table, then pushed it toward me with authority.

"An empty glass is a drink waiting to happen," she said.

"We've just got the red left, vino rouge." I smiled as I tipped the contents of the bottle into her glass, filling it nearly to the top.

"That's another thing I like about you Nicky, you don't skimp." She nodded her head with the final word to emphasize her point; perhaps implying that getting drunk on wine was a new thing for her, or that she had not even been given the opportunity before to over-indulge. Upon filling her glass, I poured the rest of the bottle into my own.

"A toast, we should have some words to commemorate our stupor," I said.

"Oh, but not a speech," she said looking around the restaurant at the few other patrons. "We can keep the toast to ourselves."

"Of course, but still, a toast is in order," I said.

She smiled, holding the back of her fingers against her lips to stifle another giggle.

"Okay, some words on our behalf, but you make the first toast," she said.

"Alright, to the wine?"

"No, no . . . make a proper toast."

"How about a toast to this beautiful evening and beautiful city?"

"No, to me. I want to hear you make a toast for me."

"A toast for you," I murmured, assembling the words in my head. *"Angeline, sips wine to get her fill; she tips her glass, but doesn't spill."*

She clapped her hands quietly, quickly glancing around the room.

"I like that toast. Yes, we should keep drinking wine and making toasts. Now me."

"Good, what will you toast?"

First she took a sip, as though finding inspiration from the wine. Thoughtfully, she let the wine sit on her tongue, then she swallowed, raising her glass. *"To Rome, to our evenings in La Buca, and to hoping that this goddamned heat goes away."*

"I second that, the heat can't last forever," I said.

"We should walk, it's dark and I want to see the city."

"Fine, but first finish your last gulp," I said pointing.

She smiled at me, but left her glass on the table. Without acknowledging my request, she stood up, placing money on the table.

"Let me," I said.

Again, she ignored my remark and simply walked toward the door, clutching her handbag. I considered counting the money to ensure it was the proper amount, but she was already near the door. Hastily, I pulled out several bills, dropped them on the table and followed her, uncertain if she even had a destination. Already half a block behind, I hurried to catch up to her. She meandered to the right, then left, despite every effort to maintain a straight path.

"Here, let me drive," I said, putting my hands firmly on her hips to keep them straight. "Walking's good, but sitting's better. The world might stop spinning if we sat."

"No, Nicky, walk with me. I want to see the city. This is Rome and I want to see every bit." She draped an arm around my shoulder and used it for balance, continuing to make steps ahead.

"Where, though?"

"I want to be in Navona with a crowd and lights. I want to be surrounded by a million strangers, watching them move and talk."

Navona was Rome's most beautiful of the Baroque Piazzas; an elongated oval, the piazza contained three elaborate fountains, altered several times over the centuries. Even the buildings that formed the piazza perimeter were built upon the altered foundation of the vast grandstands of the Stadium of Domitian. Navona had, centuries before, been the site for numerous athletic contests, and now enjoyed another incarnation as a magnet for pedestrians, always a center for activity.

"I thought you liked to be anonymous; didn't you want to get away from people?"

"A crowd is anonymous. We'll be away from people, away from people who know us. I want to talk with strangers who I'll never see again. That's the same as being anonymous."

"Every city is full of the anonymous; we'll easily find what you're seeking."

"I want to be in a crowd. Let's keep walking until we get lost among strangers."

Angeline was a fascination. Her look, her demeanor, and her speech suggested fragility. She blushed with ease, she wilted under scrutiny, and she went to lengths to avoid and deny conflict. She possessed a willful naiveté, and seemed to enjoy portraying herself in that light. However, she seemed able to shed those qualities of her personality at will. Claiming to eschew attention, she proceeded down the streets of Rome seeking a crowd in which to lose herself. I kept one hand on her hip, as though guiding her. In fact, I was only holding on to avoid being left behind.

As we walked, she altered her pace, slowing as if preoccupied, then quickening her pace to hasten our journey. Tiny cars zipped by as we moved along the side of the streets. Headlights burning through darkness, the little vehicles hummed by in procession. There was nothing quiet about these city streets, they seemed to come alive at night in a way that they never could during the day. Too much heat still lingered in the air for the young to sleep, so they hopped onto bikes and into cars. With no place to go, they drove quickly beeping horns at busy intersections. Angeline and I followed along these wide streets until we found ourselves in familiar territory.

"Here, turn here," she said, leading me with her torso. I followed without speaking. We walked without exchanging words, simply listening to the hum and buzz of the streets. Though the sun had long since vanished, the heat had remained and the air felt heavy. As we moved, I could feel moisture on my forehead, but never enough to roll down my face. It was simply a warm sticky dampness that refused to go away.

With Angeline's arm draped around my shoulder, I felt restless. It was the same feeling I remember as a child, laying awake in bed while the summer sun was still hours from setting. It was a sense that something should be happening, but I wasn't yet a part of it; a sense of expectation and apprehension.

We continued through narrower, less populated streets, where the noise of cars was only background. The clatter of dishes and pots emanated from nearby homes, announcing meals had just ended. Faint Italian voices escaped through windows, left open to allow a welcome breeze to chase away the heat. We walked, but still had hardly shared a word since the restaurant, as though our silence should remain unbroken while we walked to the Piazza.

We approached the Campo, walking past our studio, then past the building where Angeline had her room. Holding out her bag, she turned her head and motioned up to the room. She gestured toward an open window on the third floor of the palazzo.

"I'm going to drop this off before Navona, I'll be back down in just a minute," she said.

"How do you feel? Still up to going to the Piazza?"

"Feeling fine."

"Need any help?"

"I'll be right down."

"Let me join you, no reason for me to wait here on the street."

She unlocked the door to the building and we both walked up the dimly lit flight of stairs leading up to her room. I asked about her roommate, and discovered she was out on an excursion to Orvieto, and would be gone the entire weekend. We entered Angeline's room without turning on the lights, her open window providing just enough illumination to see. She sat down on the bed, still feeling the effects of the wine we had consumed. Once inside her room, neither of us spoke, we only looked at each other, barely able to see in the dim light. With the lights off, and in silence, I kissed Angeline. She lay back on the bed, as I undressed her, seeing only her silhouette in the darkness.

We didn't linger, Angeline sliding out of bed and picking her shirt off the floor. She began dressing and reached over to kiss me.

"Do you still want to go out?"

"Yes," she said.

"It'll be late soon."

"It's too hot, we won't sleep."

"Navona?"

"Yes."

She grabbed my shirt, giving it to me as she put on the rest of her clothing. We left, leaving her window open to cool off the room and let some of the humidity escape.

Outside, dim stars poked through the evening haze, replacing the dusky sky. We wove along the meandering streets, as the sound of the piazza ahead intensified. We entered Navona, filled with motion and bodies, walking, watching, conversing, and sitting. Some stood with bottles of beer in hand, others sat around cafes, the piazza moved as if it had its own pulse. Angeline turned to me and pushed her lips into my cheek; almost a kiss, but more of a greeting. She smiled and nodded her head. Her arm slid down from my shoulder, gave me a squeeze and then released me.

"Isn't it fun, Nick? Isn't this an amazing place? There's so much to see, so many people."

Navona was an enormous piazza, with a long, thin proportion, one fountain at each end and a third at its center. Opposite the center fountain, Fontana dei Quarttro Fiumi, was a large Baroque church with a concave façade. The statues populating the fountain seemed frozen in dialogue with the statue of St. Agnes standing at the Church's façade.

I sat down on the steps leading up Quattro Fiumi, while Angeline strolled around the perimeter.

"Could you ever live in Rome, Nick?"

I watched her circle around the fountain, disappear, then reappear on the other side. As she came back toward me, she reached out and grabbed my hands. We both pulled, she to get me on my feet, me to bring her down to sit on the steps. The tug of war ended in a stalemate, she standing and me still on the step.

"I don't know if I could live in Rome," I said. "For me, part of the appeal of the city is that it's such a different place from what I know. If I ever got used to it, if it ever became commonplace, it's as though it would no longer be Rome."

"What if you knew that you were to live somewhere else in a year? How about living in Rome one year, then to New York, then to Copenhagen, then to Venice. Each place new, each place a new opportunity."

"I'd miss the things that I'm used to. Traveling is exciting, but also tiring."

She stood with hands on hips, regarding me, shaking her head while smiling. Her eyes were open wide, pupils large, taking in as much as they could. The energy of the piazza seemed to have filled her up as she stood, taking long deep breaths, her shoulders back and her gaze sweeping across the crowds.

"Come," she said, giving my arm another pull. She jumped up the few steps to the edge of the fountain and sat. As I got up to join her, she quickly pulled off her sandals and spun around to face the fountain. Pulling up the legs of her pants, she dipped both feet into the rippling water and laughed. She kicked her feet, splashing water over her shirt and pants legs.

"Oh, so nice on tired feet. Join me?"

"I'll sit, but I won't dip." I paused looking at her. "You've got a second wind after our walk."

The bottom of her shirt, soaked from the splash, stuck to the contours of her back. Through the shirt, the warm pink of her skin was visible. Standing up she examined her shirt, relieved that only the bottom had gotten soaked. She turned and craned her neck to view her back.

"You got splashed pretty good, back of your shirt and down your pant leg."

"So I'll stay cool, but that'll teach me to dip my toes in the fountain."

We moved down to the dry steps and sat while she let her feet dry. We both took in the surroundings, looking at the large dome sitting atop the Baroque church. The modest statue of St. Agnes contrasted with the nude figures cast in stone around the fountain.

"These buildings surrounding us, how would you have designed them? Tell me what a Nicholas-Design would look like if it were to be in the Piazza Navona."

"Strip mall, lots of beige, maybe a couple faux mansard roofs," I replied.

"No, for reals. I want to know the sort of eye you have. Would you strive for function or beauty?"

"My formula goes, two part commodity, one part firmness, with a pinch of delight."

"Clever, but that tells me nothing. Being an enigma is appealing for just so long. Soon you'll have to say something of substance or risk becoming a terrible bore."

"A bore; is there any greater sin?"

"Boredom is the eighth deadly sin, be careful."

"Alright, then - my design for Navona," I began, not really having had a chance to consider what I would say. Or perhaps more importantly, what I should say, for it occurred to me that this was a test of sorts. It struck me as ironic that I was trying to come up with a clever fabrication in order to sound genuine. "With all this history to respond to, I'd play the modernist and reinterpret classical forms; I suppose that's me playing the post-modernist, though - "

"Nick, we need more to drink," she said.

"I'm so happy you said that."

"So, for your design, no Nicholas-Baroque churches."

"What's the use? It's like speaking a dead language."

"But a beautiful dead language."

While we talked, she put on her sandals, her feet still wet. With each step, she left a moon shaped patch of water. The print lingered on the cobblestones, tiny drops rolling off the rounded side, then away from sight. Her soaked shirt still was stuck to her back, pulling off briefly with each step, only to return to the same contour.

"*La mia ragazza*." A tall, slender young man came up to us, addressing Angeline. He gestured emphatically, seeming to have energy to burn. He brought his hand first to his side, then up to his face, back down, finally resting on his hips. As Angeline came around the other side of the fountain, the young man nodded his head in her direction. Her attention still not captured, he walked toward her and called out.

"*Ciao, la sera*." The words, while spoken correctly, lacked fluidity. From his appearance, I would have assumed that he was from Rome, his hair and skin dark enough. He wore pleated slacks and light brown leather shoes with no socks. His shirt, only half buttoned billowed with each staccato gesture from his lanky frame.

"Ciao," he called again, this time with more earnest.

Angeline looked at him, then back at me, uncertain of what to say. I shrugged my shoulders but smiled.

"You've made a friend," I said.

Our new acquaintance, determining that Angeline and I were together, included us both in the conversation. "You both, are you Americans?" He asked.

Angeline simply smiled, brushing her hair back, as if to better view her surroundings. I replied. "Yes, American, from America. You? I don't think you're Italian."

"No, no, but I love it here," he said.

"Is this vacation, or do you live here now?" I asked.

"For now, this is my home, but only for the last four months. I am from Spain, Barcelona. I'm Amando."

"Glad to meet you, I'm Nicholas the American."

He grinned. "Good to meet you Nicholas the American. Who is your friend?"

"Angeline," she said without moving closer.

With our new friend, Angeline had become more subdued. She didn't appear threatened, but simply content to listen. Having just recently been accused of being a bore, I saw this as an opportunity.

"You've lived here four months, so you can show us around?" I asked.

"Show you around, you are already here." He stretched out his arms and swiveled his head, regarding the crowd that filled the Piazza.

"This, we've seen," I said mimicking his gesture. "What else, what can you show us that we otherwise would miss?"

"You like dancing?" He asked, looking at Angeline.

"Yes, where can we dance?" She said, finally finding a tongue.

"Follow." He clapped his hands and began walking. First very quickly, then a little slower until he saw that we were following. I put my hand on Angeline's moist back, and pushed her two steps ahead, but still several paces back from Amando.

"We're going dancing, your favorite," I said.

"Oh, shut up," she said in mock protest.

"Are you going to blush?" I asked.

"Now, you *shut up*."

She giggled as she bounced behind our tour guide, still leaving small wet moons on the street with each step.

"This place," I said loudly enough for Amando to hear, "will we find wine there? Drink?"

"*Si, esso `e Italia*," he replied.

With long acrobatic strides, he moved easily along the streets, slipping quickly into alleys, beckoning us along with waves from his spider-like arms. He had unusual dexterity for having such gangly limbs. It occurred to me that he was probably right at home on a dance floor, and had no doubt been to numerous clubs in Rome. His clothes hung much looser than many of the other young European travelers I had met, but it suited his casual manner. His thin shirt puffed with each passing breeze, making his limbs appear even longer and more distorted.

"You'll like this place. Good for Americans, the bartender speaks English," our guide said.

"Is it your regular place?"

"*Scusi?*"

"The discotheque, you've gone many times before?"

"*Si,*" he nodded his head then spun in place to show off his skills as a dancer. Angeline clapped.

We darted through yet another thin street, which opened up to reveal a young crowd gathered around the entrance to the club. They were grouped in packs, talking and getting some air by way of cigarette before returning to the dance floor inside. The thin street split the surrounding buildings, working its way to the club's entrance where the name, *Bijou*, was lit in pink neon. Not a very Italian name, but it fit with the international flavor the disco had achieved. The dance club seemed restricted to the ground level, the upper floors appearing vacant with painted slats over the windows.

"See, I told you I knew the way," Amando said grinning.

From inside, rhythmic thumps signaled the beginning of another techno song. Angeline and I followed Amando inside, then skittered to a corner, watching the dancers. The dance floor was sparsely populated with young men and women wrapped around one another, while colored lights strobed. The bar, however, was packed, a swarm of young Italians pushing forward, as drinks where passed to whoever shouted loudest.

"That's for me," I said pointing to the horde at the bar.

"What are you getting?" Angeline asked.

"Bourbon with a twist of anything; what can I get you?"

"Do they have wine?"

"They'd have to; I'll muscle through the crowd. Amando, anything for you?"

"Oh, you are kind, but you should be my guest."

"Next round. This is thanks for getting us here."

"Then good, wine for me too."

"Two for wine."

I walked to the bar. Several men were shouting to the bartender, waving money in the air, not one word in English. Being a quick study, I pulled several bills from my pocket and leaned against the bar with Lira in the air. I wedged myself between two customers and slowly pushed until I was up to the bar. To my right, a young man held up two fingers and shouted his order. As the bartender turned to grab more drinks, the other waiting patrons pushed forward and continued waving their Lira to secure the next spot. I held my ground, and when the bartender came back, I grabbed his arm, pushing lira into his hand. I used what little Italian I knew to order three glasses of wine, deciding to keep it simple. The bartender nodded, then took more orders before running back to fill them.

I looked back toward Angeline; she was talking to Amando, laughing about something. The two of them began mixing into the crowd, moving closer to the dance floor. I hadn't been with Angeline to any of the clubs before, I found myself almost uncomfortable seeing how at ease she was. Not that it mattered, but it made me realize that there was a side to her that I really hadn't gotten to know.

I turned and watched the bartender, as he mixed drinks, hardly looking at what he was doing as he tried to keep up with the outstretched hands grappling for his attention. He scooped ice into several glasses, then picked at chopped limes and cherries, dropping them into the mix before squirting in the house liquor. He caught my gaze, and offered a quick smile to let me know I was not forgotten. Then, grabbing an open bottle, he poured three glasses and set them in front of me, never stopping before returning to the crowd to fill more orders.

I managed to balance all three glasses in both hands, while sticking out my elbows to push through the crowd. With the strobe lights blinking, and colored pulses of light, I zigzagged before finding where I had seen Amando and Angeline. They were gone. I looked at the dance floor, but saw no one familiar.

"Nicholas the American."

I spun around to find the voice. Amando stepped toward me, and helped me with one of the glasses.

"Let me grab this before it spills all over the floor," he said smiling. "Thank you."

"Where's Angeline?"

"You're lady friend? We were dancing, and then she left the floor."

"Did you see where she went?"

"I thought she would find you – I can see you have her glass."

"You don't know where she is?"

"Sorry, again?"

"I said, you don't know where she is?"

"No, but she went toward the back." He pointed to a hallway leading away from the dance area. I smiled, and walked as quickly as I could without spilling my glasses.

On either side of the hallway, were the men's and women's room, both with impatient lines formed outside the door. I continued through the hall, where young couples leaned back against the wall, casually groping at each other while finishing cigarettes. I set down my glasses and covered my mouth passing through thick trails of smoke. I moved to the back of the hall, running my hand along the wall where remnants of posters concealed stains and cracked plaster. The surface of the wall felt moist and sticky from the humid air that lounged around the club, unable to find an exit.

There was a door near the far side of the wall, past the restrooms. I had no idea if Angeline had run back to the dance floor, or had pressed on through the maze, deeper into the club. I had never before been alarmed in Rome - most of the time had felt like a long vacation. But I suddenly felt sick. I was confused and desperately wanted out of the club. My heart hammered inside my chest, and I could hear blood hiss through my ears. Adrenaline pumped into my stomach, but there was nothing for me to do, I just stood.

Unwilling to turn back, I pushed open the door, walking past the sweaty couples. Beyond the doorway, was a second, shorter hall which let through a breeze; I quickened my pace, understanding that I had found a passage out, and pushed open the exit. The air was free from smoke, and the noise from the dance floor now sounded muffled, just background.

I was alone, standing in a tight alley under a street lamp. No young dancers and no young lovers stepping out to smoke or talk or feel each other. I stood by myself.

The street lamp illuminated the cobblestones beneath my feet, and I looked down, observing a wet pattern trailing away from the building, out across the street; small half moons, wet prints that fell side by side, in even paces. I followed the puzzle several steps before reaching the limit of the street lamp, uncertain how to follow or if I should. I tried to think, tried to reason out what had happened and why she had disappeared. It didn't occur to me until later that night, when I was almost asleep, to wonder whether or not she had taken flight alone. Without more clues, I simply had a disjointed evening to piece together, and a sense of uneasy confusion. I had spent the entire evening trying to follow close behind, only to fall back further. After finding my way back to the Campo, and then up to my room above the studio, I crawled into bed feeling tired and defeated.

2

In the morning I walked to the Vie Dei Giubbonari and met Ron for espresso and biscotti. I woke up later than usual, but decided to make time for my habit. Ron had already ordered, and was standing at the bar with an Italian newspaper. He squinted at the text, trying to discern as many words as he could. I placed my order and handed over folded Lira to the barista.

"Anything new in the world?" I asked.

"Damned if I know, can't read a thing. I feel like I'm grasping more of the language, but I still can't make sense of the paper."

"Good thing they've got pictures."

"I'm debating if I should order another coffee. Will you stick around if I get two?"

I had already finished my espresso, pounding it quickly to get my engine going. "I'm in no hurry."

"Good enough. Tell you what, I'll order one for you too." He got the barrista's attention and held up two fingers. *"Espresso – due tazza."*

"Much appreciated."

"Don't mention it. So, have any fun last night?"

"Some, but not much."

"Seems like you and Angeline always have some fun together."

"Usually, not so much last night."

"It's been a long summer, can't be exciting every night."

"Sure, here comes the espresso." Two cups were placed in front of us, one sugar cube on each saucer. I dropped one in my cup and asked Ron for his.

"Now I'm ready for the day," Ron said. He drank his coffee.

"This is a good place, we should meet for breakfast more often."

"Too hard to wake up in the morning, I could never make it a habit. When I get going early enough I'll meet you."

"I never got to sleep last night."

"Why not sleep in?"

"No sense tossing. If I can't sleep, I can't sleep."

"The heat?"

"No, not the heat."

"Drink your coffee."

"Was hot last night, but little by little I get used to it. A little cooler now than earlier in the summer, anyway."

The bar was starting to crowd up, so we gave up some of our real estate.

"So Nick, how's your competition going? We're not far from the end of our two terms. They'll be judging our entries soon enough."

"Summer's getting late, I know."

"I like your design; I've peeked when you weren't at your desk."

"Forgiven. Anyway, I like what I've got. Never know, but I think I've got a shot at the prize. You?"

"Me? No."

"Not turning out? Usually your work is good."

"I just can't focus when I'm here – I want to spend all my time in the city, not at my desk. No regrets, though."

"Good."

"More to life than studying."

"True enough. Maybe I should follow your lead."

"Too late now; plus you've got a shot at winning."

"Only a matter of time now." I let the sugar dissolve, then sipped half my coffee. "Look, Ron, I couldn't sleep last night because my mind couldn't get settled."

"Then good thing you're drinking espresso," Ron said.

"Doesn't affect me, not this early, anyway."

"Worried about studio?"

"Not that. I went out last night with Angeline. Enjoyed dinner, but she disappeared later in the evening. No explanation, no goodbye – just gone. Feels different than how things had been going."

"Like I said, it's a long summer. Don't sweat it."

"Maybe not."

"Best not to look too deeply."

"But still."

"Maybe you need another coffee."

"Nope, I'm hitting my limit. Be my guest, though."

"Getting a little crowded; maybe I'll pass. What's the big deal about last night, anyway?"

"Was late, so we followed some guy to a disco. Just for kicks, you know. I didn't even really want to be there."

"Maybe she didn't either – she didn't leave with the guy? That's not what's got you in a funk."

"No, he was still there, but I went to get drinks and she was gone."

"That is a little peculiar."

"Thought you said not to sweat it."

"Don't. Just sounds a little strange."

"Well, she did want to be there. It was her idea. Good idea for me to ask her about it?"

"Of course, ask away."

I finished my coffee. "You're competition really that bad?"

"It's not bad, just unfinished."

I nodded.

"Well," he said pausing, "it isn't good."

As more people pushed up to the bar, we made our way to the door, Ron leaving his newspaper. We relaxed a little in the morning sun. It felt good, soaking it in before the air had really heated up. I watched crowds of older women stroll through the market, purchasing fresh fruit and some spices.

After a bit, we made our way back to the studio for class. I saw Angeline, but didn't try to get her attention. Instead, I just focused on my work. She didn't come by my desk to gab, which was unusual. I noticed Ron chatting her up, but decided to stay at my desk. Thinking that a little bit of space might be the best thing, I made dinner for myself and spent a quiet evening back at my apartment. I'd catch up with Angeline the next evening.

3

When I woke the next morning, there was little time before class was to begin. A quick shower cooled me down. I walked down the stairs from my apartment to the studio on the ground floor. The class had convened, each student waiting, bleary-eyed, at their desk. Professor Rice paced around the room with his second cup of coffee already in hand. Clearly excited, he glanced at his watch, then began addressing the class the moment it struck eight.

Shortly, we would take a field trip to the Forum; individually, nearly everyone in the class had been to the Forum to take notes for the studio project, but this was the first formal field trip that we would take as a group to this ruin.

Flanked on one side by the Capitoline Hill, and by the Coliseum on the other, the Forum served as an appropriate metaphor for the disintegration of the Empire. Those seeking one-stop-shopping for history could begin at the Capitoline hill, the seat of Roman government. Then after pausing for a snack or souvenir, stroll through the ruins of the Forum, and be a stone's throw away from the arena where civilization consumed itself, one lion at a time. The Forum had once been home to many temples as well as political monuments and a center of commerce. In today's Rome, the Forum only resembled an elaborate archaeological dig, broken columns capitols and stained stone foundations too numerous to count.

The class left the studio on foot, carrying lunches and sketching pads in our backpacks. I wondered to myself, what it would be like to travel without the typical accoutrements of a tourist. Just once, I would have liked to walk like an Italian, without sketch pad, camera, or map. However, I held no illusions that I would ever be confused with a local.

After a twenty minute hike, we had made our way to our destination. Morning was the only time to travel before having to endure the heat of the day, so our walk was actually refreshing. I felt as though I didn't even need my typical shot of coffee to wake up; that being said, I still purchased a morning cup of coffee. The difference was that I bought it out of habit, not because I needed it.

Just before Rice got started, I touched base with Angeline and we set a time and place in the Forum to steal away for lunch. We quieted as professor Rice walked slowly, turning toward the class. The students had assembled in a mass at the West entrance to the Forum, waiting for his direction.

"You've all seen the Forum on your own, I'm sure, but now having spent time with your design, you will see it with new eyes." He moved his arms both to emphasize his words and to direct the class forward. "Today, the Forum is visible only as ruins. But imagine the columns standing, the streets filled with people.

This center of Roman life grew with the city; you need to see the Forum as an always-evolving part of Rome. Forty-six years before the birth of Christ, the population of Rome became too much for the Forum, and Julius Caesar expanded it, building a new Forum. This set a precedent for additions by subsequent Emperors. Therefore, Forum was re-invented by each generation. Now it's your turn. Your designs should express the next logical shape for today's Modern Forum."

Rice spoke while walking backwards, swiveling his head to ensure he didn't catch his foot on some no-longer-evolving piece of antiquity. He continued by offering an abridged version of the historical rise and fall of Rome. His gestures seemed more like nervous ticks, his energy level still not subsiding though his last cup of coffee had been consumed nearly an hour before.

The class dispersed, after the professor's lecture having, each person studying the portion of the Forum that would hold their design. I took the opportunity to pull more information from Rice.

"Nicholas, your site is at the Basilica Julia, correct?"

"Yes, that's right."

"What do you think of parasites?"

"Sorry, I haven't thought much about them."

"Certainly, why would you? But I think you should. Imagine that a parasite simply takes nourishment from its host. I'm talking about design, mind you. This is an analogy."

"Still, I don't think I follow."

"Look, I'm only suggesting that you see the Forum as your host, and your design needs to consume its host. Don't be a slave to what you see here; learn from it, and break it down. Use it for whatever good it serves. Your design will build off of what you see here, and inhabit it."

"So, I'm designing a parasite?"

"If you want to look at it that way, yes. Your design will live inside of this ruin, but will also take something from it. But that's what each generation of Romans did when they designed."

"Do you think I have a shot at winning this competition?"

"I've reviewed your design and seen it progress, you've got a shot. Don't get hung up on that, but yes, you've got a shot."

"A parasite?"

"Yes, it's only a metaphor, mind you. The point is to understand your site because in the end, you'll absorb it. Some of your design will become what inspired it, but don't let that alone define it. Now, go understand your site."

"What will you do while we're exploring?"

"Me? I'll run back to the café, I've run out of coffee."

I spent the early part of the morning strolling around the Basilica Juliu, filling my sketchbook with drawings and diagrams. I had chosen the Basilica as a ruin suitable for my design, in part because only a portion of the façade remained, allowing a new design to inhabit the old shell. The site was also situated at a visual crossroads between the Coliseum and the Capitoline hill, giving it a station of some prominence within the existing fabric of the city.

On previous trips, I had already taken exhaustive photographs. This occasion I chose to use my pencil to measure the site; by sketching the site in simplified volumes, I was able to understand the system of proportions used for the original structure. This way, I could use a modern vocabulary of materials and tectonics, but defer to the classic proportions and rhythms inherent in the Forum. Perhaps that is a wordy way of saying that I learned about the site by sketching it. By laboring over the columns and steps with my pencil, subtleties made themselves visible that might otherwise remain hidden.

After filling pages in my sketchbook, I grew restless. I watched classmates file around the Forum, reviewing their chosen location for a design. To the east, I could see Angeline walking among a row of headless statues overlooking a pond. She sat at the edge of the pond, her feet dipped into the cool water. The pond was at the far end of an intimate courtyard, surrounded by the crumbling statues of the Vestals. Along the perimeter of the courtyard, pink flowers provided one of the few bursts of warmth and color in the entire Forum. She remained still, providing time for me to record her as light and shadow on my paper. Tracing over her body, I captured her form, beginning with her leg, bathing in water, to her hip, then up her torso, ending at her dark hair, tied up behind her head. Sitting at the edge of the pond, staring at her reflection caught with the stone Vestals, she seemed almost as still, made from stone.

My sketch complete, she moved abruptly, startled by a visitor. As Pierce approached her, she pulled her feet from the water and quickly put on her sandals. They talked for a moment, then strolled from the courtyard and away from sight; leaving the Vestals alone on their pedestals.

I spent another hour walking along the perimeter of the site. In many ways, it was far removed from the day to day of any Italian, yet only a stone's throw from any number of groceries, banks, or cafes. Pierce had described the Forum as the trailer park of antiquity. Broken columns, like the chassis of burned out cars, were balanced on blocks haphazardly around the site. Unmanaged tufts of grass worked their way through the dirt, between cracks, forming a patchwork on the hardened clay. Every monument stood as evidence of a better time long past. While the stone symbolized a stubborn permanence, it also had a surprising fragility. Even the most thoughtfully pieced together buildings had been losing a battle over the course of centuries. Each year, the rain rounded once sharp corners, and the elements opened cracks just a little bit wider. For permanence, the Forum could have been made of glass and the result would eventually be the same.

Although the Forum was fascinating, my appetite soon took precedence over my curiosity, and thoughts quickly turned to lunch. No amount of philosophy is ever so compelling as hunger. Wiping perspiration from my lip, I found shade and sat on the stone steps leading to what had once been the temple of Vesta. A circular wall and stone hearth was all that remained of the ancient shrine. I had packed a lunch early in the morning, before the heat had taken hold. I had dropped a chunk

J Edward Duncan

of cheese and a handful of grapes into a paper bag, and filled my water bottle with a cheap white wine.

Before I had eaten more than a handful of grapes, Angeline came walking towards me, waving.

"Nick, can I join you?"

"Sure, find a seat."

"Learn anything new?"

"About the Forum? Just that they could use a Starbucks. You'd think in Rome, of all places, it would be easy to find a cup of coffee."

"You'd think."

"Angeline," I deliberated, not certain how best to proceed. "I didn't see you the other day. I was a little surprised the way you disappeared at the club."

"Yeah, sorry about that, I just felt like I had to get out of there."

"Me too – started to feel claustrophobic. Glad we can grab a quiet lunch, just us."

"It's good to relax. I do need something to keep me going."

Angeline unpacked her lunch, setting the contents of her backpack on the rim of a large stone bowl centered in the temple. The bowl's surface was pocked and cracked, a portion missing, having broken into bits and removed as a souvenir or artifact.

"Careful, you're setting your picnic where they kept the sacred flame. What'd you bring?"

"Sandwiches."

"Any water? I brought some wine, we can share."

Angeline handed me her bottle, which was still cold; she had frozen the contents of her bottle, and pulled it out of the freezer before class.

"Have you read about the Vestals? You know what happened to any priestess who allowed the flame to go out? I'm not talking about a cookout, this was serious." I asked.

"Can I have some of your grapes?"

"You're not interested."

"The flame has blown out, no turning back now."

"They were whipped, honestly. Can you imagine?"

"Pity for them." She reached for my bag and pulled out several grapes, smiling and then returned the bag. "Nick, what will you do when the summer is through?"

"There's still some summer left."

"Yes, but where will you go?"

"Portland, grew up there. Probably look for work. Why, what will you do?"

"I haven't decided, but I might live there too. It would be fun if we still saw each other."

"More picnics?"

"Yes, but I don't want to hear any more about women being whipped."

"Sorry, just some history. Care for any cheese?" I sliced the cheese into several pieces and set it on top of the bag. Angeline reclined on the stone, propping herself up on her elbows. She had kicked off one of her sandals, and let the other balance on her toe.

"It makes me sad that this can't just keep going on and on. Wouldn't it be fun if the summer didn't stop? It could be us having lunches and dancing and drinking more wine."

"Did you ask for more wine?" I handed her the bottle.

"We could live in Rome together, imagine that."

"Sure."

"How much Italian do you know?"

"Very little, and the little I do gets me into trouble. Would you really go to Portland after the term ends?"

"Could be a good place to start out. Would you call me up?"

"Of course. You know, we're starting to become each other's bad habit." She looked at me quizzically, not following what I had said. "Bad habits are a good thing."

"I like being your bad habit, Nick." She poured a stream of wine into her mouth, laughing as she swallowed. "You mind if I nap?"

"No, go ahead," I said.

"I just don't want to get burned, you'll be my alarm clock."

Angeline stretched out in the grass just below the stone steps. Rolling her shirt up from her waist, she tucked it just below her breasts, exposing her white stomach. She put her sunglasses over her eyes and turned her head, using her arms as a pillow.

Sitting in the ruins of the Forum with Angeline, I felt content. It was easy to imagine life continuing at this pace, with picnics of cheese, fruit, and wine being enough to satisfy.

4

As the term progressed, I began to rely more heavily on my credit card. This wasn't just because my cash was getting skinny, but it also was far more convenient. Credit also made for the best exchange rate on dollars to lira; so it made for convenient rationalization. Another reality was that I was increasingly attracted to restaurants where I could sit down and eat a leisurely meal, rather than the hobo-fair of assorted cheeses and breads from the market. While the tidbits from the market were tasty, there was no comparison to the prepared meals that could be had in the various hole-in-the wall cafes. I had arranged to meet Angeline for a lunch at a favorite café near Piazza Farnese, a short walk from the Campo. I arrived early, and had hovered while tables were brought outside to cater to the late morning crowd. A light breeze stirred up the few leaves that had accumulated, reminding me that summer would soon be drawing to a close. Small wooden tables with shaky legs were dispersed in front of the café, then draped with white linen. There was hardly enough table top for two to eat, but each table had a glass bottle in the center holding wild flowers, and holding down the linen. Along with the tables, short planters were wheeled out to the edges, defining the area claimed by the

282

restaurant. I grabbed a table and watched the waiters finish, watering each of the planters, spilling more water onto the stones below.

The moment I sat, a waiter came by and took my order for a Pellegrino. I waited, reading an American newspaper; the entire time the waiters wouldn't leave me alone, asking if I wanted to order something.

Finally, Angeline arrived and I waved for her to join me. However, she was walking with Pierce and Ron, the three of them taking their time. I couldn't hear what they were saying, but saw Ron make a remark and they bust up laughing.

"There's hardly enough table for one, how are four going to fit?" I asked.

"Nicky, don't be stingy, we'll pull up chairs."

"Well, so much for a romantic lunch with the two of us. But grab chairs fast, they won't last." Pierce and Ron scavenged chairs from a nearby table while Angeline sat down across from me.

"What are you drinking?" she asked.

"Just fizzy water, I was waiting for you."

"Glad you were able to grab a table."

"Crowd's already arrived."

Pierce and Ron sat down, and immediately a waiter came by. We quickly scanned the menu and ordered assorted appetizers and sangria; the waiter seemed more satisfied.

"Have you been waiting long?"

"Not very."

"Didn't mean to keep you waiting, but Pierce and I were late in studio talking to Rice," she said.

"We managed to pull some information about the finals for the competition. Coming up fast, you know," Pierce said.

"Good, probably didn't have to twist his arm."

"Hope our food gets here quickly, I'm starved," Ron said. He inched his chair closer to the table, angling for a little more space. "I stumbled into studio and tagged along for lunch."

"Waiters have been fast, I think they want to get people in and out."

"I don't intend to be quick, let's relax and eat," Angeline said.

"Good enough, but we may have to order more food."

"So, you talked to Rice?" I asked.

"He gave us the lowdown on the format for judging our competitions. Should be a sizable group between our designs and the drawings from the Italian students," Pierce said.

"Final round will be jury format, how's that for pressure?" Ron asked.

On the morning of the judging, each student would be assigned space to pin up their drawings and display a model. Our class would be interspersed with other study abroad programs and Italian student competitions. Due to the quantity of entries, the first round of judging would be silent, students were not allowed to be present and could not defend their design. The best designs would be selected, and would be evaluated by a design jury while the students gave a brief presentation. In theory, the judges would make up their mind after hearing the designs defended, but the reality was that the selection would likely be made in the first round – the final round being more formality. This was fortunate, as we would be depending on the judge's ability to understand either English or our broken Italian. In this instance, a picture was worth far more than a thousand words.

The waiter came back with assorted plates and a carafe for sangria. We drank, and quickly realized we would need to order more food. We stacked the plates as they emptied to make better use of our tabletop.

"Did Rice give any hints on our chances of winning the competition?" I asked.

"Nothing specific, but overall I think he's impressed with our studio," said Ron while spilling bruschetta on his shirt.

"When studio is finished, we should all get together to celebrate," Angeline said. "We can have more sangria, sit in the shade, and eat."

"Sleep for me," Pierce said.

"A long nap in the sunshine – that's all I'll need," I said.

The waiter came by and grabbed our stack of plates. We placed another order and watched the crowd gather. The piazza had become so crowded that the waiter had to hold the next carafe above his head before setting it down on our table. More food arrived, and we ate our second round more slowly, taking our time and telling the others where we would travel if we were awarded the prize.

As if on a beach, I stood barefoot, toes wiggling, gazing out at an open sea of blank vellum. My shoes sat beside the desk, kicked away, as I rubbed my toes against the cool concrete floor of the studio. There was now only one day left until the competitions would be judged, and I now had to beat the clock. I had two completed drawings, rolled into scrolls and stashed above my desk. With luck, I could finish the line-work for my last drawings before the evening, but I would be up all night rendering the colors.

I pulled out a few crumpled drawings on trace paper that would serve as underlays for my final drawing. I had drawn a perspective view of the New Forum with my building hunkered down into the earth. I also had a wall section and a floor plan to add to the sheet.

My design was an example of *Velvet Modernism*, as Ron and I liked to call it. I adhered to the notion that 'form follows function' and 'less is more'; but I was not a strong proponent of the axiom that 'ornament is crime'. If a crime, it was surely no more than a misdemeanor. To me, ornament can make a building accessible; it is often the morsel that gets noticed, and then draws attention to the rest of the design. I enjoy the clean lines and uncluttered sensibilities of Modernists, but I also welcome the beauty and attention to details found in Craftsman buildings. I wanted to develop a Modernist style that finds pleasure in exposing joints and doesn't regard austere, scaleless planes as *International*.

I had discussed this softer side of Modernism with Ron during one of our studios in Eugene. Ron was a fervent detractor of *The International Style,* a prescriptive ideology that utilized Modernist doctrine to create a building vocabulary that might work equally well in any region. Perhaps it would be more accurate to say it worked equally poorly, but that much is still open for debate.

Ron sat at his desk, dremil in hand, cutting through sheets of bass wood in preparation for a model. I sat at my desk, cup of Starbucks in hand, staring at a rough sketch I had drawn earlier in the day. The evening had not yet turned late, but the light was already dim, making it necessary for us each to turn on lamps we had mounted to our drafting tables.

"Ask me why I like building models?" Ron asked.

"I give up."

"Ask."

"Fine, why?"

"I like to drill things. It's all about the tools. Give me power tools, and I'll build you a bass wood city. Tiny little houses, to perfect scale. I'll cut perfect joints, sand them, glue them, and give you flawless tiny details."

"Why not become a carpenter?"

"Not the same."

"If it's not the same, then it's only because it's better. If you like tools so much, become a carpenter."

"I've just never seen myself as a carpenter."

"You like tools, you like working with your hands. Not only that, but you seem to have a monster case of attention deficit disorder – do yourself a favor and quit architecture."

"Nick, I enjoy designing, and I think I'm pretty damn good at it."

Ron went back to working with his dremil, placing several pieces of basswood in a tiny jig, cutting them all to perfect size. Studying his drawings, he sanded the pieces to a beveled edge and set them in glue, clamping each until dry.

"Your design must not be going well," Ron said.

"Why would you say that?"

"You lashed out; you always lash out when you've hit a snag."

"I didn't lash out, and I've hit no snag."

"Fine, but I take nothing back."

"Alright, I was a little short."

"So, then you lied when you said I should quit architecture."

"There was no lie, it was only a suggestion."

"But you didn't mean it, you were angry so you lied."

"Again, there was no lie. It was a truth neutral statement."

"Great – truth neutral. Is that what you call it."

"Fine, Ron, you're an outstanding designer."

I sipped my coffee, finding it impossible to focus on my drawings. The creative process relies on both concentration and momentum, and Ron had successfully broken both. I sharpened several pencils in a last ditch effort at productivity, then finally gave up.

"Ron, you really are a good designer, though you sort of design like a girl." This time, I really was lashing out. I knew precisely where his buttons were, and I was determined to press them all.

"What? That doesn't mean anything," he said.

"Of course it does; it means you design very gently."

"Look, Nick – you're talking absolute nonsense. *Gently* is a stupid adverb to use for design. Designing is thinking, and one can't think gently."

"Why are you protesting so vigorously?"

"I'm not even protesting, I just don't understand. I design in a modern fashion, just like everybody else who receives an education. I suppose if I design like a girl, then you could say I soften things up a bit."

"Interesting thought, that."

"Softening up modernism?"

"Yes, wrap it up in a blanket, but keep it simple and clean."

"You know, Nick, I hate to admit it, but you're on to something. I do design like a girl. I've always had a penchant for a velvet Modernism, something sensible and ordered, but still lively."

"Like taking the Villa Savoye and wrapping it in neon."

"Now that you mention it, the Villa does remind me of a diner without the lights and chrome. I mean, it does have a drive-through."

"Yes, like an old Fifties diner. Put Le Corbusier in roller skates, and you've got yourself the softest Modernism yet."

Ron smiled, and continued sanding his segments of wood. He planned out a few sketches on trace, then started chopping wood dowels to size in meticulous, orderly fashion.

"Why do you suppose we all become Modernist designers?" I asked.

"What else?"

"Well, there are plenty of other styles."

"Sure, but Modernism isn't really a style, it's an anti-style. And I don't think we all become Modernists."

"You described yourself as a Velvet Modernist."

"So, there's a difference. And how would you describe your style?"

"No style really, don't know how I'd describe it. I suppose I'm still developing my style, learning what I think design ought to be."

"Then school is no place for you; typically one stops developing the moment they enroll. If you want to learn, better start skipping more classes."

"Ron, cynicism isn't the same as being clever."

"You're right, but it doesn't change the fact that I am clever."

"Well, clever certainly isn't the same as being smart."

"True, Nick, and being smug isn't the same thing as being right, so where does that leave us?"

"Me smug and you clever."

"That's the first time you've been right all day."

"Look, it is a good question, though."

Ron stopped cutting dowels and looked at me quizzically. "Was there a question?"

"Yes, it's determining what one thinks design ought to be. You're telling me school is the worst place for it."

"I overstate my case, but there's a point to my comment."

Ron went back to chopping bass wood. He had assembled several piles of dowels, like phalanx of wood soldiers, stacked up for ready combat. I waited for him to continue, then prodded him. "The point then - what is it?"

"It's that you can't determine how you should design without observing good design. You need to spend time understanding what you think works, and break it down so it's clear why it works."

"Dissecting it?"

"No, appreciating it. Use your eyes and appreciate what's out there. Then you'll develop an intuitive understanding of what works and why." He said.

"And that's how you get to the softer side of Modernism?"

"Yes, with some passion for the doing, and appreciating what's been done before."

"Now you really are being clever. Do you believe we're capable of that?"

"If having passion means becoming a starving artist, then I hope not."

"There must be a way to enjoy design without living the life of a starving artist. Does being an artist have to involve sacrifice and misery?" I asked.

"Sacrifice, no. Misery, yes. The nature of passion is that it is reckless. Passion inevitably consumes itself," he said.

"I think I'd rather have a sensible passion; some middle ground that's sexy but not reckless."

"Nick, that's a little like asking for water that's not wet."

After Ron had finished cutting his pieces to size, he went back to sand the ends, creating uniform parts. With that sequence complete, he began to glue and set pieces. As he assembled his model, he periodically turned it, reviewing it from all sides. Then, he would cut apart the model, eliminating elements that didn't work, refining the design as he built. At this point, even Ron did not know what the model would become; it was during the process of building, that the model would tell him.

I finished my coffee, and went through more cycles with my trace paper, sketching perspectives. The entire time, I pictured a large rotating sign, lit up and blinking, "Eat Now, at Savoye!"

In Rome, however, these memories did little to further my design. Standing barefoot in my Italian studio, I had spent the better part of two terms engaged in *process*, and found myself acutely aware of only the deadline. I had been on my feet constantly for the previous few days, grinding out the last of my underlays and then final drawings. A few other diehards were matching me for time in the studio, but most refused to let schoolwork detract from their time exploring the city. Pierce was another who was so focused on his design that he had scarcely seen daylight in the last few days. He had even confided that he had spent so much time standing at his desk, that he had lost a toenail. War wounds aside, there was a peculiar adrenaline rush in trying to beat the clock. Occasionally Pierce and I exchanged looks, and sometimes even dialogue.

"Finished yet?" I asked.

"Not close, not close."

"Are you ever going to let me see your design?"

"You're welcome to come here and take a look."

"If I did that, I'd have to leave my desk."

"Take a break, come on over."

"Sorry, too busy. Must work."

"Don't say I didn't give you an opportunity."

"Less talk, more work."

And then we let an hour pass before addressing each other again. Angeline was nowhere to be found. The rumor was that she had finished early. Too me, it seemed a ludicrous notion. No one ever finished early; rather, one was finished whenever the deadline arrived; not a moment sooner. Angeline, however, had a more poetic style of design, she tended to have simple themes that she would explore, coming up with a scheme quickly. Her decisions were more often intuitive, and she was less likely to define the logic that dictated her design. If it was true that she had finished early, I was in no way envious, just pissed off.

At what hour, I don't know, but sometime mid-afternoon, Angeline walked into the studio. Her skin was slightly pink, and she still wore sunglasses despite the relative darkness of the studio. Her top, hugging her body and not quite touching the top of her shorts, made her seem younger, almost a teenager. She had tied up her black hair, letting strands fall across her face, past her eyes. She seemed less a near college graduate, and more a girl prepared for a summer holiday.

"Nicky, when are you going to take a break?" She walked to my desk and put her arm around my shoulder.

"A break? The designs are due tomorrow, this is the big push."

"Yes, I know, the home stretch, but you haven't moved from that spot. When are you going to come out and play?" She twisted back and forth, adopting a mock girlie pose. I looked down at my bare feet next to hers in sandals. There might as well have been a chain around my leg, bolted to the desk.

"Angeline, you haven't really finished your design?"

"Finished it? No, but I've stopped working on it. It's done, if that's what you're getting at."

"I should be so lucky. How did you finish so quickly?"

"Nick, when did you lose your hearing? I told you, I didn't finish; I got tired of working on it. This is Rome, I want to spend my time outside, not hunched over a desk."

"I'm not hunched."

"You're design looks fine, why not take a break?"

"I need time to render the colors, I'll be lucky to finish at all."

"Fine. If you're too busy, maybe I can pry Pierce free from his desk."

Pierce looked up. "You two should go ahead; all work and no play- " He smiled and went back to his work.

"Are you happy with your design?" I asked Angeline.

"Yes, very happy."

"Can I see it?"

"Already turned it in."

"Were you just happy to be rid of it, or are you confident you can win?"

"Both. Look, I've put time into the design all term, and it'll give yours a good run, but I'm not going to sweat over it just to be a martyr for architecture." She now had pulled off her sunglasses and held them with arms crossed, her shoulders pulled forward.

I continued drawing, viewing her from my periphery, "How about we grab food tomorrow after the designs are judged?"

"Nick, we haven't spent any time together these last couple days, you're so addicted to your drawings, you can't even look at me. Maybe if I were a five-hundred year old statue I could get you to sketch me?"

"Can you give me just a day?"

"What is it with you? You can't even take one hour right now. Lunch, are you going to eat? You can't even take a lunch with me?"

Angeline had stopped twisting back and forth, now remaining ridged, eyeing me, waiting for a reply. I did want to be with her, but finishing the competition was important too. This, after all, was the same girl who seemed to pick her moments of affection, only to disappear when it suited her. I grabbed her hand, prying her crossed arms apart. Wordlessly, I kissed her fingers.

"What does that mean? Do you want to spend time together, or no?" Though the studio was nearly empty, her words were a whisper. After she spoke, she looked at Pierce, as if hoping for support. He simply cleared his throat, studying his drawings.

"I always want to, but sometimes I can't," I said.

"And now is a time when you can't? Class isn't in session, there's next to nobody else here. Nick, I want to be with you more, but you seem to want to be with me less."

"I've been trying to spend time with you this entire summer; won't we have time when classes are finished? Come here." I pulled her hand to my lips and kissed her again, she offered no resistance, but remained silent. "Angeline, come back after six, I'll take a dinner break. Let me have some time to work. I can even find you, you'll be in your room?"

She shrugged, but was noncommittal. Her shoulders were starting to turn even a little more pink, save two long white stripes, hidden by her top.

"You're burned, too much time in the sun."

"Pale skin; burns easily, but it'll turn to tan." She walked over to Pierce, and leaned against his desk. "Don't tell me you're camping out in studio as well."

"Honestly, I've been looking for an excuse to break. Lunch?" He asked.

"Let's."

"We'll leave Nicholas to his sketches, no sense rocking his boat."

Pierce locked up his desk, leaving his drawings taped to the top. They left together, Angeline avoiding my gaze upon exiting.

Pierce returned alone about an hour later. As he walked past me, he slid two pieces of pizza bianca on top of my desk, following them with a San Pellegrino; that was the only time I had pizza delivered in Italy.

After a few more hours had passed, I set down my pen and stretched my arms. My fingers had begun to cramp. It seemed silly that completing a design might become a physical battle. I liked to think of what I did as an exercise for my mind, each design problem a parallel bars of logic. To be slowed by something as pedestrian as a hand cramp seemed nearly cruel. I shook out my hands, and then rolled my eyes several times to avoid fatigue.

"Pierce, how late do you intend to be here?"

"Little longer, but not much."

"Any guess when that will be?"

"No."

"But you won't be up all night?"

"Don't mind me, you should take a break with your lady friend."

"This isn't a break, I'm giving my fingers a rest. Besides, you shouldn't eavesdrop."

"Wasn't eavesdropping. If you don't meet her for a break, I promise, I will." He continued working without looking up from his drawings. Pierce had used a thick paper with a heavily toothed texture, thick so not to buckle as he brushed his water colors. He had a tin can on his desk with an assortment of brushes and foam pads, all well used, but still in good condition. He stood at his desk, allowing his arms to get full extension, giving him greater control of his brush.

"Pierce, will your competition be enough to take the prize?"

"Sadly, no."

"You're that certain?" I was surprised. "Your work is always first rate, I can't believe that."

"Thank you, but my design will not be complete in time."

"Your drawings are done, can't you turn them in?"

"The watercolors will not be finished, which is fine. I've traveled quite a bit, and will certainly travel a good bit more. There are others who can use the opportunity better than I."

"You've worked pretty hard not to finish."

"I'll finish, but not in time for judging. Like I said, I'll work until it's done."

"What will you do when the studio is over?"

"Back to the states."

"And once there?"

"Work or teach."

"Anything lined up?"

"I've talked with a friend, an Interior Designer, who has just started working. Time's are fat, and they have more work than they can handle; that's the good news."

"The bad?"

"I've not been impressed with the work done by the office; not certain it's the place for me." Pierce looked up from his drawings.

The studio typically didn't overheat, despite little breeze, and seemed easily more comfortable than the blistering heat outdoors. I shuffled across the cool concrete floor to Pierce's desk. His drawings were exceptional, the level of detail demanded that the eye linger over the drawing, taking in each pen stroke.

"Sure you couldn't turn those in? They don't suffer from lack of color."

"Quite sure."

"Have you talked to Ron, is he finished with his design?"

"I don't think he's done, and I'm not sure he cares. His project didn't ever get off the ground, disappointing."

"I've seen him do good work in the past."

"But no good work in the present. I think he's enamored with Rome. Wants to spend every moment exploring the city."

"Good for him."

Pierce set down his brush, stacked his papers, and put away the rest of his tins, paints, and pens. "Nicholas, my day is done. I'm laying down the brush."

"Leaving?"

"If you don't mind, I'm going to find Angeline and grab some food; she seemed a little out of sorts."

"She seemed in great sorts to me – spent her entire day in the sun. Tell her I'll catch up with her tomorrow."

I remained at my desk, completing my remaining line-work and beginning to add color. The studio empty, I was determined to complete my renderings for the competition. As I labored, I glanced at a clock; eleven. I had forgotten to find Angeline, and she had not bothered coming back to the studio.

My eyes ached, dry and stinging, I blinked wide and rolled them from side to side. It was well past midnight when I set down my pencils. I tried to stretch out my back, but felt so fatigued that I simply slouched on the stool. I regarded the drawings that would comprise my competition entry. I don't know that I've ever been more proud of a design. I felt as though I had actually captured something in my building that was worth preserving and would stand up to any other competition entry. I was finally ready to let them go, and call the drawings finished.

The boards complete, I stacked them on top of each other, leaving them on my desk. I would clip them to pieces of foam core in the morning for display. Worn down, I lumbered up the stairs to my apartment above the studio. Before falling asleep, my mind wandered, imagining the cities I might visit if I were fortunate enough to take the prize. As I drifted in and out of sleep, a summer rain gathered in the sky and fell, washing the streets and relaxing my mind, allowing me to finally sleep.

5

Morning came quickly. The air was moist and cool; the first rain in weeks had washed the cobblestones, and pavement. It seemed unusual to look outside and see a gray sky, dominated by a patchwork of clouds. Water continued to drip from windowsills, though the rain had ceased. Cooled by the moisture, the air remained sticky, feeling heavy, coating the skin. The streets gave off a musty smell, as if the dampness had been lingering for weeks rather than hours.

Having woken just before the rain stopped, I threw my bed sheet to the ground and sat up, running my hand through my short hair. Wearing only a pair of boxers, I padded across the stone floor to the kitchen. After a bowl of dry cereal, I quickly threw on clothes, deciding to shower after grabbing a morning coffee.

Down the stairs, I took a detour to the studio; I wanted to look at my drawings again, feeling both paranoid and protective. Opening the door to the studio, still groggy from sleep, I looked across the room at the window adjacent to my desk. Even as I stared, droplets of water sputtered from the edge of my desk, splashing to a puddle below. I followed the path of water from floor, to desktop, and then to open window; I was stunned. My drawings lay, stuck to the desk, colors bleeding together and muddied. I lifted a corner of the soggy paper, gingerly at first; the corner tore easily, most of the drawing still stuck to the desk. Small patches of the design were still intelligible, but the plans were unreadable, the ink blurred and faded.

I pounded my fist on the desk, sending droplets of water into the air. I was furious, but had nowhere to direct my anger. My ruined drawings lay, plastered to the desk, still soaking up more water. Overnight, my design, which had been a contender for the prize, had been reduced to a sponge. I had been so tired, I couldn't even remember opening the window. Yet that simple oversight had left my drawings exposed, the rain shower soaking every page.

My face felt hot, and my eyes stung. I was angry with myself for leaving the window open, but mostly I was angry that I had left the drawings out. I had sketches on trace paper, but they weren't presentable, there was no design to be judged. I pulled the tatters of drawings up from my desk in pieces and threw the rags to the floor. I wanted to scream, but with no one to hear me, there was little point. I stormed out of the studio in disgust, slamming the door and hissing obscenities as I pounded down the stairs. My own carelessness had lost me the competition.

6

I spent the morning alone, all the other students gathered to see the competitions judged. I had skipped the review; with nothing to present, I had no stomach to watch the prize awarded to someone else. After morning turned to late afternoon, I had had my fill of solitude. The competition had ended hours earlier, so I sought out Pierce, hoping to gain some perspective. We took a bus out of town, both needing to get away, and chose the Catacombs as our refuge. Just outside the city walls, the early Christians had buried their deceased in underground cemeteries, as was mandated by Roman law. Aside from the history of the tourist attraction, the catacombs were also several degrees cooler than the streets, making it a refuge for both the living and the dead. For centuries, the bones of the deceased accrued, filling four levels of the subterranean caverns. A system of tunnels wound through the earth, connecting countless rooms and niches, where bodies where stacked upon bodies. They decomposed quickly, leaving only anonymous discolored skeletons. The tombs were a network of interconnecting passageways hewn from volcanic stone. Large niches, called loculi, were excavated large enough to hold two or three bodies.

We both stood in the aisle of the bus, holding onto the grab bar above for balance. The floor had a thin layer of dust that stirred up each time we shuffled our feet, coating them and settling onto our sandals.

"Was there a good crowd?" I asked.

"Hard to find a place to stand, lots of people. Many Italians, some professors that Rice knows," Pierce said. He looked at me as if waiting for me to say more, then continued. "We were a person short, though – where were you?"

"Walking, I just spent the time walking."

"Nick, I don't follow – you had a great design, people were asking about you."

"There's not much I can tell you; my competition entry blew up, I ruined my drawings. I had them all finished, and then they were gone."

"Finished and then gone? You're losing me, I saw you the day before. You're drawings were nearly ready to turn in."

"Nearly, but somewhere between nearly and completely, I ruined them."

"Nick, what happened?"

"Not now, it makes me sick to think about it."

"Sorry. We both come to Rome but neither pins up a competition. Seems that we both burned ourselves."

The bus took a sharp corner, and we staggered to regain balance. Instinctively, I reached down to pat my wallet. The bus out of town was notorious for pick-pockets. Pierce carried no wallet, rather he had stuffed cash and a small map in his pocket. A button was all that separated him from a would-be thief.

"What would you have done if you had won?" I asked.

"Travel to Greece. I haven't been. That's a place everyone should visit, at least once."

"My traveling days are done, at least for a long while."

"Tired of travel?"

"Not tired, but I've got to find a job. It may be some time before I'm able to break away. Would have been good to see a little more of the world."

"World's a big place; better find excuses to see it."

"Pierce, I haven't asked anyone how it turned out."

"How's that?"

"The competition, who won?"

"I thought you knew; you haven't talked to anyone since the prize was awarded, have you?"

I shook my head. "Not really, I've laid low."

"Haven't talked to Angeline?"

"She seems a little mad, I was going to wait until she cooled down."

"What's going on between you two? I don't mean to pry but I'm assuming the bottle has run dry?"

"How do you mean?"

"You're both pulling away."

"No, you're wrong. I don't know where you got that idea."

"Sorry, it's just clear that things aren't right."

"Short term, we're just in a rough spot, nothing more."

"Nicholas, you two aren't talking."

"Wrong," I said, shaking my head, trying to play his comment off as a joke.

"Then why haven't you two talked since the competitions were reviewed?"

"It's only been a day, not a big deal."

"Nicholas, she won – It's a huge honor for her, but you two haven't even talked about it."

"She won?"

"How could you not know?"

"She didn't tell me."

"Tell me again how you're still talking to each other."

The bus stopped once more picking up a few more tourists. By now, there was no more room, passengers standing shoulder to shoulder. I had no reply for Pierce, and couldn't tell if he expected one or not. I wanted to be happy for Angeline, wanted to feel happy for her accomplishment. Yet I realized how quickly we had come apart.

"Tell me about it, lots of fanfare?" I asked.

"Of course, she was very happy. I know she's wanted to travel quite a bit; I think Italy is the first time she's been abroad. She's not ready to pack it in, too much yet to see."

"That's good. If she's happy, then that's good. I wish I had been there to see it."

"The entries are still on display, will be pinned up for a couple days. Rice asked about your design, he was surprised that you were a no show."

"I'll tell you more, just not on the bus," I said eyeing the herd of tourists sitting and standing, leaning against each other every time the bus changed speeds. Most probably didn't speak English, but I was in no mood for an audience. I patted my wallet again, happy to know that it hadn't moved.

We reached the catacombs and found a long line of visitors waiting to enter. There were several lines, each marked by a different flag, indicating the language spoken by the guide. Pierce began walking toward the British flag, but I grabbed him.

"No, I'd rather just walk without hearing what they're saying."

"You'd prefer a German tour?"

"Yes. Look, I just want to get lost in a crowd."

"Then the catacombs will be perfect, we can get lost amongst the dead."

The air inside was cool, though there was no breeze. For the first time in months, I felt cold, bumps raising on my arms. Pierce and I lagged behind the group of ten other tourists, who were listening intently. The guide moved slowly, pointing at the cavernous walls. We walked past empty niches, which had at one time contained the remains of saints. The caverns muffled the guide's speech, although it made little difference to me.

I was disappointed to discover that all of the bones had been removed years ago, eliminating most of the intrigue of visiting a centuries old burial site. We walked past row after row of empty niches, providing no evidence of the bodies that had lay for centuries. The actual remains had long ago been removed, never to be viewed. Only the stucco and frescos betrayed any hint of the original purpose of the niches.

As we continued, we made our way into a chamber that held resin recreations of the bones that had sat in the actual catacombs. The walls held shelves of skulls, as if it were some macabre department store. Femurs stacked neatly with femurs and skulls heaped upon skulls in anonymous piles. No person had any identity, each becoming little more than a decoration, a nameless accessory to the walls. What had once been testimony to religious determination was now only bait for tourists.

"I can only hope that when I die, my skull will be displayed with this much reverence," Pierce said.

"Each of us has a skeleton hidden beneath our skin. I can only hope that mine never ends up in a warehouse like this. I like to think that I can bury my mistakes in places where no one can find them."

"Nick, you've nothing to be ashamed of."

"I feel stupid; I threw away my opportunity."

"You'll have other competitions."

"Other chances to lose, more opportunities to squander?"

"Your entry was good, you can at least feel good about that." Pierce seemed uneasy, twisting his ring around and around on his finger.

"I lost more than the competition, I lost Angeline. I'm not likely to have another opportunity to win her."

"Don't blame yourself."

"Who else is there to blame?"

Pierce looked around, "Blame the bones, blame the skeletons that lay buried beneath the city. Civilization hides its mistakes in the catacombs, you can point a finger to the idle metacarpals."

"Spare me the melodrama; I defeated myself, I left open the window that ruined my design, and I drove Angeline away. I don't need any help burying myself; I dug a hole and stepped right in."

"What happened to you in studio? Enough innuendo, how did you ruin your design?"

I shrugged my shoulders. "I had the whole thing done. I mean, the drawings were done and the only thing I needed to do was turn it in. I don't know how late it was, and I went to sleep. When I came downstairs in the morning, there was just nothing left. I must have forgotten to close the window, and every last drawing was soaked. Two whole terms of work, and in one night it was ruined."

Pierce looked away. I've never liked pity, and I wasn't asking him to feel sorry for me. He just shook his head, hiding his expression with his hands.

"So, that's why I was a no show today when they judged the designs; it's my own fault. And I should have been there for Angeline, but I screwed that up too."

"Nicholas, don't do this." He stopped and looked around at the racks of bones, each a resin facsimile displayed for the benefit of tourists. "You shouldn't blame yourself. This shouldn't be a big deal; who cares, right? We're only students, and none of this should matter. We've the rest of our lives as adults to beat up ourselves over our regrets."

"I loved her. If only I could have made her see that."

Pierce remained silent, his head down, drawing circles in the dirt with his foot. We had lagged far behind the tour group, and the guide's speech was nearly inaudible.

"It's not your fault."

"Sorry, there's just no where else for me to point the finger."

"Many things happened; many things out of your control. Please don't beat yourself up."

"I know you're right. But how could everything fall apart so fast?"

"Nicholas, don't berate yourself - How do you even know if you were the one who left the window open? How do you know that you're responsible for the drift between you and Angeline? There's a lot to life that's out of your hands."

"Sure, I know."

"Do you?"

"I know that in a couple days, I'll be on a plane back to the states. I know that school's finished, and I've got to look ahead to the fall. I'm done with my education."

"You're going to be okay, right?"

"I think this air is getting to me. Does the smell in here bother you? So musty, makes me a little ill. Any reason to finish the tour?"

"No, we're done. Let's get back up."

We made our way, backtracking through the catacombs, pushing through a group of English speaking tourists as we broke through the entrance and into the heat of the mid afternoon sun.

7

I waited.

My summer was nearly finished; only the denouement of the journey home remained. On the flight to Rome, I had wanted nothing more than to read my books on Italy and talk to others who had already been. I had practiced my Italian, ambitious to learn more, hopeful to sound like it was second nature. I had slept little, despite the long flight, unable to keep my mind from churning and imagining the next twenty weeks. However, as I sat in the airport, preparing for my return, there was no such expectation. I wasn't looking forward to returning, but I also had no desire to stay any longer; I was simply tired. I wanted my journey home to be done, I was ready for life to return to what it had once been.

However, my flight was not scheduled to depart for two hours. I sat with my bags in the waiting area. I had emptied a small box of chocolate peanuts, and had several small bags of snacks to last me on my flight home. I was to meet Angeline. We had agreed to eat lunch together before my flight. She would continue her journey, eager to travel on the stipend from her competition prize. However, it was half past noon, and no Angeline.

It was in studio that I had seen her last, both of us cleaning out our desks, the term complete. At first I simply smiled, uncertain of what to say; there seemed to be so much unsaid. She must have known I was still in love with her. But I could sense awkwardness between us.

"Congratulations, I talked to Pierce, he told me."

"Told you what?"

"I got together with him yesterday, and he told me the whole story."

"Why did you talk to Pierce. What did he say?"

"You know; I'm happy for you, your design was really good."

"You like my design?" She asked, setting down the drawings that she was packing. "Thanks, it's going to be exciting."

"How long are you going to be traveling?"

"The stipend will probably hold up for about two months. I'm supposed to write a paper. They're going to make me give a presentation, I had no idea winning would be more work."

"Life's never fair. So, we won't be flying back together."

She nodded.

"Well, I never got to properly congratulate you." I put my arm around her, kissing her cheek. "You really deserved it, I'm going to miss you."

Giving me a squeeze, she said, "We've had a hell of a good time, huh?" She smiled.

304

"Before my flight, let's get together. We can take a long lunch, soak up a little more summer. It'll be two months before I see you again."

Again she smiled, and nodded.

"Maybe I'll even have a job by the time you fly to Portland," I said.

"Ready to start working hard?"

"Well, ready to start working anyway. You know my motto, if you can't do something properly, you might as well do it half-assed."

She laughed.

"I am going to miss you, Nicky."

I grabbed a sheet of paper and copied my flight information. "Here, meet me outside the gate – let's say noon?"

"Yes, noon."

"Good."

"Too bad we can't both travel, we'd have such a damn good time together."

She placed a stack of drawings and sketchpads into a box, then finished taping it shut. Her desk empty, she began walking away.

"Yes," I said. "We always do."

I studied the clock. It counted off forty minutes, then an hour. I was alone in the airport, and I realized that she was not coming. The thought occurred to me to walk around, see if she was looking for me. But I already knew. Sometimes pretending is easier. Sometimes words left unsaid are the most profound. My flight would leave in an hour, and my summer would be over.

Chapter VII

T Squares and Sympathy

[Summer 2001]

1

R epetition can bring order. But patterns don't allow for change, and cycles of behavior become compulsive. When I first learned about design, there was joy in the doing; the process itself had value. But at some point, my habits and attitudes changed, my focus moved too much toward fulfilling other people's expectations. And I found myself engaging in the same behavior for so long, that I forgot that there was any other way to be. Making the wrong choices over and over, I felt like an addict, unable to find sobriety. My life was imitating art, and I understood that I was in desperate need of intervention.

I sat at my drafting table, sketching the same schemes again and again, knowing that Harlan would have no part of it. I had spent the better part of the morning re-working the drawing Janet and I had shown him. I taped pieces of trace over the plans, and had sketched several iterations of the schemes Harlan had described. It almost seemed pointless to start with the plans we had shown him, as the design held little similarity to our original scheme.

I couldn't focus, my mind constantly wandered, rehashing my evening out with Angeline. I tried to understand the difference between what I wanted and what I needed; and then chastised myself for wanting what I knew would only bring me down. In the end, I forgot all about what was good for me – want trumped need. I called Andrew at his studio and invited myself. I was tired of guessing; I was going to prove my suspicions.

His studio was east of the river, the opposite side of town from the university. In a shared space, on the second level of what had once been a warehouse, Andrew developed his skills as a painter. Several artists used the warehouse as a place to paint, sculpt, or draw, each getting a small portion for work and for storage. At one time, this enclave of artists would have been found in the Pearl district itself, perhaps not far from the Angry Pear. But the Pearl District was quickly losing its industrial flavor, as boutiques and restaurants fought for space in the now trendy area. And as the rule goes, when money moves in, the artists move out. Much of the creative energy that had sustained the Pearl District sought the lower rents of the eastside's industrial area; that is, until the day that the eastside is discovered and rents go up, forcing the artists to migrate once again.

I drove over a gravel road, and parked a block away from a run of train tracks. In daylight, the street seemed pretty safe, still, I jammed my CDs and stereo under the driver's seat and out of sight. The front door to Andrew's building was not locked, and offered no friendly list of tenants. In fact, once inside the building, there was really no indication of where to go, or even that there was anything to see. The entry foyer had bare, unfinished floors and a stack of scrap plywood to the side. Instead of an elevator, there was only an empty pit surrounded by a cage. The only hint that the building was occupied was a small sign on a stand at the far end of the foyer. It read, 'studios on upper floors'. With scarcely enough light to see the steps, I made my way up to the third floor. This routine was not new, I had been to Andrew's studio before, but I was always relieved to note that the staircase was still standing after I got to the top.

Only a skylight lit the hall, providing an even wash across the floor. While still in the hallway, I could already smell turpentine fumes; Andrew's door was open. He stood in front of a large sheet of paper that was taped to the wall. Hands stained with black charcoal, he moved them quickly over the paper, never acknowledging my presence.

"Knock, knock."

"Come in, what's up, Nick?"

"Thought I'd come by your studio."

"Hasn't changed since you were here last."

"New paintings, though. You've been busy."

Andrew had a series of makeshift vertical shelves tall enough to hold enormous canvases. Inside, he had several frames leaning against one another. Two easels were facing the window, obscured from view. All the windows were open, and a large fan ran on high, blowing fumes outside.

"Can I see your new work?"

"See it? You can see it, but only when it's finished. I'd rather show it to you as a series." He looked back at his drawing and added a few small strokes. He no longer seemed intent on the drawing, but would not look away.

"That's not like you, Andrew. Usually you demand I offer feedback on your work. Has my advice been so bad that you'd rather not hear it?"

"No, that's not why. I'd just rather wait until it's all finished."

"So, you're agreeing that my advice has been bad?"

"Sorry, too many fumes for me to follow your verbal gymnastics. How about we grab a drink; I could use a break."

"You really do need some air in here. But I don't want to break your rhythm if you're working."

"No drink? This part of town is a little out of your way for so short a visit, let's go relax a little."

"A drink? It's not even noon."

"No, not like a cocktail. I've got beers downstairs. Everyone renting space here shares a fridge."

We left the studio; Andrew locked the door but let his fan continue to run. The refrigerator sat in the basement, loudly humming and heating up the small room. We picked through a number of plastic bags and open bottles before finding a stash of Coors Light cans in the back. We found shade outside, behind the building, and drank facing the train tracks. I sat on a concrete curb and cracked open a can, Andrew leaned against a metal guardrail.

"Last time you visited my studio, how many paintings did I have?"

"No more than three or four."

"Now, at least a dozen. It's been fast."

"More portraits?" I asked tipping back the can.

"Mostly. I think they're good. It feels good to work quickly anyway. I work faster when I have something to say, when I'm inspired."

"A muse?" I said between swallows, finishing most of the can.

"You mean a lady for posing? To sit for a portrait."

"Don't your ladies always do more than sit?

"Only if so inclined."

"Inclined or reclined? And how much time spent posing versus imposing?"

"Nick, I'm an art major, you're going to have to keep your words simple."

"To be blunt, I'm asking how the ladies are treating you." I said, opening another can.

"They always treat me as well as I treat them."

"That bad?"

"No, that good," he said. "Look, Nick, what are you driving at?"

"Not driving, just drinking." I held up my can as if to remind him.

"You and me are different, Nick."

"How so?"

"Relationships mean something different for us. I don't load them up with expectations, and I'm content to let them run their course."

"Doesn't that just mean you like to avoid entanglements?"

"No – means that a good relationship doesn't always last."

"It only lasts until your paintings are finished? But isn't that just a way of limiting how much you invest in the relationship?"

"I don't agree; I just like to limit the amount of baggage a girl brings to a relationship."

"Baggage is what; emotional turmoil, a jealous lover, a child?

"You've got me wrong, I've dated girls with all of the above?"

"You went out with a woman with a kid? I never knew that."

"It didn't last long."

"No?"

"Dating a girl with a kid is sort of like cleaning up after a party you didn't get to attend."

I smiled, but said nothing.

"Nick, you didn't come here just to see my paintings. Why not just say what you came to say?"

I didn't answer. I simply stared straight ahead, following the tracks, watching their progress through the streets of the warehouse district. Cutting through gravel, then carving into thick asphalt, the steel rails traveled with an uncaring and relentless purpose. Once put in place, the tracks became the standard by which direction was determined and distance measured. By comparison, debris littered the gravel providing an ephemeral quality that emphasized the permanence of the rail. A flattened cardboard box supported a faded heap of fraying rags. In time, the rags would scatter or disintegrate, but the rails would remain. I took another drink from my can and continued to question Andrew, still unwilling to get right to the point.

"I did come to see your paintings, in particular your new work," I said.

"Maybe I'll someday have a show in the gallery you're designing."

"Wouldn't that be nice for both of us?"

"Hell of a nice thing, if it happens."

"That is, if the gallery happens," I said. "I begin to wonder if he wants our design, or if Janet and I are simply cheap labor. We're re-scheming."

"Does he intend to build at all?"

310

"As far as I know. He wants us to work on documents. So something will be built, I suppose. What that will be, though, I don't know."

"Janet's worked with him before? Doesn't that count for something?"

"Yes, but for how much, I don't know."

I had questions at the tip of my tongue, but was trying not to be too direct. I really had no business demanding information of Andrew. But, if he was involved with Angeline, I wanted to know. Perhaps he was content with brief affairs, but I wanted something steady, something I could count on. I wasn't into sharing, and I had decided not to be strung along. Andrew was a friend, but I wanted him out of the picture.

"Perhaps we have something in common," I said.

"Besides pissing away an afternoon drinking beer by the train tracks?"

"You're studio's been busy, with all the visitors knocking on your door."

"How's that?"

"I talked with Angeline, she mentioned that she's seen your studio, she seemed impressed."

"Impressed was she? Good, I never understand how I could leave a good impression; some people are easily fooled."

"Look, I'm not pretending it's my business – but I'm going to stick my nose in it anyway. What's with you and Angeline?"

"So, you did come by for more than a peek at my work," he said. He set down his can, and folded his arms. "That's what this is about."

"Let's quit dancing, is she your model? Has she been your fling while you finish up this series of paintings?"

"Well, you're right about one thing, it really isn't any of your business," he said shaking his head.

"You knew that I've been interested in her, you knew that she means something to me. And for you it means what? Just one more cast off relationship?"

"Nick, relax." He sipped his beer and looked away. "It isn't your business, but Angeline and I aren't involved." He paced to the side, his hands now on his hips.

"She's come by to look at my work, that's it. I haven't painted her, and we're not involved. It's great that she means something to you, good to know."

"She hasn't been your model?"

"I just said she wasn't, do you want me to write an oath? She's not a model, so don't worry."

"I'm sorry, I just assumed. I mean, you won't let me look at your work, so I thought you were hiding it."

"Why hide it? Just because you'd freak out like this if I was seeing her? Don't worry, I'm telling you that I've never painted Angeline – there's nothing between us."

I had nothing left to say. I had assumed the worst, and had blown up. I finished my beer, and left Andrew to continue his work.

2

The day progressed slowly, I had little interest in doing anything other than hunkering down in my apartment and letting the rest of the weekend pass me by. I lost myself in television, never settling on a channel, just moving up and down the dial. Evening approached, and I decided to take advantage of the weather and cook outside.

Stuffing newspaper at the bottom of my grill, I stacked coals in an efficient pyramid and drizzled lighter fluid over the pyre. I tossed in a match and watched the newspaper quickly turn to ashes. I couldn't resist shooting short bursts of lighter fluid into the barbecue; each time the flames rose, I cut off the stream, narrowly averting disaster. I let the coals smolder while steaks soaked in a bowl of honey and barbecue.

According to building codes, my tiny inferno on the third level balcony was prohibited. Current rules demanded a sprinklered balcony in order to accommodate any urban grilling. But laws are funny things. It seems to me that any law is basically an agreement; and I had never been asked if I agreed with the code. More

312

to the point, I wasn't entirely convinced that I could cook any other way. The number of recipes I could manage was limited, and my ability to cook with anything besides a grill or microwave was nonexistent. So, I reasoned that grilling steaks was primarily a matter of survival.

Sitting on my balcony, I felt a part of the city. It was as though the street became one large living room. The summer evenings were still hot, though the days were rushing toward autumn. And with my balcony on the East side, I received little direct sun after noon, making the reality of changing seasons even more real.

Despite the prospect of change, there were some constants. Above the murmur of the street, a comforting and off key voice could be heard marking time with a guitar. The elderly cowboy was standing on his usual street corner holding his instrument, shoulders slouching, while he drawled in his monotone. His accompaniment on tambourine was nowhere to be found, making his lonely song almost poignant, if that was possible. I imagined he was singing a song about loss, although I couldn't actually make out any words.

I waited for the coals to heat up, then poked them with a spatula scattering them evenly under the grill. I tossed on a steak and waited for summer to end.

"Hey there, you. Didn't realize I lived next door to a chef. Smells like protein; what are you cooking?" Carly appeared on her balcony, waving to me. She leaned out over the guardrail as we chatted.

"Steak, want some?"

"Love some, can you toss one over?"

"I've got another in the kitchen, how 'bout I throw it on?"

"Nick, you're so sweet, grilling meat for me," she laughed.

"Honestly, come on around, we'll make it a party."

"Your door open?"

"Wide."

She left her balcony, and I went back into my kitchen, grabbing the remainder of dinner. I placed it on the grill, letting it get friendly with the other steak. Sizzling together, the meat provided background for the cowboy's staccato song. A minute went by as I waited for Carly, then I heard my front door open, and she bounced onto the balcony carrying two bottles of cold beer.

"See, much nicer out here after you've planted a garden," Carly said surveying the greenery.

"What makes the difference are the steaks and beers."

"Believe what you like."

Carly sat in her chair, her legs curled beneath her. She hadn't bothered putting on shoes, exposing her painted toes, polish chipped and fading. She was wearing a tight knit pullover with a hood in back, and a pair of faded linen shorts. It seemed that she also was preparing for the change in seasons.

"You haven't given me any updates; any news on your romance?"

"Updates?"

"With your lady friend, wasn't I going to act as your romantic confidant? I can't give you advice if you don't keep me up to speed on the situation."

"Well, there seems to always be a situation."

I smiled but didn't immediately expand on that thought. There was little about the situation that I was eager to discuss. I had just badgered a good friend, prying about a relationship that I was not certain either of us was even in. Rather than attempt to express my feelings, I instead brooded and internalized my frustration. There seemed so little point in expressing anything. Among other things, it had occurred to me that Carly might be a much better pursuit than Angeline; if for no other reason, I at least could make sense of what Carly wanted.

"There's a new situation, but I can't really make sense of it."

"Well, Nick, we both know you can't make sense of romantic situations; that's why you've enlisted me to help."

"Refresh my memory, what's in it for you?"

"Steaks, of course."

"Fair trade."

"Details, I need details."

"I can't tell if I'm in love with the girl or in love with who I want her to be."

"You're a guy. Guys are always interested in who they want a girl to be."

"So what do I do?"

"Well, Nick, I can give you advice but I can't tell you what to do."

"I think I keep making the same mistakes; No, I know I keep making the same mistakes."

"If you want my perspective, tell me the story. What's happened?"

I didn't know how much to tell Carly. I wanted to spill my whole story, and have her sort out the dilemma. But there were details I wanted to keep. There was no way to give enough detail for her to understand, while maintaining any privacy. I began by relating the high points of my dinner with Angeline, but I chose not to delve into my visit to Andrew's studio. However, I rarely strayed far from vague information, my forte.

"Nick, it's not clear to me what you want   is it clear to you?"

"Does it matter what I want?"

"What could matter more?"

"What I want is not nearly as significant as *what I'm likely to get.*"

"Amazing - If you don't know what you want, it can't be any secret what you're likely to get. Why are you so reluctant to tell this girl how you feel?"

"But she knows."

"Does she?"

"I believe so. I think we both want different things."

"Nick, tell her and be done with it. If you want different things, find out so you can move on."

The truth was that I didn't want to move on. I wanted to reclaim something that had moved on without me. I turned over the steaks and brought out two knives, two forks, and two plates. We sat waiting for the meat to cook.

"Carly, what about you? What's your story?"

"My story – which story?"

"Nobody steady?"

"Not yet, just you and these steaks. For tonight, I only have a date with a rib eye. That's what I like about summer, you don't really have to have a plan. It's good just to relax."

"Easier to relax now that the temperature's cooled a bit. Won't be long before the leaves fall and it's time to watch football."

"First game of the season: you, me, and a couple steaks. Deal?"

"Deal."

We tapped our beer bottles together and took a swig to seal our oath. I poked at the rib eyes, and cut into one, the center still pink. I gave each just another minute, not wanting to risk drying out the meat. I always like to serve a steak slightly rare; there's no excuse for an overdone piece of meat, a good chef always knows when to quit.

Later that evening, my cell phone rang. It was late; usually I let it ring and take a message, but Janet's ID came up on the screen. I felt a small amount of guilt, knowing that I had made little progress on the gallery design over the weekend. However, we had been going non-stop with the drawings for so long, that I hardly felt I had sinned.

"Janet, it's late – what couldn't wait?"

"Sorry, Nicholas, I didn't think it was late." I looked at my clock, it was nearly eleven. "Anyway," she continued, "I got word today that Pierce is going to be released any day. They're still monitoring, he's gotten pretty weak with all the bed-rest, but it could be very early this week."

"Good, we'll have to help do some shopping for him. Last I talked to him, he was still out of sorts."

"Unfortunately his hand will never be the same. He'll undergo some rehab, but for what I don't know," she said. I cringed as I contemplated the likelihood of

Pierce having insurance. Then again, if he had nothing, he already would have been sent home with a pack of band-aids and some bactine.

"I'll call to get his official release time, and I'll help get him settled back at home. Maybe I'll find some old hospital gowns so he has something to wear around the house."

"You're a real peach, Nicholas."

"I try."

"One other thing, I talked with Harlan today as well. We've set up a firm date for the revision of our design."

"You mean *his* revision?"

"Whatever – point is, a contractor will be there, so we're also going to go over the budget and set a schedule for permits. Things are getting more real, so we need to work fast."

"Fast or faster? We could really use Pierce, this is a three person job."

"Agreed. But we've got two people."

"Well, I've made some progress on revised drawings. I'll incorporate notes on materials so we can get a budget worked out. Can we also ask for an increased design fee?"

"For the next job, sure." I couldn't tell if Janet was being optimistic or cynical.

3

Monday came too quickly, and I stumbled into the office at nine – late enough that I took the back stairs to avoid walking past the reception desk. I immediately plunged into my work, hoping to make up for lost time, trying to avoid idle chit-chat. But, Ron spotted me and spoiled my plans.

"Nick, I need your stapler."

"You won't bring it back."

"This time, I will."

"Paper clips work just as well."

317

"Nothing like a staple, don't be stingy."

"Ron, you need to embrace the paperless society. Besides, I'm busy."

"You're not busy."

I offered no comment, letting the silence of the office settle in. Bodies sat in front of their computer monitors, dutifully striking their keys slowly. In a great silicon symphony, fingertips gently tapped out discordant rhythms. A hand in accounting issued a call, another hand in business development provided an answer, and the hum of the HVAC system supplied a deep rumbling bass. The performance would have pleased Phillip Glass every bit as much as Phillip Johnson.

"If you're so busy, that means you need to make time for a coffee."

"Where you going to go?"

"Around the block, Coffee People."

"A break would make me a more efficient employee," I reasoned.

"You don't have to convince me, just yourself."

We rode the elevator down, and made a quick journey for caffeine.

"You've got to do me a favor."

"Ron, I owe you nothing."

"Why can't you just hear me out? No reason to shoot me down so quickly."

"Fine, I should wait before shooting you down?"

"A favor, is that so hard, just a favor."

We moved to the front of the line and ordered. Ron threw a quarter into the tip jar and I scowled.

"What are you tipping for?" I asked.

"It's just a quarter."

"What, do we get tips? Do you see me with a cup on my desk begging for change?"

"Nobody's begging."

"But why do you give them extra money, he just filled a cup with coffee; he didn't wait on you, there wasn't any service."

"It's just a tip."

"It's not just a tip, it's tyranny."

"Fine."

"Good."

I sipped my coffee.

"So a favor, you could do that for me."

"Fine."

"You should hook me up."

"How?"

"Not how, but who – with your neighbor."

"Carly?"

"Yeah, that's her name, Carly."

"You don't even know her name."

"I've only met her once."

I didn't want to help Ron. Really, I had no right to refuse; I was making my play for Angeline, and had made as much clear to Ron. Nevertheless, I was inclined to make him earn his own relationship. Why was I suddenly a romantic Santa Claus?

"I'm just asking for another introduction; I'll do all the work, you have no other responsibility or pressure."

"There's nothing in it for me."

"Correct, there is nothing in it for you – we're concerned about my benefit here."

"Will you give me a tip?"

"What?"

"For exemplary service."

"I'll pay for your next coffee."

"Okay, but I intend to get a grande."

"Good, so you're in, tell me your plan."

"My plan? This is your plan."

I was already regretting my words. I hadn't even really agreed to do anything, but Ron interpreted anything other than staunch refusal as agreement. I had the sinking feeling that I should have demanded coffee and a scone, but the die was cast.

"Here's what you could do. Talk to what's her face and get her to meet us at the Angry Pear."

"Am I the chaperone?"

"No, you're the foil."

"Foil?"

"Sure, have you ever read a book? A foil is a literary character who the protagonist plays off of."

"You're the protagonist now?"

"Look, your job is to make me look good."

"So a foil is a sort of jester."

"I'm not calling you a jester; I'm calling you a foil. You just need to introduce us, set me up for some good lines, then get lost. The easiest coffee you'll ever earn."

"I hate being your coffee whore."

"No one ever said you had to like it."

I drained my cup as we walked back to the office. I couldn't shake the feeling that I was preparing to sell out Carly. I knew that Ron was no good for her but she was a big girl and was free to decide; free to say yes or no. Really, she might not even agree to meet us. But I felt a peculiar sense of loyalty to Ron; one that compelled me to agree to his requests. He tended to couch his demands as adhering to some unspoken 'guy code', that all males are obligated to help facilitate each other's romantic endeavors. Bottom line was that I had known Ron longer than Carly, so I was inclined to look after his interests. My real question was whether I needed to make my own interests subservient to his. Talking to Ron had made one thing clear in my own mind. If fate should determine that I could not be with

Angeline, then I had no desire to help Ron hook up with Carly; I was simply not that good a friend.

4

I had called Angeline earlier in the day, but had not left a message. The thought of leaving a message *hanging out there*, waiting for a reply that may or may not materialize, was too painful. Better to talk to her real time or not at all.

I thought back to my conversation with Carly; I believed that she was correct. Even now, looking back, I still can see that she was correct. No matter what the result, I had every reason to tell Angeline how I felt about her. It occurred to me there was every chance that I might be disappointed. But there's power in knowing where one stands, and that was my motivation.

I sat on my living room floor with a cell phone balanced on my knee. Since having resolved to call her, and tell her flat out how I felt, I found myself suddenly filled with doubt. The idea of knowing retained its appeal, but the idea of asking seemed excruciating. I considered that the easiest thing might be to simply ask how she felt about me. But I realized that there was no great statement there; no confession of love to shyly ask another to take the first step.

I began to dial the number. One digit. Then another. Two more digits, halfway there. I needed more time to think, was this still a good idea? In the end, I never answered my question. Instead, I simply dialed three more digits.

"Hello?"

"It's Nicholas."

"Hi, there – What's up?"

"Just a little restless, thought I'd give you a call."

"You too? I've been that way all day, can't seem to relax. Too much on my mind, what's your excuse?"

"Just finished with work. I tried to unwind a bit on the bus, but that never works. Too many people, I stood the whole way. So, now I'm sitting in my apartment wondering what to do with myself."

"Try a chocolate martini, can't be uptight with a sugar drink."

"I didn't say I was uptight."

"That's right, I did – relax, I'm joking."

With the two of us talking about nothing, it seemed such a leap to suddenly turn the conversation into something. I didn't think I could move directly from martini jokes to true confessions, so I continued to fish.

"The summer goes by too fast, there's already a chill," I said.

"Chill? Close your window if you feel a draft. You need a getaway. Find a sunny beach somewhere and take a vacation."

"Got a recommendation?"

"I said a sunny beach, take your pick."

"I'd like to be in Mexico, the beer is cheap and they've still got beaches that aren't on the radar."

"Yeah, and you like to gawk at the ladies," Angeline laughed.

"That, and I can be drunk in public. That's a perfect sunny day, drinking on the beach."

"It sounds like your dream is to be homeless."

"I could work on my tan."

"Do it now, while we still have sunshine." Angeline continued speaking, but my cell phone lost it. I walked to the window and opened it.

"Sorry, one more time," I said

"What's that?"

"Lost it, could you repeat?"

"Oh, nothing worth repeating."

We both waited for the other to speak, finally I blinked.

"Angeline, we have a good time together, right?"

"Always do, just like old times."

"When you moved to Portland, did you think you'd bump into me? I mean, did you think we'd catch up?"

"It's always fun to catch up, you're easy going. I'm relaxed when I'm with you."

"Good."

"There's no hassles with you; laid-back Nicky."

"That's good, right?"

"Sure."

"Honestly, did you think we'd see each other – you remembered that I lived in Portland? We talked about that in school."

"I looked forward to moving to Portland. Lotsa reasons for me to be here."

"I still can't figure out what to do with myself tonight. You're restless too?"

"Something in the air." I imagined that she nodded as she said this.

"Look, I'm kind of talking in circles, but I do have something I need to say. The more I think about this, the harder it is to get the words out, but - hello, sorry are you there?" Noise on the other end, but nothing I could understand. "Angeline?"

"Still here," she said.

"Good," I leaned out the window, hoping to catch some small extra tad of signal. "Did you catch the last bit?"

"You faded out, but your back now."

"Well, I'm stumbling a little bit here, but let me get it out. I called to tell you something specific."

Silence on the other end, then, "Yes, I'm listening. Let it out."

"Angeline, you've said yourself that you're relaxed when you're with me. And for the whole time, years now really, that's gone by since we got to know each other – sorry, I'm struggling for the words, but I'll find them."

"Nick? Sorry, you're breaking up again."

"Really, I'd like to do this face to face. How about this; we need a reason to celebrate, like we used to. The seasons are changing, we should commemorate the occasion. What are you up to this evening?"

"Nicky, this evening's no good."

"How about another?"

"Yes, we'll definitely get together for another."

"Should we pick now?"

"This sounds official, go ahead and pick."

"Is this a busy week?"

"I'll pick for you. This Friday, we'll get together, how's that? I'll meet you at the Pear."

"Friday's a busy night, big crowd. Where should I look for you?"

"I'll be there, just keep your eyes open."

"What time? How's seven?"

"Great, we'll have fun. Say, can we finish later?"

"Sorry?"

"My ride's here. I'll call before Friday."

"Good, that'll be good."

"Love ya', talk soon, bye."

5

The door was ajar when I climbed up the steps; it was pushed open slightly so I didn't have to set down the bags I carried. I had offered to pick up groceries for Pierce, knowing that he would be unable to carry much for some time, if at all. He had been released from the hospital, though he would continue to return for therapy indefinitely. I didn't want to ask if there would be more surgery in his future, further skin grafts and further bandages.

With the list he had given me, I had filled the cart up quickly, adding plenty of additional items I would want if in his position. I took two trips to bring in all the bags, setting them on the counter, then calling upstairs to let him know I had arrived.

At first, no sound. Then shuffling, and his voice from the top of the stairs.

"Nick, great to see you, thanks for stopping by."

"Good to see you out of the hospital and not wearing a gown."

"Miss those, but I'm managing. They are pretty comfortable, though."

"I put all your groceries on the counter. Follow me, and you can tell me where to put them away."

"Please, no need to do that."

"Don't argue, let me do this."

"Well, with only one hand, it's not as though I can stop you."

"That's right, I don't care if you were a boxer, you're without a one-two combination."

"Don't worry, I'd hit you when you weren't looking. You'd be flat on the floor." Pierce smiled only after he said this, giving me a brief moment of pause.

I reached into the large brown paper bags, and pulled out packages. I had been careful to select items that didn't require a full compliment of fingers to open. Flip-top soup cans, at one time seeming just clever, now appeared to be the work of a genius; I had gathered enough cans to last a week. Bottles of beer seemed manageable, so I had not shied away from alcohol. Unfortunately, fresh vegetables seemed too much trouble, between cleaning and chopping, so I opted for frozen packages of peas and corn.

"Like eggs?" I asked. "I decided that with a little practice and perseverance you could probably crack them with one hand. By the way, if it bothers you when I talk about your hand, let me know now."

"Doesn't bother me, and I'll learn to like eggs. You get any cheese?"

"Sorry, I can bring you some."

"Please don't - lactose intolerant, glad you left the cheese in the store."

"Here's a box of breakfast bars, where do they go?" I asked folding up the sack.

"I get those two cupboards there, toss it in anywhere, I'll find it."

Pierce grabbed a beer bottle and tucked it under his arm. Gripping a bottle opener he eased the cap off the bottle, then offered me the open beer, before fumbling with a second. I felt uneasy watching him struggle, but couldn't look away. He still managed his good hand with dexterity, but was not yet practiced enough with his diminished capabilities.

"Mind if we step outside, I need to puff while I drink."

"Sure thing."

"And before you ask, I prefer to light my own cigarette."

We stepped outside through the back door, but there was little yard to step into. A tall wood fence, just ten feet from the back door, contained a small patch of grass with a square concrete patio.

"Janet told me that Harlan has really changed the concept for your gallery," Pierce said.

"You mean *his* gallery."

"Yes, but he's no designer. You and Janet need to push back, make him reconsider."

"I don't think he'll listen."

"Do you have anything to lose?"

"Well, he could always take the project away from us."

"I'm not saying you have to push him over the edge, but test some of his ideas. See what he's really committed to and find where you can insert your ideas."

"I'll see what we can do," I said tipping back my bottle and taking a sip. "What about you? If you're able, you could help out with the design. Have you tried sketching?"

"With this hand, no. No point." Pierce laughed.

"No, no - with your other hand."

"I'm working to build dexterity. At the hospital they had me practice putting on clothing, feeding myself. When no one was looking, I practiced drawing."

"What did you do with the drawings?" I asked.

"Trash. They were no good."

"That bad?"

"Not so bad, in fact, quite encouraging, but nothing to keep."

"What did you discover?"

"I just draw what I see."

"Will you teach again?"

"Perhaps, but I still have some progress to make."

He sat on the back porch and finished our beers. We heard a knock at the front door, and then Janet called out. She pushed open the door and let herself in.

"Sounds like Janet's back with dinner. Chinese take-out," Pierce said. We went inside and grabbed forks and plates, bringing them to the living room. We sat on the floor, our backs leaned up against the couch, and opened all the Chinese take-out containers. There was something about Chinese take-out that made a table and chairs superfluous. Inside the white delivery bags were three sets of chopsticks and several fortune cookies hermetically sealed in clear plastic. We all elected to use forks.

"They ever give you Chinese at the hospital?" I asked.

"Food was fine, but no Chinese. No, I take that back," he said pondering. "They did offer teriyaki chicken with vegetables. But the vegetables were cooked corn and peas. This is better." He raised his fork to his mouth.

I shifted my position, the wood floor becoming unmercifully hard. The couch looked inviting, but there was camaraderie to be had on the floor. I leaned to my left, then right, to keep my cheeks from going numb.

From the living room, we could easily hear cars rushing by outside. Over time, the neighborhood had evolved from residential to commercial, but this house had remained. An old Victorian home, it fronted a three lane street that lead cars to an onramp. With no insulation in the walls, there was little that could be done to silence the sound of traffic. Instead, we turned on the radio, setting it only loud enough to drown out the hum of cars passing by.

Pierce sat, legs crossed with a box of pot stickers in his lap. He had slipped off his shoes, allowing his bare toes to flex and wriggle while he ate. Sitting on the floor, he looked like a skinny Buddha.

"I got a call from Harlan. We're supposed to present development of the new scheme in a little less than two weeks," Janet said between bites of salad rolls. "We'll be transitioning into construction documents and talking to contractors soon."

"When does he send us our first check?" I asked.

"Supposed to be at the end of this week. Don't get too excited, though, it won't be anything to retire on."

"I just want to be able to pay for all the extra lattes I've been consuming. These late nights have been hell on my coffee tab."

We finished eating and Janet piled the take-out boxes into one stack, gathering the remaining debris from our dinner. While she cleaned up the dishes, Pierce and I finished where we had left off.

"What will you do now, still planning on teaching?"

"Don't know what I'll do. Tough to be much of a designer with only one hand."

"Difficult to draw. You could still help Janet and I, no need to have fingers to offer advice."

"Are you still looking for a muse?"

"I have all kinds of inspiration, unfortunately none of it's any good. I didn't take your advice, I'm still going after Angeline. I'd like to believe that things could work. Can't passion provide fuel for a design?"

"I'm sorry, Nick, you're making a mistake."

"I know you don't think we're right for each other."

"No, No - Nick, you don't get it. Please listen. I haven't wanted to spell it out. I don't feel good about this, but I've got to make you understand. There's still a lot that you don't know."

"Pierce, maybe I know more than you think."

"I know you loved her."

"But I never told her. That's what I want to change."

"Nick, she knew, and she didn't care."

"Pierce, she and I were closer than you know, all the way until the end of the summer. It was only after leaving the airport that I felt alone."

"I'm not talking about the airport – she didn't leave you at the airport, she left you before that." Pierce said, trying to keep his voice low enough so Janet wouldn't hear.

"I don't follow."

"She was through with you before that. I understand that you were in love, and I'll grant you that there was a time when Angeline was someone worth loving. But, Nick, you're clinging to an image of who she used to be, who you want her to be."

"I know she's changed, that's obvious to anybody – who hasn't?"

"You, for one. It's been years and you can't seem to change. You just fall into the same patterns."

"Why do you think Angeline is so different? How have the years changed her? You haven't even seen her since she's moved to Portland."

"Right, and I don't plan to. Nick, I'm not talking about her since she's moved here. I'm talking about her while she was in Rome. She changed right before your eyes, but you never saw it."

"Pierce, you're wrong. We cared for each other, but I was the one who could never say anything. So she never met me at the airport; there was no reason for her to show up."

"Forget about the airport. You've talked to her – don't you know what happened before that?"

"I was there, I know what happened."

"Do you still think it was your fault?"

"What are you driving at?" I shifted my position, the floor becoming unbearably hard. Finally I stood up, and Pierce followed suit.

"Look, Nick. The last weeks of the term, it seemed like you and Angeline were through. I mean, I thought it was just a summer fling – that's how she described it."

"Why would she tell you that?"

"Nick, I thought you two were through. I'm sorry."

"What are you saying?" I asked quietly.

Pierce looked back toward the kitchen, still hoping not to draw Janet's attention. "The night you were finishing your design, it seemed like she was so distraught, and you didn't care. I didn't mean for anything to happen – but I went to find her, and it just happened."

"What happened?"

"I stayed the night with her, we slept together – I didn't go over there to do it. She was so unhappy, and we were friends. I just went there to comfort her."

I was stunned, silent.

"Nick, there's something else. I tried to find a way to tell you, but just couldn't do it. The morning after, early, I had to find a way back into the building. I stayed at Angeline's, and had to sneak back in. The only way I could find was to open the studio window and climb in. You didn't leave the window open, I did."

I couldn't move, I couldn't speak. I simply stood and stared at Pierce, as though he was someone I had never met, and didn't know.

"Nick, I'm sorry – I've never known how to tell you."

Without thinking, I reeled back and threw a punch, cracking Pierce in the jaw. He leaned back, then his legs buckled and he slumped to the floor. Janet ran in, seeing Pierce on the ground and me staring back. I don't think she had any idea what to do.

"Jesus, Nick – what did you do?"

Pierce stayed on the ground, his jaw swelling. He reached up with his bandaged hand, feeling his face. Without saying a word, I turned around and walked out the door.

6

During the days that lead up to my Friday rendezvous with Angeline, I had at first resolved to call it off. But I needed to follow it through. Friday evening, I showed up at the Pear, though I didn't want to be there. I was fulfilling a promise to myself, one that I had made when I was more content but also more naive. However, the promise now seemed stale. Too many times, I had wasted time and effort wondering what might have been, wondering where I stood.

Angeline was sitting as far from the bar as she possibly could. Close to a window, in a small booth, she waved at me. She picked up her cell phone and dialed; moments later my phone rang. Holding her phone to her ear, she motioned for me to do the same.

"Nicholas, I'm sitting at twelve o'clock. Slide past the pokey waitress and meet me at the booth."

"Angeline, this is eating into my minutes. Let's quit playing telephone, I'm almost at your table." I hung up and waved back to her. In mere moments, I had split the crowd and was sitting across from her. She had a tall package wrapped in brown paper leaning against the side of the booth. In front of her was one empty glass and another that was half gone. She had tied up her hair, using chopsticks to hold it together.

"Been sitting here for a bit, maybe a drink and a half?" I asked.

"Only a half, sit down, the seat's warm. Don't mind the package, we can scoot that over to make room."

"Fragile?"

"A little, they're paintings for the upcoming show in the gallery downstairs. I'm dropping them off to be stored in the back."

"Moonlighting as an art dealer?"

"I like you Nick, you're cute. Order something quick."

"Can we talk first?"

She held up her phone. "Sure, I've got you on speed dial."

"No, without phones."

"Nick, I want to have a good time tonight. We always have such damn fun."

"You're ahead of me, I haven't even started yet."

"Then order up, you're slow." She put her hand on my shoulder, leaned her head down and laughed.

"How about this, we'll smoke a cigarette," I said.

"Perfect."

I lit up two cigarettes and grabbed an ash tray from another table.

"Angeline, the other night when I called you, you remember?"

"Of course."

"I wasn't just hoping to get together. There was something important I needed to say; I didn't get to say it."

"You need a new phone."

"Help me out here, this isn't easy. Even as I sit here, I'm debating what to say."

"See, that's you're problem – you always debate what to say, but don't say it. Why not talk first, then decide later if it's what you meant?"

"Alright, but here's what I mean; Angeline, for a long time in Rome, we had a romance. Hell, we were in love – I know I was, and I think you were to. Time has passed, but I haven't been able to get past that."

She continued listening and sipped at her drink.

"Tonight, I want to get past that," I said. "I want you to know that I loved you in Rome. I thought maybe we had a shot, and I even believed it again these past few weeks."

"What do you believe now?"

"I don't know, I don't know if it matters."

"But you've been waiting all this time to tell me. Well?"

"Well what?"

"Are you going to tell me?"

"Alright, yes. Up until a few days ago, I loved you again, but I don't know. I talked to Pierce, and he told me what happened between the two of you."

332

"Nick, that was a long time ago – I'm sorry about what happened, I'm not proud about what I did. But we were through, there wasn't anything left."

"I know that now."

"Think what you want about me, but don't let it come between you and Pierce. He's your friend, a good friend. Don't let one mistake ruin that."

"The important thing for me, is that I tell you how I feel. I don't want to leave so much unsaid. I loved you once, and could have again. But I don't anymore – and it isn't because I can't get past something that happened years ago when we were in school. It's because we're so very different. It's because we want such different things. It's something that you've known all along, and it's why you don't love me now."

She forced a smile, looking around the room, as if afraid that anyone else might be eavesdropping on the conversation.

"Nick, watch my drink, I need to take a powder."

While Angeline made her way to the ladies room, I sat by myself. All around me, couples danced and drank and flirted. It was like choreography, everyone knew their parts so well. I was sitting in a room packed with people, but still alone. I smoked my cigarette down, then crushed it in the ashtray.

Angeline's package still leaned against the booth. I tapped it with my toe. Impulsively, I stuck my finger under the flap of brown paper and pulled at the tape. The flap came open, revealing three canvases stacked together. I recognized Andrew's style immediately. But these were canvases that I hadn't seen when I had gone to his studio. Each was a portrait of a reclining nude, painted in an energetic and fluid hand. I placed my finger on the surface of the canvas and traced the contour of the thigh, to the hip, up to the chest, and out along the outstretched arm. It was Angeline.

The noise of the crowd continued to intensify, to the point where it wasn't even bearable. My head started to throb, and I could feel myself getting sick. I remained in my seat, hoping for it to pass. It felt so muggy I could scarcely get enough air. I stood up and pushed my way to the exit. Once outside I punched the side of the building, bruising my hand. I was angry, not because the paintings changed anything. I was just tired of being deceived. I would never again have a need to confide in Angeline, and I would never again set foot inside the Pear.

7

The next two days, I called in sick. The first day, I actually neglected to call. By mid afternoon the secretary got a hold of me. She had called earlier in the day, but I simply let the phone ring.

I had not slept much, instead choosing to sit at my drafting table, completing the re-schemed design presentation for Harlan's gallery. This time, however, I grabbed folded pieces of trace from the original design that Janet, Pierce, and I had developed. I uncreased each sheet, and tacked them to my walls, creating architectural wallpaper of scribbles and colors. I revived the initial scheme of borrowed light from the streets filtering into the gallery atrium. From developing the project with Janet, I had a stronger understanding of how a gallery worked, how the circulation needed to flow, and how the building could support the displays.

I didn't leave my apartment. I had my own coffee maker, so I had no need for a café or coffee house. It took a little research to remember how to use the machine, but I nailed it. At some point, I heard Carly out on her balcony. Truth be told, I really wanted to join her. She was remarkably easy to talk to; no games with her. The intrigue of mind puzzles with Angeline had worn thin; it was so refreshing to speak candidly. But I kept at my work. During the early process of working on the gallery, I had felt inept and impotent. Pierce had lost a hand, but I was the one left unable to affect my world. Now I desperately needed to prove to myself that I could be creative, to prove that I still could design. With no interruptions, I made progress.

I had half expected to feel guilty for missing work and then lying about being sick. Faking flu symptoms over the phone was more involved than I'd imagined, but the decision to skip work was easy. It was the first confident decision I'd made in a long time. I had chosen to remain in my apartment; not out of any feeling of loss or anger, but because I came to an understanding about what I needed to accomplish. More importantly – what I wanted to accomplish.

When I had worked on previous design boards for Harlan, I had maintained a preoccupation with keeping the design within his limits. As Janet and I had been strung along, the idea had been diluted and dumbed down. My goal now was to realize the design as it should be, to develop it into a piece of art. In days to come, Janet and I would offer drawings to Harlan and I intended to push him, to persuade him. I had already resigned myself to the reality that I might risk pushing too hard, but at least I could put my effort into something I could believe in. I was no longer trying to design for Harlan, I was no longer trying to satisfy Janet, and I was no longer trying to impress Angeline; I was only drawing what I believed the gallery needed to become.

On the evening that I completed my work, the singing cowboy was on his regular corner belting out his song. I didn't feel so far removed from the cowboy. He wasn't talented, no one could ever make the mistake of believing that he was. But he continued to sing. He sang without applause and without encouragement; only because he loved to sing. He was a singer, he knew no other way to be. I now aspired for the same satisfaction from my work. Not to be recognized, but to do for the pleasure of doing.

8

When the phone rang, my first instinct was to ignore it. However, I was curious enough to peak at the caller ID and saw the call was coming from next door. It wasn't late, but I was camped out on my sofa watching entertainment news.

"What's up?"

"Have you looked out your window?"

"Many times."

"Now – look out there now."

"What's so urgent?"

"Go to your window -"

"Okay, what am I looking for?"

"Are you looking? Directly to the east, it's burning."

"What's burning?" I ran to the window, opening it so I could poke my head outside. I could see dark smoke rising through the twilight. From so many blocks away, the light from the flames seemed feint, but still illuminated the horizon. The unsteady glow turned the plume of smoke into a beacon.

"They've got it on the news, flip on your TV."

"What happened?"

"Fire. They don't know how, but fire-trucks just arrived."

I found my remote and flipped through the channels until I found the local news. Large letters ran across the bottom of the screen exclaiming *Breaking News*, and there was the brick shell of the Angry Pear, with flames jumping out through the windows. I turned my head from window to screen, seeing the thick column of smoke growing outside and the view from the news cameras on my television. A helicopter overhead brought images of trucks parked askew in the street, hoses stretched out from hydrant to building. Jets of cascading water were directed at the building, mostly where the Pear connected to the adjacent building. A crowd huddled together on the north side, back beyond the barricades.

"How long has it been burning?"

"Not sure; I was just surfing channels and I saw your club. I think it started within the last half hour, so sad."

"The whole ground floor gallery is going to be gone - and the restaurant above, the stage, the bar. Was it crowded?"

"They haven't said, but there's a pack of people grouped together past the trucks. Most had been inside."

I looked back at the screen, watching the glow above the building. By now, dark smoke hung over the pearl district, visible as a silhouette in the dusky sky.

Beyond my street, beyond the overpass, in the middle of the industrial neighborhood, the old building stood with a belly full of flames. It had been there for over a hundred years, first as a warehouse, and then vacated. God only knows what else it was used for before it was renovated into the Pear. The weathered lettering, painted under the windows so many years ago, was now illegible and scorched. Steel supports for the entry canopy sagged under the intense heat, drooping like decaying tree limbs. And the sound - the heavy, rumbling noise of the building being consumed; it sounded like booming tanks, like steady driving hurricane winds, like murmuring voices roaring wordless gossip.

I watched, and the Pear burned.

"I never went inside. Guess I'll never experience it."

"Never went into the Pear?"

"Just heard about it from you. What are you going to do without your hangout?"

"I'll drink fewer martinis." I paused and considered. "Well, I guess I'll just drink them somewhere else."

"I hope there weren't people trapped inside. It's so unnerving for this to happen so close by."

"Feels farther away now. But a lot happened there – that's where I started drawing the gallery design. I was just there days ago meeting a friend."

"Lady friend?"

"Sort of, but not really. It's unfortunate, she was there to drop off a set of paintings. They were to be displayed at the Pear for next month's show. I imagine they've burned up; just like that - gone."

"I just hope no one was hurt."

Carly and I talked. We watched the news cameras pan over the building while cascades of water battled the blaze. We hung up when the news transitioned to the next story. I turned off the television, and fell asleep minutes after hitting the bed.

The next morning, I called Janet from work. According to her, the fire had started from a short circuit in the electrical system. The old building had a stroke of sorts. Janet was noticeably upset, which bothered me because I couldn't share her concern. Being partners in the design of Harlan's second gallery, I felt as though I really should be more sympathetic. However, the emotion just wasn't there, perhaps I had spent all my emotion and was content to float for a bit. She hadn't yet talked to Harlan, so there hadn't been any word on the effect the fire would have on our gallery design. I didn't suspect it would kill the job, but there was no telling how he would want to proceed; perhaps he would look to build two galleries now, or perhaps none.

Our conversation was somewhat strained, and at first I couldn't account for it. Then I recalled that the last time we had talked I had punched Pierce in the face. She was still talking to me, which was a good sign. I decided, though, that I wasn't going to be the one to bring it up.

I grabbed a copy of the paper in the café at work. There were pictures of the fire on the front page, the Pear a smoking shell, the flames now extinguished. The structure still stood, but there was nothing inside except ash, the fire had consumed everything that would burn. The building now stood empty, reminiscent of the abandoned farmhouse, now defunct but full of history. I couldn't help but let my eye linger on the photo of the masonry edifice, blackened with soot but still retaining its muscular appearance. The punched window openings now seemed even thicker without the wood frames and glass to cheat them of their depth. The photo had been taken early in the morning, allowing bright sunlight to stream through the windows, leaving contrasting patterns of light and shadow on the ground and against the brick walls. Despite the tragedy of the fire, and despite the loss, I couldn't help but be taken with the subtle beauty of the photo. The simple, common structure stood with a strange dignity among the remains of all that it had once held.

I avoided Ron. The morning came and went, and I was happy to have the time to myself. I ate a quick lunch and then hurried to the museum, sketchbook tucked under my arm. Rather than linger over different exhibits, I found a favorite painting and spent the remainder of my lunch drawing what I saw. While drawing, I forgot about other things. Using the creative part of my brain created distance. Each day that week, I spent my lunch break filling up the pages of my book.

Ron and I did go out for coffee later in the week. We made it a quick trip, but couldn't resist talking about the fire. The Pear was no more, and our tradition of First Thursday required a new denouement. For him, the question was what establishment would become the new Pear. He also speculated if and when the Pear would be rebuilt, rising from its ashes in some new form; perhaps this time with better fireproofing and a larger bar. Somewhere, the carnival would form again as it did each month.

On our way back to the office, he asked me about Carly. At first I avoided the question, trying to steer the conversation in a different direction. Ron was stubborn, however, pressing the issue. I was glad, because it gave me the opportunity to simply be direct. I explained that she was off limits, I would suffer no competition. To his credit, he let things lie and didn't even probe. He simply sipped some more of his coffee and seemed to chew it over. The fact is, I've never given Ron enough credit; probably because he's never pretended to be anything other than who he is.

Now it's early evening, so much cooler than even the week before. August seems like a dream and we're only barely into September. I've already seen some leaves start to color, losing their summery green. Won't be long before the evenings stay dark and the cold, wet weather falls from the sky. Tonight is First Thursday, though I have no plans of participating. The tradition continues in dozens of other galleries throughout the city. Instead, I've come back to the museum – to escape and to think and to draw. Only a few more pages to fill in this sketchbook, then I'll make a run to the art store; nearly out of trace paper and charcoal as well.

I'm nearly done with my sketch, much more and I'll overwork the drawing. Still, I haven't got it quite right. The young woman, posing for the sculptor seems less shy in my drawing; I haven't quite captured the mood on the canvas. However, I love to draw. I suspect I'll always draw, partly out of habit, and partly for the joy of it. But this routine is different, not some guilty addiction. The truth of it is, I'm not going to go cold turkey and quit architecture. But I understand it can't just be about designing, I want to build. I want to see designs take shape, and not simply finish their life on paper. I like to think that there's a way to build something that will last, something that can continue on beyond those who built it. I think about the Pear, and the multiple lives it had, evolving and changing but still retaining its substance. I hope that someday I can help build something that lasts, that can't be torn down or forgotten.

I'm going to take the streetcar home tonight; I want to take my time. I'll stop for a coffee, purchase the largest cup they have and walk it around the neighborhood. I'll take in the familiar streets, and then detour to the small alleys I've never seen. I'll walk past the shops and up through the townhouses. I want to walk until the sun drops below the sky and see the whole place in the glow of the streetlights. I want to take it in and remember it, because everything changes - constantly changes. And I'd like to hold onto the way I remember it now.

THE END

www.ingramcontent.com/pod-product-compliance
Lightning Source LLC
Chambersburg PA
CBHW030400030726
47497CB00002B/419